BETWEEN SMOKE & SHADOW

BREE WILDE

For the underestimated girls,
I hope you prove them all fucking wrong.

CONTENTS

PROLOGUE

Cycle 892 / Blizzard Season / Day 47
Rune

"I t's time, Rune."

I ignore my dad, watching blood pool around the drain. I should still be at work, not soaking my blistered hands in the sink. I grimace before glancing in my sliver of mirror. It's a small and misshapen shard, slim enough to fit up my sleeve but big enough to watch for descendants—and apparently, overbearing fathers.

"Come," he insists. His voice is soft and kind, and I hate it. He's staring at me with worry and pity, but not with anger. Gods, I wish he'd be angry.

I lift my fingers from the sink, inspecting their gruesome blisters. A bored guard had infused my rag with magic, forcing me to clean with it for eight hours. Only he grew bored before my shift ended and dismissed me. Eight hours, mutilated skin, and no pay.

Blood drips to my wrists. I slip the mirror back up my sleeve and dry my hands on the hanging towel. It's stale and stinks of something sour. Now, it's also stained with blood and pus.

Dad touches my shoulder and guides me from the bathroom. I let him pull me down a twist of corridors, keeping my head lowered. My mask, a pathetic scrap of veiled fabric, dangles loosely from my ears. I should tighten it, but I can't see the point.

Servants filter around us, their faces made sickly by yellow walls and dim lighting. I barely register them, instead focusing on the cracked floors and cheap wooden doors. When we reach our quarters, marked with numbers 246 and 247, Dad leads us into the darkened room. I catch a final glimpse of his appearance: blonde hair, stained coveralls, and ratted shoes before he disappears into the shadows.

I'm sure I look similar, if not worse.

"They took my pay," I tell him. I'm sure he already knows. His magicked brand should have lost a half mark today. Instead, only a quarter mark is gone. My portion remains.

Dad doesn't respond. He sits on the edge of his bed, springs creaking against his meager weight. I force myself to move, leaving the doorway open. My bed is a mattress on the floor, squished between Dad's narrow cot and my long-broken metal frame. I've insisted on the floor bed, because Dad's knees are too bad. Honestly, every bone in his body is too bad.

"I worked *all day*," I say, voice cracking. I clench my hands, letting the pain of it scorch through me. "All day, Dad. I scrubbed and scrubbed, even though I knew it wouldn't work. He made me scrub for *eight hours*, watching my hands blister, only stopping when he was bored of it. And then, a sweep of his hand, a thread of smoke. And it was gone. Every drop. Gone."

Dad rests his elbows on his knees, his gaze drifting to my drenched shoes in the corner. He looks at me, half of his face remaining in the shadows. Dark circles line his eyes, surrounded by too many wrinkles for a man his age. A large bruise, purple and black, blossoms just below his ear. He still won't tell me what happened.

"And then—then he took my pay," I say. A sob chokes my throat, but I swallow it, grinding my teeth to keep it contained. "He said I wasted *his* time. As if—as if it was my fault that their blood is demonic—"

"Don't speak like that," Dad hisses, head snapping toward me.

I don't respond. He's right—and I know better—but I can't admit that. I can't admit anything beyond the fact I've been wronged and I'm angry for it. I want Dad to be angry too, not at me and my dangerous words. At them, at the guards and the royals and the crown, at all the monsters who take, just because they can.

"We will make it through," is all he says. His words are soft and empty, a hollow lie in the dark.

"Saying it does not make it true," I whisper. I sit on my mattress and hug my knees to my chest, as if squeezing hard enough will keep me whole.

"Rune—"

"They are going to *kill* us, Dad. They are going to torture us until—"

He surges to close the door, letting darkness swallow us— servant quarters do not have lights. I fidget in discomfort, but I don't argue.

"You must stop," he says as he returns to his cot. My emotions twist and choke, suffocating in their loneliness. There must be someone, *anyone*, who feels this poisonous rage—and actually wants to do something about it.

"It's been six cycles," I say. My voice wobbles with the words, struggles beneath the weight of them. "It was only meant to be five."

"We are almost there," he says. He believes the lie. I can sense the surety of his tone, as if we haven't built debt faster than we've cleared it.

"Six cycles," I repeat. "For a crime that didn't deserve to be punished."

The springs shriek as Dad moves again, coming to kneel on the mattress beside me. His hands find my shoulders through the darkness, his overgrown nails digging through the fabric.

"Enough," he says. No, he *begs*. "Rune, there are ears everywhere. If they hear these accusations, they—"

"They'll what? Lock us up for eternity?" I don't know when I started crying, but my words break with choppy sobs. Now that I've begun, I don't know how I'll stop. "I know you want me to trust you, but I'm going to *die* here. I can feel it. I don't—I don't want to die here."

Dad pulls me to his chest, and I sag against him.

"I love you," he whispers.

I'm crying too hard to say it back. I only burrow my head against his shoulder, letting the tears fall until I run out of them. When he finally pulls away, I grab his left hand. It's the only thing visible in this blackened room. Dull magic shines through it, the red glow twisted into the shape of an Old World wolf. Magic that bears no use to him, except to trap us here. Within its mouth, dozens and dozens of marks symbolize our debt.

"Do you regret it?" I ask, the question I've never dared to voice. I don't know why I do now, if I'm so desperate for compassion I'm willing to hurt him for it.

"No," he whispers. "I loved your mother too much not to try."

My hands shake as I hold his fingers. I was eight when Mom fell ill, when Dad attempted to steal a medicinal root to save her life. After he failed and was arrested, but before the guards came to take our family as collateral, I sat with Mom at her bedside. I counted the seconds between her last breaths, reaching nearly one thousand before I allowed myself to believe she was really and truly dead.

"I wish you loved me that much," I say.

They are the cruelest words I've ever spoken, but I don't take them back. I release my father's hand and lay on my side, turning to face the wall instead of him. He leaves a few minutes later, and I fall asleep, waiting for him to return.

<hr />

Cycle 892 / Blizzard Season / Day 48
Harrick

When I was young, I had a servant named Quil. I considered him my closest friend, but I didn't really know him. I was always too busy talking. I'd tell him how I hated my brother and how desperately I wanted to be king. I complained about my annoying sister and the tutors who made me feel stupid. I'd seek his help when the Architect beat me and forbid me from getting a healer. He'd do his best to tend my wounds, and he never laughed if I cried.

Even now, I don't know if he had family or why he was working as a crowned servant so young. I knew his clothes were too small, and that he was skinny and skittish. And yet, I never realized I should help him.

Instead, I took everything he offered and only tried to give when it was too late. He had stolen bread, a foreign concept to someone like me, and had earned twenty lashings. The Architect demanded I deliver them, setting us up in the courtyard with a crowd of servants watching. And when I refused, when I publicly defied him, he removed his mask and killed Quil in front of me. He killed my friend in a matter of seconds, and I stared at the mangled body like I could will it back to life. I might have tried, had the Architect not cuffed my ear and dragged me from the courtyard.

We do not show mercy, he told me. I hadn't responded. I only trembled, feeling my body grow distant, as if it was no longer mine. My mouth wouldn't move, even as I tried to speak. The Architect pinched my chin, hard enough that it bruised by nightfall. He said again, louder. *We do not show mercy, Harrick. Especially not to them.*

I think of Quil now, as I sit on my throne in that same courtyard, surrounded by a cocoon of magicked heat. Beyond this stage, the early morning air is brittle and stark, paled by an onslaught of heavy snow. My brother and sister sit to my left and my mother to the right, with the red-suited Architect across the platform. His throne, a horrible thing of cleaved bones—animal and not—is raised to shadow ours.

I dig at the rough carvings on my armrests. They're twisted into the shape of Old World creatures: growling bears and open-mouthed lions and cackling hyenas. My scarlet attire is a drop of blood against the black throne, and the latter is a blot of ink against the snow-swept sky. I finger the rough edges as I stare out at the crowd, a shivering mass of white and yellow. There is not a blanket of heat for them. There is only crushing snow and relentless wind and the choking smell of death.

The cobblestone yard is hidden beneath a layer of thick ice, and a trail of blood traces from the prisoner holding area to the center of the square. The final man, a gaunt prisoner with startling blue eyes and blond hair so filthy it looks brown, walks barefoot to his death. His pale skin is sickly, as if the afterlife would have caught him soon, even if our guards hadn't.

"Number 246," the lead calls. Dressed in all-encompassing

black, our guards look more like shadows than people. These ones, the royal guards, wear masks shaped like wolves.

"You are charged with conspiracy to abscond," says the guard. His voice is deep but flat, and I try to decide whether he loves or hates this role. After many cycles, I've learned there's not often an in-between. "For your attempt to evade debt owed, you now face immediate execution."

I study the prisoner from where I sit. He wasn't supposed to be on the death toll this morning. He was a late addition, caught by an undercover guard mere hours ago. He'd been inquiring about a smuggling operation, one that doesn't actually exist.

Now, the man's hands are bound behind his back, and I can make out the red outline of his indebted brand from here. His legs remain untied, but he makes no move to run. I'm sure the Architect is disappointed. It is only when they run that my father plays with them. Coils his magic between their ears as they flee, infecting their thoughts with every terrible thing they've ever done, until they can't bear their own existence. They inevitably return before they reach the fenceline, and when the Architect offers them a blade, they eagerly slice their own throats.

None of our prisoners have died like that this season, but the memories are as visceral as the real thing. I steady my breathing and still my twitching hands, ignoring Mother's heavy gaze. She has an unnatural sense for weakness, especially when it comes to mine. I don't let myself look at her.

Instead, I study the commoners and servants. They stand in a huddled mass, their eyes covered by varying styles of masks. The commoners wear white ones, narrow but thick. The servants wear yellow, eyes covered less by a mask and more a scrap of thin veil. Above us, in the looming Tower, royals and elites watch from their viewing rooms.

"Your remaining debt shall fall to your estate," the guard says, startling me. When the man winces, I again look through the attending servants. He has surviving family then, but they're not here. They probably don't know.

Prisoner 246 shifts, and the movement catches a glimmer of sunlight. His brand, a red wolf with a gaping mouth, has less than two dozen gem marks between its teeth. If I had to guess, he owes one more cycle of servitude, maybe two.

"For thievery of Amarum in Cycle 886, four hundred and twelve beryls. For attempted evasion in Cycle 892, ten thousand and two hundred sixteen beryls. All remaining debt..." the guard pauses, consulting the device on his forearm before continuing. If he notices how still the man has gone, how utterly pale and withdrawn, he doesn't react. He only faces the crowd, announcing, "All remaining debt to prisoner 247."

I squeeze the armrests hard enough I might crush the animal carvings. My breath stalls as I work not to make outward movements. Ten thousand is an insurmountable sum, surpassing fifty cycles if there is only one person carrying it. I watch the servant, and then the guard. He stands tall, chin tipped high, and I have my answer from earlier. He is, without a doubt, relishing in this man's torture.

"No." The word is whispered, yet it somehow vibrates through the entire courtyard. I look back to the servant. His body is stiff and there's no touch of emotion on his expression. But there's something in his eyes, barely visible from behind his ratted veil. "I only have one—one daughter. The debt is too—"

"Fifteen thousand," the Architect interrupts. He rises from his throne, striding to stand above the guard and his prisoner. "Question my guard again, and it will be twenty."

Now the man lets out an animalistic sob. His face barely moves, but that look in his eyes flares into something recognizable. Not anger or ferocity...no, it's hopeless devastation.

The Architect tips his chin down at the prisoner, much like he's looking at an unidentifiable bug. Like the guards, my father wears a form-fitting suit that hides his entire body. But where theirs are black, the Architect's is the color of dried blood.

The servant's knees buckle as he sobs again, and though I can't see the Architect's face, I know he's grinning. He descends the platform, letting the harsh snow and wind overtake him. With a gentle sweep of his hand, he removes the servant's off-colored veil. It breaks away all too easily, flitting to the ground and settling over the ice. Behind the quivering man, the crowd averts their gaze to the cobblestone.

"May your magic be more worthy than you," the Architect says. With a twitch of his head and a spark of magic, his mask vanishes. From the side, he looks like an ordinary man of no more than forty cycles. Dull brown hair, lightly weathered skin, a sloping nose. I've often wondered if we look alike, or if our only similarity is in our eyes. Dark blends of violet, so deep they're almost black.

The Architect cups a hand around the back of the man's head with taunting gentleness. The servant trembles to the point he could be seizing. Darkness spreads over his pants—he is not the first to wet himself today.

I tighten my jaw, hard enough my teeth should crack. If I was mortal, maybe they would.

"Tell her—"

The servant's words cut off, replaced by his choking scream. The Architect leans into the hideous sound, a tight smile straining his lips. With gloved hands, he forces the man's eyes open, paralyzing his once thrashing body. I watch him work, as if he's solving a complex problem and not murdering a man.

Pieces of dull magic, so thin they look like strands of hair, twist from the servant's eyes. It is not outward magic, nothing he could have used. It is the magic of his soul, of his very being —and the Architect devours it in a single breath.

Once it stops, when the man is nothing but a corpse, the Architect releases him. His body collapses with a heavy thud and his head lands upon his killer's boot. Those startling, unseeing eyes stare up at me. The Architect, with his mask back in place, kicks the servant's head to the ground. He steps over his victim's body and wordlessly returns to the stage.

I'm still staring at the servant, at his gaping blue eyes, when I hear her. I have seen more than a hundred mourning children in my lifetime. I have heard them sob and wail and plead uselessly to the sky. But this girl isn't crying—she's screaming. A tortured but ferocious scream, high pitched and painful.

The crowd parts for her. The girl has darker hair than the dead man, but her eyes are the same unmistakable blue. She's not wearing a mask, and I'm almost too distracted to process anything else. Beautiful. Her eyes are stunningly beautiful. Her voice strains against her scream as she collapses at her father's side. With shaking hands, she pats his face like she's trying to wake him.

This is how I would have looked, I think, had I tried to save Quil.

"Ahh, and you must be the daughter," the Architect says. His words are lazy, almost amused, as he turns away from her. Settling back into his throne, he nods to the guard, who captures her without hesitation. "Thank you for saving us the trouble."

The guard presses the girl's palm against her father's hand. Magic sparks from the guard's gloves, and slowly, the brand disappears from the man's cold skin and carves itself into his daughter's instead. New blisters, violent red and throbbing, join old ones, until her left hand is more wound than flesh. She sobs and thrashes, face twisted in raw panic, and I make myself watch.

The girl slackens when it's over. With her mangled hand lifted toward the sky, she studies the burned mark. It is identical to her father's, only its mouth now overflows with debt. Her scream vanishes as she traces the wound, as she realizes just how many cycles she now owes.

When her eyes lift, they find mine. It's no more than a second, her vibrant blue against my dark violet. And yet, in that brief moment, her shocked rage burrows into my bones and tells me I'm a coward. I force myself not to react, to look on with only that unimpressed expression.

Once they have taken her away and I have returned to my quarters, I finally allow myself to cry.

1
RUNE

We meet in the burning room. Nine of us now, all tucked into the far corner, faces slick with sweat, eyes squinted against the furious blaze. We sit with damp shoulders pressed together, choking on scorched air, waiting for Vale to begin. For now, he doesn't acknowledge us.

The newest member—Arnelian—is the first to speak. He's older, skin thick and wrinkled, hair more gray than black. He's lived more cycles than any of us, and he's got a smug expression, like this alone makes him better. I don't entirely blame him–I'll be smug too if I reach his age.

"There are no cremations tonight," he says. His words are strangled and rough, an accent from the Pit. He wasn't born here. He's not paying the debt of a dead family member like most of us. He's here because of something he did, and by the markings on the back of his hand, he's not getting out anytime soon. Arnelian clears his throat, but his voice is still ragged. "We should move from the flame, where it's not so—"

"No," Vale says. He doesn't snap or yell, but the elderly newcomer straightens like he has. He doesn't argue—*nobody* argues with Vale.

He sits directly to my left with three parchments in front of him. Despite being malnourished and unkempt, Vale is attractive. Smooth dark skin, expressive eyes, and relatively straight teeth. He glances between a pair of hand-written reports and a wrinkled page from an old book. His fingers leave oily prints everywhere he touches.

In the time before he speaks again, I mentally recite my report. It's too hot to focus though, the heavy air making my brain slow and jumbled. This burning room, between its suffocating heat and the taste of charred skin, is our safest place to meet. There's nothing but the crematory and the stone alcove we've claimed, tucked behind the fire and out of sight. Nobody ever comes here unless they're depositing a corpse.

To my right, second-in-command Caleah looks at me. Her dull brown eyes, cloaked by flimsy veil, are hooded and shadowed with dark circles. She's a cycle younger than I am, but she's smarter. Probably the smartest in this room. I wasn't surprised when Vale made her second, two seasons before he made me third. I've been here longer—but she undoubtedly has more to offer.

"Our people suffer here," Vale says, drawing my attention. His voice is low and harsh, and he spits each word like a curse. "Alive, we fill the forgotten halls of the Tower. Our scarred hands build this kingdom that fails us. The crown starves us. Beats us. Weakens us until they hope we can never fight back.

"And dead, our corpses are dragged here. Tossed into a burning grave like diseased animals. Their fire devours us— takes every insignificant drop of our magic—to make sure we are useful, even in death." Vale pauses, his dark eyes shifting to the vibrant flames. "This room is our eternal hell. One day, we will all be nothing but blackened dust in the bottom of that burning tomb. This crown we live to serve...they want to destroy us. So we must destroy them first."

"Together," I whisper. The word fills the room, expanding through nine chests, bleeding from nine cracked mouths. Arnelian stares, jaw slackened, skin flushed, eyes unnaturally bright. As our group grows, I've found this moment to be one of my favorites: when hope lights even the darkest of shadows. I'm still watching the awe in Arnelian's expression when Vale clears his throat, startling me back to attention.

"Rune," he says, nodding at me. "Any updates?"

"Yes," I say. I try to sound more confident than I feel. "Tomorrow, I have my final interrogation for the position of Lady Saskia's handmaiden. Caleah has already been made Lady Viana's, so once I'm promoted, we should be precisely where we need to be."

"Why not Princess Tora?" Arnelian asks. Any trace of awe is gone from his features, replaced with his typical sneer. "You want close to the royals? Start at the top, I say."

I press my lips into a firm line. If I were brave, I'd tell him to keep his stupid questions to himself. Vale certainly would, and so would Caleah. But I'm not like them, no matter how hard I try.

"The princess already has handmaidens," I say instead. "Besides, she's too likely to detect our deception. She's a dangerous choice. Viana is easier, and according to Vale's confidants, she's likely to be Prince Harrick's betrothed by the end of the season."

"But—"

"Hold further questions," Caleah snaps, voice hard. Arnelian shifts again, fading into the shadows. Caleah glances at Vale, the two of them sharing a concerned expression, before she gestures for me to continue. I don't let myself dwell on that look, heavy with concern, as if they don't think I can handle my new role here.

Clearing my throat, I force myself to continue.

"Lady Saskia is a close friend of Lady Viana. I will use my position to keep an eye out for any trouble. Caleah will work to find information, and I will keep her from getting caught."

"Thank you, Rune," Vale says with a nod. After checking with Caleah, who has nothing to report, Vale looks back to the semi-circle of rebels. "As for the rest of us, we will finally put our plans into motion. We will be smart and cautious, but we can no longer *talk* about our future—we must now create it. Weapons, explosives, armor—we're going to steal anything we can get our hands on."

The rebels nod, but Vale's words leave a heavy pressure in the air. He moves into specifics, assigning tasks to each individual. He's mostly after weapons for now, but I imagine it will change as we progress. Once everyone has their assignment, he glances toward me and Caleah again.

"These women are risking their lives to find our escape. When the moment comes, whenever that may be, we *must* be ready."

I force myself to act unaffected, as if the thought of dying for this mission doesn't terrify me. As if I'm more confident in our faction than I am in anything else.

"You're dismissed. Reveal nothing if you are caught," Vale says. Without looking at us, he adds, "Caleah, Rune, hold back."

The other members hurry from the room, leaving in groups of two or alone, and I suck in as many breaths of cool air as I can. When the final person leaves, once again sealing the door, the trapped heat crushes against me until I'm nauseated.

"Explain this text," Vale says, placing the aged paper in front of Caleah.

She'd glimpsed it over Lady Viana's shoulder during one of her study sessions, and after giving me detailed instructions, I went to retrieve it. I'd snuck into the library, ripped the 301st page from its spine in the dead hours of morning, and returned it to its shelf. I ran straight here with my heart pounding, my stomach halfway up my throat, and the wrinkled text tucked into my underclothing. It wasn't the first time I've risked my life for our group, and it certainly won't be the last. I only wish I read well enough to understand it.

I look at the page now, at its weathered edges and worn ink. There are too many words, and I hardly recognize any of them. Vale tried to teach me to read when we first met. I'd been in the midst of reckless grief and he'd been desperate for an accomplice. I practiced for a while, but as our faction grew, my time seemed to shrink.

Caleah places her hand near Vale's, her pale cheeks flushing when their fingers brush. She's been smitten with him for nearly a cycle now, and I have no idea how he hasn't noticed. Or maybe he has, and he's not interested. It seems unlikely. Caleah is pretty. Red hair, brown eyes, chaotic freckles. She looks like a breathing masterpiece *and* she's brilliant, too.

"I know it's not much to go on," she says. Smoothing the edges of the worn parchment, she trails the text, pausing at the third paragraph. With a glance at me, she asks, "Do you know what this is?"

I look at the page, leaning toward it like I can will myself to be literate. Finally, I force myself to swallow and shake my head.

"It's from *Illia's Tome*," she says. "The *original* version, that is. They've updated it a hundred times by now, at least. I assumed they did it any time laws changed or there were new procedures. I've only ever read the newest version."

Now she looks at Vale, as if to confirm he's still paying attention. He is, and by the look on his face, he's already figured something out from the text. He's several steps ahead of me— they both are. I wish I could say it's an uncommon occurrence, but it's not.

"Viana's tutor was going over something in this original version, and I was scanning over her shoulder. That's when I saw *this*."

She stabs in the middle of the page, over a hand-drawn chart. There are several numbers and a handful of words. I recognize *magic* and *crown*, but that's about it.

"It's a chart of Savoa's magic during the first ten cycles. How much was collected during Lightning Season. How much was distributed to each sector. How much was stored for future uses." Caleah pauses, dipping her chin toward Vale. "Notice anything about the numbers?"

"They're...high," he says. He raises his eyebrows, squinting toward the chart, as if he might be reading it wrong.

"They're *very* high," she corrects. Her smile is broad as she looks at me. "According to this, we used to collect *three times* as much magic every cycle. Three times! So unless nature is collapsing and no one is concerned..."

Caleah looks between me and Vale, clearly waiting for an answer. I'm still scrambling to digest what she's explained, but luckily for her, Vale is far ahead of me.

"They're lying," he says. He doesn't bother to look at me, his eyes solely tied on Caleah. "They're...but *why*? What could they possibly be doing with that much excess?"

"Who knows." Caleah shrugs, folding the parchment in half. "Maybe they're sneaking more magic to certain sectors. Maybe they're giving more magic to themselves. Maybe the original numbers were skewed. Or maybe...there's something sinister going on. Something we could use to our advantage."

"If there is," says Vale. "We'll find it."

After Vale leaves for the night, I do a sweep of the alcove while Caleah reads over her texts one last time. She stands beside the far brick wall, where Vale carved a small cubby to hide our stolen goods. He'll need to expand it, now that he's planning to steal weapons and *explosives*. I'm tempted to ask Caleah what she thinks of that.

"How did you read the text?" I ask instead. I pick a tiny piece of lint off the floor and toss it into the fire. "Without Viana noticing, I mean."

Caleah shifts her mirror in and out of her sleeve. Hers is almost too large to fit, but she once told me she can't breathe well without it. It's why we all carry mirrors, after all. Not because they'll actually protect us, but because they at least give us the illusion when we need it.

"The key is to act with purpose," she says. She steps past me, chin lifted, as if demonstrating as she leads us around the fire. Like me, she carries the debt of a dead relative, but I don't know anything more than that. I've never asked who committed the crime or what it was. All I know is that her brand has nearly as many beryls as mine. She glances at me before continuing. "Always have your excuse ready and be sure-footed. But small and unsupposing too, if you can. Too much confidence will catch their attention."

"You've thought a lot about this," I say, hating how my voice shakes. It's not that I *haven't* thought about how to stay alive. This just suddenly feels too real, too dangerous. One wrong move and I'll join my father's ashes in this pit.

"We're going to be fine, Rune," Caleah says. Her hands twitch at her sides, as if she's debating reaching for me. She doesn't. Instead, she nods toward the fire, a chasm between us. "Remember the motto."

She offers one last smile before slipping through the

burning room's only door. I linger at the flames after she's left, probably for longer than is smart. I hated this Tower when they first dragged me here, and I've hated it every day since. I've dreamt of escaping, of running until I find myself back in the City of Mirrors, back in the childhood home I barely remember. I plot the countless ways I could kill the crown, if I ever got the chance.

Anger has taken root so deeply inside me, I can no longer tell what's flesh and what's fury. And yet, I still taste the fear, feel it pulsing through my bones where I wish magic lived instead.

When I finally leave the burning room, I repeat the faction's motto in my mind. They were the words Vale told me all those cycles ago, when our desperation planted the seeds of a rebellion.

We'll find a way out, Rune, he'd said. He even took my hand, squeezing as he said what eventually became our motto: *While others fight to survive, we fight to* live.

2
HARRICK

I am a child playing pretend, and everyone here knows it. The four elite representatives are my biggest concern. They glower at me from behind elaborate masks, their unimpressed expressions hollowing my stomach. My skin itches with their blatant disapproval, but I can't afford to show vulnerability. I keep my shoulders squared as I stand at the end of the table, organizing parchments into careful piles. Despite the sharp spike of my heartbeat, I force myself to act bored.

"Let's begin," I say. "From my notes on your previous—"

I'm cut off by an abrupt rumbling.

At first, I think it's an earthquake, but a quick glance to my right proves even worse. A dark-haired servant stands at the far side of the room, his thin hand shaking against the lever to the window's cover. The protective shields, glowing pale red with low magic, peel from the window like skin pulled from bone. The servant trembles, his already pale face growing near-translucent with blood loss.

"Stop," I demand, hands tensed at my sides.

The servant immediately complies and sucks in a weak

breath. His shoulders sag as he cradles his burnt hand to his chest. Mortals aren't made to touch magic. The window's lever is laced with it, and now, the man is vibrating in agony, his hand already swollen with blisters. He doesn't cry—he barely even moves.

"Explain yourself," I say. My words are clipped, as if I'm annoyed. I am, I suppose, just not at him.

The upper half of this room's window is now exposed. The shields exist to fortify the Tower during Earthquake Season, to keep the windows from collapsing and the building with them. It takes days to get these shields in place before the start of the season, and only seconds to free the magic, to let it leech back into the room.

"I hoped to see the mountains," the man stutters.

It's a blatant lie, and it's so poorly conceived, I can only assume Demetrius Llroy is behind it. Representative for the City of Mirrors, he's as cruel as they come. Built like an overgrown weed and bearing the personality of an aggressive hound, Demetrius is Mother's favorite lackey.

I stare out at the Savoan mountain range. Its jagged ridgeline, silhouetted by the dying sun, rises hundreds of feet higher than the top of the Tower. Every few moments, a crash of waves strikes against the barren peaks and surges between them. I follow the saltwater as it cascades over the mountain range in elaborate patterns, until it disappears behind the thick foliage of the Wilds. Though not visible from here, pools of translucent water collect at its base, making animals sick with its salt and slowly devouring the forest floor.

When I was young, Quil explained Savoa was like a bowl and our world was like the tub I bathed in. Our land sat in a wide expanse of water, and during Flood Season, water rose higher than the lowest peaks of our mountains, spilling into our bowl. Even in the days before the Flood Season officially begins, water leeches between the mountain peaks, seeping into what little fertile soil we have.

I clench and loosen my fists, feeling the bite of restless magic within them. The servant keeps his eyes low, but behind his thin veil, his tongue darts between his lips as he watches me.

I'm going to kill him, he thinks—and still, he pulled the lever. I wonder what Demetrius threatened him with.

"You are dismissed," I tell him. My voice is stale, blunt. I sound angry, and I hope he knows it's not at him. He probably doesn't.

The man scampers from the room with a grateful nod. Behind me, Demetrius scoffs and Oris Fhell, representative of the Reaping Grounds, echoes his sentiment. Beyond the four representatives, three servants and six guards remain in the room. I glance between the servants, at their ill-fitting coveralls and their cowered stances. Weak, defenseless, terrified.

"All servants. Dismissed," I bark. They hesitate, only momentarily, before hurrying from the room. I'll ensure they're paid, but I'm not going to worsen this moment by announcing it. I've already given the representatives plenty to report to Mother.

It's her fault I'm here.

The elite sector representatives meet at the end of every season, and typically, Mother leads them. They discuss magic distribution and upcoming contracts, and I've heard it's often past midnight before they adjourn. Only *heard*, because while these meetings are routine for the others here, it's my first time. I read as many meeting transcripts as I could when Mother abruptly announced my new position, but it doesn't translate to the real thing. I've never been to a sector meeting, and now I'm supposed to lead one.

You will face many surprises if you become king. You must know how to adapt, Harrick, she'd told me.

If.

I didn't miss the insult. From the moment I was born, taking over as Savoa's king has been my destiny. And yet, Mother often acts like it's not, as though this kingdom will never truly be mine.

With a final steadying breath, I look over the representatives. Demetrius Llroy takes a generous chug of nightwater, effectively finishing off his first stein, and refills it for a second. His upper face is concealed by his ornate mask of crushed mirrors, but his lower features are twisted in a scowl.

"Going to let him off with that?" he asks with a grunt. He lifts his gaze to mine, and I can just barely make out his dark eyes behind the tulle of his mask. The elite class don't have magic, but they do have money. And if Demetrius gets his way, his daughter will soon be my wife. Magic, money, power. It's all any of these people want.

I ignore Demetrius and turn toward my secondary guard, Dae.

"Fetch me as many menders as you can find. Tell them our shield is compromised," I say. I should probably just do it myself, but maybe that's Mother's true intentions. If I exert all my energy fixing a stupid window, I'll be too drained to lead this meeting. I'll fail, and she can add it to her ongoing list of reasons I'm not fit to rule.

Though it's impossible to see Dae's face through his wolf mask, I know he's scowling. He'd once been my and Tora's friend, but once he became a guard, that ended. Mother had him assigned to me two cycles ago, and though he's *my* guard, I know exactly where his true loyalties lie.

"The queen won't be pleased," Demetrius continues. "A strong leader knows when to discipline the help."

"A strong leader knows how to recognize a feeble ploy," I say. I snatch the pitcher of nightwater from the table and pour myself a stein. Taking a long drink, I relish its burn down my throat. "Torturing innocent men isn't particularly useful. Wouldn't you agree, Demetrius?"

"That *thing* is a criminal," he spits. He leans onto his elbows, the decorative beryls of his suit clanking against the metal table. The man is wearing literal money.

"Enough," I snap. "We all know what you've done, Demetrius. The queen may tolerate—or encourage—your tactics, but I will not. Your hijinks have made this wing vulnerable, so I recommend you settle down before I have you physically removed."

Demetrius stares at me. My heart races as he assesses me, upper lip twitching. I keep waiting for his response, whether it's a scoff or an outburst. When neither comes, I shift my weight, refusing to let my gaze wander. The two female representatives, Ksana Renat for the Wilds and Maeve DinSon for the Reaping Grounds, remain perfectly still. Oris Fhell, on the other hand, notes something in his journal.

I wait, holding my breath behind my teeth. I outrank everyone here, but I don't know what I'll do if Demetrius Llroy actually challenges me. His mouth curls into a heinous sneer, threatening, even as he shifts back into his seat.

"Now," I say, steadying my voice. "Let's begin."

Oris Fhell will likely have a sore throat tomorrow from all his guttural scoffs, but the meeting has been borderline productive following our rough start. Maeve DinSon approved her contract for the Pit without a single adjustment, and Demetrius eagerly signed his for the City of Mirrors. I assumed he would. Despite everyone else receiving a reduction, Mother managed an *increase* of magic for his sector.

"This isn't going to work," Ksana says, smacking her contract against the table. It jostles her mask, and she has to pause to readjust it on her face. Fashioned to symbolize her sector, her olive mask is a blend of creatures from the Wilds. Fish and crocodiles on the left to represent its bottomless lake. Panthers, serpents, and boars on the right for its treacherous forest. Near-transparent mesh covers her eyes, making them easier to see than most.

Ksana Renat is dark-skinned, beautiful, and taller than the majority of men. I always hoped I'd be matched with her daughter, but Mother would never be so kind. According to rumor, she's going to pair me with Demetrius's daughter. Viana Llroy. One of the most beautiful faces, paired with the nastiest of hearts.

"It's the most we can offer," I say, as if I had any part in the decision. Ksana is right though—Mother nearly halved her magic allocation. I look over my copy of the numbers and resist the temptation to offer more.

"And yet, Demetrius saw an increase," she argues. "You're asking us to keep our animals alive and our lake free of salt with...this? It's preposterous. It's *impossible*. We won't have enough magic to protect both."

"Well, I vote to save the woodlands," Demetrius says, voice drawling. "I'm not a fan of fish."

Ksana's mouth bobs, much like the fish Demetrius doesn't like. He smirks at her, flashing his magically-straightened teeth. I often wonder if his entire face has been mutilated by low magic. It would explain the unnatural stretch of his skin and the odd sheen to his dark hair.

"The Flood Season is hardest on the Wilds, and everyone

here knows it," Ksana snaps. She shoves her contract toward the table's center, glare fixing between me and Demetrius. I hate that she's somehow teamed us together. "The City of Mirrors gets more magic during Earthquake Season. *That* makes sense. Help the commoners survive and give them something with which to rebuild their collapsed structures. But Flood Season is our beast to face. If you—"

As if awoken at Ksana's mention of the season, the floor trembles beneath us. Unlike earlier, there's no mistaking this sensation. It shakes the reflective marble, shooting vibrations up my legs until my knees buckle. My attention darts to the partially-covered window. We'd had a series of earthquakes this morning, mostly small ones that barely affected the Tower. Still, I was convinced we'd had our fill for the day.

Foolish.

The tremor slows, trailing to an eventual stop. I bend my knees, adjusting to the stillness, and keep one hand on the metal table. The four representatives remain in their chairs, but they've pressed themselves to the table's edge, as if it will protect them. We look amongst each other, our quiet breaths filling the room.

"Perhaps only the one?" asks Joran from the wall.

He's my primary guard, recognizable by his impressive stature. He's taller, broader, and stronger than any other guard in the lineup. Stepping from the wall like a detached shadow, Joran crosses the room to stand beside me.

"For Demetrius's sake, that better be the case," I say. I follow Joran's lead across the room, where metal handles blend into the scarlet wall. Chairs screech as the representatives do the same.

There's no sign of Dae or the menders.

Demetrius spits back something about the incompetent

servant, but he doesn't have the chance to finish. He doesn't even make it to the wall before the next tremor hits. This one is infinitely harder than the first, like getting punched in the gut or falling down stairs. I stumble against the wall, gripping the metal handle as Joran steadies me from the back.

I don't hear the splinter of glass, but I see it: a hairline fracture that dances from one corner of the window to the opposite side. It spiderwebs until it mars the entire upper window with serrated fissures. The earthquake finally stills, followed immediately by the ring of a two-toned siren. It radiates from this room, a global warning that we've suffered damage.

Mother will be so pleased if the room collapses under my watch. And unless I do something, it will.

"We must go, my prince," Joran says. Heavy boots sound on the marble floor behind me and voices blur in the back of my mind. I tune them out, only reacting when Joran pulls hard at my shoulder.

There are over fifteen royal guards in the room now, and where the four representatives once sat, there is now only an abandoned table. The mending royal has arrived, but it's far too late for that.

"It's going to shatter," I say, my voice hoarse. This was likely Demetrius's plan all along. Not to report my lenience with servants, but to show my incompetence. I should have evacuated the room as soon as the window lost half its shield. I should have ensured royals arrived to mend it. I should have—

It doesn't matter now.

"My prince—"

I rip out of Joran's grasp, legs still unsteady. Multiple pairs of hands reach for me, as if I could possibly leave the room in this state. I shove them off and center myself in the room.

"Guards," I say, my voice steady and loud over the blaring siren. "Vacate the room immediately. That's an order."

Nobody argues—they *can't*—but still, I feel Joran hesitate behind me. His bulking frame lingers for one second, maybe two, before he reluctantly leaves. I stretch my fingers, into my palms and away, until my hands are loose.

Magic pulses through my bones, growing hotter as it nears my fingertips. I twitch with discomfort.

I raise my arms, keeping my attention on the window. The mangled cracks taunt me, worsening with each passing second. I suck a deep breath into my lungs and close my eyes. Without sight to distract me, I can feel every morsel of magic in my bones. It's a living thing, jolting around the marrow, somehow both desperate for release and reluctant to leave.

I open my eyes, find my target, and cast.

The magic rips from my fingers, dark red and coiled tight. Bits of my soul go with it, and though I know it will return, it's uncomfortable all the same. I scream against the sensation, throat burning with it.

As a son of the Architect, I can harness every type of magic: violence from the Wilds; darkness from the Pit; pain from the City of Mirrors. But I've always been drawn most to the power of the Reaping Grounds.

Raw magic comes in discordant bursts, often taking the form of smoke or fog. It's reckless and difficult to control, and most descendants are not strong enough to wield it.

But I am not most.

With a thrust of my hands, the magic transforms before me. Red mist solidifies into a swarm of vines and roots, multiplying the farther they stretch. A thick bough, wide as my chest, slams against the floor. The magic expands, swirling through the room like a living tornado. Tendrils of reedy branches stretch across the wall and over the window, lacing together like a woven mat. One row and then another, slowly building from the top down.

They solidify as I move on, transforming from pliable magic to hardened overgrowth, thick with bark and tangled vines. I'm almost done. Twisting, twining, until branches cover the majority of the window.

Another earthquake strikes, the hardest yet, and the glass shatters with it. It slices against my living magic, hurting worse than if it was my skin. I stumble with the pain, magic snapping like an overstretched band. I scream harder, finding my balance again and pushing the magic back toward the window. It doesn't matter—it's too late. The ceiling sags without its exterior support, slanting as if ready to plunge two-hundred stories.

The room is going to collapse.

I bring both hands together, transforming narrow branches into full-sized tree boles. I'm giving too much, letting the magic take more than I have to offer, but I don't stop. With jerking heaves, I place one massive trunk after the other, smashing them against the failing shield. By the time I'm done, panting and exhausted, six tree trunks stand as impenetrable pillars. A soft wind filters through the gaping hole in the wall of vines and trees, but the ceiling holds.

I drop my hands, the magic shooting back into my bones. Instant relief courses through me as it settles into its rightful home. Breaths come easier. My legs stop shaking. Even my thoughts clear.

"Your hands, my prince," Joran says.

I startle at the sound of his voice, though I shouldn't be surprised. He likely stood just beyond this room in case I needed him.

I rotate my hands. Burning like fresh embers, my skin glows with the extreme heat. I flex my fingers, groaning against the tremor of pain. Now that my magic is where it belongs, tucked in the recesses of my bones, a weariness presses against me.

The earthquakes have ended, at least for now, and the

Tower is safe from collapse. I stagger forward, one step, then two. Finally, I collapse into one of the chairs and lay my head onto the table.

"My prince," Joran says again. He says something else, but I'm already succumbing to sleep.

3
HARRICK

"I don't think you're supposed to leave," Tora says. She watches me from the infirmary doorway with crossed arms.

This place is designed like a cave, with her at the mouth of it and everything else subdued in blackness. It's supposed to be calming, according to the healers. Tiled floor of the finest black spinel, heavy drapes to block the sun, and paint darker than shadows themselves.

"I'm healed," I say. It's mostly true. I spent all of yesterday resting, but I don't have time to lounge around for three days like the healers expect. There's too much to do, especially with the upcoming celebration. In nine days, the Flood Season begins, and the Royal Committee will announce our betrothals.

"Does Mother know?" Tora asks. She pushes from the wall, adjusting her crown. Hers represents Haver Lake in the Wilds. Thousands of tiny water droplets form a crown, complete with miniature jumping fish. The metal snags her unruly braid, and she curses, fixing it in place. Like the queen, she hasn't cut her hair in cycles, and it hangs far past her waist.

She looks like a younger version of our mother, and the antithesis of me and Malek. Where we are pale with dark hair and darker eyes, Tora is all golden: bronzed skin and fair hair with the lightest shade of violet irises. She is Mother's only true-born, nearly two cycles older than Malek and I.

When the queen and king failed to provide a worthy heir, the Architect had no choice but to intervene. For the first time in fifty cycles, he fathered children: twin boys with magic stronger than any other descendant in time. Immediately after our birth, the Architect gave us to the king and queen to raise.

People whisper of our true mother, but no one knows who she is or what became of her. Some say she killed herself, either from the horror of seeing our power or from the depression of having us stolen. Others say the Architect had her killed or imprisoned following our birth. One way or another, I never knew her.

I've only ever had Mother. The king died when I was too young to remember, and the Architect has always been clear: Malek and I are his descendants, but we are certainly not *his*.

"Harrick?" Tora presses. "Does Mother know you're leaving?"

"I've no idea," I say. I shrug into my suit coat and lace up my shoes. "But it's her fault I'm here, Tor. I don't much care what she knows."

I pluck my gloves from the unmade bed and slip them over my hands. My palms still radiate heat, tinted the lightest shade of red, but they're better now. That said, I don't need people whispering more than they already will be.

"Let's go," I say as I pass her. "This place feels like a tomb."

Tora is quick to keep up with me. We walk without speaking, and I study the red-painted walls as we pass. The 195th floor is reserved primarily for medical purposes, so the decor reflects that. Portraits of visionary healers are painted directly on the walls and more than one sculpture of a medical device peaks between the window drapes.

"Are you truly feeling better?"

"Truly," I affirm.

I nod toward the center stairwell, and Tora beams at me in response. It makes her look cycles younger. It's been too long since we've been to the courtyard anyway, and I can spare another hour before returning to my responsibilities.

Hidden behind a magicked door, the stairs are only accessible to royalty. Tora enters her code and takes the steps two at a time. I go slower, pretending it's because I'm in no rush, rather than out of breath. Using as much magic as I did, I won't feel normal for a while. Stripping magic in and out of the body like that is exhausting, and my bones won't soon let me forget it.

At the two-hundredth floor, Tora holds the door open for me, and I lead us onto the rooftop courtyard. A lazy sunset highlights us in shades of orange and pink as we round the center pool. The soft breeze ripples the water, distorting its reflection of blue sky and feathery clouds.

We cross over rough black stones, weaving between folded chairs and stored decorations. In nine days, this will all be transformed into an extravagant celebration. Exotic meats and delectable fruits, all enchanted to look and taste better than they truly are. Partygoers will crowd this large square, doing too much of everything: drinking, dancing, gossipping.

For now, the space is empty. Green, yellow, and blue trees, all varying in shape and size, line two sides of the yard. A few leaves drift over the Tower's ledge. Tora stares as they plunge hundreds of feet to the ground below, but I shift my attention to the farside of the courtyard. The event stage, half-hidden behind bright foliage, will one day serve as my altar.

We stop once we reach the far corner, where only an iron-wrought fence separates us from the nauseating drop. It's a long way down. I sit at the base of the metal rungs, facing the oval pool, and close my eyes. Tora slides into the spot beside me, and I let out a hard breath.

"I snooped," Tora says after several minutes.

I crack an eye to look at her. She's lounged against the railing too, head tilted toward the sky. Though she's not crying, I get the sense she will be soon.

"On?"

"Our betrothals," she says, voice cracking. "I went through Sorace's desk after he'd left for the day."

My stomach tightens, and I can't think of what to say. Traditionally, princes and princesses are only told of their betrothals on the day they propose. We are to be informed on the morning of the season change and set to propose at the night's celebration. Dozens of elites will attend, all wearing green in a vomit-colored sea of desperation. The rest of the crowd will be no better. They'll fight to join our mangled family tree, if not as our spouse then as our friend, our associate, our *anything*.

Without my asking, Tora continues, "You were right, you know. They've picked Viana Llroy for you. Pretty girl with an ugly personality and an even uglier temper. I suppose they're hoping for beautiful, vicious babies."

I blow out a breath and close my eyes again. I've suspected Viana for a long time, what with my mother adoring her father, and yet the confirmation makes me sick.

"Well?" Tora asks. She nudges me with her shoulder.

"Well...what? There's nothing to say."

"Only a few days ago, you seemed okay with it," she says, shrugging. "You'd been making jokes. Saying you'd just have to put a spike between your ears and it wouldn't be so bad. She *is* pretty."

"Yeah, well I can't actually stab myself through the skull, now can I?" I snap.

Tora doesn't respond. Her pale eyes scan my face and her mouth switches. Just when I think she's going to cry, she lets out a sharp laugh.

"This is cruel, but you being upset makes me feel a bit better." Her lips tilt into a quirked smile.

"That *is* cruel," I agree, but I laugh too. "Why, who did they assign you?"

"His name is Nordan Kerr. I don't think I've even met the man. But his name is *Nordan*. That has to be a bad sign."

"I don't know him," I admit. "I think his parents meet with Mother every season though. They oversee the fruit production in the Reaping Grounds."

"Maybe he knows how to cook then," Tora says, her words softening. "Is he good looking? Gods, at least let him be good looking. Or kind. What are the odds he'll be handsome *and* kind?"

"He's short," I say. "That's all I remember. His hair might be brown."

"You're useless," Tora snorts. She drops her head against my shoulder, only to pull back just as quickly. When I open my eyes, hers are puffy and red, like they can't keep the tears in much longer. "Can we go over our plan? At least one more time."

It's a stupid game we've played for far too many cycles. We shouldn't waste time pretending, but soon enough, we'll both be fully grown and we won't be able to do this at all.

"We'll start in the Reaping Grounds," I say. I twist to face the skyline. With my hands on the iron rungs, I glance at Tora.

She's already turned as well, propped onto her knees, grinning at me like she rarely does these days. We must look like children, and for the moment, I don't mind.

"I thought we'd finally agreed on the Pit," she says, creeping closer to the ledge. "We can collect some gems, maybe some magic. Save up enough—"

"Hear me out," I say, cutting her off. "We'll start at the Reaping Grounds. That's where we'll have the quickest access to food."

We're facing the Reaping Grounds now. Once that sector was full of flourishing crops—lush vegetables and ripe fruit—and hundreds of plump cattle. Now, the ground is graying dirt and the animals are sickly.

"Once we have food, *then* we'll move to the Pit."

We shift to face Savoa's mines. All the gems and metal we use come from the Pit's underground network of tunnels. The sector looks the same as it probably always has: black gravel with massive equipment littered across it. Beneath the surface, however, cycles of earthquakes and floods have collapsed over half the tunnels.

"Then we'll work our way through the City of Mirrors."

We have to scoot now to see the eastern sector. Most commoners live there, and even from here, it's the hardest to look at. Their city is in constant disrepair, destroyed almost every season and rebuilt worse than it was before.

"Maybe we'll make it our home, or maybe we'll just try to help a family or two while we're there," I say. I've always liked the idea of helping people, and Tora is one of the few people who understands. "Then we'll make record time across the Deadlands."

We turn again, our backs to the iron fence now. We can't see the Deadlands from here, but we face its general direction. It's the southernmost part of Savoa, and it's a final, haunting reminder from Wyhel, the god who banished the Architect and his people. The Deadlands are what Savoa would be without Wyhel's cyclical magic distribution, every Lightning Season. The entire sector is inhospitable, covered in scorching stone and toxic gasses.

"And then, the Wilds," I say. It's a salving breath through my lungs. "We'll stay there as long as we like. Tame a beast or two, live off the land if we can."

Backs still against the iron fence, we look to the western side. It is the lushest sector of all: towering trees of all colors with trunks as thick as my height; a freshwater lake, rumored to have no bottom; and wild animals of all kinds, many of which produce the finest meat. Aside from the Tower, the Wilds is the strongest remaining sectors, thanks mostly to Ksana Renat. Still, even it struggles. The lake is murky and too dangerous for swimming; the animals are often toxic and unsafe to eat.

"That's a solid plan."

Tora closes her eyes. I take another moment to scan our kingdom, my attention drifting to the mountains that surround it. The peaks are enormous and daunting, sharp daggers angled up and away from the earth. Beyond them, saltwater rushes in undulating, crashing waves.

"But if it fails..."

"If it fails, we'll start climbing," Tora finishes.

As children, we believed a utopian world lived on the other side of the mountains. We had seen the ocean rise and pour over the ridges, drowning half of Savoa with its saltwater. We had seen it, and yet, we still hoped a safe haven existed there, just out of sight. We stopped believing a while ago, and yet, we couldn't bear to forgo the dream entirely.

"Yes," I say, my voice a whisper. "We'll start climbing."

Tora falls silent as the sunset fades to a blackened sky. My throat tightens through the quiet. I can feel the weight of Savoa pressing heavier against me, tearing through my skin, piece by piece. Savoa will soon be mine, and these people will beg me to save them.

But just as there is no utopia beyond our mountains, there is no salvation for those who deserve it most.

4
RUNE

I am on the forty-sixth level of the Tower. Every section has its own aesthetic, and the military floors are almost as bleak as the low servant quarters. While we are known for filth and decay, the military levels are known for their emptiness. Each floor is made up of mirror-like walls, overly-polished silver floors, and gaping rooms with minimal furniture. There are no colors, no decorations, nothing to pull attention one way or the other.

I sit in a wide room lined with identical doors. Thirty minutes after I've arrived, the nearest door clicks and a crying servant hurries from the interrogation room. She brushes past me, hiccuping breaths echoing as she disappears into the blank corridor. I tense, trying not to panic. I can do this—I *have* to.

"Rune Ealde," says a woman.

I startle, looking back to the door. A petite guard stands motionless in the shadows, nearly invisible in her black, full-body suit. She's wearing the dog-shaped mask of a low-ranking guard.

After a moment too long, I force a smile and stand. I arrived early, wearing the nicest coverall I could find, but it doesn't matter. I'm an unwashed rodent standing next to this guard. Her suit is pristine and high-tech, and my coverall is dingy with a small hole near the armpit.

"Good morning," I say. I sound too eager, too obviously fake, but at least I'm not crying.

The guard doesn't respond. She leads me through the door and down a hallway, her boots clunking against the marble. She stops when we reach the corridor's end, where a gaping room splits into view. It's twice the size of the waiting area and holds nothing but a square table and three chairs in its center. A royal and his guard, both stiff in their seats, occupy one side. The guard, hidden behind his wolf mask, looks more beast than man.

"Rune Ealde," the royal says. His voice is sharp, like I've already disappointed him.

He's dressed in a violet suit, stitched with red seams, and a pair of slick black shoes. His purple mask, cut short like most royals, starts at his eyebrows and stops an inch above his mouth. Unlike most, however, his is made of angled metal, not fabric, and interwoven with black mesh to conceal his eyes.

"Sit," he says, folding his hands on the shiny table. The black reflects his image perfectly, from his smooth dark hair to his already downturned mouth.

I take the chair opposite the two men. I can see myself in the table too, and I have to work not to react. I look horrible. Clean coveralls or not, I'm hideous. Sallow skin and unkempt hair, lips so dry they're bleeding. My mask—a strip of fraying tulle—is discolored and brown. The red emblem of an indebted servant scars the back of my hand. I subconsciously tuck it beneath the table.

"I am Sorace Awyr, descendant of the Architect," he says. He didn't need to tell me what he is—the intricate insignia on his shoulder already did.

I shift in my seat. Sharp panic sears my every nerve, but I can't let him see it. I force a slow breath.

"You're our final candidate for Lady Saskia's handmaiden," he says, face twisting unpleasantly. He tilts his head toward me, appraising me, I think. "A member of the cleaning crew, all the way to an elite's handmaiden?"

It's an unrealistic promotion—or it should be—and we both know it. One of Vale's insiders snuck my application, filled with false qualifications, into the final round of candidates. That, paired with my innate ability to lie like my life depends on it, has gotten me to this point. Caleah and I each created elaborate explanations, in case anyone demands details. I have the story in the front of my mind, but I can tell he doesn't want to hear it.

"Yes, my lord," I say instead. I give him an absent smile, as if I don't realize his question is an accusation.

Sorace stares at me. After an uncomfortable pause, he finally nods, grimace remaining in place. "All right, Rain, tell me what you know of the crown."

I don't correct him on my name. I smile as I regurgitate facts of the Architect and his descendants and their *incredible* dynasty. My expression holds as Sorace barrels through the interrogation, even as he shifts from Savoa's history to mine.

"You are an indebted servant," he says, after some time. His eyes narrow. "Criminals do not often serve elites."

"My father was a criminal. I am not," I say before I think better of it. Sorace's lip curls, and I bite the inside of my cheek until I taste blood.

"Our family's guilt is our own," he says.

"Yes, my lord."

Sorace rolls his fingers across the table, jaw tight. I wait for him to get angry, to end the interrogation early, but after several seconds, he continues.

He asks about my mother.

She died when I was eight. ~~*Your laws killed her.*~~

Then about my father.

He was a ~~*failed*~~ *criminal. The crown executed him.* ~~*Maybe it was me.*~~

Finally about my skills.

I am capable of working long hours. ~~*I am capable of plotting revenge.*~~

I am an obedient servant. ~~*I am an excellent liar.*~~

I have no aspirations beyond ~~*dismantling*~~ *the crown.*

By the end, I'm smiling and shattering and imagining Sorace's blood on my hands. I force myself to *look* calm, so that he might believe I am. I don't let myself break—I'm not sure I want to. I'd rather scream than cry, rather lunge than cower.

I should ask Sorace how he'd like to share his secrets, his family's shame. How he would feel about claiming his ancestors' guilt as his own. I want to know how he thinks a failed thief compares to his line of merciless killers.

But I don't.

I answer his questions and nod and keep my voice light. Because Vale needs me to, because this is our best chance.

"Your interview is complete," says Sorace. He retrieves a flat red token, marked with a complex pattern, and slides it across the table. "Your new quarters. Fifty-one CC."

"You've chosen me?" I ask, unexpected pride swelling in my chest. "I have the position?"

Sorace doesn't reply. He barely moves, nothing but a downward twitch of his mouth. I glance sideways at his guard. *He* hasn't moved since I first arrived.

"Thank you, my lord," I say, lurching to my feet.

I grab for the access key, only to let out a yelp when it attaches to my skin. Scalding heat grips the pad of my thumb, burning my flesh to the point I can smell it. I should have known it'd be laced with magic. With an embarrassing cry, I flail my hand until the token clatters back to the table.

For the first time, Sorace lets out a soft chuckle. He snatches the enchanted token and easily returns it to his pocket.

"Your thumb is the key," he tells me.

"Thank you, my lord," I say again, voice wavering for the first time.

I wait for him to nod his dismissal and then hurry from the interrogation room. My steps quicken, and before long, I'm running. I hit the stairwell, going down, down, down, until I realize I'm running toward nothing. My roommates will be thrilled to have the extra space, and I don't have any belongings. Even the clothes on my back are borrowed.

I lean into the corner of an unmarked landing. Dozens of servants filter past me, juggling buckets of cleaning supplies and trays of dishes. None of them look at me.

Despite the swelling, I can already see the changes on my thumb. I stare at it, trying to bring back the pride I felt only minutes ago. Many servants work their whole lives for this, for a chance to earn a decent wage, to live amongst the important people.

But this is not a token of honor or a triumph. This is yet another brand tying me to my captors—and a reminder of why I must fight.

***

After five days as Lady Saskia's handmaiden, I find myself on yet another military level. I stand behind her, juggling her water stein and heavily jeweled clutch. She's already threatened twice to take my finger if I steal anything. Now though, she's too distracted to harrass me. She sits to the right of Lady Viana and to the left of another well-dressed elite. There's an entire line of them, over twenty elite ladies and gentlemen, all vying for their shot at royalty.

No, not just royalty. The *crown.*

All the elites look nervous, even Saskia and Viana, who take turns fidgeting and picking at their skirts. Like the others, they're here to watch the crowned siblings train, or more realistically, to watch them show off. They sit near the center of the room, facing an elongated window. Through the glass, the training arena stretches in a wide rectangle of concrete walls and black-matted floors.

Dozens of weapons, almost all foreign to me, hang along the room's interior walls. They're different sizes and shapes, some with glowing magic, others without. Swords and knives, shields and gloves, oblong darts and sharpened rings. I survey the dangerous objects and wonder if Caleah's doing the same. Though she stands beside me in the line of servants, she hasn't moved since we arrived. Not a twitch or a glance or even a hitch of her breath. Acting unaffected comes naturally to her, but it takes every ounce of my effort to keep from peeking at her.

A sharp horn sounds over the intercom, announcing the arena's first arrivals. Unconsciously, I lean toward the glass separation. A troop of twenty-five low guards, some with descendant insignias and others without, take their places around the massive room. They stand, tensed and ready, facing away from us.

"Wench," Saskia hisses, stealing my attention. She's painfully ordinary for an elite. Unremarkable features, lifeless hair, a round face. I wonder if she doesn't use magic to enhance her appearance, or if she typically looks even worse. She whips toward me, arm reaching. "My bag, wench!"

I don't have time to move before she surges over her seat, snatching the clutch from my hand. Then she turns to Viana again, and the girls hastily apply blood red lipstick.

"You're going to win. I know it," Saskia says, smiling at Viana.

Saskia has lipstick on her teeth, but Viana doesn't tell her. She only glares, as if her friend has somehow insulted her.

"Of course I am," she snaps. Her words are sharper than any weapon here.

I dig my fingernails into my side. Aside from her potential selection as queen, I've heard only two things of Viana Llroy: she is stunningly beautiful and viciously cruel. After only an hour, I know both to be true. She has tanned skin, upturned eyes, full lips and white teeth. Her dark hair is healthy and shiny and twisted in a beautiful plait. I wonder if Caleah braided it.

As for cruelty...Viana is vicious to everyone, not only the servants. She has the unique ability to draw people in, even as she blatantly tears them apart.

Saskia is right. No one else stands a chance.

I'm still studying Viana when Sorace Awyr enters the room. He exits from what appears to be an office, located to the right of the arena. Before he shuts the door, I catch sight of a metal desk, a stack of parchments, and what appears to be a pinned series of blueprints. Maybe of the Tower? I resist looking at Caleah. Instead I make a mental note that this interior door doesn't seem to have a separate lock.

Sorace moves to the front of the room. He's directly between Saskia and Viana, looking almost as unimpressed by the elites as he was with me during my interrogation. He lifts his arms, flashing what I think is supposed to be a smile. He's unbearably rigid, moving in tight gestures, as if the false enthusiasm physically pains him.

"Ladies and gentlemen," he calls. "Welcome to your exclusive viewing of this crowned training session!"

"The bag," Viana hisses. "Get rid of it, Saskia! It's hideous. We can't—"

Saskia twists and throws her clutch at me. There's not enough time for me to react. Her clutch strikes my chin, and when I try to catch it, I drop the water stein. There's a thud for the clutch. A clang for the stein. A slosh for the water across my threadbare flats.

A furious heat burns my cheeks as the entire room shifts to look at me.

"Pick it up, wench," Saskia says. Her face is as scarlet as mine feels.

I sputter an apology before dipping to the floor. Caleah's foot turns toward me, just slightly. I let myself believe it's a signal, that it's her way of showing compassion.

By the time I'm back to my feet, belongings in place, most of the ladies have turned away. Sorace's glare lingers for another second before he returns to his overly-rehearsed spiel.

"Only those of the crown are permitted to utilize the training arena." Sorace gestures stiffly behind him. "However, as a reward for making it this far into consideration for a place in the crowned family, your access codes will allow you entrance into this viewing room through the duration of the Flood Season."

The elites glance amongst each other, whispering their excitement.

"Now, back to tonight's main attraction," Sorace continues. "The crowned siblings will demonstrate all things from physical combat to weapon control to magic casting. And as this will be an authentic experience, please prepare yourselves for great violence and potentially lethal bloodshed."

The elites all suck in gasps, except for Viana, who turns toward Saskia with a bloodthirsty grin.

"Don't worry, you'll be safe here. The glass is magicked to

ensure it." Sorace nods behind him. "There are twenty-five guards in this arena. Their goal is to remain on their feet. Whichever sibling incapacitates the most guards wins."

There's a soft murmuring amongst the elites, but they fall silent as Sorace begins again.

"A final reminder to the servants: be mindful of your masters. They have worked their entire lives to reach this moment. You have not. You are here as shadows, not contenders. I advise you to remember your place."

I chew on my tongue, forcing myself to nod, first to Sorace and then to Saskia, who has turned again to glare at me.

How have they worked for this? I want to ask.

Saskia is the one who hit me, I want to say.

I couldn't forget my place if I tried, I want to scream.

Instead, I remain silent, motionless, as if I'm nothing but a brainless corpse. I focus on the squishing of my water-logged shoes until another horn sounds.

"Welcome Prince Harrick, Prince Malek, and Princess Tora!" Sorace calls. His plastic smile returns. "And please, enjoy the show!"

As the elites politely applaud, Sorace bows out of the room. We're left to wait, the anticipation building in the air like thick poison. I shift my attention back to the arena. As much as I hate it, I *want* to see the crowned siblings. I've only ever seen them at executions, and even then, it's from a distance.

I once saw Queen Elaria on her way to a celebration. She had passed by in a glass lift, wearing an elaborate red gown and an excess of golden jewelry. The sight of her should have made me sick. Her opulent clothing, the wasteful magic, the glittering jewelry that could have paid my father's debt a hundred times over. Yes, I should have hated her.

I only hated that I would never *be* her.

Of course, I can't admit that. Not to Caleah or the other

rebels or anyone at all. I wouldn't admit it to myself, if I could help it.

When a tall figure enters the arena, a collective breath draws through the viewing room. It's one of the princes, broad-shouldered and dressed in a vermillion training suit. His face is bare, which is the most startling thing of all. Only members of the crown don't wear masks, and this close, it's unsettling. Viana grabs Saskia's hand, hard enough that her fingers lose color.

"He's beautiful," she whispers. Her voice's usual severity is gone, replaced with only the purest childlike wonder. "My husband is beautiful."

Prince Harrick, heir to the throne, immediate descendant of the Architect. And yes, he's stunning.

Despite myself, despite the fact Caleah is here, I move forward, desperate for a better look. I've heard snippets of gossip, seen portraits of the crowned on elite-level walls. This is different. I can see Prince Harrick, so near and unmasked and hauntingly beautiful. His eyes, closer to black than violet, contain more magic than any other descendant in history. That includes his twin brother Malek.

Prince Harrick steps farther into the arena and pauses. Without looking at the guards or the array of weapons on the wall, he nods at us through the window. Of course, he's not nodding at *all* of us. He doesn't notice the malnourished, dirty servants in the back. He only sees his choice of brides, the beautiful ladies all desperate to be his.

I fight the unexpected smile on my lips.

Because someday, things will be different. Everyone in this room will see me. They will learn my name, memorize my face. They will come to fear this little shadow, because someday, it will take *everything* from them.

5
RUNE

I can't decide if Viana's putting on a show. She's smiling and giggling, waving shyly at Harrick through the glass. She doesn't scowl when he ignores her. She doesn't scowl at all now that he's here. It's probably an act, but she sure looks genuine. Her eyes track his every movement, smile widening as she watches him.

She doesn't react when Prince Malek enters the arena, but the other elites do. While he and Harrick were born identical, they're easy to distinguish now. Gruesome scars line Malek's face, all different shapes and lengths: one across his cheek, another through his left eyebrow, two more along his jaw and throat. His hair is long, unkempt, and his eyes are just barely lighter than his brother's.

He moves differently too. Where Harrick takes slow, calculated steps, Malek strides wildly. He knocks shoulders with every guard he passes, flashing a snarled grin at his audience. He does a full rotation of the room before settling in beside Harrick.

The brothers do not acknowledge each other.

Princess Tora arrives last, and the first thing I notice are her eyes. While her brothers' irises are dark, like strong nightwater, Tora's are the color of wilting lilacs. She's weak. Far weaker than a crowned descendant should be—and without masks, it's easy to see the stark, startling contrast between them.

My heart spikes in my throat.

I know about their magic, of course. Everyone, even lowly servants, know the basics. Descendants get their magic from one of four sectors: the Reaping Grounds, the Wilds, the City of Mirrors, the Pit. Most royals have an ability, ranging from reviving wilted plants to causing deadly rockslides. Their strength depends on several factors, but it's always visible in their eyes. The darker the violet, the more the power.

And the crowned are supposed to be strongest of all.

After Princess Tora's disappointing birth, the Architect started a new line. Twin boys, both shockingly beautiful and immensely powerful. Like the Architect, they can channel not one sector, but all four.

Looking between the brothers now, I can feel it.

Their untouchable power.

For the first time since we've entered the room, I glance at Caleah. It's not intentional, but I'm desperate to know what she's thinking. I've never witnessed crowned magic in person, aside from the Architect's executions. Has Caleah? Have most people here? She doesn't return my gaze, so I force it back to the arena.

A buzzer sounds, and that's the only warning we get before the guards lunge. The non-descendant guards grab at the weapon-lined walls. One tears a collection of metal squares and fastens them to his chest plate. Another claims a magicked hook, treacherously sharp and glowing red. She flips it in the air, letting it rotate, before smoothly catching it in her gloved hand. Then, she snaps to face the crowned siblings, legs braced in a wide stance.

As the guards seamlessly move, the siblings maintain their positions in the back. They don't race to choose weapons. They don't take defensive stances. They remain still, watching the guards like I imagine lions watch their prey.

The guards shift to the left side of the room, in what appears to be a practiced arrangement. Malek ticks his head, a small and devious grin twisting his scars. Harrick glances at Tora, and though she doesn't return his gaze, she offers a subtle nod.

A second buzzer blares, longer than the first. This time, there's a heavy pause. The guards raise their weapons or their glowing hands, shoulders clenching with tension. With each passing second, they cower closer together.

One breath. Two.

Malek moves first, his jaw unhinging with a brutal scream. Despite the glass wall, it sounds like he's yelling in this very room. His hands light with magic, flaring like hot coals. They burn infinitely brighter than any of the guards', and the red pulses as it grows in size and changes shape. The viewing elites suck in breaths and give squeamish cries, but I find my awareness narrowing. Suddenly, I feel like I'm alone in this room, watching something equal parts horrifying and beautiful.

Magic pulses at Malek's fingertips, brighter and stronger, until the smoke takes a life of its own. It coils from his outstretched hands, morphing from heavy fog into a beast unlike anything I've ever seen. Rising over ten feet tall, its misshapen body nearly touches the ceiling. It stands on multiple sharp, spindly legs that bend at unnatural angles. Every time it moves, one of its pointed feet pierces clean through the mat.

An elite male screams and sprints from the room. Despite Sorace's promise of safety, two others are close behind.

I stare, transfixed, as the beast charges with impossible speed.

It isn't real, I tell myself.

Except it is, in all the ways that count. The creature may be born of magic, but it moves as if it belongs here. It roars, body undefined and shifting, translucent in certain angles. It reaches the guards in three strides, striking its first victim before he fully lifts his sword.

With a sweep of its leg, the creature launches the guard across the room. The man crunches against the wall of weapons, spears and arrows clattering over him.

Malek gleams behind the beast as it turns on its haunches. The scarlet magic stretches from his hands, pulsing life into his creation. Creeping with predatory slowness, the beast faces the guard. And then, it lunges. With a jolting kick, it punches a hole through the guard's stomach, clear through to the other side.

I scream before I can think better of it, but no one scolds me. They're too busy screaming themselves, too busy watching a man die before their own eyes. Because surely there's no saving him. Dark blood spills around him, creating a shallow pool of red.

I dig my fingers into my coveralls, trying to keep a level head. I can't afford to lose focus here, to draw any more attention to myself.

"Malek!" Princess Tora screams. It isn't until she's yelled that I realize she and Harrick have moved. They remain near each other, with Tora straining to see the beast's victim within the chaos. She twists back toward Malek, grimacing. "No killing blows!"

Her voice is too casual to my ears. As if she's scolding Malek for cheating their game, not for murdering a man.

I force my gaze back to the remaining guards. They break from formation like a cluster of frightened insects. A few challenge the beast, hacking at the meatiest part of its legs, swinging for its underbelly. Most guards, however, retreat to the opposite side of the room. I wonder if they knew the man, now corpse. They must be terrified they'll be next, and for this, a stupid show of bravado.

The beast spins, stabbing through a guard's foot as it faces Tora. Harrick wrenches the princess behind his back and lifts his hands. They're brighter and sharper than Malek's, not like burning coals, but like fire itself.

I tell myself to remain still, emotionless from the show that isn't meant for me. But when Harrick screams, I flinch. It's a strangled, pained cry, like he's being tortured.

His magic strikes three guards at once, ripping them away from the beast. The pinned guard screams as she's pulled across the mat, the beast's foot slicing through the side of her ankle.

"That's three for Harrick," Viana says without flinching. She lowers her voice, forcing Saskia to lean closer. "Smart to take the guards nearest Malek's magic. Claim the points for himself."

I ignore Saskia's reply and squint at Harrick's magic. It's almost too fast to track, snapping left then right and breaking into multiple strands. It is only as it curls around his victims that I realize his magic has taken the shape of vines. The Reaping Grounds. They weave over the three guards' bodies, mummifying them as they strain against his hold. Only the fronts of their masks remain exposed.

"Wyhel," Saskia says, words trembling. "Three at once. That's terrifying."

"What did you expect? He's our king. Of course he's powerful." Viana sounds anything but frightened.

"Still," Saskia murmurs.

I silently agree.

More and more guards collapse. I count twenty-one, and according to Viana, Harrick is far in the lead. I'm not so sure. My head spins with the endless blasts of magic. Vines and branches from Harrick. The spiky-legged beast from Malek. Nothing at all from Tora.

"That's sixteen for Harrick," Viana says, her voice echoing through the viewing room. "Sixteen for Harrick. Five for Malek."

"I've got eleven for Harrick and ten for Malek," an elite woman says down the line. She leans forward, raising an eyebrow at Viana. "It's okay, V. Counting is hard."

"I think Malek is going to take it," another woman says.

"No way. Harrick will get the last three," a man says.

The others pitch in, drowning out Viana's insistence that Harrick has already won.

I scan the arena. I'm better at counting than reading, and I decide the other elites are right. There are eleven mounds of calcified vines to nine surrendered guards and one dead. The latter are curled on the floor, incapacitated in one way or another. Blood seeps around them, and something tells me the first victim will not be alone in the burning room tonight.

Malek's creature lunges at one of the final three guards. Before its strike lands, however, the guard drops to his knees. I lean forward, shadowing the line of elites before me. The beast lowers, growling and exposing hooked fangs. It roars as water spills from the bottom of the guard's mask.

"Well finally," one of the elite women calls. "Tora decided she wanted to play after all."

The princess doesn't acknowledge the heckler. I'm not sure if they can hear us, or if only we can hear them. I'm surprised anyone, even an elite, would be so bold. But she's right. Of the twenty-two fallen guards, this is the only one Tora has claimed.

Water spills harder from the guard's mask, drenching the

front of his uniform. He falls to his knees, flails an arm in submission, and collapses on the mat. Tora drops her hands, letting her pink-singed fingertips hang at her sides. The guard curls into himself, his ragged coughs loud enough to hear over Harrick and Malek's ongoing battle.

"Yes!" one of the elite men screams when Malek's creature takes another guard. "That's a tie. He just needs the last one."

I shift from my toes to my heels. It shouldn't matter to me which brother wins, but I want to watch Malek lose. I want to see his face when he realizes he killed in vain. I'm not sure it will matter to him anyway.

The final guard stands between Harrick's lashing branches and Malek's growling beast. He staggers between them, masked face turning toward one and then the other. Tora leans against the nearby wall, as if submitting a single guard took everything from her. I can see her heaving chest and flushed cheeks from here.

"Come on, Harrick," Viana whispers. She clasps her hands, leaning against them as she watches the twins. "Focus, baby. End this."

She speaks as if she knows Harrick. Maybe they're already dating, even though it's against tradition.

Harrick thrusts two vines around the guard, forcing the man's arms to his sides. Malek's beast lunges a moment later, but it doesn't go for the guard. Instead, one of its spindly legs strikes against Tora, knocking her hard against the wall. A hanging sword falls at the impact, the blunt handle cracking against her shoulder. She lets out a high-pitched cry, crumbling to the mat and tucking around herself. The beast surges, as if to attack her, and the viewing room sucks in a collective, horrified breath.

Surely Malek didn't *mean* to hurt Tora...right?

Harrick's vines instantly disappear from the guard, and

seconds later, they're tight around Malek's neck. The scarred brother smiles maniacally, even as his face turns red, then purple. He doesn't fight Harrick's hold. He only raises his hand, twisting it to command the beast before him.

The creature staggers away from Tora, and just before Malek passes out, it tears into the remaining guard's throat.

6

RUNE

"I can't believe Harrick lost," Saskia says less than an hour later. With her arm looped through Viana's, she exits the waiting room.

"He didn't lose," Viana snaps. She scowls at her friend, shoving out of her hold. "Malek cheated. When they release the official results, they'll take that into consideration. Harrick would have won if he'd broken the rules."

I want to point out that, technically, Harrick did break the rules. Sure, Malek broke them first and more often, but Harrick still attacked his brother. If they asked me, I'd point out that Tora was the only one who *didn't* cheat. But of course, they don't.

"You're right," Saskia says. When it comes to Viana, this tends to be her response for everything.

I stay two steps behind them, my shoulder brushing with Caleah's as we walk. The two elite women whisper back and forth, quickly moving from the exhibition results to lighter conversation. Viana talks about what she'll wear to the upcoming celebration and then describes in great detail what she imagines Harrick will look like naked.

It's easy for me to ignore them now. After leaving the chaos of the viewing room, my brain is too spent to pay much attention to anything. My shoulders ease as the glass lifts come into view. Saskia and Viana will take them to their respective rooms, and Caleah and I will go down to the elite kitchens to fetch their lunch. And then, finally, she and I will talk about what we've just seen.

We're halfway down the corridor when Viana slams to a halt. I barely stop in time to avoid colliding with Saskia, my wet shoes squelching against the marble.

I look up.

Right now, I don't care who or what made Viana stop, so long as it's not me. Even if it's Caleah. It's cowardly and pathetic, but I've suffered enough torture for one day. For a whole lifetime, it feels.

Viana glares at me.

She's wearing an ornate green mask with sharp points at either brow, and it's almost impossible to see her eyes through the center black tulle. Still, I can feel her watching me, assessing me.

"Ugh," she says finally. She scrunches her nose before whipping toward her friend. "Your servant is fucking revolting. Look at it. People are going to talk, Saskia."

An unintentional gasp sucks through my lips. I don't mean to react. But...*it*? It's been cycles since I've heard that, since someone has implied I'm not even human.

I drop my eyes, praying Viana didn't notice. It's too late. She strikes my face so hard I lose my balance. I manage to stay upright, but my shoes slip across the floor, streaking water over the reflective marble.

"Not another sound from you," she snaps. "You have embarrassed Saskia quite enough. She ought to have you fired, removed from service entirely. Send you out on the streets. See how you like it there."

My eyes are on the floor again, and I hate it. I hate myself. I press my fingernails into my palms, even as I start to break skin.

"Viana—"

"No, Saskia. If you don't get control of this thing, it's going to destroy your reputation. Trust me, it makes them all too giddy to ruin what isn't theirs."

Breath in through my nose. Out from my mouth. Nails cutting into flesh.

"It's bloodied and its feet are smearing dirty water everywhere we go." Viana steps closer, her breath hot against my face. "It is taking away from your status. What will people think of you, Saskia, if *this* is what Sorace assigned you? You've got to manage these things. Remind them of their place."

And there it is again, these people with their assumption that I—or any other servant—am confused about how insignificant I am.

"Apologize," Viana demands.

I look up at her. She's grinning like a fiend, like she *loves* that I gave her the excuse to belittle me. Behind her, Saskia's face is pale. She's cruel, as all elites are, but even she doesn't seem to be enjoying this.

"Forgive me, Lady Saskia," I say, voice cracking.

Saskia doesn't respond. Viana grabs the back of my neck and jerks me sideways, until my face slams against the reflective wall. There's blood on my chin and my cheek, and now, on the glass.

"You will stand here and you will look at yourself. You will think about your duty to Saskia and to the crown." Her fingers pinch hard against my throat. "And you will *not* move until I send someone to release you."

She pushes against my neck, pressing my face into the glass until I can barely breathe.

"Let's go, Saskia."

She releases me and steps back, only to press forward again. Her hand curls over the strap of my mask. I tense, and Viana's blurred reflection smiles.

"Do as you are told, wench," she taunts. "If you look away, it might be the last thing you do."

I suck in a breath, locking the sobs in my throat. With a harsh grunt, Viana tears the mask from my face, taking pieces of hair with it. My ratted veil, the one I've had for several cycles, disappears in her clenched fist. Cold air presses against my exposed skin and I stare at my bloodied reflection. I keep my eyes open, even as my instincts beg them to close.

Caleah's feet appear in my peripheral, showing her silent support again. But that feels empty now, worthless. Viana is going to leave me here, maybe to die. And Caleah isn't going to stop her.

She can't, I remind myself.

"Let's go, Saskia," Viana repeats. She finally steps back, and I catch the last glimpse of my mask being tucked into her expensive clutch. She starts down the hall with Saskia at her side. To Caleah, she calls "Hurry up, wench! Fetch our lunches, and be quick about it. I'm starving."

Once their footsteps fade, I shut my eyes. A harsh sob bursts from my throat, and I work to keep any more from escaping. With my head leaned against the wall, I remain still for over an hour. Then two. Then a few more until I lose track of the time. I keep my eyes closed and pretend it's enough to protect me from attackers. The dark is nice, too—far better than my bloodied reflection.

Every so often, someone passes me. It's usually a guard on patrol, but sometimes it's royals or elites. After a while, I can identify the different classes by sound alone. The guards with their heavy boots and rhythmic steps. The elites with their clanging jewelry and clicking dress shoes. The royals with their near-silent walk. I only recognize them by the swish of their extravagant clothing.

None of them speak to me.

I shift on my feet, body growing stiff as the halls quiet. Night falls, and other than the patrolling guard, who has yet to acknowledge me, it's empty here. My legs tremble, my throat feels like sandpaper, and I've needed to pee for an hour. I don't allow myself to move.

I do open my eyes though, out of boredom more than anything. I've memorized every streak of blood on my face, from the shallow wound on my chin to the long scratch on my cheek. I've decided Viana was wearing a ring when she struck me.

A pair of boots sounds down the corridor, startling me. It's too soon for the guard's round, and this person is coming from the wrong direction anyway. The footsteps don't match any of the others I've heard. They're too light for a guard, too soft for an elite, too loud for a royal.

I keep my eyes open, but I don't dare turn my head.

The man is halfway down the corridor when he stops at the edge of my vision. He's several feet away, but the bright lighting makes him easy to see. Tall and lean and wearing the blood red of the Architect. He's dressed in it from neck to toe, a lavish suit and leather shoes. He's maskless though, his face fully exposed. Not the Architect, then, but one of the princes.

My legs buckle without permission. I press both hands to the glass in front of me, trying but failing to stabilize myself. I'm always a vulnerable target—a descendant could rip off my mask and kill me whenever he wanted. But Viana has made it too easy. She's primed me for slaughter, forced me maskless and alone in an empty corridor. Most people are sleeping by now. They won't get to me in time, even if I scream.

They wouldn't save me anyway, especially not from *him*.

The man starts toward me again. I hold my breath, begging Wyhel to show mercy, if only this once. Let the man walk past me, let him ignore me as everyone else has. Let him spare my life, even though he could take it without anyone ever knowing.

His footsteps stop, no more than an arm's length from me. I squeeze my eyes shut as my legs buckle again. This time, there's no steadying them. They shake harder, until I can barely stay upright. For the first time, I realize how truly scared I am of death. Not just the fact that it will hurt—of course it will hurt. But the fact that I won't exist after this.

A strangled sound cuts from my lips. I don't want to cry in front of him. I want to be brave and fierce, if only in death. But there are already tears on my face, and those buried sobs claw their way up my throat.

"I am not going to hurt you," he says, voice deep but quiet. "I am going to move your hair, okay?"

I don't respond except for a choked sob.

The prince pulls my hair over my shoulders, and I try to focus my thoughts. If I'm going to die, I have to at least do *something*. He's going to spin me around, force my eyes open, and drain whatever magic he finds there. I am going to die, but I can at least leave a bruise or a scar or some other mark so Caleah knows what happened. I hope she realizes I never stood a chance in this hallway, and that I chose to fight anyway.

I'll strike his throat. Run as fast as I can. Pray that I've got a secret power in my bones, magic that will reveal itself when I need it the most.

Strike. Run. Pray.

Strike. Run. Pray.

Strike. Run—

Something soft presses over my eyes. The man's hands rest against the back of my head, tying the fabric over my hair. I'm still facing the wall, but there's a heavy darkness over my closed eyes. Hesitantly, I open one eye, then the other. It's complete blackness.

He's tied some sort of a blindfold.

I blink against the fabric, struggling to understand. How is he going to kill me if I'm wearing a blindfold? Maybe this is some sort of new, sick challenge. Or maybe, he prefers torture over magic.

"Face me," he says, taking a step back.

I turn slowly, because I don't know what else to do. If his aim is to confuse me, it's working. I bend my arms to my chest in a pathetic attempt to shield myself.

"What is your name?" he asks. His voice is too soft, too gentle. This is a trap—I just don't know how.

My mind is still whirring when he speaks again.

"Mine is Harrick," he says. "On the honor of my crown, I am not going to harm you."

"Rune Ealde," I say finally, because it doesn't feel like there's another choice. My words are rasped and painful. "I am Rune Ealde, my prince. Indebted servant. Handmaiden to Lady Saskia."

Prince Harrick doesn't respond. He's quiet long enough that I foolishly hope he's left.

"And she did this to you?" he asks, making me flinch. "How long have you been here?"

"I do not know, my prince," I say. I lick my lips, but it does nothing. Even my tongue is dry.

He lets out a harsh breath, like he's angry. I squeeze my elbows against my ribs, trying to disappear into myself. I wish I could.

"What do you need?" he asks. "Water? Food?"

"I am not to leave this wall," I say, voice shaking. "I am to wait for Lady Viana's messenger."

He doesn't respond for a long moment. I realize Viana is his girlfriend. Did she tell him I'm here? Is he here to finish her work?

Harrick touches my shoulder, and my entire body clenches. His touch is soft, but I don't trust it. I wait for his strike or cruel words, feeling unsettled when neither happens.

"Come," he says. It's not a question, so I stumble at his side as he leads me back the way he came. I clasp my hands together, picking at my thumbnail until I think it's bleeding.

We turn this way and that, and I'm trying to memorize every corner. It's hopeless though. We could be anywhere. The prison, maybe, or if I'm really lucky, the service stairwell.

"Here," Prince Harrick says. His hand remains on my shoulder as he stops us. "The female washroom."

I curl my nails into my palm, pressing as hard as I can.

"I am not allowed," I say finally. My voice is shaking and soft, so much that I doubt he's heard me. But this is a trap, and if I enter a guards' restroom, it'll be his excuse to kill me.

"I am not asking, Rune," he says. He guides me forward, pushing through a set of doors. There's a pause. "You are alone here. Wash your face. Drink water. I will wait for you."

I don't say anything. My body trembles, rattled by a nausea that only worsens. Prince Harrick drops his hand, and a moment later, the bathroom door opens and closes.

7

HARRICK

It's her.

Even without seeing those blue eyes, I know. I can't explain *how* I know. Her brown hair is shorter than the girl's from my memory. Her limbs are thinner. Her cheeks are sunken, and the wounds on her face distract from almost everything else. Still, I know her.

All those cycles ago, I'd seen her on her worst day. Something about that moment marked my soul, bruising me from the inside out. I spent far too long wondering what became of her, until eventually, I convinced myself things got better. The same cowardly lie I always tell myself. Because things don't get better, not for people like her in places like this.

I tilt my chin to look at my reflection in the ceiling, fighting waves of nausea. The woman, *Rune*, is crying. Soft sobs and sniffles that never run out. It's better than silence though. At least I know she's still breathing.

Who knows what else they've done to her.

Other than Tora, I've never really helped anyone before. There are always Committee members or guards lurking over my shoulder, advising me on what I can and can't, should and shouldn't, do.

But this morning, I was alone. I'd been headed for the arena after my disastrous loss, needing to sit and sulk and maybe break a weapon or two. I couldn't go during the day, when the trainers would be there to lecture or give theories as to what went wrong. I already know what went wrong. I've *always* known.

It wasn't that I was too slow. It wasn't that protecting Tora stole my focus, not really. I failed because I'm not the Architect's most powerful descendant. My eyes may be darker, my magic may run thicker, but my abilities have a limit. And Malek bests them every time.

As I stand here, I wonder what it's like to be Rune. I've never seen someone as defenseless as she was in that hallway. I could have killed her, and we both knew it. I'm still thinking about it, that unspoken horror that hangs between us, when the bathroom door cracks open.

Rune hesitates. She's still wearing the mask, my folded red handkerchief, but it looks like she washed her face. The smeared blood is gone, leaving only the wounds themselves. A deep gash on her chin and a long scrape on her cheek. She's trembling again, mouth bobbing softly, like she can't decide whether to speak.

"I'm here," I say. I want her shoulders to relax, for her to smile, even if barely. Instead, she flinches, like she was hoping I'd be gone. She braces herself against the door as if it's a shield. After wetting her lips, she speaks in a rush of words I almost don't catch.

"If you are going to kill me, please do it quickly." She raises her chin as she speaks, and I know she's trying to sound brave. Unaffected, like she couldn't care less. But her words vibrate like they're about to shatter all over this corridor.

I don't respond. There's no *good* way to respond to a request like that.

"Please," she says again, lowering to a whisper. "I have suffered greatly, and as much as I don't matter..." She trails off then, sucking in a quiet sob. "I'm still a person, and—"

She says something else, but it's impossible to make sense of it. She's crying too hard, and my insides are burning and I don't know how to describe this horrible, rotten feeling she's pushing into my bones. It's more painful than injured magic. More horrific than any cut I've suffered in the arena.

I do the only thing I can think of, what I'd do if this was Tora crying. I wipe the tears from her face.

But she doesn't react like my sister. She doesn't shove me away to wipe her own tears. She doesn't get control of her breathing and make an off-color joke. Instead she tenses. She jerks away like I've struck her, and she trips in the process. As she crashes to the ground, something—I think her elbow—strikes the tile. She freezes, collapsed on the floor, breath erratic. She looks like an animal, trapped with no escape.

I catch the door before it closes and slip into the bathroom, standing over her. I wish she wore a servant's veil instead of my dark handkerchief. If she could see me, she would know I'm terrified too.

I weigh my options:

I can leave, but she'll never find her quarters like this.

I can drag her, but she'll panic and think the worst.

We can sit here all night, but that will only lead to more problems for both of us.

"Rune," I say finally. She flinches but otherwise doesn't move. Even though she can't see me, I move slowly, lowering to the floor until I'm knelt before her. "Rune, I'm going to take off the mask. I'm going to take it off, and you are going to look at me. And I am *not* going to harm you. You have my word."

I've given her my word several times now, but it's clear that doesn't mean anything to her. She's still crying as I untie the blindfold, tears falling from her closed eyes. I press the blindfold into her hand, and then, I wait.

After several minutes, her breathing slows. Her eyes are still closed, and she hasn't said a word, but I think we're getting somewhere. I'm trying to think of something, anything, to make her trust me.

And then, her eyes open. Vibrant blue and wide like an Old World deer. Depthless, innocent.

A strange breath releases from my lips. I can't explain the blend of emotions that crash against my chest. The Architect claims eye contact is common in the Old World, but here, it's rare. Beyond my family, I've barely seen anyone's eyes. Whether it's a woman I'm sleeping with or my closest friends, they tend to keep their masks.

Out of respect, they tell me.

Out of fear, I know.

I don't blame them. But Wyhel, looking at Rune now, I wish this wasn't rare at all. I almost feel like, if I just look hard enough, I might see into her mind. Like every thought she's ever had, good and bad, is hidden within that endless blue.

I wish she would actually *look* at me. Instead, her gaze is fixed on my nose and her shoulders are tight.

"I will not harm you," I repeat. "If I was going to hurt you, it would already be done."

Rune still doesn't meet my eyes, but she nods. It's a stilted gesture, like she doesn't believe me.

"I'm going to take you back to your quarters. It won't be safe for you to return alone, especially without a mask."

Her eyebrows scrunch, creating a crease between them. I inexplicably want to smooth the wrinkle, but I don't try. Instead, I let my eyes roam her face. Everything about her is pale and sickly: her limp brown hair, her translucent skin, her cracked lips and unsteady breaths. Even so, she's fucking beautiful—so much more beautiful than I remembered. It's not just her eyes, either. It's all of her: high cheekbones, full lips, delicate nose.

I want to touch her, to wipe her drying tears, to cradle her against my chest. I can't explain the feeling that tugs beneath my ribcage, unlike anything I've felt before. It's an uncomfortable mixture of protective instincts and blatant attraction, like I want to hide her where no one will ever hurt her again—and then ravish her body any way she'll allow.

I swallow. Force my attention to the handkerchief in her grasp. I can't help Rune. I know all too well what happens when I try...and the thought of the Architect doing to her what he did to Quil is enough to squash my urges.

"Put the mask on," I tell her, trying to memorize the colors in her eyes, one last time.

She does as I say and then stands, legs shaking from fear or maybe pure exhaustion. She turns toward me, wordlessly, unmoving. I press my hand to her shoulder, pretending I don't notice the way she flinches.

"I'm in 51 CC," she says, voice soft. She tilts her palm toward me to show her thumbprint. I shouldn't be surprised at the lingering blister on her skin. She's too malnourished to be a long-time elite servant.

"You're newly-promoted," I say as we leave the bathroom.

"Yes, my prince." She doesn't offer anything more, and I force myself not to ask.

Instead, I lead her down the corridor, distracted by the tightness of her shoulders and the trembling of her hands. She's radiating fear in everything, from her clenched body to her soft but unsteady breathing. When we reach a corner, her foot slides, nearly sending her to the floor. I wrap an arm around her, steadying her by the elbow. She jerks out of my hold immediately.

"Sorry, my prince," she says. As if she'd leaned into me, and not the other way around.

Don't be, I want to say. Instead, I look at her feet. "Your shoes are wet."

She doesn't respond, but her mouth bobs again. Somehow, that's all the answer I need. Viana and Saskia are somehow behind it, and she's going to lie for them. Because she's scared to tell the truth? Because she thinks I won't believe her?

"I will send for new ones," I say, sparing her from having to answer.

"They will dry, my prince," she says. Her voice is hurried, ashamed.

"Yes," I agree. Then, "The new pair will arrive tomorrow."

She thanks me, tacking the same *my prince* onto the end. I want to tell her to call me Harrick, but I don't. We'll likely never see each other again anyway. I ignore the way my stomach sours at that thought, and as we stop in front of 51 CC, I find my gaze devouring her. As if committing her to memory, as if I'm afraid to forget her.

You did, once, I think. Not *her*, exactly, but the details. Her eyes are bluer. She's prettier. Her voice is rougher. She's just... more, and I don't want to forget this time.

I don't want to lie and convince myself her life gets better once I'm gone.

"My prince?" Rune asks.

I startle, realizing we've stopped and I haven't explained why.

"Apologies," I say. The word brings a rush of pretty blush to her cheeks. I wonder if she's ever been apologized to, and I know, without a doubt, she hasn't. Especially not from someone of my rank. "We've arrived at your quarters, Rune."

She blindly steps forward, patting at her door until she finds the keypad. A spark of magic zaps between her thumb and the pad, and Rune flinches. Her door clicks open, and she releases a heavy breath. I wonder, if until this moment, Rune doubted I was bringing her where I promised.

"Thank you, my prince," she says. Her breath is heavy, unstable. She faces me, keeping her foot against her opened door. "Truly."

"It was my pleasure," I tell her, wishing she knew how much of an understatement that was.

She unties my handkerchief from behind her head, and a rush of disappointment swells my chest. Her eyes are closed, the blue hidden from me. I resist the urge of asking her to look at me, if only because I know she would. She would, not because she felt the same thrill when our eyes met, but because of what might happen if she disobeys the crown.

"You can keep it," I hear myself telling her. It's insane, absolutely deranged, but I want her to have it. I want her to *want* to have it.

Rune doesn't respond. She keeps her hand stretched toward me, the handkerchief dangling from her shaking fingers. Her mouth opens, and I realize she does this a lot. Thinks about speaking, only to keep the words inside.

I take the mask from her. She doesn't want it—that much is clear. And I know, logically, it's for the best. She could end up with lashings if anyone discovered her with it. They wouldn't even waste time learning the truth. She'd be bloodied and bruised, and it would be my fault.

Again.

"Am I to be punished?" she asks me.

I almost ask what for, but then decide it doesn't matter.

"No Rune, you will not." I make my voice as firm and gentle as I can, and I hope she can hear the honesty in my words. She will not be punished, certainly not by me, and not by anyone else if I can help it.

Once I've had the thought, it solidifies in my mind. I can't protect Rune, not in the blatant way I once tried to protect Quil, but I can help. And I will.

She nods and retreats into her room, keeping her face toward me as she slips past the door.

"Your shoes will be here in the morning," I tell her, if only to prolong this moment for another second.

I'm surprised when Rune hesitates. She holds the door, using it as a shield, as she did in the bathroom. Her eyes remain closed.

"My mask is gone," she says. She's stuttering as she speaks, and her hand noticeably trembles. "I don't need shoes...but my mask is gone. I don't know how to retrieve another without..."

She trails off. Without walking the halls maskless? Without risking punishment for losing it?

"I will take care of it," I assure her.

Again, she doesn't smile or look relieved. She's tense and vibrating and waiting to realize this has all been a nasty trick.

"Goodnight, Rune Ealde," I say. And then, because I can't help myself, I add, "It's good to see you again."

The wrinkle between her eyebrows appears, and I wonder distantly if she remembers seeing me that day. Probably not. I study her face one last time, and it stays with me, long after she's shut the door.

***

It's late in the evening, over half a day since I left Rune Ealde at 51 CC. I stand in the Tower's underground bunker with my mother and siblings. We haven't spoken since our exhibition, but right now, I couldn't care less. After the mess of this morning and all the tedious routine that followed, I'm just trying to stay awake.

"Well, Mother? Did he say it's enough?" Tora asks. She stands to my left, once again fidgeting with her crown.

Mother tilts her head as she looks over the space. There are endless rows of bottled magic, stretching into the room's deepest shadows. She sighs, finally turning toward us.

"We are close," she says. Her hair, dark like Tora's but streaked with gray, is twisted around her own crown. A combination of rocks and gemstones, hers represents the Pit. "He doesn't want to act until he's certain. If we attempt too soon, and we don't have enough, it will have been for nothing. We will have to start over."

I scan the room as she speaks, trading my red handkerchief between my fingers.

"How long?" Tora demands. "Look at this room. We've got thousands of bottles here. It's enough magic for Savoa to thrive our entire lives. And what, we're supposed to let it collect dust until he's certain? Our grandchildren will have grandchildren before he's satisfied. And in the meantime, our kingdom is going to suffer until it inevitably collapses."

She's not wrong, on multiple accounts. This bunker holds enough magic to save Savoa's dying crops and protect its crumbling buildings, to cure the commoners' sick and heal their wounded animals. Our land wouldn't be suffering as it is, if the Architect hadn't been hoarding for so long. I feel nauseated, looking at aisle after aisle of black bottles, each containing magic, all kept for an escape mission that never seems to come.

If the commoners found out about this place, it'd be ravaged before nightfall. They'd steal every bottle, even if they died doing it. Luckily for the Architect, only those in the Royal Committee and a few hand-selected high guards know this bunker exists. Fewer still know how to access it.

"How long?" Tora repeats. "How much longer does he need? How many more bottles until it's *enough*?"

"The Architect estimates two more cycles," Mother says finally. Despite Tora's pitching voice, our mother's remains steady. She takes a bottle from the nearest shelf and holds it to the light. Faint red is visible within the black. "Two more cycles, children, and we can finally go home."

"Two cycles?" Malek repeats with a scoff. His crown is all bone and teeth, jagged fragments of slaughtered Wilds' animals. "I believe you said that two cycles ago. And four. And six. The lie is getting thin, Mother."

He plucks the bottle from her outstretched hand and tosses it carelessly between his fingers.

"We don't need two cycles." He glances between me and Tora. "If he wants extra magic, we'll take every drop of it this Lightning Season. We'll bottle it all, spare nothing. It should be enough to open the portal. Might not hold for long, but it'll get us and the Architect through."

"You suggest we leave our people?" Tora snaps. "And, worse, use all of our magic to do it. The entire kingdom would collapse. Everyone would die, Malek. Does that not bother you?"

"Our only people are the descendants, and there'd most likely be enough magic to get them through." He rolls his eyes before returning the bottle to its shelf. "Do you honestly think we're going to get *everyone* out? We're not, Tora. And if you think for a second we're wasting magic on mortals, you're delusional."

I switch the handkerchief to my other hand. We meet in this bunker at the end of every Earthquake Season, and it *always* goes like this. Mother says the Architect needs more time. Tora fights with Malek about right versus wrong. And I sulk in the background until I feel forced to intervene.

I've always tried to keep the peace, but right now, I don't know why I bother. The Architect's never going to open a portal to the Old World. He's been here over two hundred cycles, kept alive by engorging himself on raw magic, and he hasn't managed it. Even if he could, I don't know why he would. He's got it in his head he'll be welcomed back, if only he can get there. As if their god didn't personally banish him.

"We're going to save as many people as we can," Mother says, staring pointedly at me, as if offended I didn't offer the solution myself. "Until the Architect decides we're ready, there's no point in arguing."

Her eyes flicker to my crown. It's molded to represent all of Savoa with components for each sector. Roots for the Reaping Grounds, teeth for the Wilds, glass for the City of Mirrors, rocks for the Pit, all twisted together with strands of magic. It's fit for an heir, and by the look on Mother's face, she doesn't think it fits me.

"Fine," Tora says.

Malek doesn't respond.

"Now, let's go," Mother says. "We're expected to make an appearance."

Malek's jaw ticks, and one of his darker scars hitches. I've heard elite women whispering about him, theorizing the marks on his face and body. They tend to assume the wounds are from training or scandalous nights with his so-called concubines. I know better. Malek only ends up with new cuts after a late night in the City of Mirrors, and there's nothing admirable about them.

We walk through the bunker and back toward the main hub of the Tower. Malek and Tora start arguing again. I lag a few paces behind them and Mother, hands tucked into my pockets. I've never understood their desperation to flee our world for one only the Architect has seen. As if his judgment should be trusted, when he's the reason we're not there. Or the fact that the Old World was *his* home, never ours.

I'd prefer to stay here. If we used this hoarded magic, Savoa might not be so bad. We could repair this land rather than abandon it, but I've only ever been mocked for that idea. Even Tora wants to leave, though I think that's more about escaping her title than Savoa itself.

The four of us gather into a darkened lift, one hidden and unknown to most in the Tower. Malek and Tora are still arguing as I press the keypad, and my sister is about to break into tears. She always lets Malek get to her, even when she knows he's a liar, an entitled child who only thinks of himself.

"Enough," I snap as the lift stops. "Let's just make it through the night."

Fifteen minutes later, we stand on the 199th floor, just outside the event center. Mother pauses at the metal door, sounds of the rehearsal party filtering around us.

"No less than twenty minutes," she says, eyes shifting between us. She looks only to Malek as she adds, "And behave. There is no need for theatrics tonight."

"Very well," Malek says with an exaggerated sigh. He flashes the mischievous grin everyone but Mother hates. "I'll save it for the Celebration."

Before she can respond, Malek is through the door and into the bustling party. Mother and Tora go next, and I enter last, letting the door settle behind me. The muffled quiet of the hallway is gone, replaced with a cacophony of last-minute preparations. The center is filled with elites and royals, along with their servants, and lowly shop owners. Trinkets spill over tables as the sellers compete for their place at the Celebration. Low and high guards line the wall, bodies tensed and motionless. As I lean against the door frame, a high guard appears in my peripheral vision, hovering.

I ignore him.

Malek thrives in this type of environment. He loves the chaos, the endless possibilities. There are pretty women to seduce and tipsy men to fight when he's bored. Three elites surround him now, one hanging on his arm as he grins at her. I never asked Tora who will be betrothed to Malek, but I pity the woman, whoever she is.

I scan the room until I find Viana. She's stunning, wearing a juniper gown and a mask of braided gold and green. Her cheeks are flushed, her hair in an intricate knot on her head. Several men gawk at her, glancing between her red-painted lips and her low-cut top. My stomach twists unpleasantly, and I scan the area around her. As expected, Saskia is at a nearby table, and behind her: Rune Ealde.

Saskia approaches Viana, and the two ladies compare raindrop necklaces. The pendants are white stone, and if they're the same as last cycle, they'll turn red when wet.

Rune remains in the background with Viana's servant. Their heads are low, hands clasped, mouths closed. Rune wears the dark yellow veil and shoes I sent to her room this morning, and there don't seem to be any additional scars on her face or neck. I'd sent something to Viana and Saskia's rooms, too. Not accessories but a letter, warning them of the laws and the consequences of abuse against servants, authorized by Queen Elaria herself.

It's not true, of course. There are no laws against abusing servants, and Mother has never sent an authorized letter over something like this. She'd find it trivial. I'm just hoping Saskia and Viana don't figure that out.

"It's horrible, isn't it?" Tora asks, startling me.

"What?" I ask. I shift my attention to a nearby statue. One of the vendors has crafted a life-size model of the Architect, made entirely of that ivory stone.

"What they do to their servants," she says. Her voice is low as she steps closer, nodding toward Rune. "See that one's face? All cut up. I'd bet you her master did that."

I don't respond, but I allow myself to look back at Rune. She's in the exact same place, same position. I wonder if she notices me staring.

"It hurts, you know?" Tora whispers. "That we let that happen."

"*We* don't let that happen," I say, turning toward her. "*We* tried to help. *We* tried to introduce laws. It is the Committee who refused to pass them."

Tora is silent for a long moment before letting out a humorless laugh. "It's so silly. For all the power they believe we have, we are just as helpless."

I move my attention back to Rune. She still hasn't moved, and I'm beginning to think she's too scared. Maybe my letters to Saskia and Viana didn't help at all, maybe they've only made things worse.

"Things will be different when I'm king," I say. The words are empty, and we both know it. Tora nods though, even smiles, as if she believes the lie.

Thirty minutes after we arrive, Tora returns to my side, shadowed by two guards.

"Leaving so soon?" I ask, glancing at the men behind her. She doesn't often travel without at least one.

"Aren't you?" she asks, lips quirking. "I'm surprised you're still here, actually. You're usually gone the second Mother allows it."

I shrug. I've moved to the other side of the room, so that I'm less than ten feet from Rune. I'm desperate to catch an interaction between her and Saskia or Viana. There's no reason for my lurking. Like Tora said, we can't actually do anything. It's not like I can hurl an elite across the room for bullying her servant. And yet, here I am.

"You can just talk to her," Tora says, nudging me. My stomach drops, because I didn't realize I was being *that* obvious. Tora sighs. "She's going to be your wife, Harrick. You may as well find out if she's as bad as they say."

Viana. She thinks I'm watching *Viana*.

"Well, I'm going to go," she says when I don't respond. She glances back at her waiting guards before playfully knocking her elbow against me. "You really should talk to her. I'll expect a full report in the morning."

Not long after Tora leaves, Viana notices me lurking. Her eyes light up, mouth curving in what I think is meant to be seduction. Gods. I should have known better than to get this close, but I'm desperate for any sign that my intervention *helped* Rune.

Viana steps toward me, brushing her red-haired servant to the side. She's almost in front of me when Malek lets out one of his ear-carving whistles. The room falls silent, and for once, I'm actually relieved at his interruption. Anything to save me from Viana Llroy's attention.

If I'm lucky, whatever stunt Malek's going to pull will bring the night to an early close.

"There is a thief in our midst!" he shouts. Several people flinch away from his wild gaze. His eyes move lazily over the crowd, and as if satisfied by the fear he finds, he smiles.

He jumps onto a wooden table of gift bags, causing it to stutter beneath him. He strolls from one side to the other, his smile growing wider with each step. The crowd stares, both terrified and mesmerized.

Malek kicks gift bags as he walks, sending them to the floor.

Something shatters, and the seller steps forward, only to think better of it. She slinks against the nearest wall, face crumbling.

"Did you see her?" Malek demands. He faces a pair of guards, who have come deeper into the room. They're tensed, ready to apprehend Malek's non-existent thief. They should know better by now. When the guards don't respond, Malek scoffs. "She's stolen right from under you!"

The crowd shifts as people look at each other, accusations heavy in their expressions. Malek moves again, striding to the edge of the table. His chin lifts almost up to the ceiling, and he looks down at his subjects with amused eyes.

There are nearly two hundred people here. Elites from the adjoining rooms creep into the spectacle. They look hungry, like they've waited too long for one of these elaborate stunts. I survey the crowd, wishing to find Mother, but knowing I won't. Malek has always been strategic with his timing.

"Brother!" he shouts.

I look up to Malek's sadistic grin. He typically prefers all the attention for himself, but right now, his eyes are on me. I keep my face emotionless. If I don't, he'll latch onto anything I offer.

"Surely you saw her too, Harrick!" he calls. He gives me a look I haven't seen in awhile, the one that begs me to join his twisted game. "We must—"

"Stop this, Malek. There is no thief," I say. My voice is low but sharp, sounding more confident than I am. "However, I *have* heard there's cake. Is it ready to serve?"

My question hangs in the air, and I've got my hand half-stretched toward Malek. As if I honestly expect him to hop off the table and share a slice of dessert. Still, it isn't until he scrunches his nose that I realize I've made an error. It's been his tell since we were two cycles old. He's a spider, and I've just fallen into his web.

"No thief?" he says, voice pitching. He kicks another gift bag off the table before leaping to the floor. "No thief, my brother says! No thief, *your* future king says! I wonder, Harrick, are you protecting this criminal or are you truly so oblivious?"

I don't respond, don't move a single inch of my body. Malek may have me in his web, but I'm not going to squirm for his amusement. I keep my eyes locked on him as he strides across the room.

The crowd parts for him, servants and elites bumping against each other without their usual caution. Despite sharing a womb with Malek, I never know his next move. Is he going to claim the thief escaped? Has he forced one of his servants into the act, ready to fake an elaborate capture?

A guard winds through the crowd to my left, stopping just behind Malek. And then I'm shoving my way through the crowd, almost aggressively. They've stopped in front of *her*. As if she hasn't suffered enough in the past twenty-four hours. Rune takes a tiny step backward, only to be pushed forward again by Saskia.

The entire room holds its breath.

"Hand it over," Malek says. "Resist and you will be punished."

I'm on the other side of Malek now, hand landing heavy on his shoulder.

"Stop this," I hiss into his ear. "Right now, Malek. It's too far."

"It will stop. As soon as this wench surrenders what it's stolen."

"I haven't stolen *anything*, my prince," the woman says. Only it's not Rune. It's Viana's handmaiden, a red-haired woman with a chipped front tooth. She raises her chin, as if in defiance, but her fingers are shaking. She's terrified, and Malek can sense fear better than anyone. He leers at the redhead like she's his newest toy.

"You've taken the capsule," he says. "And if you want to live, I suggest you return it. Now."

"This should be handled in the interrogation room," I say. My words are so snarled they don't sound like mine. "Let the people return to their party."

The guard doesn't glance at me, but Malek does, his mouth twitching with a smirk.

"I don't know of any capsule, my prince," the woman says. She spits each word and straightens her shoulder as she leans toward the guard. She doesn't have pockets, but she's carrying a small basket of blue-toned tulle. "Search if you must. You won't find anything."

My stomach clenches. She has to realize her basket is the perfect place to hide something. Or, in this case, for Malek to plant it. This wench must be as new as Rune—she's certainly skinny enough to be from the basement. She doesn't know the rules here...or the lack of them.

The redhead extends her basket, and the guard snatches it. He digs through the ribbons of fabric, hand moving like a hungry animal off its chain. The crowd leans toward him, and I'm ashamed that I do too. I'm desperate for him to find nothing, for Malek to look like a fool.

I know better than that. Malek is many things, but he is not stupid. He wouldn't put on this performance unless...

The guard pauses. He drops the woman's basket, spilling her collection of tulle across the marble. Everyone leans close, staring at the clear vial in the guard's hand. Within it, a thin spool of red magic swirls, glowing bright against the guard's dark glove.

"A capsule," he says. His voice is quiet, almost like he's speaking to himself. But then he shoves his fist into the air, holding the vial for all to see. "The wench has stolen magic!"

"No!" she shrieks. She cranes her neck to see the bottle in his hand. "That is *not* mine. I am not a—"

"A thief?" interrupts Malek. His voice is barely a whisper, but he may as well have screamed for the way the crowd gasps. "Unfortunately, creature, the evidence suggests otherwise."

"Give me your hands," the guard demands. The woman shakes her head and steps backward.

"I did not steal that," she says. "I did *not*. My prince, you can't—"

The guard lunges, grabbing the woman with his magicked gloves. All low military wear them, each pair holding enough magic to incapacitate several criminals—or to kill one. The woman writhes against the man's touch, screaming as his magic, borrowed from our bunker, crawls up her arms. Nearly a minute of blistering red, until finally, she loses consciousness.

As she falls, Rune steps forward. I can see it on her face, her trembling lips. She's going to try to help. It's too late for the redhead though. If Rune tries anything, she's going to get herself killed too. And this time, I won't be able to save her.

I move through the crowd, twisting to block her with my back. I remain there, shifting every time she does, until the guard has taken the redhead away. In a few hours, she will wake in a prison cell, and she will cry her innocence. She will beg them not to kill her.

But she will lose.

The servants *always* lose.

8
HARRICK

"Crocodile," Tora hisses. She drops into the metal chair to my right and taps her fingernails against the table. She's wearing a floor length dress, almost too dark to be considered red and tight enough she might suffocate before dinner.

Without acknowledging my sister, I settle my elbows on the black table's edge. Even as she shifts and sighs, I stare down at my reflection, at the angled sides of my crown.

"Crocodile," she repeats, voice hard. "Did you see it? They're serving crocodile."

"I saw it, Tora. I saw it, and I know what it means." My words are a growl, but Tora only leans back into her chair, sharp nails tapping again.

A pair of servants enter the gaping room. We're in the royal dining hall, a lavish room with red satin walls and marble floors, a mix of red and violet and black. Scarlet curtains hang over the windows, hiding the bulky shields from view.

The servants, each carrying an overflowing tray of dishware, don't acknowledge us. They move silently around the table, placing wrapped silverware to the left of each menu.

When a young servant lays my silverware, he glances at me. It's quick, almost unnoticeable, but I'm watching for it. And there, beneath his flimsy mask, stretched across his pronounced bones, pure hatred radiates from the boy.

I wonder what he'd do if he weren't trapped. Would he hit me? Try to kill me?

If I were brave, I'd find a way to help him. I wish he knew I'm trapped too.

The boy turns away, back to the kitchen.

Tora jabs her elbow into my side, and I startle.

"What?" I snap.

"Listen. You can't start anything with Malek tonight," she says, eyes watering. "I know you want to, and believe me, I do too. But he's scheming to take your throne. Don't fall into whatever game he's playing."

"That girl will be put to death," I say, whispering when I'd rather yell. "That's not a game. She's going to die for something we *all* know she didn't do."

"I'm just saying—"

"You're saying I should let him get away with it to protect my crown," I interrupt. "That's pathetic, Tora."

Her eyes flicker to her lap. She wipes each eye, hard and fast, like she's angry for crying. Pain slices through my stomach. I meant what I said, but I should have kept it to myself. Tora isn't the enemy here.

"Tor—"

"It is pathetic," she says, looking back at me. Her eyes are rimmed with red, dark makeup smudging her cheeks. "It is pathetic to let your brother get away with murder, but it is also your best option. I've thought about it all day. If Malek steals your throne...he'll kill far more than one innocent."

"Malek will *never* get the throne," I snarl. "It's *mine*, and his games aren't going to change that."

"But he wants it," she says. Her voice falls low again. "And what Malek wants—"

Tora cuts off as the door crashes against the wall. Malek strides into the room, as if he was listening for the perfect moment to enter. I tense, lip curling as he struts to the seat on my left. He grins and glances between me and Tora like we're all playing the same game.

"Brother, sister," he says, dropping into his seat. He knocks over the empty stein at his setting. "Why the glum faces?"

I relax, only slightly. At least he didn't hear our conversation. The last thing I need is for Malek to think I *am* concerned he'll steal my crown.

"Leave it alone, Malek," Tora says, leaning across me to straighten his stein. She's always been the buffer between me and Malek, but it worked better when we were kids. Now she's several inches shorter and sixty pounds lighter with watered-down magic. If she tries to keep us apart, she'll only end up hurt.

"Harrick, do you recall whether we're doing combat or powered training tomorrow?" She keeps her voice airy, even manages a smile.

I lean back in my chair, ignoring Tora as she attempts to distract me. I can sense Malek's taunting grin, his desperation for a fight. If I lunge now, no one will—

The door opens again, this time softly, as Mother and Sorace enter the room. My cousin—second or third, I can't remember—looks the same as he always does. Slicked black hair, upturned chin, and an overly pressed violet suit.

"Thank you for having me," he says, glancing between us. His voice is clipped and proper, like he's reading a prepared speech. "I wish it were under better circumstances."

My stomach clenches, and Tora touches my elbow. Images flicker through my mind, turning everything to mush. The red-haired servant, looking more shocked at the vial than anyone. Rune's attempt to help, and the way she looked at me when I finally moved out of her way. Disgusted, as if I was a monster for stopping her. Malek's knowing smile, his daring eyes. The life of an innocent. The death of thousands.

Mother calls for the first course of food, and I focus on the servants as they move around the table. I wonder if they are terrified to be so near Malek. They have to know one of their own was framed. They have to know Malek ruined her, simply because he could, and that he could ruin them too, if he wanted.

Aside from Sorace's compliments on the broiled crocodile, *his favorite*, we eat in silence. I'm not hungry, but I gorge myself to keep from acting impulsively. It's the only reason Malek doesn't end up with my knife in his throat.

Once the servants clear the plates, Sorace pulls a stack of folded parchment from his coat pocket. I'm not surprised, but my dinner still presses against my throat. I should've known better than to overeat. Now I'm going to vomit before this conversation is through.

Sorace lays six parchments across the table, each one bearing the information of a different servant. Six women and girls stare up at me, their skills listed beneath their pictures. I'm not sure how, but I know she's in the lineup before I see her.

Rune Ealde. Indebted servant. Currently assigned to Lady Saskia.

I reach for her profile, but Malek is too quick. He swipes all six off the table, flipping lazily through them.

"Oh, how delightful," he croons. He pauses to inspect one of the girls' photographs. "Are these the replacement options already?"

"Yes." Sorace nods. "I apologize for my department's error

in judgment with 213. I assure you, the servant has been dealt with accordingly."

I don't point out that Sorace himself is responsible for selecting upper elite servants, or that he obviously knows the girl didn't steal anything. Instead, I dig my fingers into the arms of my chair.

"I am simply relieved I caught the mistake before something worse occurred," Malek says. He shudders, as though imagining all the terrible things he prevented. Like normalcy and peace.

"As we all are," Sorace agrees. Then, he gives me a cruel smile. "Do not feel too terribly, Prince Harrick. Perhaps your brother can help strengthen your observational skills."

The chair suddenly feels too flimsy, like I could crush it with my bare hands. Before I respond, Tora leans over me to peer at the parchments in Malek's lap. Of course, he's quick to shield the options from her view.

"Six options," Tora says, ignoring Malek's obvious provocation. "Is it not more narrowed than this?"

"I like this better," Malek says. He tosses the first profile back onto the table. "I feel a bit like I'm picking a concubine."

"Ew. Focus, Malek. No one wants to hear your vile comments," Tora says. She falls back into her seat and grabs Malek's discarded parchment. After a moment, she says, "This one has good experience."

She tilts the profile toward me. I don't look. My eyes are on the shielded windows behind Sorace and Mother. I imagine the sky is darkening, falling to night. We haven't had a single earthquake today. This season is slowing to a close, and soon heavy floods will pour between the mountains. Savoa will become a different world, and yet, everything will be the same.

It is always the same.

"I choose this one," Malek declares. He tosses the other profiles to the floor, even as Tora attempts to grab them. Then he snatches the one still in her hand, throwing it too. "Trust me, sister. We want 247."

He plants his choice in the center of the table. My stomach bottoms out, because *of course. Of course, he's chosen her.* Maybe he noticed I protected her in the event center. Or maybe I just have terrible luck.

"A criminal?" Tora asks with arched brows. "You want us to put *a criminal* with Lady Viana?"

"Well of course he does," I say, snapping forward. I pull Rune's profile off the table, as if doing it will protect her. I glance at her information. Her picture is outdated. She's younger here, but much the same. Small and malnourished and withdrawn.

"Harrick—"

"No," I say, cutting Tora off. "We are not going to sit here and pick another victim for Malek to torture. His first isn't yet dead, and we're already scouting his next plaything."

"Harrick!" Mother shrieks, staring at me like *I'm* the monster. As if pointing out the treachery is somehow worse than committing it.

"Well, I certainly wouldn't mind having 247 as my plaything," Malek says, wiggling his eyebrows.

"Gross," Sorace snorts, but he smiles. "If you'd like to up your standards, I know a guy with a pet sheep."

"Stop," Mother demands. Sorace shrinks back in his seat, but Malek ignores her. He's grinning at Sorace, making vulgar gestures.

"Enough!" I scream.

I don't realize I've shoved from my chair or that I've cast magic until Malek strikes the far wall. My vines wrap around his neck, holding him a foot from the ground. He flails against my magic, hands at his throat, legs kicking uselessly against the scarlet walls. I didn't mean to attack Malek, but I don't release him now. I clench my fingers, tightening the vines until his face turns as crimson as his suit.

Tora yells at me, but I don't register what she's saying. I don't register anything beyond the surge of power in my bones. Malek slouches against the wall, his mouth gaping, not in a scream but in a useless gasp for breath.

I don't fight my smile.

I squeeze again, only to suddenly grow dizzy. I try for a breath, but nothing comes. Again and again, until I realize Mother has stolen my air. I'm suffocating, and it feels like I'm somehow losing consciousness faster than Malek. I clench my fingers, but they drop as I stagger on my feet. My breath returns at the same moment Malek collapses to the ground. He sags against the wall, eyes slowly returning to focus.

He snarls at me, his skin regaining its natural color.

"That is enough!" Mother shouts. And in the same breath, Tora asks, "Are you okay?"

She appears in front of me, her right hand aimed toward Malek, as if she could possibly protect us.

"Tora, *move!*" I scream. With a flick of my wrist, I shoot magic against her chest. It's not vines this time, but a gust of wind from the Wilds. She tumbles over the table and across the marble, only stopping when she strikes the window shields. Mother crouches at her side and barks for Sorace to fetch the guards.

Guilt prickles the edge of my consciousness, but there's no time to stop. I twist back to Malek, hands raised and magic ready. I'm a second too late. Malek has already conjured a beast, a terrifying monstrosity with the body of a crocodile and the muscular limbs of a lion. It charges me, crashing through my half-formed vines, as if they're nothing but dust.

The beast smashes against my torso, heavy paws slamming me to the ground. We slide nearly a foot across the marble with the hybrid's weight settled over me. My breath sputters, oxygen disappearing in painful bursts. A sharp pain radiates through my skull and blurs my vision.

The hybrid's claws bite through my shirt, tearing my skin and puncturing my ribs. I need to focus. If I can get myself centered, I can get out of this. A few vines is all I need to tie this creature and get it off me. But everything hurts and my vision is going black.

I hit my head *hard*.

Even as the world darkens, I hear Malek's cackled laugh. I can imagine his grin, the excitement in those narrowed eyes. This is what he's always wanted: a dead brother and a guaranteed throne.

With a snarled roar, Malek's beast shoves off my chest, only to crash back against me. I hear cracking, snapping, my ribcage shattering against my organs. I try to scream, but nothing comes out. There's only the crunch of bone, the warmth of blood splattering against my chin and out my mouth.

Black overtakes my vision until I can't see or hear or feel anything at all.

I'm not sure how long my senses are gone, but they return in an abrupt snap. Everything, all at once. Breath and sound and the steady pulse of magic through my bones. Tora is screaming again, wailing, but at least she's okay. Her sobs grow quiet, replaced by multiple guards pushing into the space around me. They shout orders and Mother's voice filters between them.

I don't try to get up. Even without Malek's hybrid on my chest, I'm not sure I can move. My body might be shattered. It certainly feels that way. I'm sucking wet breaths through my lips, the taste of blood bitter on my tongue.

A healer kneels at my side and presses his hands against my

ribcage. He frowns at what he finds, but he doesn't tell me the damage. I can't find the energy to ask.

"I'm putting you to sleep now," he says. His voice is calm, almost hypnotic. "All will be better when you wake."

I know he means my injuries, but I pretend he truly means *all*. That when I wake, I will be stronger, faster, smarter. When I wake, I will be the most fearsome caster, more powerful than the Architect ever was. They say I was born with more magic than any other descendant in Savoan history, and maybe when I wake, I will believe them.

<hr>

"He is waking," says a voice. It's foggy and distant, like it's coming from another world. "Quick. Fetch the Architect."

A moan rumbles from my chest. Everything hurts. A sharp throb pulses against the back of my skull and it feels like my lungs aren't working. My bones are worse. It's like someone chipped them into a million pieces, only to sloppily reconnect them. I move my hands up my ribcage, groaning as the bones flex against my touch.

"Don't, my prince," the foggy voice says. "Leave it be."

It takes three tries to open my eyes. Bright lights shine overhead, and the man holds another light in his hand. He hovers it above my face, tilting my chin with his fingers.

"Very good," he says.

I have no idea how this could be good, let alone *very good*. I wince as he moves his hands over me, pulling at one eyelid, then the other. He promised I would wake better, but I'm far from it. Maybe Malek's magic has infested my body like a disease, and the healer's power isn't working. Maybe this is how I die, shattered in the infirmary, each breath harder than the last.

"What's wrong with me?" I ask through a wheezy gasp.

"The Architect requested we postpone further treatment," he says, still moving his hands over my body. "We will heal you soon, but we must wait until he arrives. I've already sent for him."

"No," I say. It sounds more like dust than my voice. "Don't send for him. He'll only—"

"I will only *what?*"

I close my eyes at the Architect's voice. It is deep and menacing, despite his impossible age. The healer scampers from the room, his clicking shoes replaced by heavy footsteps. Even with my eyes shut, I recognize my father's walk. Purposeful and slow, like a bloodthirsty predator, closing in for the kill. As a child, I did everything to resolve the Architect's hatred of me. I trained hard, studied hard, practiced magic until my hands were burnt and raw. It was never enough. I am nothing more than a vessel for the Architect's magic—my mind, to him, is a nuisance.

I open my eyes when he reaches the bedside. His clothes conceal his entire body and face, but more importantly, they hide the fact he's dying. After countless cycles, the Architect's human body is struggling to survive, even as he regularly gorges himself on excess magic. It's kept him alive this long, but his time is running out. Unless he can get back to the Old World to beg his banisher for mercy, he will likely die before I do.

The Architect leans over me, face concealed but disgust prominent. His crown of weathered bones gleams from between the center of his red wolf mask.

"What will I do, my boy?" he asks. He remains still for several seconds before his hand finds my chin. He squeezes hard enough that he might add a broken bone to my collection.

"I only meant—"

"Save your lies. Your mother told me of your squabble with Malek," he says. He perches on the edge of my cot, and I groan at the jolt of movement. The Architect scoffs. "Picking a fight over such a trivial matter? Pathetic. But *losing* that fight? Unacceptable."

I don't have a response to that. He's right, at least about the shame of losing.

"He framed a servant for murder. He's going to have her killed," I say, glaring at the Architect, hoping I come off more confident than I feel. "I will not be a king who allows the unjust abuse of my people!"

The Architect laughs. It's a hollow sound that bubbles into my gut, making my entire body cold. I keep my eyes on him anyway and force my chin higher, despite the radiating pain.

"Malek must learn—"

"No, *you* must learn!" he shouts. He presses his hand to my bare chest and pushes down, stealing a sharp gasp from my lungs. "You are to be king because you are powerful. Because you have more magic than any other descendant.

"So do not be confused, my boy! Your duty is to escape Savoa, not save it. The mortals are here to keep us alive, to grow our food, to hunt our grounds, to unearth our metals. You are not here for them. You are here to open that portal for *me*." He leans closer, until I can feel his harsh breath through his mask. "I will *not* hear of this foolishness again. Do you understand?"

I grit my teeth, a growl locked at the peak of my throat.

"Do you understand?" he screams. He shoves his hand against my sternum, and a hideous croak breaks in my throat.

"Yes, sir," I say. Without breath, my words are barely audible. But the Architect slowly lifts from my chest, straightening until he's no longer over me.

"Good," he says. He backs away from the cot and strides for

the exit, only to stop at the door. His hand hovers over the metal handle as he looks at me. "I expect you to increase your training. If I hear you've lost to your brother again, I will not let them heal you."

And then he's gone. The ebony door slams behind him, only opening when the healers return. They press their hands against my chest and face, their magic seeping through my skin like boiling water.

As they work, I stare at the ceiling. I imagine Rune has been promoted to Viana's handmaiden, and now, there's nothing I can do to protect her. There never was, and I'd deluded myself into believing otherwise.

In moments like this, I wish I knew the extent of the Architect's sickness, his vulnerability. If I did, maybe I'd get the nerve to kill him and take his role for myself—saving the very kingdom he's determined to betray.

9
RUNE

Two days after they take Caleah, I sit on the floor of a servants' bathroom. The ones up here are far nicer than the ones on the bottom levels. There are dark sage tiles, a row of well-maintained toilets, and even an elongated mirror. I'm between two toilets now, arms tucked around my legs, knees pulled to my chest. I haven't puked in several minutes, but I still can't find the motivation to get up.

A deep-toned buzz sounds from the ceiling. It's the start of a new hour, and I officially can't procrastinate any longer. Vale will be waiting for me, and if I don't go now, he might leave before I arrive. Or worse, I'll be late returning to Viana's quarters, and I'll have the bruises to show for it.

My gut lurches and I curl over the toilet again. There's nothing in my stomach—it was mostly empty when I got here—but I retch until the pain fades. Then I crawl from the floor and fix myself in front of the mirror. I leave, still frail and hideous, but at least without the bit of vomit on my collar.

The service stairwell is empty as I jog down to level fourteen. I haven't been here since my first promotion, and I strangely thought it might be comforting to return. Familiar, if nothing else.

Instead, the heinous smells are worse than I remember. Heavy body odor and old laundry that's been sitting too long and thick dirt that will likely never be cleaned. It's darker too, lit by a flickering off-yellow, rather than the illuminating white of upper floors.

I walk past dozens of yellowed doors, reciting the message I'd sent to Vale: *fourteen feet, nineteen hands, twenty-one long.* That's the twenty-first door on the fourteenth floor at seven in the evening. When I reach my selected door, I use my sliver of mirror to check that I haven't been followed. Once I'm sure I'm alone, I slip into the closet.

The tiny room is filled with broken cleaning buckets, ripped coveralls, and a mismatched collection of brooms. Today, it also contains Vale. The light from the hallway dances over his brown skin, until I pull the door shut, subduing us both in darkness.

"Is it true?" he demands. His voice is a harsh, trembling whisper. I'd sent a message to meet here, but I couldn't convey more than the place and time. I couldn't tell him about Caleah or her capture or the uncertainty of her future. Still, I'm not surprised he knows. News travels fast, even to the bowels of the Tower.

"Yes," I say. I rest my hip against the nearest shelf to keep myself from shaking. There's something in here that's molding, emitting a hideously sweet stench. I steady my breaths, staring in the general direction of Vale. "I'm so sorry. I was watching out for Caleah, but I swear there was no warning. Prince Malek...maybe Prince Harrick...they framed her. I know that doesn't make sense—"

I break off mid-sentence. If I speak another word, I'm going to cry. I had one job as Saskia's handmaiden, and that was to keep Caleah from getting caught. One job, and I failed almost immediately.

"It's not your fault," Vale says. His voice is smooth and gentle, comforting even through his lie. After a lengthy pause, he asks, "Where is she now?"

"I don't know," I admit. My tongue feels like it's doubling in size, making every breath labored. "She might be in the prison. But I don't know where that is. Somewhere in the military section, maybe?"

Vale doesn't say anything for a long moment, and I finally realize he's not going to.

"I've been made Lady Viana's handmaiden," I say to fill the quiet. The words bring an unsettling twitch to my stomach.

Vale swears under his breath.

"Caleah didn't last five days up there," I whisper. "She's the best of us, Vale. If she didn't make it, I won't either."

The words are bitter against my tongue, but they're the truth. I press my palm to my chest and count my racing heartbeats. I've always known this mission could get me killed, but I hoped it wouldn't. And I certainly hoped I'd at least survive the Earthquake Season.

"We need to run," I say desperately. "Forget stealing magic or dismantling the crown. At the start of the season, let's just *go*. Once things settle, we'll come back and finish the mission. Get revenge. Steal magic. Whatever else we want. But for now, we just need to survive."

I need to survive.

Vale is silent for a long moment. My pulse grows heavier against my palm, more erratic. Like it knows it's running out of time.

"We aren't giving up, Rune," Vale says. His voice is hard, harsher than I've ever heard it. "I know you're scared, but you can't back down. We'll lose *everything*."

"We don't have anything," I bite back. "We have *nothing*, Vale. That's the whole point. All we have are our lives. And I'd like to leave before I lose that too."

His breaths are ragged through the darkness. He takes a step back, jostling a shelf as he leans against it. As the moments stretch, I press my hands over my eyes to keep from crying. I keep hoping he'll say he understands, that he'll readjust to get us out sooner than planned, but he doesn't.

"I'm scared," I admit after an eternity of silence. "I don't want to die."

"You're not going to die," he says. "You're going to do what's needed to survive. Find escape routes. Find information. Find Caleah. See if you can figure out where she is."

"And what will you do?" I snap. I hardly recognize the ferocity of my tone.

"The rest," he says simply. I have no idea what that means, whether it's a lot or nothing at all. It certainly feels like I'm expected to do everything by myself.

Still, I feel the fight drain out of me. I'm too tired to question him. Right now, I only want to return to my room and sleep for the next three days.

A buzzer sounds from the ceiling. Another change of the hour. It feels impossible that we've been here for so long.

"I have to go," I move to the door, pausing with my hand on the knob. "Hopefully I'll survive to our next meeting."

It's a low blow, but I don't feel guilty for saying it. Vale doesn't respond before I slip out of the room, shutting it behind me. I tell myself he didn't know what to say, even when I worry he didn't care to say anything at all.

On the night of the Flood Season Celebration, I polish shoes in Viana's quarters. As I do, she stands on a round platform, surrounded by a handful of unfamiliar servants. Everyone here has their place, their task, and no one speaks. We've been silent, with only the sound of tapping makeup brushes and fastening metal buttons, for over an hour. Viana remains motionless through it all. She's a perfect doll, staring at herself in the elongated mirror, practicing her smiles.

By the time I finish with the third and final pair of shoes, an older servant makes her final hair adjustment. Viana eases off the platform and inspects herself in the mirror. She alternates between grinning and frowning, adjusting her dark curls and touching the edges of her black lipstick. Her green dress, a long-sleeved gown with a high neckline and raindrop-shaped gems, is impeccable. Viana can't find a loose thread to tug, but she looks anyway, twisting this way and that in the mirror.

"You look lovely, my lady," the older servant says. "Like a queen."

"Do not speak," Viana snaps. She glares at the woman, and without looking at me, snatches a pair of emerald heels from my lap. "Your opinion means nothing."

"Yes, my lady," the servant says. She smiles placidly, as if Viana's words don't touch her. I wonder if her insides are secretly boiling as she smiles, or if she's lived this life so long she's finally numb to it.

The remaining servants step back against the wall of Viana's quarters. Her bedroom is as lavish, if not more so, than what I expected. Like Saskia, she has green velvet curtains and a matching bedspread and an over-fluffed rug. Much of Viana's decor is in the shape of Harrick's crown, and I've realized her feelings for him blur between admiration and obsession.

To be fair, she'll likely be his wife. Clearly her tactics are working.

I move to my feet, returning the shoe polish to a service basket in the corner. Along the walls, there are multiple paintings of previous Savoan queens and glorious landscapes of places I doubt exist. If they do, they're from the Architect's memories of the Old World. They certainly aren't from within our ruined kingdom.

We stand silently as Viana practices more laughs and smiles and sultry stares. When the overhead siren buzzes, a warning that the party will soon begin, Viana slips into her heels.

"I do look like a queen," she says, grinning at herself. Her smile drops as she turns to me. "Let's go, wench. It's time to claim my crown."

T he royal courtyard is unlike anything I imagined. It's almost frightening, the way we stand in a room without walls, looking down at all of Savoa. A thousand feet below, and far into the distance, the Wilds beckon. Lush forests and grazing beasts of all sizes, and in the distance, sharp-peaked mountains clawing for the sky.

I keep near the courtyard's center, away from the thin iron fence and the drop beyond it. A magicked ceiling floats overhead, and I glance at it often, doubting it's strong enough to protect from the coming downpour. I'm less than two feet from Viana, hands clasped in front of my waist. She has barely acknowledged me since we exited the lift, and I've never felt greater relief.

She and Saskia are seated in transparent chairs, legs crossed and shoulders poised. There's a collection of desserts on the table between them, all delivered by me and Saskia's new handmaiden. Between bites of cake, the two ladies whisper and snicker, openly gossiping about their competitors.

As they taunt the other ladies, I let my eyes wander the space. There is so much to look at that it's hard to focus on any one thing. Hired commoners serve exotic food from two rows of white stone tables. There are platters of sizzling meat and tiered displays of colorful fruit; bowls of leafy vegetables and too many nightwater pitchers to count; an entire table of chocolates and cakes and raindrop-shaped pastries.

Additional tables line the right hand side of the courtyard, but these carry white stone trinkets. I've heard whispers that they'll all turn red with the rain. I hate that I'm excited to watch. I hate that I love this at all, that I'm savoring the excess and wishing it was mine.

Beyond the crowd, high-backed chairs line a raised stage. Four are black and intricate, covered in metal carvings of animals, most unrecognizable to me. The final is much more throne than chair, standing tall above the others. And where the smaller ones are black metal, this one is yellowed bone. I study the fingers and skulls and femurs, the way they've been twisted, forced into place, splintering like dried wood. It brings me back to *that* day, the one I've tried desperately to forget.

The cold touch of my father's skin. His eyes, wide and empty.

The man in a wolf mask, red like my father's spilled blood.

And his emotionless children, their blank stares, bored posture.

Is this not enough? I wanted to yell. *Does this not appease you?*

Now, I stare at that throne of shattered skeletons and wonder if my father is somewhere in its design.

"Thank you for joining us for the Flood Season Celebration!"

I startle, realizing a woman has entered the stage. A stunning elite with soft curves and an elaborate dress. Her mask is as lush as her build, covered in dainty gemstones and thick tulle. She smiles so wide it must hurt and lifts her arms to the crowd. Like called animals, the partiers surge toward the stage.

"You are in for an absolute night to remember," she continues. "Not only will you be treated to delicious food, complimentary nightwater, and enough dancing that you'll want to kick off those heels...you will also be the *first* to learn of the crowned siblings' betrothals!"

Several people hoot and squeal, and multiple men lift their chalices over their heads. Viana and Saskia disappear into the crowd, wedging themselves forward until I can no longer see them. Normally I'd be a foot behind Viana, but she ordered I keep my distance tonight and only come when requested.

That's more than fine by me.

Saskia's new servant shifts beside me, eyes darting my way. I ignore her. I haven't spoken to her once, and I'm not going to start now. It's not worth the risk.

"Let the party begin!" the elite woman calls. "Please, ladies and gentlemen, kneel for your leaders!"

I lower to my knee, keeping my head low but my eyes watchful.

The courtyard's metal door opens, revealing first two high guards and then the Architect himself. He strides forward, drawing immediate silence. I shrink into myself, angling behind Saskia's new servant. Every cell in my body revolts at the sight of this man, this unflinching killer. He's smaller than he is in my memories. Average height and build, almost dwarfed between his guards. It should make him less terrifying, but it doesn't.

There's something lethal in the way he carries himself. Shoulders thrown back, chest out, arms readied at his sides. He is a hunter, always ready for the kill. No, not ready. *Eager.*

His guards maintain a clear path as they lead him toward

the stage. At the door, two more guards appear with Queen Elaria. I force my attention to her, not letting myself spiral into panic. The Architect has taken too much already—I can't give him my sanity too.

The queen wears a pale scarlet dress and heavy makeup with her braided hair twisted through her crown of shattered stone. Prince Harrick is next, wearing a red suit. I'm too distracted by his face to notice much beyond that. His near-black eyes have haunted my dreams for several nights, but I've worked hard to forget him during the day. He could have killed me in that hallway, and instead he'd returned me to my quarters. He'd sent a new mask and shoes to my room. I'd even ended up with an extra biscuit at breakfast, though I can't prove that was him.

I stood before him without a mask, and I'm still here to tell the tale.

Not that anyone would believe it.

A small part—or maybe a major part—of me was entranced by him in the days that followed. I'd been thinking of him, wondering if perhaps he was good. If perhaps there was more to know about this crowned family than I had assumed.

But then he helped frame Caleah. I've replayed the rehearsal night a thousand times, and it only ever becomes clearer. Harrick played the honorable protector, while Malek played the cruel and heartless executor. It was their twisted display to show Harrick's diplomatic leniency, fit for a king, and Malek's unflinching brutality, perfect for a military lead.

I glare at him as he approaches the stage. His siblings trail after him, but I don't look at them, not even Malek. He at least has the decency to be undoubtedly cruel.

The elite woman onstage invites us to rise. I barely get to my feet, half-wobbling, before Viana storms into view. She looks like she did on the day of the royal training. Her face is red, mouth pinched, and her barely-visible eyes are locked on me.

"What did you do to my shoes, wench?" she demands, almost barreling into me. She glances over her shoulder, as if to check that no one is watching, then presses closer. "Tell me."

"What is wrong with your shoes?" I ask carefully. My voice rasps, so weak I want to cut out my vocal chords. I clear my throat, but my words come out even smaller, "Are they not—"

"Do not lie to me," she says.

She fists my collar, tightening it until it hurts to breathe. She looks behind her again, hand still on my coverall, and drags me toward the courtyard's edge. Stopping in a nook between the iron fence and the stairwell door, Viana lines me against its stone wall. She presses her fist hard against my chest, and a pained gasp sucks from my lungs. Viana's lips twitch at the sound.

"There's nightwater on my shoes," she says. "Did I not ask you to polish them?"

I don't tell her the shoes were clean when she took them or that her breath reeks of nightwater or that half the court is drinking.

I only say: "You did ask me, my lady. I apologize."

"That's not good enough," she says. Her long nails press against my throat. "Do you not understand what's at stake? Do you not realize how important my appearance—"

"Ah, here you are," a deep voice says.

Viana's hand vanishes from my neck, leaving my coverall bunched at the collar. I remain frozen against the wall, posture strained over the rough stone. I don't let my attention move from Viana, even as she turns away from me.

"Good evening, Prince Harrick," she says, her words airy and bright. "I was hoping we would connect tonight."

"As was I," he returns. He moves close enough that I can see his profile. There's a light scruff along his jaw, and his crown is off-center. Where his mother's is made of broken stone, Harrick's crown is chaotic with roots and mirrors and teeth, bits and pieces of every sector.

"I'm sorry for disappearing," Viana says. She laughs softly, and it sounds exactly like the one she practiced in the mirror. "I was having a bit of a wardrobe malfunction."

"Well, you look radiant," Harrick says. He's flirting with her, and as much as I hate these two people, a pang of jealousy dips through my stomach. Nobody has ever spoken to me like that. Viana is red in the face again, not from rage this time, but infatuation.

Harrick offers his arm, and she takes it, breath hitching as their elbows link. A week ago, I would have been elated to see them like this. It would have meant we were right about Harrick's betrothal, and we'd soon have access to the highest level of information. Now, I'm worried I'll be dead before I learn any of it.

"Have you tried the roast?" Harrick asks.

"I'm afraid I haven't," Viana says. She's beaming at him, leaning so hard against him they look molded together.

"Perhaps your handmaiden will find some for you," he says. It's the first time he acknowledges I'm here. Sparing me a brief glance, he adds, "She can leave it at the crowned table."

"That sounds wonderful," Viana says. Her voice is still breathy as she turns toward me. "Wench, fetch me the roast."

And then they're gone, rounded the corner, leaving me to creep from the shadows behind them. There's an uneasy quell in my stomach, a strange feeling that, maybe, Harrick just tried to *help* me. Again.

I shake the thought as soon as it comes. If he wanted to help me, he could have peeled the vile woman off my throat. He could have thrown her from the party, from the Tower. He certainly wouldn't be guiding her to the dance floor, holding her to his chest.

As I gather a plate of roasted boar, I find Harrick watching me. His lips are moving and Viana is giggling at whatever he says. They're talking about me—they have to be. The attention, the kindness...Harrick must have given it to Caleah too. Maybe I'm not the first defenseless servant he's rescued from Viana's brutality.

This might all be a game, and I could very well be their next target.

10

HARRICK

The Royal Committee is furious. They frown at me from the stage, where I'm supposed to make my big announcement in less than half an hour. They were clear I shouldn't interact with Viana until I asked for her hand. It's tradition, and after the Architect's visit in the infirmary, I had planned to obey.

It's the Committee's fault for pairing me with a vile woman.

She sways in my arms, all smiles now. Her hands are on my shoulders, the lace sleeves scratching my neck, and her collection of rings tickle the bottom of my ears. I'm barely present in the conversation, but it doesn't seem to bother her. She's busy putting on a show for everyone else, giggling and blushing, tucking her head to my chest.

There's something unsettling about a person who can shift like this. Torture an innocent in one breath and play coy the next.

I absently spin Viana, looking over her head until I find Rune. She's walking the tables of wild game, carefully organizing a plate of roasted boar for her mistress. It's the only food

"

here I haven't liked, and I feel a pathetic twitch of power, knowing Viana will eat every bite to appease me.

Rune looks up, as if she feels me staring. Her coveralls swallow her, making her look like a kid playing dress up. She doesn't blush or smile or nod her head in subtle appreciation. She only scrunches her eyebrows, like I'm a puzzle she's trying to solve.

"I know I should wait for the formal announcement," Viana says, grinning up at me. "But am I right that you have chosen me?"

Demetrius Llroy beams at us from the front of the crowd. I can only guess what perks he'll reap from our engagement. Mother already favored him over her other cronies, but I imagine he'll weasel his way into a shiny new position or a hefty pay raise.

I look back to Viana. Black lipstick frames her flawless smile, and I can make out the deep brown of her eyes behind her mask. She looks like a demonic being, trapped in the body of a pretty woman. I want to tell her that *I* haven't chosen her and that if it were up to me, I'd choose anyone else. Instead, I pull her tighter against my chest, keeping my eyes on her frail servant across the yard.

"That is my intention," I say. "However, I do not tolerate violence or abuse. Not from anyone, but especially not from my wife. If we are betrothed, I expect to never witness what I have tonight. You will not lay a hand on someone undeserving. You will not harm someone who cannot fight back."

I spin Viana away from me, finally looking back to her. A purple-red blush swims under her tanned skin, and her lip trembles like she might cry. I twirl her back into my arms, ignoring the clamor of applause that follows. The crowd cheers like Viana is my long-lost love, not a woman I've just met.

"Do you understand?" I ask, wrapping my arm around her waist. Her decorative jewels are sharp against my hands.

"Yes, my prince," she says. I expect her to follow with an excuse, but she only clings tighter to me. "You have my word. I will never lose my temper again."

I lower her in a dip and grin at the crowd. When I pull Viana back to my chest, her eyes lock on my lips. She kisses me, open mouthed and sloppy. Her tongue tastes like nightwater, and all I can think about is her black lipstick on my face.

"You have my word," she repeats. Her lips brush mine as she speaks, and I can feel her smile. "You can trust me, *husband.*"

I quickly nod and pause to wipe the edges of my mouth. Then, I turn to face the crowd. Their eager eyes are already on us.

"Savoa!" I shout. I lift Viana's hand in mine and try not to grimace. "Kneel for Viana Llroy, your future queen!"

Despite the cheers and eager bows, despite Viana clinging proudly to my arm...I can't help looking for *her.* She's still near the tables, knelt with Viana's plate of food in her thin hands. Long brown hair, shielded eyes, an expressionless mouth. She doesn't look horrified at my proposal, like she's shocked I would marry someone so cruel.

Instead, she looks unaffected, unsurprised. And I finally realize, as she's looking at me and Viana, she sees not one monster here, but two.

The following afternoon, I return to my quarters after a grueling training session. Joran and I tested a few new weapons, and I've got the bruises to show for it. I'm covered in sweat, body aching and in desperate need of a bath.

When I enter my room, Tora sits on my bed, grinning at me.

She's eating something fried and sweet-smelling, and there are already crumbs on my duvet.

"Your date is in less than an hour," she says pointedly. "You look disgusting."

"I'm aware," I say.

I kick out of my shoes, leaving them in the middle of the room. At the Architect's insistence, all heirs occupy these quarters, which he designed himself. Everything is a sharp, headache-inducing shade of red. The carpets, the drapes, the bedding, the walls. Only the dark wood furniture breaks up the monotone nightmare.

"Are *you* aware these are my quarters?" I ask. "How did you even get in here?"

"You know I have my ways," Tora says, taking another messy bite. "But we don't have time to talk about that. I've been desperate to speak with you all day."

"Well, get on with it then," I say. At the end of my bed, a red suit hangs, pressed with shattered glass. I can only assume it's to honor Demetrius Llroy and his ties to the City of Mirrors. I look back to Tora and arch an eyebrow.

"You broke the rules," she says, bursting with excitement. She discards her half-eaten pastry on the nightstand and leans forward. She's wearing pants and a simple shirt, a rarity for my sister. At my hesitation, her smile wavers and she lowers her voice. "Was the Architect furious?"

"He didn't care," I say with a shrug. It's the truth. He can't be bothered with silly things like betrothals and weddings and changing customs. All he cares about is getting more descendants and more magic. If it's not related to his return to the Old World, he doesn't waste his time.

"Well, *I* was surprised," Tora continues. "Could you simply not help yourself? Viana *did* look beautiful."

I study her, frowning. If I tell Tora the truth, that I despise

Viana and was only trying to stop her cruelty, she'll pity me. She might even cry, for me and for her own stale match. Her breakdown will make me late to meet Viana, and as much as I'd like that, it'd inevitably lead to drama from Mother.

"It seemed like a good move," I say, turning toward the nearest mirror. My hair is damp with sweat, and the training suit is starting to rub against my neck. "It will give people the impression we're soulmates, that we're in love. They'll look at us and see blissful harmony in Savoa's future."

"Sound a little more bitter, will you?" Tora snaps. When I glance at her in the mirror, she's deflated. Shoulders slumped and arms wrapped loosely over her waist.

"What did you expect?" I ask. I lean against the vanity to face her. "You know Viana. You know me. You know the situation. Nothing changed because she looked pretty last night."

Tora doesn't say anything for a long moment. Her eyes start to water, and I know I've got ten seconds before she has a complete meltdown.

"Our marriages are part of the job," I say. I cross the room to stand at the edge of my bed. "It's strategic. Savoa operates best with both a king and a queen, and if people believe they're in love, that proves to do even better. It might not be romantic or passionate, but it's important—"

"Oh stop it, Harrick!" she interrupts. She scoots toward me, letting her legs dangle off the bed. Her eyes still water, but she's frowning now, lips harsh rather than shaky. "You don't believe a word you're saying. Don't act like you're okay with this. That you wouldn't rather marry someone you love or at least someone you *like*."

I don't respond for a long moment. I fidget with the shoulder of my suit, fingering the glass adornments

"Love is not for us, sister." I force myself to look her in the eyes. "And despite what you think, I do believe it's for the best.

If I loved someone, the last thing I would want is for her to be trapped with me."

"Harrick," Tora says, voice cracking. "Come on, you can't—"

"I need to get ready," I say. I collect my clothes and stride for the washing room. I don't look back as I close the door behind me.

At the committee's insistence, Viana and I have our date in the open-air courtyard. The same place I proposed. The same place she shoved Rune Ealde against a stone wall.

My stomach twists thinking about it, and I force the visual from my head. Luckily, any traces of the Flood Celebration are gone, making it easier to pretend it never happened at all. The tables and decor have been removed; the nightwater stains have been scrubbed clean. Now, there's only this solitary table for me and Viana, and a small area for serving trays.

As Viana talks endlessly, I study the skyline. The sun hangs low over the mountains, casting orange and red hues over the flooding water. The Wilds are likely sitting in a foot of water by now, and I can't help wondering if Ksana Renat got her increase of magic. Probably not. The Wilds will be flooded by season's end, and people will go hungry thanks to the damage.

"I just feel so much like a princess already," Viana is saying.

I try to focus on her as she admires her new dress. It's a long green gown, similar to any other elite dress, except for its streaks of red. Part of Savoan tradition, scarlet will be added to all of Viana's clothing up until the day we're married. Only then will her clothes be solidly red like mine.

"Thank you very much," she says. She fusses with the skirt, smiling up at me, almost shyly. She must know I see through the act, but she's giving it her all.

I nod for a reply. I had nothing to do with that dress, but I doubt the Committee would mind me taking credit.

The door to the stairwell opens, and a line of servants enter the courtyard. Three men waltz across the black stone, carrying overloaded trays of food. They spread their dishes over the nearby table, delicious scents of meat and vegetables filling the damp air.

I twist my stein between my fingers. Our table is intentionally small, I think. A round, satin-covered table with barely enough room for two plates and steins. Cramped enough it's impossible to escape Viana's reach.

One of the servants hurries to offer us a selection of soups. Viana chooses a thick gray option that smells a bit like musty dirt. I'm still deciding when the stairwell door opens again. Rune hurries into the courtyard, wearing her dark yellow mask and oversized coverall. She's barefoot though, her toes turning pink from the dramatic drop in temperature that comes with Flood Season.

She centers herself behind Viana, chin low and eyes anywhere but me. Viana turns toward her servant, and I realize I've been staring a moment too long.

"Come closer, wench," she croons. Her voice almost sounds kind, and I'd feel better, if it weren't clearly fake. "You may stand near the heat."

Viana returns her attention to me, smiling like she's hoping for a treat. I keep my eyes on her, forcing myself to smile back. Rune silently moves toward us, stopping when she's tucked in front of the nearest heater. She keeps her hands folded at her waist but slowly leans into the warmth.

"The poor thing misplaced its shoes," Viana says, following my gaze once again. She touches my hand, pausing until I force my attention back to her. "Don't worry, I will arrange for new ones. And hopefully it's learned its lesson. Right, wench?"

"Yes, my lady," Rune says. Her voice is steady, unaffected, and I'm desperate to know how someone manages that. Few people call servants "it", as if they're an entirely different species. The Architect and Malek both do, so this shouldn't come as a surprise. Still, I have to grind my jaw to keep from saying anything.

Maybe I *should* say something.

"Good," Viana says. She holds both of my hands between hers, squeezing softly. She's damn-near grinning at her show of kindness.

I glance once more at Rune, who remains as stone-faced as ever, before changing the subject. I'm going to come unglued if I don't. So I ask Viana about herself and her family and her desires.

She tells me she's an only child. That she hates Blizzard Season the most. That she dreams of meeting the Architect, face-to-face, someday. She says her mother died cycles ago, and that her father is the only family she has left. She doesn't mind —her small family is far preferable to Saskia's ever-growing one of nine children. She's quick to add that she'd happily bear twenty children, if that's what I wanted.

She tells me she only desires to do what is best for Savoa and for me. But a lovely parade would be nice, as would a hand-crafted crown and a magicked carriage for us to tour Savoa with our children and their pets.

Viana asks me questions too, all surface-level and easy. I've been asked them enough during events that I don't have to think about the answers.

"Do you like the City of Mirrors?" she asks. She's slicing her cake into symmetrical pieces, smaller and smaller, putting more time between each bite. Her smile is eager, like she's got enough questions to drag this date well into the morning.

"I've only been a few times," I say. My cake is gone, the plate cleared fifteen minutes ago. "I imagine it's in rough shape at the moment."

The City of Mirrors is *always* in rough shape, but especially after Earthquake Season. Unlike the Tower, the buildings there don't have enough magic to protect them. Hundreds of structures collapse by the end of the season, and the residents have no choice but to build from the ground up during Flood Season. In the midst of heavy rain, the commoners put their city back together, using the same materials that failed them in the first place.

It's one of the few sectors I *don't* like to visit. It's a place of squalor and filth, and I feel like a monster any time I'm in it.

"Have you ever been with Malek?" Viana asks. There's a subtle edge to her voice, just prominent enough that I catch it. She isn't asking if I've visited the City of Mirrors with my brother. She's asking if I've *hunted* there with him.

A violent shudder pinches the back of my neck, and without meaning to, I look at Rune and the other servants. None of them look at us, but Rune's mouth twitches. I'm sure I don't imagine it.

"No," I say, voice sharp. I force myself to look back at Viana. "No, Tora and I don't do that. We've no interest in Malek's habits."

"Of course, my prince," Viana says. She's nodding, trying to act relieved, but I'm not fooled.

She didn't fear I was a monster.

She *hoped* I was one.

Viana starts to ask something else, but I cut her off.

"What's her name?" I ask, nodding toward Rune. When Viana only stares blankly, I say it again. "Your handmaiden. What's *her* name?"

I watch Viana, her cheeks warming as her eyes flicker between me and the woman who waits on her at all hours. I look at Rune then. She's blushing harder than Viana, her cheeks so red they look sunburnt. She's started trembling, and I feel a prickle of guilt. I might be embarrassing her more than her tormentor.

"Luna. No, wait. No, it's Rain." She smiles like she's just passed a test. Her lips tilt then, almost coy. "Forgive me, my prince. I'm *pathetic* with names."

I don't respond. I'm watching Rune again. Her skin has returned to its sickly pale shade, and she's gone motionless. Back to unaffected.

"It has gotten late, my lady," I say, forcing a smile. I raise a hand toward the servants. "Let's pack up your dessert and be on our way. We've got an early morning. Wedding arrangements to be made."

"Oh yes," she says. Her momentary disappointment vanishes at mention of the wedding, and she's back to giddy babbling.

Within ten minutes, we stand at the doorway of her quarters. Rune is a few steps behind Viana, motionless as usual. Still, I'm distracted by her. She's frail and defenseless, and yet she never cracks. There's something fascinating about her, but I know better than to get invested—especially with her.

"Thank you for a lovely evening," Viana says.

When I turn toward her, she's already leaning in. I meet her partway, force myself to taste her lips and hold her waist, as if I don't know who she is. As if I don't know what she does when no one is watching.

She deepens the kiss, clinging to my shoulders and pressing her tongue into my mouth. Her nails are sharp against the skin of my neck, and she moans. I'm sure half the building can hear us—and even if not, I know there's at least one person witnessing this.

Watching me kiss the person who degraded her, who made her bleed.

I pull back, feeling a stiff sickness in my stomach. This is what I'm *supposed* to do, I remind myself. Viana will be my wife, and eventually she'll mother my children. There's nothing *wrong* with what I'm doing.

And yet, I want to vomit. At the very least, I should take a hot shower and maybe gargle boiling water. I can taste the mule soup she had for dinner and a hint of the chocolate cake she took so long to eat.

"I look forward to seeing you in the morning," I say, prying her fingers from my shoulders. She wants me to come into her room. I can almost hear the words before she asks them, so I take a quick step backward. "I will send a guard for you in the morning. And don't worry about your handmaiden's shoes. I will send a new pair for her immediately. It's best if you focus on us, don't you think?"

She nods, eyes glossy.

"Come along, Rain," she says finally. She slips into her quarters, and Rune is quick to follow. I try to catch her eye, but she doesn't look at me. Then they're gone, closed behind a door and painfully silent.

Part of me wants to linger in the hallway in case Viana releases Rune early. I could explain that I'm forced to wed Viana, that I never would have chosen such a cruel bride if I had the choice. And maybe Rune would understand, maybe she'd smile and say it was all right and that she didn't blame me.

I force myself to leave, because even if Rune *did* understand, it wouldn't change the truth. I am marrying a heartless woman and together we will leave this world, condemning all the commoners and servants with it.

11

RUNE

I sit on the floor of my bedroom, submerged in darkness. The automatic light shut off hours ago, and I don't trust myself to stay awake in bed. Luckily the elite servant quarters are nicer than the low ones. Rather than stains on the tile and bad smells in the air, my new bedroom is clean and all my own. Since coming to the Tower, this is the first thing that's ever been *mine*.

I stretch my legs in front of me. I've been wearing the shoes Harrick sent me, but I took them off. They're too new, the soles too thick and noisy. Viana burned the last pair in a fit of rage, just hours before her date with Harrick. The beautiful gown he gifted her was too small, and I had no idea how to fix it.

Viana felt badly afterward, once a mender had adjusted the dress to perfection. She even came close to apologizing, I think. I've since decided her temper is a beast within her, a vicious creature she doesn't know how to control.

I'm still thinking about her—and that explosive hatred—when a dull buzzer sounds, marking the hour. I move to my feet, blinking any exhaustion from my eyes. It's two in the morning, late enough that most in the Tower will be asleep. I tighten my mask over my eyes and fumble through the darkness until I reach the door. I lean on it, the metal cold against my ear as I listen.

After a few silent beats, I ease my door open and sneak into the corridor. Then I'm off: bare feet tapping across the marble floor, breaths shaky but silent. The lights are dimmed, providing just enough visibility to navigate turns.

The Royal Training Arena is only one level below mine. I've dreamt of returning since I first saw that unlocked office, and now that I've snuck Viana's access code, I finally have the chance to do *something*. A way to redeem myself for failing Caleah, and to hopefully make it right. Even if I can't find a map to the prisons, I'll be happy with just about anything. The next time I meet with Vale, I'd rather not show up empty-handed.

So, despite the pathetic odds of finding something truly useful, I'm creeping down the service stairwell. I stop on the fiftieth floor and crack the door, listening, watching. I can hear my own heart, the way it slams against my ribcage. With each beat, there's an echo of *don't get caught, don't get caught, don't get caught.*

I repeat Viana's access code, my lips moving silently, as I take off again. I don't know what happens if I enter it wrong. Maybe a blaring alarm or a poisoned arrow or a swarm of guards with magicked gloves. I'd rather not find out.

The panic stews in my gut as I run, working its way up my throat and into my head. The endless stretch of mirrors makes me nauseated, and without Viana here to lead the way, I keep getting confused. I have to backtrack three times before I finally see the silver doors to Hall D.

I don't pause before entering the access code, terrified I'll back out if I hesitate. At the last number, I suck in a thick breath and hold it. My lungs relax when a high-pitched *ping* radiates from the doorknob. No blaring alarm or poisoned arrow or flock of guards...not yet, anyway.

I slip into the room, trembling against the door once it closes. The center lights whir to life, revealing the viewing room and the training arena beyond it. The door to the arena hangs open, but the adjacent office is closed. I move slowly through the room, eyes jetting from one corner to the next.

When I finally reach the door, the tension in my chest loosens. There's no keypad, no place for a thumb print. I'll be able to slip inside, search for anything useful and get out within a few minutes. I lift my hand to the doorknob, only to pause.

I can't explain why, but I find myself staring at the arena's gaping entryway. The heavy black mats, the cold gray walls, the rows upon rows of weapons. Sharp-edged swords and heavy rods and daggers and rings. The most powerful weapons in all of Savoa, left carelessly under-protected in this room.

I move away from the office and creep into the doorway of the arena. I don't step into the room, but it lights up anyway. There are shoe marks on the mats and blood stains along the walls. From where I stand, I can see the tiles one guard used to fight the siblings. They're smaller than the palm of my hand, tiny enough that I could hide a stack of them in my coveralls. I might do it, if they weren't streaked with red.

What a difference our fight would be, if we had even a fraction of this magic.

I walk into the room, pausing again. Still no alarms, arrows, or guards. I keep my hands clasped in front of me as I walk, surveying the options. I'm almost back to the viewing room when I see a long sword propped against the wall. It's not hung like the other weapons, and it appears to be made of solid metal. Not even the softest shade of red touches it.

I glance over my shoulder, triple checking I'm not being watched. Then, I step closer, only stopping when my feet frame the sword's handle. I stare at it, trying to imagine its weight, whether I'd feel powerful or foolish holding it.

I lunge without thinking, clenching my breath as I pull the sword into my hands. There's no burn, no sign it's touched by magic. It is heavier than it looks though, and I have to use both hands to balance it. The handle, rough and bulky, feels like power for the taking. I suddenly hold a million revenge fantasies in my hands, and I raise the sword higher, struggling with the lopsided weight. The tip of the sword stretches two feet from me, bobbing at even the slightest movement.

I could hurt someone with this. I could *kill* them. The thought should scare me, but it's delicious instead.

I carry the sword into the center of the arena, arms trembling, and pretend Viana stands before me. I imagine her beautiful dark hair, her delicate mask, her elaborate green gown, streaked with red. And that angry, violent expression she gets, right before she hits me.

With a sharp grunt, I swing as hard as I can. The blade slices through the air—and through imaginary Viana's throat—but there's no time to celebrate. The weight of the sword throws me more than I expect, and it flings from my grasp. It skitters across the mat, and I'm a second behind it, landing on my stomach.

After taking an unsteady breath, I curl toward the mat. Any feeling of power is gone, replaced with a fresh wave of humiliation.

What was I thinking, that I'd pick up a sword and transform from feeble servant to heroic warrior? As if *anything* in my life had ever gone so smoothly.

I clench my teeth and force myself to my knees. Pathetic. Absolutely pathetic. Not only wasting time but also damaging weapons. If there's even a scratch on that blade, someone will know. I crawl toward it, and then freeze.

Red boots and slacks stand beside the handle. And I realize I am far worse than pathetic—I'm about to be dead.

I move my eyes up slowly, not sure who I'm hoping for. The Architect will kill me swiftly, I think. Prince Malek slowly, for the pure enjoyment of it. And Prince Harrick...I imagine he'll use me as an example. He'll show some form of mercy in front of a crowd, something that looks like a gentle sentencing that will actually be worse than death.

I swallow when my eyes meet Prince Harrick's. He's not wearing his crown, but he looks no less terrifying. Jaw set, lips turned down. There's even a red tinge to his face, like he's about to lose control like Viana so often does.

Vale will be disgusted if he ever learns *how* I failed. He won't understand why I got distracted from the mission, why I risked so much to play pretend.

I don't understand it myself.

My lips part, but I can't force myself to speak. If they're going to kill Caleah for stealing a vial of magic, I can't imagine how I'll suffer for *this*.

"Rune Ealde," he says. His voice is smooth and deep, but his tone is eerily flat. "What are you doing here?"

Somewhere, in the recesses of my mind, I'm surprised he remembers my name. But my mouth still isn't working, and it really doesn't matter whether he thinks my name is Luna or Rain or Rune. A heavy tremor shakes through my body, harder than any earthquake I've ever felt. I'm going to pass out. I can feel the blackness pinching my eyes, the fogginess swarming my skull.

"Take a breath," he says. He looks away from me to grab the sword, plucking it from the ground as if it's weightless. "I've already vowed not to harm you."

I nod, even though I don't believe him. Vows, words, mean nothing at all—especially when that person is armed.

"You were holding it wrong," he says, stepping toward me.

I scramble to my feet, moving backward as he comes forward. He stops then, eyebrows scrunching as he frowns at me. Still holding the sword in one hand, Harrick digs through his coat pocket and removes his red handkerchief. The same one he'd lent me for a mask.

"I understand that you fear me, Rune, but it's not necessary," he says. As he speaks, he lowers the sword, propping it against his side. He twists the blindfold over his eyes, tying it tightly around his head. When I suck in an audible breath, his lips tick, just slightly. It almost looks like he's smirking.

"What are you doing?" I ask. These are the first words I manage, and they're so quiet, even I barely hear them.

"Showing that I have no interest in hurting you," he says simply. With the handkerchief over his eyes, he brings the sword back to his hand. "I have questions of you, Rune. Some suspicions too. I think that's fair. But if you're going to do something as wild and forbidden as brandishing a weapon, you should at least know how to hold it. It'd be a shame for you to cut yourself in half without anyone to stop the bleeding."

"Why is that?" I ask. I don't know why I'm talking or what I'm saying. I'm trembling and there's still a good chance I'll faint.

Harrick doesn't respond. He only steps backward, slowly, the sword tip pointed at an upward angle.

"Step back," he says. "Even more unfortunate than you stabbing yourself would be *me* stabbing you. Go to the wall across from me. Knock on it so I know you're there."

I hurry away from the prince and press my back against the wall. I knock twice before inching silently to the side, just in case he's planning to use me for blind target practice.

Harrick widens his stance and shifts one leg forward, tilting the sword as he moves. He looks like a masterpiece, so beautiful this moment should be painted and hung upon a wall. I'm mesmerized by the sharp cut his sword makes through the air, until I'm not thinking of the million ways he could kill me. Eventually he stops, relaxing his practiced stance.

He's not going to hurt me.

The thought comes without permission, but I think it might be true. The fact that he *could* have killed me a million ways— and hasn't—might be proof that he won't. Maybe there was something more about Caleah's capture, something I haven't figured out. Or maybe he's deranged, ruining some and sparing others.

Harrick lowers the sword and steps toward me. He's about halfway across the mat when he lowers the sword to the ground. Then he moves to the wall opposite me and blindly gestures toward the abandoned weapon.

"Try it," he says, voice soft. "Don't swing it yet. You need to get a feel for the weight first. Just try to copy my movements. Pick a dominant foot—"

"You don't have to do this," I say. I blush, realizing I've just interrupted the crown prince. "I only mean—I believe you. I take your word that you will not harm me. Please forgive me for my horrible actions. If you let me, I will return to my room and I will never inconvenience you or defy your laws again. I will repay your mercy with anything you ask of me."

I don't know if I'm telling the truth or not. All I know is that, once again, the sour taste of death is in my mouth.

"Pick your dominant foot," he repeats, words level, void of emotion. "Take the sword and bend your elbows as I did. I'm going to remove the mask to watch you. Okay?"

"Yes, my prince," I say. I collect the sword and put my left foot forward. I've no idea what he means by *dominant* foot, but it doesn't matter. If I survive the night, I will never get myself into this foolish of a situation again.

"Call me Harrick," he says as he unties the handkerchief. He folds it back into his pocket, dark eyes studying me. "Now, shift your stance, move the sword, get a feel for it. Widen your feet a bit. You're going to fall if you swing it like that."

I force myself not to think about anything other than Harrick's commands. He says one critique after another, until I'm too exhausted to hold the sword at all. I finally lower its tip to the floor, panting as Harrick explains the importance of my hips while sword fighting. My face is damp with sweat, and I can already feel a soreness spreading through my shoulders.

"It will get easier," he says. He pushes from the wall, taking slow, tentative steps toward me. I force myself to stay put, even as my legs beg me to run. "And next time, we will pick a better weapon for you. The sword is too heavy. You'd do better with a dagger or maybe darts. Unfortunately, you won't be able to use anything magicked. It'd kill you long before it protected you."

I tilt the handle of the sword toward Harrick, unable to think of a response. I can't decide if he's being sincere, if he's honestly offering to help me illegally train for a second time. It'd be dangerous and reckless, not just for me, but for him too. His punishment would be nothing like the death I'd face, but teaching a servant to fight couldn't fare well for him either.

Is this how they tricked Caleah?

"You're going to be sore tomorrow," he continues, taking the sword from my outstretched hand. He moves across the room, hanging it on an empty holder. "You'll want to rest, but that will only hurt worse in the long run. We'll meet here tomorrow night, same time."

I'm not sure what to say, so I watch him in silence. He removes his gloves, revealing long fingers and slightly calloused palms. He walks back toward me, doing the buttons of his coat as he stops a foot away.

And Wyhel, this man is unjustly attractive. He is tall and

broad and muscular—and I have to remind myself that some servants would be built like him too, if they weren't starving. No amount of food would make them this stunning though. Harrick's jaw is square and his cheekbones are high. His lips are full, and his nose is strong. If I dared to look into his eyes, I am sure they are beautiful too.

I look back to the ground.

"I don't understand," I say after a heavy pause. My words tremble as I push through them. "I've done something terrible, and it seems you should punish me for it."

I don't know why I keep opening my mouth, why I'm reminding him that I should be killed for my actions. There's nothing good that will come of it, but my body is a mass of tightly-wound anxiety, making it impossible to think straight.

"You want me to punish you?" he asks. He's staring at me intensely, looking from my eyes to my nose to my chin and up again. There's a heavy crease between his eyes.

"I just...I don't understand," I repeat. I fidget under his hard stare, further explanation drying in my throat.

"I am not going to punish you," he says, frowning. "But if you would like to repay my *mercy*, as you call it, I will accept."

"Anything, my prince," I say, and it comes out as a rushed breath. The thought of him holding this much over me is nauseating, and I'd rather pay my debt sooner than later.

"First, I want to look into your eyes," Harrick says. I shift as he watches me, crossing my arms over my stomach. "Second, call me Harrick, not your prince. And third, I want you to train with me. Here, tomorrow night."

I force myself to nod, mind churning with his requests. It's not like I could possibly refuse, but now my insides twitch with unease. All I can think about are the probable consequences, most of which will lead to my death.

"Good," he says. He steps a fraction closer, dipping his head slightly. I force myself to be still as he continues. "I would also like you to hear my apology."

"Your apology?" I repeat, stammering.

"Yes," he says. "I am sorry for how I've hurt you."

"You've never hurt me, Prince Harrick." My entire being vibrates with reckless energy, waiting for the moment he finally drops this act and kills me.

"Not on purpose, no," he says softly. "But you suffer because of my family, because of my betrothed. I am disgusted at how they treat you, and even more at how little I do to stop it."

"I am a servant, Prince Harrick," I say. His name tastes strange in my mouth, leaving a buzzing sensation on my lips. "You owe me nothing."

He doesn't respond. His eyes continue to roam my face, a strange sadness falling over his own. I never expected to see pity on an elite's face, let alone the prince's.

"Now, the repayment," I say. I push back the thought of training here again, of the likelihood this is an elaborate trap. "You want to see my eyes. Am I allowed to ask why?"

"With me, you are allowed to ask anything," he says. "I may not be able to answer, but I promise you won't be punished for asking."

"You make a lot of promises," I say.

"Only ones I can keep," he returns. His lips quirk upward. I've seen him smile in public and while dancing with Viana, but this is different. This is a small, not-quite smile, and it's directed at no one but me. He goes on, "I want to see your eyes because people tend to hide them. Especially from people like me. I haven't seen many, but I've seen yours, and they were nice. I'd like to see them again."

It's hard to imagine any elites hiding their eyes from him. I know Viana would crumble from happiness if Harrick asked her to remove her mask. But perhaps that's too vulnerable for her.

Perhaps he's afraid he won't resist the urge, and he'll accidentally kill his queen.

With a hard swallow, I untie my mask. I hold it between both hands, keeping it close to my chest. I tell myself I'll throw it back on if he starts draining my magic, but I don't think that's even possible.

Like last time, I don't look Harrick in the eyes. I study his lips and his nose and his hairline as he watches me. His lips are set in a hard line, and his nose is perfectly straight. There's a freckle near his left temple, and another one on his right jaw, barely visible through his scruff.

"Rune," he whispers, so quietly I almost miss it. And yet, the hum of his voice shoots electricity through my blood and across my cheeks. So beautiful and gentle it's almost cruel. He takes my chin between his thumb and forefinger, pressing gently against my skin. "Will you look at me?"

He can force me if I say no, but that's not why I do it.

I look at him, and I wish I could say it's because I'm afraid. That's part of it, of course. I know he can force me if I resist, but that fear isn't the full truth. I meet Harrick's gaze, not because I'm terrified beyond logic, but because I *want* to believe he won't hurt me. I'm so desperate for his kindness, I might just die for it.

Harrick stares down at me, jaw tight and brows furrowed. I'm trembling against his touch, studying the infinite colors in his eyes. Without anything between us, I can see all the different shades of violet. They aren't nearly as dark as I thought. There are flecks of lavender and plum, of lilac and nightwater.

I was right, of course. They *are* beautiful.

Harrick's thumb grazes over my skin, partway up my jawline. Without permission, a sharp gasp breaks from my lips. So shameful. So pathetically needy.

Harrick freezes at the sound. For a split moment, his eyes are more black than violet, and his hand tightens against my jaw. And then, he's stepping away, leaving a foot of cold air between us.

I think he wanted to kill me, I realize.

At the very least, he was horrified that I *enjoyed* his touch. I should explain that I'm simply not used to softness. Not from a man, not from anyone. It's been cycles since I've known anything other than brutality and cruelty. I was startled by his affection, that's all, and I couldn't help but react.

Instead of explaining, I remain silent, face boiling from the inside out.

Finally, he clears his throat. "I'll walk you back to your quarters. Don't forget to meet me tomorrow."

"I won't," I say. My gaze remains on the floor.

As we walk, my entire body vibrates with humiliation and self-hatred. His family destroys people like me for sport. Caleah is already paying that price, and if our escape plan fails, our entire faction will too. In that split second, my loneliness made me *like* something I should hate. I was leaning into Harrick's touch, craving his gentleness, forgetting that he was—and only ever will be—the enemy.

12

HARRICK

She'd look good taking my cock.

It's the last thought I had before falling asleep, and it's the first thought I have when I wake this morning. A single gasp. That's all it took for my attraction to cross from awareness to desperation. I'd known she was beautiful from the first time I saw her, obviously, but this was the first time I truly wanted to *act* on it.

I knew it was wrong. So wrong, so fucking inappropriate. This frightened servant at my mercy, my dirty thoughts between us. It doesn't matter that I'd never actually kiss her—I hate that I wanted to.

I hate more that I *still* want to.

Wide blue eyes, pretty lips, and that breathy gasp echoes through my mind as I remain in bed. It's well after daybreak at this point, meaning I've missed the morning meeting. Nothing ever happens at them anyway, but I've rarely been late...let alone *missed* one. Yet here I sit, propped up in bed, watching water streak my windows and thinking of Rune Ealde.

Pale, sickly handmaiden.

Daring, secretive trespasser.

Beautiful, fucking temptation.

In the middle of the night, I got an alert that Viana's code had been used to enter the Training Arena. Luckily I'd still been awake, and I assured the guard on duty that I'd take care of it. I'd been annoyed the entire way there, wondering what the hell she was doing. It didn't seem likely that she'd be snooping or stealing or doing anything to risk her new status. And still, none of those options would have surprised me more than the sight of Rune Ealde swinging a sword. She'd stolen an elite's code. She'd broken into a forbidden place. She'd taken a weapon and was *using* it.

I'd been mesmerized, watching her, stunned as she attempted to swing a sword far too big for her. Her arms had been shaking, but her mouth was set in a determined line. She hadn't seen me, and thank Wyhel for that. I would've been happy watching her all night, and yet, I'd found myself moving toward her. Wanting more than distant observation.

In the daylight, I have more questions than I did last night. She's obviously up to something, and it's most likely *not* in my favor. I should report her to Sorace, inform him that even our smallest of servants is creeping where she shouldn't. But the thought makes me sick. I think of him and Malek, snickering about the vile things they'd like to do to her.

No. I'm not telling a fucking soul about what I saw. I'll figure out her intentions myself, and in the meantime, I'll use it as an excuse to see her again.

My eyes fall shut, and soon, I'm thinking more about *her*. Her eyes and their unusual color: pale blue, like falling rain. Her soft, low voice, somehow both timid and brave at the same time. Her blatant curiosity and quiet intelligence.

I don't let myself think of my urge to stroke her face, or the breathy sound she made when I did.

A heavy knock pounds at my door, shattering the moment. I

shuffle beneath the covers and pretend to be sleeping. Whoever it is—and I fear I know *exactly* who it is—can wait until our training session to bother me.

Unfortunately, Malek doesn't take the hint. He slams his fist a few more times, and then, the door clangs open. Familiar footsteps—heavy and wide, like a charging general—stride into the room. Despite my closed eyes, he strips the blankets off my bed and drops them to the floor.

"A little old for pretending, aren't we, brother?" he asks. He's dressed more extravagantly than usual. He wears an unfamiliar red suit, sharply pressed and stamped with mangled claws. His crown of teeth sits squarely over his slicked black hair.

I rise to my feet and shove past Malek. As I pass the ornate wall mirror, I catch a glimpse of my haggard reflection: messy hair and shadowed eyes. I look terrible, and I've got a throbbing headache to match. Rather than dwell on either, I flick through a dozen red suits on display before selecting a random one.

When I turn, I'm unsurprised to find Malek watching me. He's wearing his mischievous grin, and despite it being late morning, it's too early to deal with this bullshit. I move to the left and head for my washroom, only for him to step into my path, blocking me.

"Aren't you going to ask why I'm here?" he sneers.

"I assumed boredom," I say, meeting his eyes. A smirk is already working its way over his mouth. I step to the left, and he shadows the movement. With a sigh, I stop again, centering myself in front of him. "If you want something, say it. I've already missed one meeting this morning. I shouldn't miss another."

"The Architect has called a gathering." Malek's smirk deepens, bringing with it an eerie spark to his expression. "He's ready to discuss the portal."

"With the Committee?" I ask. I hadn't planned on entertaining Malek at all, but now I can't help it. He grins like I've reacted exactly as he hoped: equal parts shocked and horrified.

"Yes," he drawls. "The Architect is willing to hear my plan to escape this hellish world. Sooner rather than later, that is. Seeing as you weren't at the morning meeting, I volunteered to inform you."

I study him, glancing from his suit to his crown before finally landing on his slanted mouth. There's something he's not telling me, something sinister. I can always tell by his boyish excitement, by his barely contained grin. He's conjured a new game, and I've unintentionally set it in motion by missing this meeting.

"Whatever treachery you're planning, leave me out of it," I snap, shoving past him. He loses his balance, enough that I feel a flicker of satisfaction. His voice follows me, even after I've shut myself in the washroom.

"There's no treachery here, brother!" he calls. "There is only redemption, and I will claim it for our people—with or without your help!"

"This is ridiculous," Tora says.

We sit in the Hall B auditorium of the 198th floor. Mother strolls around the room, greeting people as if they're close friends. She's memorized every royal's name and position, and she knows exactly how to use that information to her benefit. I watch her, partly fascinated, partly disgusted, until Tora nudges me with her elbow.

We're off to the side of the room, waiting for the elites to ready the stage. They move our thrones—four metal and one bone—this way and that, never seeming quite satisfied. Malek stands at the center of it all, flirting with a pretty elite, his eyes skimming the room as they talk. In front of the stage, ten rows of tipped-chin royals settle into place. A few stare at me and Tora, but thankfully, none of them get the courage to approach us.

"Look at him," Tora says. She tugs at her elbow-length gloves, a gift to her from Nordan Kerr, before gesturing toward our brother. "What a rat. Digging his way into places he doesn't belong. Trying to force the Architect's hand. Defying Mother's requests. Going over your head. He's an absolute fiend, Harrick! He ruins *everything*, and he's completely reckless about it."

"He's up to something," I murmur. His eyes catch mine, just for a moment, and he grins before looking away.

"Well, obviously," Tora snorts. "He's *always* up to something. He's trying to condemn all of Savoa, just because he's an impatient brat. And, despite the fact he's betrothed, he's up there, openly flirting with that random woman. We'll have to hear all about him bedding her at breakfast."

"No, there's something more," I say, chewing the inside of my cheek. "He came to my quarters this morning to make sure I knew of tonight's gathering."

"Do you think he's—" Tora cuts off, her attention suddenly at the door. She lets out a short groan. "Gods. I didn't know *they* were coming."

I follow her glare to the entryway, where Nordan Kerr, Viana Llroy, and Malek's betrothed Petra Renat stand. Nordan Kerr wears an emerald suit with dashes of red throughout the fabric —and yet, he looks entirely bland and unimportant. His face is a collection of unremarkable features, and his fidgeting fingers make him look like a lost child.

Viana is as beautiful as ever, dressed in a gown far too elegant for the occasion. Her attention is already locked on me. She grins, showing off teeth whiter and straighter than I

136

remember them being. She's probably using two hundred beryls of magic, just to look like that. Following a shy wave to me, she leans to whisper something to Petra.

Malek's betrothed looks almost as out of place as Nordan. She shrinks behind Viana's left shoulder, her red and green dress half-swallowing her. She hunches her shoulders, like she's hoping it actually will.

"They're without their servants," I say. I cringe, realizing my mistake only after I've spoken. Servants don't come to royal meetings, let alone to gatherings.

Luckily, Tora is too busy glaring at Nordan to notice. She picks him apart from where we stand, ranting about his hair and his poor posture and the way his fingers twitch against his thighs. I'm about to pull her attention back to me when an elite appears before us. She beckons us to the stage, and whatever theory Tora had about Malek vanishes between us.

The elite calls everyone to their seats. Over one hundred royals, dressed in every shade of purple, filter into place. Their voices quiet to whispers, but their eyes remain loud. They stare at us on the stage, expressions hungry for whatever drama Malek has prepared. They briefly look away to watch Viana, Petra, and Nordan find their places in the front row. Viana makes a show of blowing me a kiss.

I ignore her—I ignore *all* of them—from my place on the stage. As usual, I sit between Mother and Malek with Tora to his left. The Architect's throne sits empty on the stage's far right, and I imagine that means he'll have a special entrance. I don't bother trying to get my sister's attention from here. Instead, I look out at the mountains through the distant windows, trying but failing to distract myself.

The elongated room darkens and the crowd falls silent. One of the elites—the one who'd been flirting with Malek—comes to the stage and positions herself behind the glass podium. She looks back to smile at my brother before facing the crowd. If nothing else, Tora was right about Malek bragging tomorrow morning.

"Welcome all to a spectacular gathering, presented to you by Prince Malek Ademas and the Architect himself!" the woman calls. More than half the crowd claps and cheers, but I'm relieved to see some looking less than enthused. It eases the tension in my chest, and I manage a deep breath. If the upper royals are skeptical, maybe they'll revolt against Malek's idea. Maybe they'll hate the Architect's secrecy to the point they rebel against this plan of his.

More time. I'm supposed to have more time before I have to deal with this.

The elite continues to ramble, and I don't realize I've zoned out until there's heavy applause from the crowd. The white lights brighten as the Architect strides into the room. He's dressed in his usual blood-red suit and wolf mask, but his walk somehow feels more purposeful, more dangerous. He doesn't acknowledge anyone in the crowd—or even us—as he claims his macabre throne.

I sit forcibly straight, determined not to look at the Architect. I haven't seen him since the infirmary, but I know he's been keeping tabs on me. His guards linger after training sessions. My cousins ask thinly veiled questions. And I do my best to act unaffected by his increasing attention.

The elite curtsies to the Architect before leading the rest of the organizers from the room. After they're gone, the lights soften and shadow most faces in the crowd. I can still sense their eagerness. Despite anything else they might feel, these people are hungry for information.

The Architect doesn't often make appearances, and he rarely calls gatherings. If we're here, everyone in the room will have a fresh piece of gossip to whisper in the corridors. I imagine even the servants will know by nightfall. I can't help but wonder how the Architect plans to keep people from storming his supply once they know—or if he's even considered they will.

For now, he sits perfectly still, the room subdued in silence around us. After a painfully long wait, during which even Malek starts to twitch, the Architect finally rises and lifts his arms toward the sea of purple, the splashes of green and red. The crowd remains quiet, their attention unwavering.

"My greatest children," he says. His voice echoes, and the purple sea leans into his words. "It brings me great pleasure to address you here today. Many of you have experienced hardships and heartaches in this violent land we call home. For countless cycles, I have hoped to find a way out for us, to find a way to escape this land and return to our Old World. Until recently, that has felt like nothing but a dream."

The crowd is a mass of perplexed expressions and ravenous eyes. People look from the Architect to me to the Architect again. Sometimes they look at Malek or Mother or Tora, but I feel their gazes lingering on me. They think I have something to do with this gathering, this idea of escape.

"When I was approached with a plan that took evacuation from possible to plausible, I had a great realization. While I cannot yet tell you the details of our plan, I can admit I made a grievous error," the Architect says. His voice hums through the anxious stillness. "Many cycles ago, I selected an heir for this kingdom. And ever since, I have questioned whether the correct choice was made. Today, I stand before you to correct what I now know was a mistake."

No.

My heart thuds so loud I can hear it. They all must hear it, the way my body is rearranging beneath my ribcage. The crowd is unquestionably focused on me now. Meanwhile, I've finally turned to look at the Architect. I do not dare look at my brother.

This isn't about leaving Savoa, not really. This is my worst fear realized. It is countless cycles of taunting and intimidation and mockery, all building to this one horrible moment. And for whatever reason, I still feel caught off guard.

He's going to steal everything *from me.*

My body trembles, and without fully deciding to, I look at my sister. She's already staring back at me, cheeks pale and lips parted in horror. She knows. Everyone in this gods-forsaken room knows now, and before long, the whole fucking kingdom will too.

I'm going to be the first heir ever stripped of his title.

The anticipation in the room sucks through my mouth, into my lungs, expanding until I hear the cartilage splitting my ribs. I am anxiety, everywhere, all at once. I want to freeze this moment, stop time long enough for me to flee the stage with what little dignity I still have. The Architect clears his throat, and though I can't see his face, I know he is smiling.

Gods. Not here, not in front of everyone.

"Today, the fifteenth day of Flood Season, I officially renounce my chosen heir. The successor of Savoa, from this moment onward, is no longer Prince Harrick."

The anxious breath in my lungs explodes into a pained grunt, as if the Architect has shoved a dull spear through my chest. I don't know how the crowd reacts. A high-pitched buzz fills my ears and radiates into my throat until I can't hear anything else. My consciousness is trying to rip from my body, and I wish it would. I'd like nothing more than to pass out and wake far away from the gaping mouths of my subjects.

Despite cycles of Malek's prodding and snide remarks from my cousins, I never truly thought I'd lose it. Now, the Architect's words cut through every nerve ending and my body pulses with the realization that I have failed. I have truly lost. And to someone as heartless, as cruel as Malek. He swept in like everyone warned he would, and I have no excuse for it but my own inadequacy.

"Kneel for your future leader and king, Heir Malek Ademas!"

My brother claps a hand against my shoulder as he stands. I blink the crowd into focus, and they're bowing. All of them. Even those who seemed skeptical about today's gathering kneel as he comes to the podium. I'm not sure if they're happy to gain Malek as their heir—but they're certainly not sad to lose me.

My skin is hot and my blood is cold. The desperation to disconnect, to disappear, still vibrates through my chest, but something else—something angry, spiteful, violent—awakens. It pushes through my bones, right between the marrow and the magic, and threatens to consume me. I don't fight it. I let the anger swell and blister until my thoughts don't feel entirely like my own.

No.

Everyone in the room stares at me. I've said it out loud, shouted it maybe. I've stood without meaning to.

"No." I say it again. My voice is a strike of thunder in this gaping room.

I look away from the crowd, and I ignore Tora's whisper of a touch on my arm. Malek and the Architect shift as I stride forward, centering myself in front of our people. They are more blurry outlines, tinged red with my shaky vision, than they are human.

"I am the rightful heir," I say. The words vibrate around me. "You cannot take my title without a challenge."

"I'm not sure you want to do that, brother," Malek says. His voice is low and warm, as if this is all in good fun. He's not wrong though. He's the better fighter—I know that more than anyone.

"If you want the crown, you will pry it from me," I spit. The words don't sound like mine. They're cold and sharp, snapping between my ears. Looking at the Architect, I steady my voice. "I have the right to a challenge."

The Architect doesn't respond for a long moment. He tilts his head and lets out a slow chuckle, like I've surprised him.

"Very well," he says finally. He sounds more amused than offended, as if I'm a disobedient child, and he's willing to humor my defiance.

"Fine," Malek says. He rolls his eyes, making a show of it. "Have your challenge, Harrick. You'll only bring more disgrace upon yourself."

"I'd rather fall in disgrace than willingly condemn all of Savoa."

If Malek responds, I don't hear him. The high-pitched buzzing is back in my ears as I storm off the stage and into the adjacent corridor. A pair of eavesdropping elites scramble out of the way, first for me and then for Tora a moment later. She's a step behind me, heels clicking on the marble floor, calling my name between sharp breaths. I ignore her, pressing toward the stairwell and praying none of these elites get in my way.

"Harrick!" she yells again. There's a brief pause as she kicks out of her heels. Then, she's running—no, sprinting—past me, gasping as she braces herself against the stairwell door, blocking my way.

I could hurl her halfway across this floor if I wanted, and she knows that, but she stands tall, a scowl distorting her features. I wonder, distantly, if this hesitation is my greatest weakness. Malek certainly would've thrown her by now.

"Move, Tor," I say. My body is still shaking, cold with a million foreign emotions.

"Mother will fix this," she insists. "She'll talk to the Architect. He clearly—"

"Move, Tora," I snap again. I shouldn't be surprised at her lack of faith in me. Of course she thinks I need Mother to protect me, to protect Savoa. I let the hurt and shame swell in my chest.

Tora doesn't move.

I shove past her and rip the door open, knocking her off balance. She stumbles into the stairwell behind me and our footsteps echo as we descend. Once we reach my quarters, I punch my code. It'll only be a matter of time before he claims my home too.

"Harrick," pants Tora. "You can't challenge him. You *can't.*"

I stop, hand trembling on my partially opened door. Away from the gathering, the violent anger slips from my system, draining out through my toes. She's right, of course. If I challenge Malek, I'm going to lose. Regardless of who has more magic, he's always bested me. He's always been the better fighter, and if I battle him in front of our people, they're only going to feel more confident in the Architect's decision.

Maybe it *would* be a better idea to ask for Mother's help.

"Harrick—"

"I heard you," I snap. My limbs feel like deflated balloons, like dying flowers. "I can't take it back, Tora. I won't."

"He'll *kill* you," she whispers. "He'll kill you as eagerly as he killed that redhead. Maybe *more* eagerly."

I didn't know he'd already killed Viana's first servant, but I don't let my surprise show. If anything, his careless murder only strengthens my resolve.

"Perhaps," I say finally. Tora sucks in a breath. "But he'll sacrifice all of Savoa if he becomes king. He'll kill everyone if I let him. And, heir or not, I can't let him do that."

Tora says my name again, a near-silent whisper. I ignore her, shutting the door between us.

13
HARRICK

I don't know what I'm doing. After the horrific day I've had, Rune Ealde should be the furthest thing from my mind. Training an indentured servant shouldn't be anywhere on my list of priorities. They'd try me for treason if they caught me, especially after the Architect's announcement today.

Yet here I am. Leaned against the wall by 51 CC, waiting for two a.m. to strike, for Rune Ealde to sneak down to meet me. Thoughts of this, of meeting her here, have been my only sense of sanity. Despite the mess of my life, I still get to steal a moment with Rune tonight. I get to show her how to hold a weapon, how to cling to even the smallest drop of power.

The overhead clock buzzes with two low strikes. I've got my head leaned against Rune's wall, but her room is silent. It isn't until her door opens that I'm sure she's in there at all.

She sucks in a sharp but quiet gasp when she sees me standing here. Her hair is damp, making it look darker than normal. She must have showered. She smells like cheap soap and something else, something I can't quite place. Whatever it is, I like it.

She fidgets, her pale eyes hidden behind her yellow veil. I can see them still, the way they dart around my face. The way they don't seem to fear me quite as much as they did the first time. Maybe that's yet another lie I tell myself.

"Prince Harrick," she says, dipping her chin. Her voice is raspy, and I wonder how often she talks when she's not with me.

"Just Harrick," I correct. A soft blush colors her cheeks, and she glances to both ends of the hallway.

"I wasn't sure we were still meeting," she says, the blush deepening.

It takes me a moment to realize she's referencing the gathering. She's heard, then, that my crown is threatened. That by the end of the Flood Season, I may not be the heir. I may not even be alive. An uncomfortable pinch slices through my stomach, wondering what she thinks of that.

"Let's go," I say. I push away from the wall and start for the stairs. Rune follows, but I find myself checking every few seconds. Her bare feet are silent on the marble floor. She could very well be the shadow she pretends to be.

By the time we reach the training arena, my nerves are electric, spasming against each other. *If we get caught, if we get caught, if we get caught...*

I enter my code to the arena, slipping inside and sealing the door as soon as Rune is safely in the waiting room with me. She keeps a careful distance between us, hands folded behind her back, face impossible to read.

"Okay," I say after a long moment. "Okay, I think we're good."

"Are you all right?" she asks. Her voice trembles, and she bites her lip, like she wishes she could take the question back.

I don't want to answer the question. I watch her mouth for another moment, wondering what she'd do if it was me biting those lips instead of her. Rather than doing that—*or* answering the question—I scan her face for cuts and bruises.I'd been worried Viana might take yesterday's news out on Rune, but it doesn't look like she has—at least from where I can see.

"I think we'll try a dagger tonight," I say finally.

She follows me silently into the padded arena. I'm wearing the red suit from the gathering, and I'm going to pass out from heat exhaustion if I train with it. I slip out of my laced shoes and lose the heavy jacket. It's covered in red-tinted stones and weighs at least twenty pounds.

Rune watches as I do. Her hands are in tight fists, body tensed and ready to run. I'm overly aware of her movements. The way her lips twitch, like she's keeping herself from asking anything more. The way she rocks from heel to toe, eyes continuously flitting to the arena entrance.

"No one is going to come in," I tell her as I undo the top two buttons of my dress shirt. Her eyes track my movements, and her cheeks again turn red.

All at once, I realize how this must seem. Me forcing us to be alone together. Taking off clothes. Telling her no one is going to interrupt me.

"Fuck," I say quickly, finally registering how terrified she looks. Now I'm certain *I'm* the one blushing. "I'm not going to touch you. I would never..."

I trail off, watching her skin flush again.

"Yes, my prince," she says, tipping her chin.

She sounds almost rejected, and I'm tempted to clarify I'd touch her if she wanted me to. That, if she asked, I'd make her feel better than any man before me. But if I'm wrong, then we're back to square one and...

Wyhel.

I finish adjusting my clothes and snatch a dagger from the wall. I rotate it, double-checking it's not laced with magic, and hold it handle-first to Rune. Her fingers tremble as she takes it. She doesn't trust me—not even close—but she's here.

"What do I do with it?" she asks, turning it over in her hand. Her gaze flickers from the dagger to me. "It's *short*."

"Yes," I say, unable to keep a smile from my face. "Like you."

Her mouth twists into a scowl, creasing the space between her eyebrows. I think I've offended her but I'm not sure.

"Do I throw it?" she asks.

"Not if you can help it," I say, still smiling. "If you miss your target, they're unharmed and you're without a weapon."

"But if I don't?" she asks. When I only raise my eyebrows, her mouth puckers slightly. "If I *don't* miss?"

"Who exactly is your target, Rune?" I ask. I don't mean to— it's the type of question that will scare her away. If she's afraid I'm going to throw her in a prison cell once I figure out her scheme, she's going to stop coming here. She's going to stop talking to me.

For whatever reason, I want her to stay.

"Don't answer that," I say as soon as she opens her mouth. "Tell me something instead."

I step toward her, and she tenses. I hold my hands in surrender and wait for her to relax before stepping forward again. This time, she remains still. I adjust the dagger in her palm, moving her thumb up and to the left.

"Like this," I say. Her hand is so small and pale, easily engulfed by mine. "Feel the control that way?"

She nods, face tensed in concentration. I lift her arm then, slowly moving it through a basic defensive block.

"If someone lunged for you, you would do that sideways thrust. Okay? Keep your forearm up by your face." I gently guide her through the motion. "And this, if you were to stab someone, you'd do it like this."

I'm out of my mind, so far gone there's no coming back. I

can't explain what I'm doing or why, but I move her hand in a sharper motion, angling the blade toward my throat. Her cheeks flush, eyes on the dagger instead of me. I show her twice more, relishing the feel of her skin against mine.

When I finally let go and take a step backward, she practices the motion. She's the picture of intense focus, but her pace is slow and inefficient. Every time she pretends to strike her opponent, she loosens her grip. She doesn't have good technique, or even good instincts. With or without magic, it'd be easy to disarm her. It's a thought I should find comforting, but don't.

"Tell me something," I remind her.

"Like what?" she asks. She's still doing the arm movement, but I've distracted her. She's getting sloppier with each attempt, so I should shut up and let her concentrate.

I don't. I'm selfish and the gathering was horrible and I'm hungry for distraction myself.

"Anything," I say. Then, "Something about you."

My desperation is loud. If she notices, she doesn't show it. She switches the dagger to her opposite hand and practices the same movement. Her left hand is even worse than her right.

"I used to be a kitchen wench," she says. Her veiled eyes move to my face for the first time since we've started. Vibrant blue studies me. "I was promoted to Saskia's handmaiden. Then Viana's."

"Something new. I already know that," I say.

I might imagine it, but I swear something lights in her expression.

"I wasn't sure you remembered," she says. She trades the dagger back to her right hand, fumbling for a moment to find the grip I showed her. She watches the reflective blade instead of me. "I'm not a criminal. I mean, not really. My father was the one who broke the law. I know our family's crimes are our own, but *I* never committed a crime."

"Aside from this?" I ask with a smirk. She looks up at me, face paling, and I realize it's too soon to tease her. "I'm committing a worse crime than you right now, Rune. You don't have to worry about me turning you in. All right? You can trust me."

She doesn't respond. She lowers her gaze to the dagger, fingers tightening on the handle. After a long pause, she practices the defensive move again and again. I watch her, inexplicably mesmerized at her clumsy movements. Finally, she holds the dagger back to me.

"Handle first," I tell her, gently rotating the dagger in her hand. "Unless you're wanting to stab me."

"No, my prince," she says, sucking in a breath. "I was—"

"Just Harrick," I interrupt. "Tell me something about *you*. Not your father."

I return the dagger to the wall and scan the weapons until I find a collection of darts. They're meant to be filled with poison or magic, but for now, they're empty canisters.

"I've never had a friend before," she says, watching me carefully. Her eyes lower to the darts in my hand as she continues. "I've never had much of anything."

Her words send a pang through my chest. It feels like I've lodged a poisonous dart right between my lungs. As miserable as I've felt under the Architect's thumb, I've never felt alone. I've never wanted for anything. I've had comfort and luxury, and most importantly, I've always had Tora.

"I will be your friend," I say. A warmth spreads beneath my ribs as the words leave my mouth. I'm in dangerous territory, and for the first time, I wonder if Rune is manipulating me. If she's playing doe-eyed innocent to get my guard down. Still, I turn away from her, more worried about her seeing my vulnerability than attacking me.

I take the darts' matching blowgun from the wall and roll the barrel between my fingers. When I look back to Rune, she's watching me again, same stoic expression as before. She remains silent as I load two darts into the gun, but then shakes her head when I hold it out to her.

"I'll show you how to use it," I say, nodding.

At the same time, she says, "Why would you be my friend?"

I flinch, and it must show, because Rune's expression softens.

"Why would you *want* to be my friend," she says. She swallows, forcing her eyes up to mine. "Why are you nice to me at all, Harrick?"

There are a million ways I could respond. I could point out that, whether she believes it or not, I *am* a nice person. I could tell her that being friends is easy, that it doesn't take any extra effort from me to be hers. Or I could be honest and tell her that she intrigues me, that she's somehow braver than I've ever been. Without a stitch of magic, without a safety net to catch her, she's stretched her neck as far as she can. And I'm desperate to be around her.

"I don't know," I say instead. I'm ready to leave it at that, but her expression closes at the lie. I've moved five steps back, and I suddenly feel like a coward. Even more so than usual.

I clear my throat, desperate to empty the weakness from my lungs. My mind is scrambled, and I'm trying to force a cohesive thought from it. I'm still gaping when I hear it.

The softest click.

Rune doesn't react, but I've heard the sound often enough to recognize it. Someone is here, and whoever it is, they won't react well to...whatever this is. Rune will end up dead and I'll be in a cell for treason.

I lunge, grabbing Rune by her shoulders and rotating her back to the nearest wall. She lets out something between a gasp and shriek, but there's no time to explain. The dart gun falls between us as I press my thigh between her legs. Even behind her mask, I can see her eyes, wide with horror.

"Please—"

I don't let her finish. I crash my lips against hers, kissing her, even when I know she doesn't understand. I hate myself for it. Hate that I don't know how else to keep her safe, hate that Malek will hurt her if I give him the chance.

I make it loud and sloppy. It's not how I would kiss her if this was real, if she was letting me. I'd make it good for her. I'd savor the taste of her until she was begging for more. Instead, I'm reckless, concerned only with how this looks.

Malek laughs, loud and stark, and gives an exaggerated, slow clap.

I pull back, feeling the crush of self-loathing as I do. I desperately want Rune to look at me, to understand I'm trying to save us. But her eyes are closed, tears dotting her eyelashes.

I'm trying to keep you safe.

I won't let him hurt you.

Please, please don't hate me for this.

"Look at this, high and mighty brother of mine," says Malek. He laughs again. "Always judging my tendencies. Does your betrothed know you're down here with a rat-whore?"

One last look at Rune before I turn, leaning cruelly against her. It's the easiest way to keep her fully concealed.

"Leave, Malek," I snarl. "I don't interrupt your trysts."

"Mine don't typically occur in public," he drawls. He lounges against the doorframe, mouth curved. His suit is disheveled, as if it's spent the evening on that elite's floor. His clawed crown rests lopsided on his head. "I have to say, I'm actually impressed. I figured you'd be writing love sonnets for Viana, not fucking a servant in the arena. I take it no elites will have you?"

I don't respond. He's baiting me, and I can't give into temptation. I need him to get bored and leave—the faster the better. I shift in front of Rune as he attempts to look around me. His smile broadens as he realizes what I'm doing.

"Oh relax, Harri. I'm not interested in your whore." He steps closer and I press harder into Rune. She trembles, her breath hot against my back. Malek tilts his head. "A suggestion, brother. Perhaps, rather than getting your dick wet by a foul creature, you should be training. You certainly need the practice."

"Is that why *you're* here? To practice?" I snap, unable to resist.

"I saw you were here," he says with a lazy shrug. I shouldn't be surprised he's accessed my code. "I thought it best to investigate."

I say nothing, and he waggles his brows at me. Once again, he cranes his neck to search for Rune, but I shift, allowing him nothing. Malek rolls his eyes.

"Fine. I will leave you to it," he says. He smacks a hand against the doorframe and gives me a final, smug look. "Enjoy your rat pussy, but do some training once you're done. First duel is in ten days!"

I grind my teeth together, forcing myself to be silent. Malek saunters from the viewing room and lets the main door clang behind him. I wait as long as I can, counting my strained breaths until I'm sure he won't return.

Finally, I step away from Rune, slowly as if there's any chance of *not* scaring her now. When I look at her, I'm surprised to find her eyes already on mine. Not just on me, but my eyes, staring at me with a blend of shock and confusion.

"Forgive me," I say. The words sound funny, my breath choppy.

"Thank you," she says, almost at the same time.

"Don't thank me," I say. I close my eyes, feeling self-hatred drip through my veins. "Gods, don't thank me. I would *never* do that. To you, to anyone. I just...I didn't—"

"I understand," she interrupts. She's trembling, but I still at her words. "I didn't realize he had come in. He would have...he would have—"

"Forgive me, Rune," I say again. Despite her gaze on me, it's hard to look at her. I hate what I've just done, even if it felt like the best option. Not to mention she witnessed Malek's mockery of me, of *her*. I feel small and pathetic, evil to my core.

"I understand," she says again. She takes the smallest step toward me, repeating quietly, "I understand, Harrick."

I suck in a breath. This is the first time she's willingly come *toward* me.

Something squeezes in my chest, compressing until I feel nothing and everything at the same time. Rune doesn't have a speck of power in her bones, and yet she's affecting me in a way no one else has. Her expression is gentle and soft, filling me with the purest sensation of light.

Looking at her now, I wonder if there might be more than one type of magic.

14
RUNE

"I can't believe it's real," Petra says.

She's talking about the fighting dome, an enormous arena that must be half a floor's width and several more deep. It starts on one of the lower levels of the military section, and it may very well go to its top. I stand behind Viana at the bottom of the tiered seating. We're only feet from the glass enclosure, where soon, Harrick and Malek will fight their first duel. A rowdy crowd surrounds us, gulping nightwater and placing wagers.

I am numb to it all. I've moved through the last ten days in a confused fog, utterly consumed by the fact Prince Harrick kissed me. *Me.* A lowly servant. A rat-whore, as Malek called me. I'd never been kissed before that night, though I'm not sure this actually counts. I thought Harrick was about to kill me, and he was trying to save my life. In the aftermath, we didn't talk much before he walked me back to my quarters.

I'm sure Harrick doesn't consider it a real kiss.

Still, Viana would kill me if she knew. She and Saskia would string me up somewhere and take turns stoning me to death. Luckily, Viana hasn't had much time with Harrick over the past several days, and when she has, I've been able to keep my distance. As long as Malek didn't see me that night—and I don't think he did—I should be okay.

The lights start to dim, and I force myself back to the present. Petra fidgets with her pale dress, and beside her, Viana sits primly with her nose in the air. She's wearing a skin-tight viridian pantsuit, touched with flecks of scarlet. She looks absolutely flawless now, but an hour ago, she was a sobbing mess.

I'm sure she's terrified to lose her crown, though she's yet to say a word about it. Earlier, her only concern was whether her pant legs were long enough. She didn't like the way her exposed ankles looked, or the way her heels dug into her skin. Luckily, one of the seamstresses was able to find *better* shoes. Viana had been placated and I escaped physically unscathed.

"I wonder why they don't have shows anymore," Petra muses. She adjusts her skirt over her crossed legs, fussing with the pleats. Her voice is soft and her demeanor is quiet, but she's as finicky as the rest.

"They're monstrous," Nordan says from the other side of Viana. His face is unremarkable but handsome enough. His suit is all green, save for his blood red tie, buttons, and cufflinks. He props his elbows onto his knees and arches his eyebrow in challenge. "Fighting to the death, Petra? It's inhuman."

"They're not entirely human though, are they?" Viana asks, the awe bright in her voice. "Our loves are more god than man."

I don't let myself react. I'm carefully positioned behind Viana's chair, wedged between Petra and Nordan's servants. We've been standing here for forty-five minutes, long past the scheduled start time. Nobody seems surprised it's running late, and I imagine the nightwater vendors are happy for the delay. There are over three hundred royals and elites packed into this place, and most are already intoxicated.

Only the important people—the crown, the betrothed, the

upper royals—fill the bottom ring. The rest of the attendees' ranking goes down as the seating gets higher. By the fifth level, there are families of the guards, who will probably have to squint to see.

"I think it's beautiful," says Viana. She stares at the circular mat. It's smaller than the Royal Training Arena, probably thirty paces by thirty paces. Glass walls encompass its floor and stretch all the way up to that distant ceiling. The barrier seems too thin to protect the crowd, but I imagine it's been magicked to do exactly that.

"Beautiful?" Nordan scoffs. "Since when is beating someone to death *beautiful?*"

"The princes aren't going to kill each other. That would be a waste," she says. She tilts her head to the side, and I catch a glimpse of her ruby-red smile. "Yes, this is beautiful. Pure and animalistic and beastly. As humans, we tend to bury our instincts, you know. We pretend to be civil, kind, good. But this? This reveals *exactly* who we are."

I shiver at that. If this is Viana's tame side, I don't want to see her truest self.

Before Nordan has the chance to respond, the lights dim. I sweep my eyes over the audience one last time. The Architect sits on the opposite side of the arena with Queen Elaria and Princess Tora to his left. The women look bored, as if they couldn't care less to be here. The Architect, of course, is hidden behind his mask. Still, I get the inexplicable sense he's grinning.

I force my attention back to the enclosed arena. An elite, dressed in a lacy gown, strides into its center. She smiles at the audience, rotating slowly to address all sides. When she begins speaking, she faces the Architect himself.

"Welcome!" she calls. Her voice amplifies through the crowd, loud enough it echoes against the highest ceilings. "Tonight, you are honored to witness the first royal challenge in over forty cycles. This duel, the first of three, pits brother against brother. Prince against prince. Descendant against descendant."

A burst of applause sounds from the crowd. People stamp their feet, chant their chosen competitor's name, and laugh the way only drunk people can. Despite the significance of this battle, what the results will mean, the spectators are relaxed in their seats. They're grinning. This is the type of entertainment most never dreamt to witness.

"The battle lasts until one prince surrenders or until he is deemed incapable of continuing," the elite says. The crowd hushes, but their anticipation is still palpable. It's a buzzing in the room, a stinging presence that grows louder with each second.

The elite introduces the Architect, the queen, the princess. Chaos builds through the crowd again, until it's almost impossible to hear the woman at all. She's going over rules, though there don't seem to be many beyond *no leaving the arena* and *no killing blows*. The audience boos that rule.

A flicker of movement catches my eyes, and I see him a moment before Viana seems to. She straightens in her chair and pinches Petra, nodding toward the two darkened figures. The opposing brothers stand with a guard between them. Malek is loose, his posture slouched and his head thrown back as if laughing. Harrick is rigid, arms tight at his sides. He's too far, too shadowed to make out his expression.

Without consciously deciding to, I touch my lips.

"Your betrothed looks nervous," says Nordan, his voice more of a snarl. "Perhaps he doesn't find this as *beautiful* as you do, Viana."

She doesn't respond. Her attention is now locked on Harrick, as if they are the only two people here.

"Please welcome longstanding heir, Prince Harrick

Ademas!" the elite calls. The crowd explodes with applause, feet stamping louder and louder until it's deafening.

Harrick strides into the arena, looking nothing like the man who has saved me more than once. There's a heavy set to his mouth, a wild darkness in his eyes. If I didn't know better, I'd think his irises were ebony.

"He doesn't look nervous," Viana says, lifting her chin. "He looks feral."

She's right, and I'm unsettled to find it as beautiful as she said. Harrick is a caged animal at the back of an enclosure, preparing to strike. I should be terrified, unnerved, but there's something magnetic about his ferocious energy. Magnetic and inexplicably comforting, if only because he seems as *good* as he does powerful.

"And now, welcome Prince Malek Ademas, the Architect's newly selected heir!"

The audience again cheers, but this time, a deep-toned chant rumbles through the lower rings. Young royals call Malek's name, voices growing with each iteration.

Malek! Malek! MALEK!

"Looks like the crowd has picked their favorite," taunts Nordan, resting his elbows on his knees. Petra starts to agree, but Viana cuts her off.

"The crowd has no power," she snaps. "Magic will choose the winner, and Harrick's got more of it."

Opposite Harrick's calm disposition, Malek waltzes into the arena like a preening peacock. He waves his arms, egging the crowd louder and louder. The chanting royals are all too happy to oblige. Meanwhile, Harrick remains motionless at the edge of the mat.

I'm so focused on the twins, I don't notice when the elite exits. I only realize the brothers are now alone, squared off on opposite sides of the arena. Malek bounces on his feet, movements quick, effortless. Whenever he turns, the lights reflect his gruesome scars and easy grin. As feral as Harrick looks, Malek is somehow scarier. Where Harrick has proven time and again to be good, Malek has only shown the opposite. His excitement is unsettling, as if he's waited far too long to wound his brother.

"Come on, baby," Viana says, her voice a low whisper.

Nordan doesn't taunt her now. He—and everyone else —is abruptly quiet. The entire audience hitches forward, collective breaths held, bodies growing tighter with each passing second. The two princes regard each other. Identical twins in identical red bodysuits, made different only by their individual lives. Malek's unkempt locks and gnarled scars. Harrick's untouched skin and sharp posture.

Though the elite remains out of sight, her voice radiates through the arena.

"Prince Harrick, Prince Malek. Prepare for battle." Her words float through the strained silence, followed by an automated buzzing. It sounds like the changing of the hour, only faster.

Beep. Beep. Beepbeep. Beepbeepbeepbeep.

With the final note, a crash of cymbals and a momentary blackness ignites the battle. A second of blindness. Then, a piercing white light in the arena, made brighter by the lingering darkness everywhere else.

There's no time to suck in a breath or to fully realize the fight has begun. Malek's already conjured a beast. This one is different than his first. Where that creature had been tall and spindly with a wide body, this one is low to the ground. Its muscular body is shaped almost like an alligator, only instead of one sweeping tail, it has two. Its head is worse, flat and flared, with fangs protruding almost to the ground.

"Wyhel," Nordan breathes. His voice trembles as the beast strides across the arena. It prowls with the surety of a bloodthirsty predator, undeterred by the vines coiling from Harrick's outstretched palms.

Stark red, Harrick's magic whips against the mat and the domed enclosure, growing larger and wider with each passing second. An ear-splitting crack echoes each time a strand hits the glass, and soon his magic looks more like a spiraling tornado than individual vines. Petra gasps at every sound and movement, her hands taut against her armrests.

I search Harrick's face for something familiar, but everything is different. *He* is different. Violent. Terrifying. Powerful. My knees tremble as I watch him. Magic swirling, building, coursing through him like a being of its own control. Harrick's mouth clenches as he moves, raising his arms until they're level with his shoulders.

Viana is right: he is not fully human. In this moment, he looks nothing less than a beautiful, monstrous god.

One of his vines strikes, curving around the alligator's neck. Malek grunts, and the noise amplifies through the stadium. His beast snaps wildly until his teeth sever the nearest vine and then another. Malek screams, twisting his wrist, the beast moving with it. One of its tails whips to the side, like a lunging serpent. It cuts through the remaining vines. Eviscerates them as if they're parchment. Harrick screams, stumbling as he sends another twist of vines toward the beast—and misses.

It's a costly mistake. The beast lunges between the whipping vines, its fangs clamping around Harrick's ankle. Blood spills onto the mat, and Harrick screams, throwing chaotic magic from his palms. It's three tries before a vine latches over the alligator's throat, but finally, the beast loses its hold. Harrick stumbles away, struggling to put weight on his injured leg.

"Kill him!" a royal screams from behind me. I don't turn to

face her, but I can feel flecks of her spit against my neck. "Kill him, Malek!"

Harrick screams again, this time not from pain but from power. Arms raised, he hurtles both the beast and his brother with a violent gust of air. They slam against the glass barrier, and the alligator evaporates into red mist at the impact. Malek howls as his magic dissolves around him, but he's already conjuring as he gets back to his feet. The hazy red takes shape again, jolting into a solid beast.

This one is taller, thinner. A horrifying bird creature with an oblong, hanging mouth and endless sharp teeth. It jerks as it moves, as if a puppet with damaged strings. Harrick staggers a step back, arms still raised. Calculating. His vines have returned, snapping wildly around him, forcing the beast to stay back.

Harrick rotates his wrists, and as though spurred by Malek's shift of magic, his changes too. It coils and writhes, then jerks and shudders. The vines morph into shattered stone until there are dozens, hundreds of them. They float around him like a swarm of vermilion wasps.

In one sharp lurch, the rocks catapult through the air. They slam against the bird creature, puncturing its body and exposed teeth. The creature lurches, moving forward despite itself. Malek lets out a heinous cackle.

"Is that it?" he calls. His voice wavers though, and I swear, Harrick's lips tick at the show of weakness. With an echoing grunt, Malek twists his magic toward the creature, mending its injuries.

Harrick bares his teeth, but ignores his brother's taunts. His hands are steady, fingers pulsing as he silently packs the stones into a gigantic boulder. It forms behind Malek's back, and though some in the crowd shout warnings, the older twin doesn't seem to notice. He's focused on his beast, patching it together like a worn sock.

Through a faltering smile, Malek taunts, "I thought you'd do better than—"

Harrick doesn't give him time to finish. He hurls his boulder toward himself, clipping Malek's shoulder on his way and obliterating the bird's upper half. Malek collapses to the mat, crying out as his magic once again vanishes. Harrick balances his boulder in the air, letting it rotate. There's a flicker of indecision on his face, so quick I might have imagined it.

And then, he drops the stone on his brother. It hits the same shoulder again before crashing onto Malek's leg. There's a brutal crunch, like a dozen sticks snapping at once. Malek screams and sends a violent blur of magic back to Harrick. It's glass, I realize. A dozen jagged shards that slice across Harrick's cheeks and throat. There's blood everywhere now, streaming down his face and into the collar of his suit.

I expect Harrick to collapse, but he screams again, sending wave after wave of broken rock across the arena. It is only as Malek wails that I realize Harrick's magic is not like his brother's. His rocks are not erupting. They're not fading or evaporating. Instead, they're turning to solid, obsidian stone.

Multiple people in the audience gasp. This isn't normal, I realize—and Malek might not stand a chance.

"Come on, baby!" Viana screams. She's on her feet, leaning over the metal fencing between us and the glass enclosure.

A rock strikes Malek's temple. Then another smashes his stomach. His shoulder. He's taking too many hits to act unaffected, and before long, he's not striking back. His magic has died, leaving his hands violent red with heat.

Harrick holds another giant boulder over his brother. If he dropped it on his chest, this would be over.

But Malek also might be dead.

The two brothers stare at each other, both with teeth bared like wild animals. Neither casts magic, but their hands glow red with heat. Their breaths are the only sound, heavy and unsteady, as if on the verge of collapse.

"Come on!" Viana shouts. "Call it! Malek is done!"

At Viana's outburst, the arena comes alive again with chants and cheers, boos and demands. I can hear bets swirling in the rows behind us, and despite it all, some people are still laughing.

Harrick casts another stream of magic. It's misshapen, uncertain, as it unspools from his palms. I watch, breath held tight in my chest, as he pauses. It's as if Harrick can't decide how—or even *if*—he wants to destroy his brother.

He's afraid, I realize, not of losing but of *winning*.

With his legs buried beneath stone and his body bloodied and bruised, Malek struggles to rise. His eyes flicker between Harrick and the looming boulder. And he must see it, that same horrible reluctance that I do.

He makes his final move so quickly I almost miss it. With a heave of his chest, he shoves his bloodied hands toward Harrick. A burst of water, no more than a bucket's worth, surrounds Harrick's face. It latches onto him, moving every time he does, until he's drowning on his feet. He staggers, dropping the boulder where it hangs. It misses Malek by less than an inch.

"Pull through," Viana yells. "Focus! You just have to—"

Harrick collapses to the mat. Malek holds the water over his brother's unconscious face, only releasing it when the elite officially calls the match. The stadium erupts in cheers and boos, and Viana deflates in front of me. She returns to her seat, eerily still as Petra celebrates beside her.

A pair of healers remove Harrick from the ring, while several casters work to free Malek from the mess of stone. He curses at them the entire time, and when they finally destroy the last boulder, he lurches to his feet. White bone sticks out from his ankle, and his left elbow bends at an unnatural angle.

Malek doesn't acknowledge his wounds. He hobbles around the mat, managing a sloppy bow in each direction. His fans once again fill the stadium with his name, and he pumps his good hand with each chant.

Malek. Malek! MALEK!

The room shifts with bodies. Harrick's supporters grumble their losses. Malek's crowd lingers, still drinking and counting their coin. Viana remains in her seat, long after Nordan and Petra have left. I stand dutifully behind her, wishing she'd go check on Harrick. Pathetic as it is, I want to see if he's okay.

When Viana finally leaves, she heads not for Harrick but back to her quarters. My stomach is tight the entire time, even as she maintains her stoic facade. She doesn't look at me as we enter her bedroom, and I'm tempted to leave without permission. It won't help, not in the long run, and so I stay.

I stand at the closed door, hand clasping the bronze handle. I may not be allowed to leave, but I feel safest here all the same. Viana storms around the room, ripping the velvet curtains from her windows and taking a knife to her duvet. I'm not sure if the violence is making her feel better, or if it's only digging the anger deeper. Either way, she's destroyed her room in a matter of minutes.

She lets out a vicious scream, high and piercing, as she tangles her shredded comforter around her shoulders. She's gone hysterical, alternating between screams and sobs and strangled laughter. I want a guard to overhear her breakdown, to come calm her. Nobody does, and I'm too terrified to intervene.

She stumbles around her room, pausing occasionally to stab something else with her knife. I shrink against the door as she does, hoping her focus remains on her dresser and not on me. The knife leaves hollow dents along its wooden surface, and Viana shrieks with each skewered punch.

When it's clear no one is coming and Viana isn't losing steam, I finally clear my throat.

"My lady," I say from the doorway.

She doesn't react, so I clear the guck and hesitancy from my throat. If she doesn't stop soon, she's going to destroy everything in her room. Fine by me, except I'll be the one to clean it. I'll be the one to face her wrath when she realizes all her belongings are damaged beyond repair.

"My lady," I say again, forcing the words louder. "Perhaps you should lie down for a while—"

I don't have time to react, let alone finish my sentence. Viana hurls the knife across the room, and it strikes the side of my face. A flare of pain shoots through my cheek, bringing with it a warm trail of liquid. My legs shake, and I slide down the door before I can stop myself. I clasp a hand to my cheek, feeling the blood pool between my fingers.

She just barely missed my eye.

"Dammit!" she screams. She lunges toward me, arms rattling the door as they frame the space above my head. "Look at me, wench."

I do, but only with my right eye. She might not have cut the left one, but it's already swelling.

"That was an accident," she snaps. "That wasn't intentional, and I didn't do it. You fell, all right?" When I don't respond, she drops to my height. Her long nails dig into my shoulders. "You did that to yourself. Understand?"

I should tell her to go fuck herself.

I don't say anything at all. Instead, I nod, hand trembling against my face. There's blood on my lace veil, sticking it to my skin. It'll be stained now, and that saddens me more than it should. Harrick gave me this mask, and while it certainly wasn't a gift, I hate that it's ruined.

"Good," she says. There's a tremble in her voice that almost makes her sound scared. She moves away, returning a moment later. She tosses a scrap of green velvet onto my lap. A piece of her duvet, I realize. "Clean yourself up. You're dismissed."

I scrub at my face with the fabric. I'm sure I've only spread it around my skin, made a mess of blood and tears. Viana turns away from me, and I take the moment to scramble through her bedroom door. With the velvet still pressed to my cheek, I run from her quarters to my own.

Pathetic. Weak. Helpless.

The words spin through my brain on repeat. Even as I collapse into bed, they whirl faster and faster. I'm sick with it, my own shame and frailty.

I tell myself I would have fought back, if only I'd had the sword or the dagger from the training arena. If I'd had a weapon, I would have destroyed Viana for all her wicked sins. Nobody would ever hurt me again.

I force these ideas to overtake my thoughts. I make them wash away any feelings of inferiority and sadness. If I ever stand on level ground with Viana, with any of these horrible people, I will ruin them until they can't hurt anyone at all.

15
HARRICK

"This is foolish," Mother says. She trails behind me as I storm the corridor, her heels clacking against the reflective tile. "At least wait until we speak with the Committee. You don't have the Architect's—"

"Mother," I say. It comes out loud and harsh, like a strained cord finally snapping. She's barely left my side all night, one step behind, criticizing my every move. "I have already decided."

I press my thumb against the lift's access screen. A quiet swishing, like the sound of birds taking flight, fills the silence as the lift rises to meet us. We're in the military sector, but now that I've assembled a last-minute security team, there's nothing left to do except leave.

The lift door gasps open and I stride inside, disappointed but not surprised when Mother joins me. She's still wearing her gown from last night's battle, but her typically flawless appearance is ruined by the dark bags under her eyes and the fade of her once-bright lipstick.

After my humiliating loss against Malek, I'd barricaded myself in a room behind the arena. I'd sat with my throbbing hands in a bucket of ice, silently letting the healers treat me. I ignored anyone who knocked on the door and felt slighted when Malek didn't bother to come taunt me. My loss was so pathetic I'm no longer worth tormenting.

Maybe that's what spurred all of this into action.

I've spent my entire life trying to prove my worth as heir. I trained harder and longer than Malek. I took on more responsibilities. I did what Mother and the Committee and the Architect asked of me, and still, Malek was faster, stronger, *better*.

It struck me at some point in my self-pitying that *at least* if I lose my title, I can behave the way Malek always has. Not as a monster, but as a man with few worries. I've dedicated my time to training and preparing for kinghood—now that it's slipping away, what's the point? If I'm never going to be king, if all that work was for nothing, the least I deserve are those luxuries of wealth and power.

By the time Mother came around, I had the beginnings of a plan. I was taking a trip through the exterior sectors of Savoa: the Wilds, the City of Mirrors, the Pit, the Reaping Grounds... even the Deadlands, though only out of convenience.

"Harrick," she says, pulling my focus back to the present. We're almost to the entry level of the Tower, where my guards will be waiting with three carriages. They should have our bags packed, along with whatever Viana decided to bring. I don't care if she's packed half the Tower, so long as Rune is with her.

"My son," she whispers. Her voice grows quiet, laced with urgency. "You cannot go. If you try, I will have to alert the Architect. You have too many responsibilities here. There's too much—"

"The Architect won't care, Mother," I say as the lift settles on the main floor. "He'll only be angry that you've disturbed his sleep."

The lift stops and I exit. This time, Mother doesn't follow.

There's a chance she's going straight to the Architect, but I doubt it. I think she knows as well as I do that I've been written off. Even if there are two more battles to come, he knows Malek will win.

After last night, *everyone* knows.

I slow my steps. The Tower's entry level is one of the grandest floors in the entire building. It's an exquisite maze of bright papered walls and multi-colored marble. Black and red, green and violet, even a few splashes of white and pale yellow. The Architect designed this level to be as confusing as it is luxurious, in hopes that visitors would believe the entire Tower to be this beautiful and impossible to navigate. I imagine anyone unfamiliar with the layout could spend days lost on this level alone.

I take my time walking the halls, pretending this is the last time I'll ever have to see them. The garish violet and green wall coverings, the gnarled plants with vines curling around hanging portraits, the marble floors so polished I can see my own reflection. The decor becomes increasingly extravagant as I near the main entryway: rare gemstones in glass cases, masks worn by ancestral warriors, retired crowns of previous royalty.

Voices filter from the entryway, and I realize I'm among the last to arrive. Joran and Dae are discussing possible routes to take, and Viana occasionally interrupts them with questions about our *vacation*. When I enter the foyer, a pair of drenched servants give their updates to Dae.

Through the ajar doors behind them, the half-flooded courtyard is visible. Three carriages, pulled by magic, sit near the Tower's entrance, and one appears to be packed full of luggage. Opposite the shivering servants and my guards, Viana stands beside two oversized bags. There's a female servant near her, but it's not Rune.

"My love!" she calls. She dances across the colorful marble, a grin splitting her mouth, and throws herself against my chest. I give her a halfhearted pat on the back, scanning the room behind her. Aside from the soaked servants, the female servant, and my guards, there isn't anyone else here.

She isn't here. And a pain in my gut tells me there's a reason...one I won't like.

"Ah, my prince," Joran says. He crosses the room, pausing a respectable distance from me and Viana, who is still pressed against me, even though I dropped my arm a while ago.

"Give us a moment," I say to Viana. She skips back to her baggage, keeping her eyes on me. If she's upset about my humiliating defeat last night, she doesn't show it. I wonder if she's written it off as a fluke, if she thinks she'll still be queen.

"We are almost ready to leave," Joran says. He glances back at the two wet men. "The carriage is packed. They're struggling to fit the last of Viana's bags, but I told them to figure it out. Everything else is prepared. Safety procedures are in place and there are enough supplies to last us several days, on the off chance we are delayed."

"Who's coming?" I ask.

"Only a small team, my prince, as requested," he says. "There will be yourself and Miss Viana, myself and Dae, two additional guards, Viana's handmaiden and an additional servant to cater to your needs."

My attention flickers to the woman near Viana. She's no longer alone. There's a young male servant, a cycle younger than me if I had to guess, now standing beside her. He wears the insignia of a crowned servant, but he's unfamiliar. And, obviously, he is *not* Rune either.

Joran excuses himself, and I force myself to remain still. A panicked wrath pulses through my bones, pressing against my magic, growing stronger as Viana skips back to my side.

"Where are we going first, my love?" she asks, purring. She

looks ready for a luxury event: glittering makeup on her cheeks, an elaborately twisted hairstyle, and a long green gown, accented with red jewelry. She's wearing an overpowering perfume, sharp cinnamon, more acidic than alluring.

"Where is your handmaiden?" I ask. It comes out as a demand, and I have to clench my jaw to stop from continuing. Viana stares at me with wide eyes, her red-painted lips parting.

"There, my prince," she says, tilting her chin toward the unfamiliar servant. In many ways, she resembles Rune. Her hair is light brown and she's about the same height, but she's heavier, healthier. Rounded cheeks, subtle curves, unblemished skin. She keeps her face tucked down, away from me, as if she's been instructed to hide it.

"No, your usual handmaiden," I say. I force a soft lilt to my voice, trying to sound coy. It's blatantly false in my ear, as if the anger refuses to be stifled. Viana relaxes all the same.

"Oh, Rain isn't feeling well," she says. The lie rolls easily from her tongue, like she's been practicing it. "When I saw it —*her*—this morning, I felt just horrible. I'm afraid she's overworked, and I couldn't bear to stress her with last-minute travel. I've decided to let her remain here, to work on our wedding arrangements instead."

She's beaming at me, once again waiting for my approval. I wish she was telling the truth, that she's taken my warning, that she's being sincere. After all, this is the first time she's made the effort to call Rune a person and not an object.

"Nonsense," I say. Even if I were naive enough to believe Rune is upstairs resting, I'm only going on this trip to indulge my obsession with her. There's no point in going if she's not. I force a smile. "I know you've grown accustomed to her service. I will send for her immediately."

"Oh no, my husband—"

"Joran!" I call, interrupting her. "Please send for Rune Ealde.

Servant 247, room 51 CC. Lady Viana would prefer her company."

"Yes, my prince," he says. He nods to one of the newly-arrived guards, who takes off down the twist of hallways. Once he's gone, I return my attention to Viana. Her cheeks are pale, eyes wide, and I know without question she's done something terrible.

I step away from her, tightening my hands into fists. My fingers itch with magic, as if begging me to launch her across the room, to solve two problems at once. Instead, I move farther from her, crossing the foyer to join Dae, Joran, and the two servants.

"You are dismissed," I tell the two young men, interrupting one of them. "Go find warm clothes."

"They're scheduled to—" starts Dae, but I wave him off.

"Go on," I say to the men. They share a hesitant glance between themselves, as if questioning whether this is a trap. "You may rest until your next shift. If anyone questions you, ask for Princess Tora. She'll take care of you."

The men trade another glance before bowing their heads and thanking me. As they disappear from the room, I feel Joran and Dae's skeptical gazes on me, but I don't make eye contact. I don't want to explain anything, and I *hate* that a simple show of kindness is so jarring. Not for the first time, I wonder if I am as horrible as Malek. Just because I don't relish in the servants' misery doesn't mean I don't contribute to it.

I leave Joran and Dae, returning to Viana and her remaining bags. She is still pale and unusually quiet, staring absently in the direction of the lift. My stomach tightens, wondering what she already knows. Is the guard going to announce Rune's legs are broken? That she's too injured to walk? Or, worse, will he say she's gone missing? That her body was found in the service stairwell?

I'll never forgive myself. I should have known. Should have sent for her last night, rather than leave her under Viana's watch.

I work my jaw. The brunette servant still at her side glances at me nervously.

"Thank you for your services, but they will no longer be needed. You may return to your quarters," I tell the woman. Her shoulders loosen, and for the first time, she lifts her head enough to look at me. Even with her mask, she stares at my nose instead of my eyes.

"Yes, my prince." She dips her chin in acknowledgement before hurrying out of sight.

Viana doesn't flinch, doesn't seem to register my words at all. Her eyes remain in the direction of the lifts, and my anxiety spikes with each passing second. Finally, the guard returns, flanked by Rune. Her head is tucked almost to her chest, and her brown hair creates a curtain over her face. She's walking though, without any perceptible limp.

Viana shifts beside me, breath unnaturally fast. I keep my eyes on Rune. She wears a smaller pair of coveralls that exposes just how skinny she is, and her mask is pale yellow. It's tattered and the strap sags from overuse. Even from a distance, I know it's not the one I gave her.

She arrives at Viana's side, head down, body painfully stiff. She doesn't look up, but I can still see why she has a new mask. A deep gash cuts up the side of her face, disappearing beneath the yellow veil. Dark purple bruising swells over her cheek and beneath her eye, and though it isn't bleeding now, it certainly was when she got it.

My vision sparks with red, almost as if my magic is attempting to break free, any way it can. I tighten my hands again, but I feel like I'm losing control of them, as if they might punish Viana without my permission.

"Your face," Viana gasps in false surprise. "My goodness, Rain. What have you done to yourself?"

"I fell," she says. Her voice is low, cracked. "On the service stairwell. I fell after leaving your room last night."

"That is *terrible*," Viana says. "Oh, I'm so sorry. You must be hurting. Perhaps you want to stay to heal—"

"It's time to leave," I say, cutting her off. I signal to Joran across the room, and once he heads our way, I look down to Rune. "Please lead Lady Viana to our carriage. Joran will show you the way."

Once Joran has joined them, I excuse myself to one of the nearby bathrooms. I empty the meager contents of my stomach, hands pressed against the tile wall. I shake, trying but failing to reclaim my senses. I'm aware of every speck of magic in my body, and it suddenly feels painful to keep it *in*. I send a wisp of it through my fingers, let the red spin through the room like a miniature tornado, breathing through the unexpected release of tension.

You knew, my head whispers, *you knew what she was capable of.*

Only once my vision clears and my hands steady do I push off the bathroom floor and return to the entryway of the Tower.

"Get in," I say to Rune. She startles from beside the middle carriage, her blue eyes meeting mine through her mask. The gruesome wound on her face sickens me all over again, but I'll take care of that soon enough.

"She may ride with the rest of the servants," Dae says. Of course he's here, always ready to poke holes in my plans.

"Absolutely not," I state. I keep my eyes on Rune, watching blush rise through her cheeks.

"Protocol states—"

"Get in, Rune," I repeat. I open the door and gesture for her to climb into the carriage. Dae lets out a sharp breath, but I ignore him until she's inside. Only then do I turn toward my secondary guard. "Do not press me today, Dae. It will not end well for you."

He nods, a sharp tilt of his chin. He doesn't agree, but he's not going to outright disobey.

"Do not enter until I call for you," I say.

Then, I climb into the carriage and shut the door behind me. The carriage is comprised of three long benches, outlining the interior windows. Rune sits on the left side, Viana claims the center, and I take the right. My betrothed glares at her servant, as if repulsed by her simple existence.

"I thought I was clear," I say. My voice is low, lethal. I wait for Viana to look at me before I continue. "I told you not to harm someone who cannot fight back."

Viana blanches, and Rune visibly stiffens at my words. Though it takes all my conscious effort, I don't let myself look at her. I focus only on Viana.

"My love, I assure you, I didn't—"

"I know exactly what you've done," I say. I try to maintain a steady voice, but my anger is spitting out like overflowing water. "You gave me your word, and you broke it."

"No," she says. Her words choke, and she reaches for me, fingers trembling. I lean from her touch, using all my self-control not to shove her away.

"Consider our betrothal absolved," I say.

She sucks in a sharp breath, flinching as though I *have* shoved her. She's still trembling, and now, large tears well and spill onto her cheeks.

"You can't break a betrothal," she whispers. Then, sucking

in a raspy breath, she adds, "It was one mistake, my love. I promise. Never again."

I line my teeth together, grinding them until they hurt. I know she's lying about changing her ways, but I'm terrified she's right about breaking a betrothal. I'm not sure it's ever been done. I'm not sure the Committee will allow it...

I glance at Rune. She's hugging herself, eyes bolted to the floor. She's not crying, her mouth set in a determined line. I imagine she's terrified, but she's doing her best not to show it, and I am again mesmerized. She's wildly brave and relentlessly strong, and I'm desperate to find some of that power in myself.

"Our betrothal is absolved," I repeat, facing Viana again. "Appeal the queen, if you wish, but I will not marry you. Perhaps Malek will take you—you certainly deserve each other."

She lets out a sob, and if I didn't know her cruelty, I'd feel bad for the way she shrinks now.

"My love—"

"Your nothing," I correct. Then, "You will leave this carriage. Tell them the truth, if you wish, or lie and say you're feeling unwell. Either way, leave this carriage and never speak to me again."

She's fully crying now as she shoves to her feet. She throws open the carriage door and half-falls onto the wet cobblestone. It is only when she looks back, glaring expectantly at Rune that I realize she's more deranged than I imagined possible.

Rune rises from her seat, only to stop when I place a hand on her wrist.

"She no longer serves you," I say. "Now leave."

Viana doesn't respond. She whips away from me, stumbling across the courtyard and ignoring Dae's call of concern. His head turns toward me, but I ignore him, giving Rune my full attention.

"Nobody will harm you again," I tell her. Those blue eyes are on me, wide and terrified. I'm not sure she believes me now, but soon enough she will. "Anyone who makes the mistake of trying will suffer the consequences."

Rune's mouth hangs open, moving slightly as she searches for a response. Before she can, Dae appears at the carriage door.

"My prince—"

"Don't," I say, cutting him off. Then, just before shutting the door, I add, "Let's go."

16

RUNE

oly fuck.

I'm sitting in a royal carriage, and that by itself is enough to jostle my brain. Add in the fact I'm alone with the crowned prince *after* he broke his betrothal...my mind doesn't know how to process that information. As we pull away from the Tower, departing through tall black gates and entering the Wilds, I don't let myself look at Harrick.

Instead, I watch the passing landscape with feigned interest. Thick trees, interrupted by occasional moss-covered boulders, line our path on either side. In the distance, deep blue creatures—boars, perhaps?—graze in an overgrown field. They lift their heads as we pass, only to lower them again, unbothered. Above us, flickers of gray sky taunt me from between lush, overhanging branches.

I've dreamt of leaving the Tower for so long, I'm too shocked to comprehend I actually am. The more I dwell on it, the more I decide I *must* be dreaming. Any moment now, I'm going to awaken in my bed to the servant's bell, and I'll rush to get Viana's breakfast.

I glance at Harrick. He still hasn't moved. He's watching me closely from his side of the carriage, but he hasn't spoken since we left. His attention is a heavy, physical thing though, and despite my best efforts, the same thought blares continuously through my head: *Harrick broke his betrothal for me.*

I look away, swallowing hard.

No. Not me. He just didn't want to marry an abuser. He said that himself.

But if that's true...why am I still here?

I force my breaths to slow. I shouldn't be stressing over Harrick and Viana. Practical as my fear is, there's nothing to be done now. I *should* be enjoying this unexpected freedom. I've dreamt of leaving the Tower since I was eight, when they bound my hands and dragged me here. It's been twelve cycles, and the farthest outside I've been is in the courtyard. I've attended executions, just so I could remember life beyond the Tower walls. To remember crisp air and the feel of wind on my skin.

Even after several cycles in the rebellion, part of me doubted I'd ever experience this again. Not that I'm free, by any means, but it almost feels like it. With Viana gone, I might even enjoy moments of this journey—whatever its purpose.

"Are you all right?" Harrick asks.

I startle and look at him, allowing myself to pause before answering. We've been traveling for almost an hour now, and I still can't process what's happened. What's *going* to happen, now that Harrick has broken his betrothal and run off from the Tower.

Nobody will harm you again.

It's an impossible promise, one that does something strange to my heart. There are times I worry that particular organ doesn't work, but right now, I'm painfully aware of its existence. It feels terrified, angry—and worst of all, hopeful.

"Yes," I say. Something on Harrick's face tells me he doesn't believe me. It's the same *something* that compels me to add, "She will have me killed for this."

My cheeks flush at my admission, and I can't help lowering my gaze. I shouldn't challenge the prince, not when he clearly thinks he'll keep me from harm. But this is the ugly, inescapable truth. Viana will blame me for everything that's happened, and as soon as Harrick loses interest in me, she'll make arrangements. I doubt I'll survive the Flood Season.

"Rune," he says. The carriage jostles as we move from asphalt to rocky dirt. "I will protect you."

Without responding, I close my eyes. I can't decide if I'm being unfair. Right now, I can't decide much of anything. Should I be grateful? Can I use this to my benefit? Could I convince Harrick to help me escape the Tower forever? Or perhaps to free the entire rebel faction?

I could barter an agreement, maybe. Convince him to let us go, and in exchange, we won't destroy the Tower or attempt a coup on our way out. He seems genuinely kind, and if I can just play this right—

"Rune," his voice softens. He crouches to the floor, until he's the one looking up at me. The sight of him on his knees before me, as if *I'm* the royal one, does ungodly things to my stomach. One of his hands rests on the cushion to my side, and the edge of his palm touches my thigh. "Can I try something?"

I glance at his mouth without meaning to. Barely an hour, and my fantasies are already taking on a life of their own. My memories distort our kiss from a panicked miscommunication to something meaningful, and suddenly I can't think clearly.

"Okay." I don't recognize my own voice. The way it sounds unsure and desperate, all at once.

Harrick's opposite hand grazes the side of my face, so tender I barely feel it. His fingers drift over my uninjured cheek, beneath my chin, and then up to the bruised and scarred side. I can't keep myself from wincing, and Harrick's expression echoes my flinch.

"Sorry," he whispers.

His hand stills on my bruised cheek, firmly cupping the side of my face. Keeping his eyes on me, he rests his thumb on my cut, the pressure uncomfortable but not overly painful. I take a breath through my teeth. Harrick is no longer looking at me. His eyes are closed, brows scrunched in concentration.

"I've never done this before," he murmurs. "It might not work, so tell me if it hurts, and I'll stop."

That's the only warning I get before magic sparks at his fingertips. I tense, my entire body jolting at the strange sensation. Heat filters through my skin, but it isn't painful at all. It's impossible to describe, the way magic bleeds from his hand into my cheek. I have no idea what he's doing, and yet, I make no move to fight him. He could be killing me for all I know, but I'm not sure I care.

It feels that good. So ridiculously warm, until I'm full of heat and light and this beautiful glow and—

I don't recognize the sound that comes out of my throat. Worse than the gasp when Harrick stroked my face, this is an actual moan, as if I've just tasted the sweetest chocolate. I *moaned* at the prince's touch, and I've effectively ruined anything pleasant about this moment.

I pull away, fighting blush as it scours across my cheeks.

Harrick's eyes open too, but I can't tell what he's thinking. He certainly doesn't look angry or judgemental. He's simply watching me, blinking, his gaze moving from my chin to my hairline.

"It's not perfect," he says. "But it's not bad either."

Now my face heats for an entirely different reason. *Not bad* probably isn't the best compliment someone could receive, but coming from a prince—coming from him—it feels like the highest of praise.

"Your cut," he clarifies. "I'm not much of a healer, but it's mostly gone. It didn't hurt?"

I shake my head. I'm too afraid of my own emotions right now, terrified I'll admit that his touch not only didn't hurt—it felt really fucking good.

More, I want to tell him. *Touch me more.*

"Thank you," I say instead. Then, because I can't help myself, I ask, "Why are you helping me?"

Harrick scans my face, and I can hear my own heart pounding. I'm terrified he can too. His attention drops to my mouth, and for a suspended moment, I'm sure he's going to kiss me. A ridiculous thought, by itself, and an extremely dangerous one, considering. The queen and the Committee might be unhappy with Harrick's broken betrothal, but if they think I'm the thing that led him astray...

The carriage shudders to a stop. Harrick pulls his attention from my face and looks out the elongated carriage window. He eases back onto his seat, watching as his guards move in and out of view.

"We're here," he tells me. He gives me an almost boyish grin, but whatever he's planning to say next is interrupted. The carriage door slides open, and one of his masked guards leans into view. Rain cascades around him, splattering against the floorboards.

"We've arrived, my prince," he says. His concealed face turns toward me, only briefly before focusing again on Harrick. "Dae has gone ahead to call the proxy."

"Perfect," Harrick says. "We can get settled until then. What rooms are available?"

"Two master quarters, two guard quarters. A spare room the servants can use." The guard doesn't look at me this time.

"The other servant is a man," Harrick says, pointedly.

"Yes," the guard agrees.

I shift on my seat. I feel like I should excuse myself to unload the bags, but that would require squeezing past the guard. I stay where I am but turn my eyes to the floor.

"No," Harrick says, his voice hard.

I force myself to be still. On the lower floors, servants aren't separated by gender. They're shoved wherever there's room, and on more than one occasion, I shared a room with a man. It was always unsettling, and sleep often came in fits, but I never suffered an attack from one. The same can't be said for other women.

"Sir—"

"No," he repeats. For the first time since the guard appeared, Harrick turns toward me. I keep my gaze on the floor, but I feel his attention all the same. Heavy and intense, like he's trying to convey a secret message, meant only for me. Finally, he looks back to the guard. "Leave us."

"Yes, my prince," he says. He leaves without another word, sliding the door shut behind him.

It's several seconds before I dare lift my head, and even then, I look out the window, rather than at Harrick. I'm not surprised he's already watching me, but I can't bring myself to meet his gaze. I feel like I've entered another world, one where reality has an entirely different set of rules.

"Rune," he says. His voice is level, calm. "Look at me."

I do, failing to fight the nerves wracking my body. I've started trembling.

"You can't," I whisper. It's hoarse and pathetic, but his eyes widen all the same. I've never spoken this way to a superior before, let alone someone of Harrick's rank. But if I have any chance of surviving this, I can't let him do this.

"Do you know him?" he asks. He's barely moved. "This other servant? Are you familiar with him? Is he safe?"

"It is the only option," I say, ignoring his questions. I force my attention to stay on his eyes.

"I will put you in the spare master's. It will be unused otherwise, and you will be safe there."

I let out a startled laugh. I shouldn't be surprised that Harrick is this delusional. He's a member of the crown. He can do whatever he wants without consequence. Has it ever occurred to him that most people *can't*?

"It is not allowed," I say. I'm surprised at the steadiness of my own voice. I'm treading dangerous territory here. I can't challenge a member of the crown, but his kindness is going to get me killed.

"Says who?" he snaps. "I am the crown prince, Rune. My word is above theirs. They cannot stop me."

I look back to the floor. Even with my hands clenched between my knees, my fingers tremble. I want to argue that the queen, the Architect, the Committee...their words are above his. I might not be punished for this here, but I will once we return. The guards will report to the queen, and I'll be whipped or worse.

I don't argue. As far as words go, mine matter the least.

"Yes, my prince," I say instead.

There's a heavy, pulsing quiet between us. Harrick lets out an unsteady sigh, moving again in front of me. As before, he kneels, looking at me until I finally return his stare.

"Tell me what you're thinking," he says, surprising me. He touches my chin, tilting it upward. "You won't be punished. Please, I—I need to know what you're thinking."

"He won't touch me here," I say finally. My voice shakes, but I force myself to continue. I force myself to trust Harrick, to believe his promise not to punish me. "With the way you're acting, I imagine they're all drawing the same conclusion as Malek. They think I'm your pet whore. Even if the other servant is vile and cruel, he wouldn't dare touch the prince's entertainment. He won't touch me, Harrick."

Harrick's eyes flash, but the anger disappears almost immediately, replaced with something unrecognizable. While I remain in perfect stillness, he seems to relax.

"Okay," he says. "You're right."

My lips twitch without permission. It's bizarre, hearing a crown member speak like this, especially to *me*.

Harrick rises to his feet, stooping to avoid the ceiling. With a sharp tug, he slides open the carriage door. Through the rain, his men move hurriedly between the luggage carriage and a short, rectangular building. It's constructed entirely of wooden logs, and dark green vines claw up its sides, as if they're trying to consume it. It's beautiful, unlike anything I've ever seen. The City is bleak and gray; the Tower is cold and magnificent. This... this is lush and beautiful and *alive*.

"Joran!" Harrick calls.

Within seconds, the masked guard stands in the carriage doorway again.

"My prince."

"Bring Miss Rune's belongings to my quarters," he says. "Ensure the others know she's mine. I will kill anyone who touches her. Understood?"

I suck in a breath, and I swear, Joran does too.

"Yes, my prince," he says after a lengthy pause. If he wants to say more, he doesn't.

"Good," Harrick says. Then, without sparing me another glance, he exits the carriage, calling back, "Come along, Rune. I'll show you our room."

17
RUNE

I am alone in Harrick's room, sitting on the floor beside the four-poster bed. I've never been in such a magnificent place, and I'm too terrified to touch anything. Two walls are composed of wide, golden logs with windows twice my height. This room is on the home's second level, giving me the perfect view of the surrounding forest. It's hard to see much beyond vibrant green leaves and rolling hills, but I think Haver Lake is visible in the distance.

Aside from the bed, which is fitted with an elaborate red duvet and matching pillows, the room contains a spacious wardrobe, an intricate rug that spans the entire floor, and a large desk beneath an enormous painting of the Wilds. I imagine this is one of the Architect's properties, but I don't know for sure.

I pick at a loose thread on the rug, careful not to make it worse. After hours of raucous laughter and drunken shouts, the guards have fallen silent downstairs. It sounds like they're all asleep, though I doubt that's true. I strain my ears for sound, but it's quiet for nearly an hour straight. The first thing I finally hear is creaking steps. I slink against the bed, expecting a guard to appear in the doorway. Instead, it's the male servant, watching me with an assessing gaze. I hold my breath. I'm sure he knows not to touch me, but what if he does anyway? Harrick might not be back for hours.

"They've passed out," he says, and he speaks like his words should be a comfort.

Until now, I've never been around a crown servant. They're a bit in both worlds, unlike the rest of us. Only elites can serve the crown members, meaning this man was born into wealth and prestige. It's only his circumstances that have landed him here, wearing the same stark yellow coverall as I am. His elite insignia taunts me from his breast.

He's like me, but he's also like *them*.

I don't respond to the servant. I can't decide if he's here as a friend or a predator, and I'm too scared to risk speaking.

"They'll think it's the nightwater," the servant explains. His posture is relaxed, but it doesn't make him less threatening. If anything, it's only unsettling. His large frame fills most of the doorway as he leans against it. "That's our strength, you know. They always underestimate us."

"What did you do?" I ask. My voice sounds raspy, like I haven't spoken in days.

"They'll be fine," he says. "I only put a few drops per cup."

I run my tongue over my teeth, deciding not to ask anything else. Outside, the sky is getting darker, but there's no sign of Harrick's carriage. There's no way he'll be back in time to stop... whatever this is.

"Sorry, I'm scaring you," the servant says. He puts his hands up, as if in surrender. A boyish grin touches his lips. "I'm doing this all out of order. I should have introduced myself. I'm Alven. A friend of Vale's."

All my worries cease existing, replaced by entirely new ones. This man isn't here to do me harm. He's here for the rebels, and he's most likely going to tell Vale *exactly* where I'm sleeping. Does he think I'm a traitor?

I swallow. If any of the guards are eavesdropping, they might hear what isn't being said. But it's still silent downstairs.

"I've got information for you," he continues. He steps into the room, crouching in front of me. His size is no less daunting—he's not quite as tall as Harrick, but he's definitely wider. With a quick glance over his shoulder, he leans toward me and lowers his voice. "There's a guy in the City, someone Vale's been itching to talk to. It's risky. Too risky for my comfort, if I'm honest with you, Rune. I know where to find him. I know how to set up a meeting. But sneaking into the City like that...I think you know as well as I do, there's a chance I don't come back."

"Why are you telling me this?" I ask. My voice shakes, and I'm terrified I already know.

"When I heard Viana was coming today, I got myself added. Was hoping her servant would be here too," he says. He grins, maybe at my confused expression. "I've got my ways, Rune Ealde. I'm a man who knows things. I know you're working with Vale. I know there's a man in the City. A man called Berg. He knows things even I don't."

I don't say anything. I strain my ears, relieved to hear nothing from downstairs. A quick glance out the window ensures Harrick's party hasn't returned.

"I'm not about to risk my neck," Alven says. "But I got the feeling you might want to risk yours."

"What does he know?" I ask. Then, before he can answer, I add, "Something to get out?"

"If the rumors are true?" Alven grins at me. "Yes."

"Okay," I say.

My heart thrums in my chest, but there's no reluctance in its beat. If there's even a chance Berg can help us escape, I have to take it.

"Good," Alven says.

He looks around Harrick's quarters, and for the first time, his face sombers. It's as if, suddenly, he has realized where we are.

"I hope Berg has the information you need," he says. His dark eyes bore into mine. "I hope you get out before it's too late."

"Thanks," I whisper.

"And I'm sorry," Alven says, surprising me. "For what you'll endure tonight."

"Tonight?" I echo. I sound stupid, and Alven's pitiful expression makes me feel even worse.

"I've never worked for Prince Harrick," he says, his voice growing distant. "But if he's anything like his brother..."

Alven swallows and looks away from me, out to the road where Harrick's carriage left this afternoon.

"Will it be your first time?" he asks. When I only stare at him, mouth open, he clarifies, "Are you a virgin?"

"Oh," I say. My stomach twists. Hard. Stupidly, pathetically stupidly, this didn't occur to me. Harrick wouldn't actually rape me, would he? He was so apologetic for kissing me in the training arena, but I'd called myself his pet whore, hadn't I?

Everyone assumes that's what will happen, and I'm suddenly terrified they could be right.

"I'm sorry," he says again. He rises to his feet, looking almost as uncomfortable as I now feel. "Once we return to the Tower, you should seek a kitchen servant. They have remedies to prevent..."

He trails off then, a myriad of things left unsaid.

"Thank you," I say, even though it's horrible. I should ask what I'd be preventing. Pregnancy? Disease? I can't bring myself to do anything but stare.

Alven nods sharply and starts back for the door.

"You'll tell me how to find Berg?" I ask, mostly because I don't want *that* to be the conversation I'm left with.

"Yes," he says. He seems haunted now, like he's suddenly realized my fate and can't bear to look at me anymore.

I can't decide if he's pitying me for what's going to happen, or if he's hating himself for not being able to stop it.

"Goodnight, Rune."

"Goodnight, Alven," I say. I don't watch him leave. Instead, I lay my head against my knees and close my eyes, willing myself not to cry.

***

"Rune."

His voice is soft, like crushed velvet, and it doesn't startle me like it should. I wake in a hazy confusion, but my body doesn't panic. It's as if it's decided Harrick is a safe place to rest, even with Alven's earlier warning in my head.

"Rune," he says again.

I blink at him twice before remembering where I am and how I got here. I'm laying on the rug, my head nearly beneath the bed, and Harrick is knelt at my side. His hand rests next to my hip, and he's looking at me with gentle concern.

Any thoughts of him forcing himself on me fade into the background.

"My prince," I say. I'm finally alert enough to realize how shameful I'm behaving. Slumped over on the floor, probably drooling all over this expensive rug. I sit up, patting at my face to check for spit.

"Harrick," he corrects. A wrinkle appears between his brow as he looks at me. "Why are you on the floor?"

"I didn't mean to fall asleep," is my only answer.

"The meeting went longer than I expected," he says.

He moves to his feet and offers me his hand. I stare at him in shock, taking a moment too long to snap into action. I rest my palm in his and try to breathe normally as he helps me stand. We're chest to chest, our breaths mingling, his lips tauntingly close. If I went onto my toes, I could kiss him. Instead, I step back, hugging my arms around my waist.

"I brought you food," he says. He returns a moment later, holding a glass plate toward me. On it, there's more food than I've had in days. Thick pieces of meat—maybe chicken or squab, a leafy purple vegetable I don't recognize, and a mix of ripe berries. My mouth waters without permission. I glance at him as I slowly reach for the plate, bracing for the chance he might pull away.

Of course, he doesn't. He settles the plate in my hands, offering me a small smile. I shovel the food down too quickly, not because I'm terrified he'll take it back, but because I'm too hungry to help myself. The meat and berries are delicious, easily the best things that have ever touched my tongue. Servants are usually fed gruel, some disgusting blend of all the elite and guards' leftover meals.

But this...this is purely decadent.

Even the leafy purple vegetable is good. It's bitter and sharp, but I eat every speck of it.

"There's more," he says.

"That's okay," I say. I clutch the empty plate to my chest. "I...I'm full."

It's not a lie, either. I've eaten more than is comfortable, and there's a good chance I'll feel sick later.

"Here," he says, reaching for the plate. I hesitantly give it to him, watching as he places it on the room's desk. Only now do I realize the door is closed. My stomach swoops low, sending a tingling sensation up into my chest.

"Tell me if you want more," he says. It's a demand, but a gentle one. "Even if I'm sleeping."

I nod. I'm sure he knows I wouldn't dare.

He slips out of his shoes, and I stop thinking of food at all. His jacket goes next, unbuttoned and carefully draped over the desk's chair. Harrick holds the bottom of his shirt, as if he's debating whether to remove it. I tense without permission, and Harrick's attention comes up at the movement. My insides war with each other, an uncomfortable blend of instinctual fear and tentative trust.

"May I ask something?" I'm so rigid, and from the crease between Harrick's brows, he already knows I'm terrified.

"Always, Rune," he says. He steps closer, and I force myself not to move.

"Am I to have sex with you?" I ask. My knees start to buckle at my question alone. I've only been kissed by Harrick, and it wasn't a pleasant experience. The thought of being fully intimate is terrifying.

"Wyhel," he says. He steps toward me, only to pull himself back. His mouth opens a few times, then shuts again. Finally, he takes a slow breath. "Gods, Rune, *no*. I told the guards what was needed to keep you safe. I am not going to harm you. Understood?"

"Understood," I echo. My legs still tremble, but now, guilt creeps through me. Harrick has only ever been kind and good to me, and yet I constantly expect the worst. It must be exhausting, insulting, even. "I shouldn't have...I apologize."

"You don't need to," he says. He runs his hand through his hair, looking away from me, toward the bed. "You take the bed. I'll sleep on the floor."

"It's not—"

"Please, Rune." Harrick looks almost sick, with me or himself, I'm not sure. "Gods, please. Just—just get in the bed."

I shift on my feet, debating for a long second, before forcing myself to nod. I can't imagine what will happen if a guard enters to find Harrick on the floor and me in his bed, but the desperation in Harrick's voice has me moving anyway. I slip out of my shoes and ease onto the bed. It's ridiculously comfortable, a level of softness I didn't know existed.

"Wow," I whisper. I'm terrified my clothes are dirty, that I'm ruining the luxurious bedding. I don't let myself panic. I force the thoughts away and tuck myself beneath the covers. Once I'm settled, I finally allow myself to look at Harrick.

He smiles, but it doesn't look like the tender one he's shown me so many times. It looks pained, forced in a way that makes me feel responsible.

He takes a pillow from the empty side of my bed and lowers to the floor. With a flick of his hand, the light vanishes from the room. We're instantly submerged in darkness, with only the moon's natural light coming through the window. Though I can't see Harrick, I can hear his steady, even breaths.

Somehow, I'm sure he's still awake, even an hour later.

"Harrick?" I whisper. My voice sounds too loud, and I'm not sure why I've called to him at all.

"Yes, Rune?" he asks. Something about his voice calms me and makes me feel an inexplicable flicker of bravery.

"Would you like to look at my eyes?"

18
RUNE

The light comes back on as Harrick gets to his feet. I sit up, still wearing my mask. I'd normally take it off to sleep, but I'm too anxious tonight, here in this unfamiliar place. Through the haze of my veil, I watch Harrick stand against the bed, blush darkening his face.

"I would," he says. He shifts on his feet, looking painfully uncomfortable. "If you're offering."

"I am," I say. I crawl from beneath the covers, sitting cross-legged over the quilted fabric. I try to keep myself from trembling as he sits across from me, but I can't help it. If Harrick notices, he doesn't comment. He sits in the spot across from me, keeping too much distance between us. His attention skims over me, hands half-raised toward me.

"May I—" he asks, keeping his hands lifted but motionless between us.

"Yes," I say. I scoot closer, breath hitching at the base of my throat.

Harrick cups my face. His touch is firm but gentle as his fingers glide across my cheeks to the back of my head. He is delicate as he unties the mask, pausing as it comes undone. His eyes lock on mine, and I don't look away, even as my instincts beg me to. It isn't until I nod that he lowers the mask, letting it fall between us.

There's a heavy pause, so quiet I'm sure he can hear my thundering heart. I force steady breaths and count the colors in his irises. Violet, nightwater, indigo, near-black.

Harrick doesn't say anything for a long time. A contented smile dances over his lips, as his eyes roam lazily over my features. He looks at me like he'd be happy to do this for hours. I'd let him, I realize, if he asked.

"Sorry," he says. "I've been looking far too long, haven't I? It's probably scary for you."

"I don't mind," I say. Then, because I want him to know, I add, "I—I trust you."

"Do you?" he asks. There's no malice in the question.

"More than almost anyone," I admit. "Trust doesn't...come naturally to me."

"Nor should it," he says with a sympathetic nod. His eyes are on mine again. "I want you to trust me though, Rune. I really do. I promise not to let you down."

"Okay," I say, as if it's that easy. It occurs to me that I might be the less trustworthy of the two of us. *I'm* the one planning to dethrone *him*.

Harrick sighs.

"Gods, you're beautiful," he says, as though to himself. His face suddenly turns pink, and he blinks at me in shock. "I didn't mean to say that out loud."

My body feels like it's malfunctioning. This day has been impossible from the moment I was retrieved from my quarters to right now. I've never felt anything near beautiful, but Harrick is certainly staring at me like I am.

"You think I'm beautiful?" I ask, unable to keep the tremor from my voice.

"Of course you are," he says. He says it like it's the only possible answer. Blush rises through his entire face, touching the very tips of his ears. "But I wasn't...I'm not trying to make you uncomfortable."

"You're not," I say.

My heart hammers so fast it's hard to think of anything else. I am tempted to tell Harrick he's beautiful too, but he probably would find it strange, unwarranted. He already knows he's the most stunning man alive—he certainly doesn't need a *servant* telling him.

Still, I don't want this moment to end. I can feel it slipping away, and I scramble for something to say before he decides to leave.

"When you kissed me in the training arena," I say carefully. Harrick stiffens at my words, but I keep going. "Was it enjoyable? For you, I mean?"

"No," he says. He may as well have punched me in the gut, but he's quick to explain. "I hated myself the entire time. I knew I was scaring you, and I was sure you'd never talk to me again."

"I understood."

"I know," he says. He studies my lips now, more brazenly than he has in the past. "I didn't like that kiss, Rune, because you didn't want it. But if you wanted me to...I can't think of anything I'd enjoy more."

"I've never done it before," I say. My voice shakes, and I'm sure it's from my tumultuous pulse. "I'm probably terrible at it."

"You couldn't be," he says. His eyes meet mine again, shadowed by a desperation I feel echoed in my most secret thoughts. "I wouldn't care if you were, honestly. Just tell me to kiss you, Rune. Let me kiss you."

I don't know who I am or what's become of me because I don't even take a moment to think. I'm nodding before he's finished speaking, saying, "please" as if this is my only chance.

He gently presses his mouth against mine, and he's right. This kiss is nothing like the first. There's no fear, no confusion. There is nothing panicked or reckless about his movements. He is slow and purposeful, lips delicately soft as they explore mine. He tastes me like he's been desperate to, teeth grazing my lower lip, tongue meeting mine.

"So beautiful," he murmurs. His lips break away from my mouth, placing kisses across my jaw and down the sensitive skin of my neck. "So fucking perfect."

His hands settle on my hips, tugging me closer. I've never done this before, but it's as if my body was made for this moment. For *him.* I clutch his shoulders, digging my nails into the stiff fabric of his shirt. He hums in approval, and it's all the confidence I need to slide my fingers up, up, up. His hair is softer than it looks, thicker too.

"Rune, you taste so fucking good," he says. His voice is raspy, almost desperate, and when his mouth returns to mine, he runs his tongue along my lower lip.

I part for him, and he claims my mouth as if it's always been his. I moan, and Harrick captures the sound with his kiss. His hands brush up and down my sides, never going too high or too low. I lean against him, silently begging him to do more. To touch me anywhere and everywhere he wants.

Unsteady gasps break from my throat, and it feels like I've forgotten how to breathe. I'm not sure I need oxygen at this point. I only need this, *him*, pressed against me with this overwhelming urgency. He's unwinding me, devouring me, and I find myself desperate to be fully and wholly undone, so long as it's by him.

By the time we finally pull back, my lips swollen and my heart racing, I meet Harrick's eyes without hesitation. I can count five shades of violet, each more beautiful than the last. My pulse jumps as I wait for his next move, and I'm somehow both relieved and disappointed when he excuses himself to get a glass of water.

I slide beneath the covers, flipping the blanket down on his side too. Minutes later, he comes back into the room, eyebrows raised at my gesture. He doesn't speak, letting the question hang silently in the air.

"You can sleep in the bed," I say. "If you want."

"You don't mind?" he asks. He's staring at me with such intensity, it's impossible to look away.

"I don't mind," I say, when I really mean, *I want nothing more.*

Harrick crawls into bed, still wearing his slacks and shirt. We face each other, and even once Harrick turns off the light, I stare at him through the darkness. We don't touch, but I eventually fall asleep to the steady sound of him breathing and wake with his arms wrapped around me.

W e leave the Wilds early the next morning. I'm sad to go, especially once I learn where we're headed. The City of Mirrors was my home for eight cycles, but it's not somewhere I long to return. If I ever escape the Tower, it's where I'll end up. Not because I've missed it, but because it's the only place I can realistically survive.

It's where all the rebels will go. Between the City's crumbling buildings and its rabid hunters, it's by far the cheapest sector in Savoa. Most commoners live there too, making it the easiest place to avoid capture. It's also the most depressing, so a part of me wishes we could skip it. I'm not sure how long our journey will last, but I would much rather see the Pit or the Reaping Grounds than the decrepit and impoverished City.

It doesn't really matter where we're going though. I'm still struggling to grasp that Harrick is taking me anywhere at all. He sits beside me in our carriage, head tipped back and eyes closed in the image of perfect contentment. Meanwhile, I watch the Deadlands pass through the carriage window, trying *not* to think about our kiss.

I fail. My entire body feels like it's pulsing with exposed nerves. Flickers of last night invade my every thought: how he touched me, held me, made me feel like I was beautiful and important. He kept looking at me like whatever was happening between us mattered, and I'm still not sure what to make of it.

I know I should just enjoy this while it lasts, but I can't help mourning the inevitable end.

I shake my head and stand, crossing the small space to look through the window. Outside, the sun scorches against the endless expanse of dry black stone. The air seems to bend with the outrageous heat, and even in here, the oxygen feels too thin. I'm convinced I might suffocate, even as I'm breathing.

"Are the horses all right?" I ask. I can just see ours from here. Because the Deadlands don't have magic, we needed animals to pull our carriages. They must be fatigued, dehydrated.

"Yes," he says. His eyes are open now, and I'm unsurprised to find him watching me. I took my mask off as soon as we were alone, and his wide smile made me wish I could leave it off forever. "They've made this journey many times. I'll make sure they're well attended once we get to the City."

I nod, struggling to think of something more to say. Harrick rises and comes to sit beside me, stooping to avoid the ceiling.

"How do you feel?" he asks.

"Warm," I admit. Without magic, it's sweltering inside the cabin. "Otherwise, I feel fine."

"My head is killing me," he says after a long pause. "My magic sort of rebels here. Feels like it's trying to escape through my skull."

"Not your hands?" I ask. I turn to face him. "I thought it came from your palms."

"It can come from anywhere," he says. He turns, fingers gently capturing the edge of my sleeve. "I use my hands to cast, but the magic has a life of its own. If I get upset—or I'm *here*—the magic gets restless."

"I'm sorry," I say. I move to touch him, only to decide against it at the last second. "Can I do anything to help?"

Harrick grins now.

"Yeah, stop overthinking," he says. His smile is the lightest I've seen it. He pulls me back to the bench and nestles me into his side. Despite the heat, I find myself leaning closer. I can feel his smile against the side of my head. "I'm going to rest my eyes, just for a moment. Wake me if I fall asleep, okay?"

Harrick does fall asleep, but he looks far too peaceful to wake. I take turns watching him sleep and searching the horizon for the City of Mirrors. Not long after I've memorized every sharp angle and smooth edge of his face, the City of Mirrors finally comes into view.

It sends a sharp pang through my gut, and for the first time in cycles, I think about *home*. I wonder, if I followed the zig-zag of streets, would my home still stand where it once did? Would our things still be in place, as if waiting for us to return? I close my eyes and let myself imagine it. Mom's sick bed would still be unmade. My collection of found objects would still be tucked behind my dresser. Dad's drawings would still line the walls.

We were poor, even for City standards, but that was our home. And maybe I wouldn't hate returning so much, if I could return to the last place I felt loved and safe.

I study the buildings as they come into closer view. They are all sizes and shapes, made from cycles of destruction and reconstruction. Built of shattered glass and warped metal and broken concrete, these buildings are each hideous in their own way. Patchy framework, rusted pipes, lopsided walls. Some doors are oddly short, others too narrow. The only commonality between these structures are their perilous designs and their collection of mirrors. Dozens line each building, secured with impossibly intricate knots.

It's another flicker of memory. Mom once taught me how to tie those knots, how to make them too troublesome for hunters to bother removing. Without consciously deciding to, I finger the sliver of mirror beneath my sleeve.

The carriage turns, and the Chapter Building comes into view. It's the tallest structure in the City, settled on the highest hill. This is where elites and descendants stay during their visits, and these streets are where they *hunt*. Monsters like Malek and Sorace and so many more find their prey here, and these mirrors are the commoners' only chance to survive. If they can avoid eye contact—they just might make it.

The streets are emptier here than they were on my family's side of the City. While we were surrounded by impoverished houses, and lived in one ourselves, we were far enough from the City's center to avoid the worst of the hunters. We were cautious, always, but not like the people here have to be.

Despite all the mirrors around us, the streets are mostly empty. A handful of people walk from one building to another, but they're quick to get inside as we approach.

The carriage jostles over cracked pavement, inclined to force water away from the nicer buildings. As we drive, the mismatched and cobbled buildings transition into purposeful and aesthetically pleasing ones. The Chapter Building stands at the center of them all, a miniature version of the Tower itself.

"They still hunt here," Harrick says, startling me. I didn't realize he'd woken, but he's staring at me with a careful expression. "The descendants. It's outlawed, but nobody enforces it."

I nod, unsure what I'm supposed to say.

"Keep your mask secured. Always," Harrick says. "And don't go anywhere without me. It's not safe."

"I won't," I say. The lie is bitter on my tongue, as if I've swallowed ash. After last night, it feels wrong. But Harrick's attention won't last long, and once it's gone, I'll need Berg's information if I want to survive.

I spend the next day in a constant state of anxiety. Harrick's team claims an entire level of the Chapter Building, with his quarters—and subsequently, mine—on the western side and everyone else's on the eastern side. After over an hour of soft kisses and Harrick's gentle praises, I'd fallen asleep with his arms wrapped around me.

Early this morning, I'd awoken to his lips on my forehead. We ate breakfast together until my stomach ached with fullness, and then, he left with two guards. They've been gone ever since, and I've spent most of the day in the sprawling kitchen. Alven flickers in and out of view, but he takes his time before approaching. It's late in the afternoon, with the sun beginning to dip beneath the mountains, when he finally does.

As I scrub the spotless counter for a fifth time, too anxious to be still, Alven slides into place beside me. He sorts through the rationed food, separating it into nonsensical groups. Across the room, a pair of guards sit with a round table between them. They're too absorbed in their piece of parchment to pay us any attention.

From beside me, Alven shifts. He's still faced away, but he's close enough I can hear him.

"Are you all right?" he asks.

"Yes," I say. My cheeks bloom, partly because I know what he thinks and partly because I can't correct him. I have to let him think Harrick hurt me, but I still feel ashamed for doing it. Before Alven can say anything more, I get to the point. "Where do I find him?"

Alven moves the grains into a pile before organizing the vegetables by color.

"He'll be at the base of the mountain. An hour's time," he says. He shifts a few vegetables to the pile of grains. "It's a farther distance than I hoped, and a bit more complicated, but I've drafted instructions."

I don't know when he pulls out the parchment, but by the time I've looked, it's already settled in my palm. The paper feels hot on my skin, and I'm terrified the guards have noticed. A quick glance their way ensures they haven't.

"Just take it one step at a time, all right?" Alven says. "Once you get—"

"I can't read," I say. My embarrassment lodges in my throat until it feels like I'm choking on it. "Vale—Vale should have told you. I can't. I don't know how to read."

"Fuck." Alven snatches the paper back, once again moving before I've realized it. He's quick and sharp, a stealthy spy in ways I've never been. *And* he can read. Not to mention write.

"I'm sorry," I whisper. Clearing my throat, I force myself to stay focused. "You'll have to explain it. I'll remember it."

I hope, anyway.

"Fuck," Alven says again. He shuffles the food forcefully on the counter, and I scrub the already cleaned sink. There's a few beats of silence between us before he speaks in the same, quiet rush. "I'll go with you. I can get you there, but you're meeting him alone. I'm not getting in too deep—and if anything happens, I'm leaving your ass behind. Understood?"

"Understood," I echo.

"We've got to go now," he says. "Keep cleaning. I'll be back in two minutes."

He's gone before I can respond. By the time he's returned, with a full bag of laundry tucked beneath his arm, my entire body vibrates with nerves.

"We are going to walk out the front door," he whispers. "If anyone asks, we're taking laundry to the wash. But we're really, really going to hope no one asks."

I nod, trying to bury my fear deep inside me.

"Good," he says. "Now grab a side. Let's go."

I take the opposite handle, and without allowing myself to look back at the guards, I follow Alven out of the room.

19
RUNE

After abandoning the laundry in the stairwell, we move quickly through the Chapter Building. Though its exterior is identical to the Tower, the interior is far less extravagant. The walls are gray and decorated with simple paintings, and the floors are solid black. There's less activity too. Rather than swarms of gossiping elites and patrolling guards, there are only occasional servants slipping from one doorway to the next.

I hold my breath once we near the exit. If anyone sees us now, especially anyone who recognizes us as Harrick's, this mission will be over before it starts. We'll be dragged back upstairs and one of the guards might filet us before Harrick has the chance to intervene.

Alven shoves through the final door, leading us outside and into the steady rain. It's colder today than it was yesterday, and wetter. Rain slashes from the sky, drenching the streets and forming puddles on walkways. We remain beneath a red-painted canopy while Alven checks his instructions.

"This way first," he says.

And then, we're off. Rain slices against my skin, bitterly

cold, and soaks through my clothes. I don't allow myself to feel the sting or to worry about how we'll explain ourselves later. Instead I listen carefully to Alven's instructions. We go east, west, east again. All the while, I scan for signs of danger, for *hunters*. We're alone though, our sloshing footsteps the only ones to be heard.

The buildings become more and more dilapidated as we move through the City. Some were likely destroyed during this last Earthquake Season. The rest have probably been like this for cycles, rusting and warping and half-collapsed.

Alven's breaths come quick but even. Mine, on the other hand, are erratic and painful. My body isn't familiar with exercise. Every time Alven pauses to consult his instructions, I take heavy breaths and remind myself that I *have* to do this, not just for myself but for all of the rebels back at the Tower.

Farther and farther we move, and with increasing distance from the Chapter Building, the City comes alive. The streets gradually become more populated, with white-clothed commoners going about their daily business. If the rain bothers them, they don't show it. A mother walks with her young child in one hand and a bag of fabric in the other. Two men stand outside an apparent storefront, having a heated debate.And farthest yet, a group of older children kick an empty can in the street.

Nobody acknowledges us, but their eyes all flicker over us, silently deciding whether we're threats, I imagine. They might be out of the dangerous part of the City, but they're not foolish enough to feel safe.

Finally, when my lungs feel ready to burst and my legs are shaking, we reach a decrepit neighborhood. It doesn't look entirely different from the others, but it's noticeably more abandoned. The only sound comes from hurried footsteps and wheezing coughs. Alven slows as we navigate the ruins, pausing to consult his parchment. It's soggy now, almost unreadable.

"This is it," he says.

My body is relieved, but my mind spikes with anxiety.

Trap. This could be a trap. Alven might be a traitor. I might be moments from death.

"That building," he says, oblivious to my internal panic. He juts his chin toward a short structure with only half a roof. "Berg will be there soon, if he's not already."

"Okay," I say. I try to sound brave, determined, but my voice squeaks. "Will you be here when I'm done? I won't—I won't be able to find my way back."

"Be quick," he says. "I'll wait as long as it's safe. Not a second more."

"Understood."

He nods sharply, then gestures again toward the building. I don't let myself dwell on what I'll do if he leaves me here. Instead, I move for the slanted warehouse, not looking back until I've reached the entrance. Alven has already disappeared.

I'm barely through the door before a knife is at my throat. I gasp, stumbling backward until my shoulders hit cold metal.

"Name?" the man demands. He's wearing a strange concoction of white, threadbare clothing. His pale hair is greasy, beard tangled and overgrown. There's a wildness in his eyes, which are shockingly exposed. It doesn't look like he's even carrying a mask, as if he's hoping someone will end his life.

That being said, he clearly wouldn't go without a fight.

"R-Rune," I finally manage. The tip of his blade rests at the base of my neck, and he's applying enough pressure for me to know he won't hesitate.

The man looks up and down my body. We're close to the same height, but he's clearly stronger, faster, more experienced.

I writhe slightly, as if attempting to shake him off. It does nothing, and the man only continues to stare.

"Are you Berg?" I finally manage. My voice is hoarse, small. "I was...I'm here to meet you."

"Who sent you." It's somehow a statement, not a question. He applies more pressure to his blade, and I swear, he's drawn blood. His opposite hand settles into the spot beside my head, and he leans closer, eyes narrowed, unimpressed.

"Vale," I say. My voice shakes, but at least I've managed to answer him. I consider mentioning Alven, then decide against it.

The man continues staring. His mouth is downturned, but his face is otherwise unreadable. He lowers the knife until it's no longer on my skin but still high enough if he needs to attack.

"I was told you have information for me," I say. I resist the urge to touch my throat, even though I can feel the distinct warmth of blood at my collar. "Something to help us."

"Twenty-seventh level," Berg says. His voice wavers as he speaks, as if some internal instinct begs him to be quiet. "Northeast wing. End of the last hallway. Elevator disguised as a locked door. 846538. You'll find it at the bottom."

"Find what?" I whisper. A hideous chill rolls up my spine and back down to my toes. Without permission, my thoughts flicker to Harrick. Does he know what I'll find? Is it something horrible?

"846538," Berg repeats. He steps backward, eyes steady on mine and knife still raised. He keeps moving, only hesitating when he reaches the opposite side of the building. "If they catch you, pray for a swift death."

Then he's gone. I linger for less than a minute before I exit out the way I came. It's raining harder now, and the icy water collects in deep puddles around me. It doesn't matter. I'm already soaked through to the bone, and I'm too busy repeating *846538* to feel the cold.

Once I reach the place I left Alven, I twist in a slow circle. Just when I'm sure he's left, he appears from the shadows, snatching my hand. He yanks me back toward the hill, not speaking until we've gone several blocks.

"Quickly," he says. "They've likely noticed our absence."

My stomach sours at the thought. I have no idea how we'll explain, especially since it's clear we've been outside.

One thing at a time, I chastise myself.

The standing water thins as we move for the Chapter Building. I'm shivering, and my lips are numb from the splattering rain. I haven't spoken anything other than Berg's number when Alven suddenly jerks to a stop.

I look at him, but before he can offer an explanation, I hear it too.

The sound starts slow, growing louder with each passing second. A scream, I realize. It's not one of terror, but of concentration, of animalistic hunger. I spin toward the sound, my hip colliding against Alven as he pulls me closer. We're almost back to the Chapter Building, and yet, it suddenly feels so far.

Too far.

The man screams again. It takes me a moment to find him through the slanting downpour, but he's there, standing in the center of the street. Even if he weren't wearing the jarring violet of a royal, I would have known he didn't belong here. He's too built, too muscular to be a commoner. And he's far too relaxed, too loud to be anything other than a descendant.

There's a heavy pause as we stare at each other through the torrential rain. Alven's hand pulses in mine, like he's debating, debating, de—

"Run." He doesn't scream it, doesn't even raise his voice. It's a quiet, lethal demand. One I don't need to hear twice.

We sprint for the Chapter Building. Alven might break my hand with how hard he's dragging me, but it doesn't matter. I can't keep up. He glances sideways at me, jaw clenched. Flashes of white surround us as the few people outside take cover in their homes. Alven tugs again, nearly pulling me off my feet.

"Come on!" he screams.

But I'm not healthy like he is. I'm struggling to keep up, slowing to the point we're both going to get caught if he doesn't let go. Even Alven, an *elite*, won't be spared by a bloodthirsty descendant in the middle of his hunt.

If we both die, so too will this secret.

"846538," I say. It takes everything in my lungs to force out the number, to make it audible through the rain. "Tell. Vale."

"You can make it," he says, his breath ragged. But he's already released my hand, striding ahead. "C'mon, Rune. Run!"

I don't respond and he doesn't look back. I can only hope he heard Berg's number, that this wasn't all for nothing.

Alven sprints away from me and after a few paces, I realize I need a better plan. I'm never going to outrun the hunter, but maybe I can hide. I lunge for the nearest building, not allowing myself to look for him. I don't know where he is or whether he has me in his line of vision.

Something tells me he does.

I slam against the nearest warped building, wrenching the first door I see. It's locked. I stumble sideways, my stomach and legs cramping so hard I can barely stay upright. There are several doors along this building, and I sob as I tug on every latch. Fingers wet and shaking, slipping against the soaked metal.

Locked.

Locked.

Locked.

A woman reaches a door at the end of the building, less than fifteen feet from me. She fumbles with her key, body trembling as she unlocks the stooped door. I stumble toward her, leaning against the building. She gets it open, her wide eyes meeting mine.

"Please!" I scream, panting. "Wait!"

She drops her gaze, slipping through the door and shutting it just as I reach it. I grab for the handle, but I'm one second too slow. It's shut, locked, and I'm on the wrong side. I smack my palm against it. Once, twice. Finally, I look up, desperately searching for a window short enough to scale.

Instead, all I find is a large mirror. It's cracked, a jagged line cutting down the middle. On one side, there is me, staggering and drenched and sobbing. On the other, *him*, a hunter clad in an expensive, inexplicably dry violet suit. A twisted insignia rests on his left breast pocket. A descendant.

"Please, keep trying," he purrs. He makes no move for me, his hands tucked into his pockets. I recognize him now, his dark skin contrasting against the vibrant purple of his mask. He was one of the first descendants I'd ever met, the one who assigned me to Saskia. Then Viana.

I keep my eyes on the mirror as he unties his mask, revealing a handsome face and pale violet eyes. They're so faded they almost look pink, so much weaker than I expect. And yet, I know they'll kill me. The second our eyes meet outside this mirror, I'll stop existing.

I press my hands against the metal building as my legs tremble. I close my eyes, feeling a gutting familiarity. This was how I met Harrick, how he found me: weak and unprotected and alone. But Sorace is not Harrick. He's never given any indication at being kind or merciful, and the fact he's here, in the City of Mirrors...

"Look at me," he says. His voice is alluring, almost coy in its mockery.

I squeeze my eyes as hard as I can, causing a sting of pressure behind them. A distorted sob breaks my lips, echoed by a louder one when Sorace steps closer. His feet wade through the water, splashing softly, as his body reaches mine. His chest touches the back of my head, as if to remind me I'm not only mortal, but also pathetically small.

"Shhh," he whispers, leaning his mouth to my ear. It's nothing like when Harrick's breath tickled my hair this morning.

"Please. Don't," I say. I'm shaking so hard my words don't sound like words at all.

Sorace's hands touch my hips. His fingers trail lazily up my sides, brushing my ribcage, up to my armpits. He moves back down, this time sliding his hands over my chest, then stomach, stopping just below my navel. I'm trembling beneath him, my mind spinning uselessly beneath my skull. I don't know if he's checking for weapons or if he's testing the curves of my body. I'm terrified he's going to shatter my soul before he steals it.

"You smell surprisingly delicious for a worthless thing," he says, leaning against my neck. His breath is hot and uncomfortable, and I can feel his lips on my skin.

Oh gods. No. My voice echoes through my entire body, pulsing like it's trying to escape. *Think. You have to think.*

Sorace's hands move again, back to my hips. I expect him to grab between my legs, but he spins me instead, smacking my spine against the building. He allows a bit of distance between us now, bending slightly until I can feel his breath across my face.

With my eyes still closed, I lash out. It's a useless, uncalculated move, but I'm scrambling. Nothing I say will convince him to release me, and I refuse to make this any easier for him than it already is.

He likes watching you struggle, whispers my mind.

I ignore it, swinging my fists chaotically, using one leg to kick while the other keeps me upright. My knuckles connect with the stiff fabric of his suit, once, twice. He laughs at me, like he's witnessing a child's tantrum. He only falters when my fist strikes his skin—his jaw, if I had to guess. With a grunt, his hands catch my wrists, so easily, I know he could have done it all along. Could have, but wanted to watch my wild terror.

"Enough of that," he scolds, flattening me back against the metal. He collects both wrists in one hand, holding them high above my head, until I'm stretched as far as I can. His hip holds my stomach in place while his free hand rips the mask off my face.

I scream, a wild cry that somehow sounds far away. I feel like I'm slipping out of my body, like I'm not here.

I wish I wasn't.

I wish my soul would tear from these horrible mortal bones and disappear. So I don't have to feel him touch my body against my will. So I don't have to look at him while he drains my life away. So I don't have to taste my last breath.

"Open your eyes," he commands. With my mask now gone, his hand tightens over my chin. He pinches my jaw, his large hand claiming most of my face. Distantly, I wonder if he recognizes me. If he knows he'll now have to find yet another handmaiden for Viana.

"Please," I whisper it again, hate myself again.

"Open them!" he screams. His hand goes to my throat, squeezing until a strange, breathy squeak comes from my lips. "Open your eyes, you pathetic waste."

His hand starts to move again, sliding down my throat, over my chest, gripping my waist.

"Open them!"

"Just kill me first," I say. I'm sobbing, voice so hoarse I don't recognize it. "Kill me first. *Please*. Don't do it while I'm alive."

There's a brief pause. At first, I think he's considering my request, but then, he barks out a laugh. So normal and childlike it makes me nauseated. As if I'm an amusing creature, as if he's not planning to destroy me in every meaning of the word.

"You think I want to *fuck* you?" he asks, incredulous. "You're a piece of scum. And you think...you think I'd want to fuck your corpse?"

He laughs again, the sound slicing through every layer of my skin, until it's cut straight through the bone.

"I'd fuck a boar before I'd fuck you," he spits. His hand still grips my waist, painful and mocking. "Now open your eyes before this gets ugly."

It's already ugly. It's so far past ugly I just want it to be over. I want my soul to be elsewhere, floating up in the clouds. I wonder if my consciousness is tied directly to my magic, if my mind will be forever trapped in his body once he drains me.

There's power in me. I say the words in my head, firmly, as if that will make them true. As if I will awaken a dangerous magic, if I just believe hard enough.

Sorace drops my waist and my wrists, and both hands clench the sides of my face. He forces my eyes open, sharp nails piercing the skin around them. I thrash my hands against his, tearing at his knuckles.

My left eye is open, just barely, and Sorace's blurry face comes into view. I'm crying and I think I'm bleeding too.

Kill him, I scream to my brain, to the magic I pray sleeps within me. *Wake up and kill him!*

Sorace doesn't say anything as he stares at me. His violet eyes glow, so bright they're stunning. For a second, just a split second, I am mesmerized by their beauty. I can't look away from them—and I don't want to. Any other thoughts in my brain melt away, until I'm searching his eyes for the meaning of life. For the happiness I've always dreamt of.

And then, just as suddenly, I snap back to reality. A horrible pressure builds in my bones. Not on them or around them, but *in* them, as if they're being carved from the inside. The pain consumes every inch of my consciousness. It's worse than anything I've ever felt. Worse than a starving belly. Worse than skin so dirty it itches. Worse than a hundred fists on my body.

I open my mouth. I think I scream, but everything goes black before I know for sure.

20

HARRICK

Mimeo's is on the first floor of the Chapter Building, and it's smaller than any of the dining options in the Tower. I sit at a two-person table with Proxy Kean, cutting the last of my lion steak. It's delicious and tender, putting even the best meals at the Tower to shame. I'm tempted to ask for the chef's name, but I'm here to establish connections, not hire new staff. If Malek takes the throne, I want to claim the position of emissary. It's not a title anyone has held in my lifetime, but in the beginning, someone from the Tower worked with the sectors to better unify Savoa. It won't be the same as leading the kingdom—not even close—but it might give me the chance to make life better for those in the outer sectors.

"We need everything," Kean says. He has all but cleaned his plate and looks tempted to lick the crumbs. Each sector has a representative from the Tower, but they also have a proxy. A commoner. Someone born and living in their sector, someone who knows how the people struggle and what would lessen their pain.

As far as I know, it's been multiple cycles since there's been a meeting between my mother and the proxies.

"What would be the priority?" I ask. I take a final bite of steak, savoring the flavor as it melts in my mouth. Kean leans back to ponder my question, and I wave down the server. She's immediately at the side of our table, eyes downcast, even with the white sheen of veil in front of them. "Another of these for Proxy Kean. And six more to my room."

Kean's eyebrows raise. He'd seemed surprised when I insisted Joran and the other guard order meals. I'd wanted to snap at his assumption that I'd make them starve, but I know I have no right. Kean's assumptions—everyone's—aren't unwarranted.

"The priority?" I press, not wanting to indulge his curiosities. My room's kitchen is fully stocked. There's plenty of food for Rune and the others to gorge themselves, but I know she's never tasted anything like this. I want her to try it, and for whatever twisted reason, I want to *watch* her try it. To see her enjoy something, to know it's me giving her that pleasure.

Kean still hasn't responded when the server hurries toward him, whispering in his ear. He gives a tight nod, eyes narrowing in my direction. As the woman leaves, he bares his teeth at me, any cordiality gone.

"The priority," he says, jaw tight, "Should be to keep your damn hunters out of my city."

He shoves from his chair, and both Joran and Dae echo his movement. Joran stands with readied hands, flashes of magic emanating from his bare fingers. His power comes from the Pit, and he's capable of crushing someone to death in under a minute. Though Dae isn't a descendant, he's nearly as lethal with a blade. His hand wrests at his hip, waiting for my word.

"Don't," is all I say. I get to my feet slowly, hoping to loosen the tension in the air. To Kean, I say, "I will work to resolve this. You have my word."

Kean's eyes flash, and I know he thinks I'm lying. The truth is, I've wanted the hunting to stop since I was young. I've never known how, and now that Malek will likely be king, it feels like fighting the wind. Knowing my brother, he'll want to make it legal again. He'll want to encourage it.

Maybe that's how I can repair Savoa. Not by leading in the Tower, but from leading beyond it.

"You'll have to excuse me," Kean says tightly. Then, after a brief pause, he adds, "There are several out there. We'll be cleaning bodies this evening. *Multiple* bodies."

Before I can respond, Kean turns on his heel and strides from the restaurant. I remain in place, watching until he disappears.

"My prince?"

"Make sure they send up that food," I say. My mind is still reeling from Kean's announcement, from the promise of *multiple bodies*. "I'm going out on the streets. I'll see if there's anyone I can chase off for Kean."

I say it like I'm trying to win his favor, when really, the thought of those bodies makes it hard to think of anything else. I wait for Dae to challenge me, or at the very least, to question me. Instead, he only nods.

I leave the guards in Mimeo's and head up to our stay. I know Rune is safe in the Chapter Building—it would ruin a hunter's fun to kill someone here. Still, I'll feel better when I see her, when I can make sure the door is locked and she's safely behind it.

As soon as I enter the stay, I am met by the sound of arguing. The two remaining guards stand at a table near the kitchen, heads bent over a piece of parchment. They're squabbling with each other, loud enough it takes them a moment to realize I'm here. They immediately straighten, standing at attention.

"Apologies, my prince," one says. He is short and thin, barely reaching my shoulder. "We were just—"

"There are hunters out," I interrupt. I walk past them, heading straight for the master suite. Over my shoulder, I add, "Once Dae and Joran return, you are to come meet me. We'll chase off as many as we can."

I don't hear their response. I move from the empty master suite through the entire western wing, checking the bathrooms, library, and office. My heart stutters when I don't immediately find her, but I force myself not to panic.

"Joran and Dae will stay with the servants," I say as I pass the guards again.

The main areas on the eastern wing are empty, too. I pause, only briefly, before throwing open one closed door after another. My magic pulses faster with each empty room, as if it realizes the truth before I do. I open that final door to an unoccupied washroom, and everything stops. My entire body seizes as I try to accept the impossible: *she's not here.*

My vision narrows, and I storm back to the kitchen, feeling sparks of magic at my fingertips. I close in on the guard until I'm towering over them.

"Where is she?" I demand. "Where. The. Fuck. Is. She?"

"The—the servant, my prince?"

I don't respond. My chest heaves as I try to regain control of myself, but I can feel everything slipping. If she's not here, if she's out there...

"T-they went to take care of the laundry," the second guard stutters. He's taller, heavier than the first. "About an hour ago. They left together, the two of them."

"They left?" I repeat between my teeth. With a rattling breath, I grab them each by the throat, pulling them closer.

They flinch beneath my hold, but I only tighten my grip. "You will find her. Understand? If you wish to live, you will find her. Alive and fucking untouched."

"Yes, my prince," the short guard says. He sounds terrified, but not half as terrified as he should be. As he will be if anything has happened to her.

"My prince—" the tall guard starts, but I'm already halfway out the door.

I sprint down the hall, sending orders to Joran and Dae through my arm piece. I surge into the stairwell, and immediately, my steps falter. A bag of laundry sits in the corner, slouched and abandoned. They left an hour ago, and they didn't even make it off our floor.

"Fuck!" I scream.

I slam my hand against the wall and take off down the stairs, finally letting my magic go. It coils in my palms, growing hotter and brighter with each passing second. My surroundings blur around me, but I don't try to calm myself.

She's out there.

Someone grabbed them in the stairwell. It's the only explanation that makes sense, but I realize it doesn't matter now. She's out there, and whether they've found her yet or not, she'll have nowhere to go. No one to help her. She'll be so scared, so alone—

I burst through the Chapter Building's entrance. Rain pours over the empty street, blurring my vision and making it difficult to hear anything but the sound of water against metal. I can't see anyone. There are no hunters, no commoners...no Rune.

I look left, right, left again. If she was stolen from the building, that means the hunter already has her. I can't let myself imagine it, and so I hope for some miracle alternative. Maybe she left on her own. Maybe she and Alven were exploring or escaping, and if that's true, they might be far enough to be safe.

It's enough to calm me down. I suck in heavy breaths and force myself to think.

If they came out here to escape, they probably went south, where the buildings are most crowded. They could hide there for days without anyone finding them. The thought sours my gut—would have Rune truly left me, without even saying goodbye?

Of course she would, a cruel voice whispers from within my own mind. *You weren't going to help her. Fucking prince of Savoa, and you couldn't save her.*

I will, I vow. It doesn't matter that I'm arguing against myself. I promise it anyway, that when I find her, when I bring her home, I will give her whatever she wants. Even if that's a life far from me, I'll get it for her and it'll be somewhere safer than this fucking place.

A brutish scream erupts from the other side of the building, cutting through my thoughts. It's the opposite way I planned to go, but I don't hesitate now. I lunge toward it, sprinting until I almost collide with my brother.

Malek.

Of course it's him. Of course he's hunting when he knows I'm here.

"You—" I cut off, realizing who's pinned beneath his forearm. Malek has Alven Tjor by the throat, pushing hard enough that his face is tinged blue.

Malek shoots me a lazy grin. His eyes are glazed over, so drunk with excess magic I'm not sure he knows where he is. Clearly Alven was not going to be his first kill, and I use my brother's gluttony against him. I have a vine around Malek's throat before he knows what's happening, and I scream as I launch him across the alleyway. His body smacks against the side of the metal building, falling motionless in the shallow water.

When I turn back to Alven, he's gasping for breath.

"Thank you," he sputters. A bluish tint clings to his skin as he touches his throat. "I was sure—"

I cut him off, choking him with one hand, covering the bruise Malek just left. Alven's eyes widen, mouth bobbing without noise.

"Where. Is. She." My voice is a growl, an animal's last warning before striking. I only press hard enough to keep him in place, but I'm planning my next move if he refuses me. Or, worse, if he says my brother killed her.

My magic flares again, a burst of it that sends an unintentional shock against Alven's skin.

"Where?" I scream, tightening my hold. I don't have time for this—and neither does Rune.

"Building. Green roof," he says, voice strained. "She ran for the...for the building with the green roof. That way."

He manages a nod toward the nearest sloped street. I can't see a green roof. He might be lying. He might not actually know where she went. He might know she's already dead.

I don't have time to hesitate.

I shove away from him and take off down the road. The colors and shapes of the City run together, but I don't let myself slow, even as my lungs burn. I only stop when I hear a voice. It's familiar, I realize, as I brace in the center of the roadway. Cold water bites at my ankles.

"I'd fuck a boar before I'd fuck you," it says. Taunting and loud, yet vibrant too, like he's having fun. I swivel toward Sorace's voice. "Now open your eyes before this gets ugly."

I sprint toward Sorace, dread filling my stomach when I realize he has someone pinned beneath a green roof. Hoping it's not Rune, that she got away, that Alven was wrong. Hoping it is Rune, so I can save her and get her home. If it's not her, I'll break Sorace's neck and keep moving. She can't be far.

Unless she's already dead.

Unless Alven sent you the wrong way.

I am surrounded by my own untamed magic when I finally reach them. It whips around me in violent streaks, flaring so bright and hideous I'm almost blinded by it. My mind struggles to process everything at once. Sorace and Rune. Him pressed against her. His hands on her face. Her body unmoving.

Blood trails from Sorace's fingers, dripping down her pale cheeks. Rune's mask is gone, probably in the water. Maybe stuffed in his pocket like a sick trophy.

I scream, throwing him as if I'm trying to move something ten times his size. I don't know how my magic presents, whether it's tangled vines or shattered stone. All I know is that when he hits the neighboring building, the entire structure shudders. The metal dents from his impact, and his body is reduced to a mangled pile of ripped flesh and broken bones.

Five steps, and I'm in front of her. I catch her waist as she collapses toward the water. She's unconscious, her eyes frozen upward.

No.

She doesn't look unconscious—she looks dead.

She *is* dead.

A sob wracks my chest. I pull her to me, sinking to the ground with her in my arms. I rotate until I'm leaning against the building, maneuvering her to my lap. Unmoving, not even the softest of breaths. Her head lolls backward, and I cry as I level her chin. Pretty blue eyes stare blankly at me. Distant. Empty. She's not here—I can feel it.

I tighten my hands on her face, not letting myself look at the streaks of blood from Sorace's murderous touch. I force myself to focus.

I can fix this. I *have* to fix this.

I close my eyes and dig through my bones until I feel every

scrap of magic within them. When I open my eyes again, I don't think of anything except pushing magic from my bones into hers.

I don't know if it's possible. Mortals aren't like us. It doesn't matter if it's a servant, a commoner, an elite, a mortal guard. Anyone without powers has only enough magic to keep them alive. It keeps them breathing, walking, functioning. It doesn't give them strength or the ability to wield.

What they're born with is what they have. There's no way for them to steal magic from us. But she's not stealing—I'm giving.

"Come on," I hiss. I study the soft outline of her blue irises.

I've taken magic before. It's part of every descendant's training. We practice on other descendants, only taking enough to learn, never kill. They never showed us how to give it back though. All I can do now is try the opposite. Instead of pulling, I'm pushing, forcing my body to go against instinct.

It takes a second for anything to happen. I'm holding Rune's face, my forehead touching hers, and I'm digging through my bones. I've always been able to feel my magic. That's how I cast it, how I send it through my fingertips and into the air, bending it to my will.

This is different. I'm not trying to use my magic; I'm trying to evict it.

My mind is a dull blade, cleaving my bones, ripping the magic in a way that feels permanent. It's not going to come back. It won't float in the air, do my work, and return home. These pieces of me will always be hers.

I scream against the pain. An unbearable pressure builds in my head, like the magic might explode my entire skull. My knees buckle, and when I drop my grip on Rune's face, I realize I'm losing consciousness.

I break the connection between us, careful that the magic

doesn't try to return. My head continues to waver, but I can't afford to pass out. I blink hard until my vision clears, at least enough that I can see her.

Still at first, but then her eyes flutter. They waver between opened and closed, but finally, they drift shut and a steady breath ripples from her lips.

Another sob cracks my ribcage.

She's alive. She's breathing.

I tug her against my chest, laying her head on my collar-bone. She's completely limp, completely unconscious, but I think she's alive. Still, I know alive doesn't mean she's okay. She might not be the same with my magic instead of her own. I might have given her too much or too little. She might never wake up to find out.

I hold a hand over the back of her head, knotting my fingers through her hair. My breaths haven't eased, and I don't think they're going to. With her clutched in my arms, I rise.

I'm unsteady. Wyhel. I had no idea I could transfer magic, but now I know why my people don't. It's horrible. Like I've been drained of half my blood. I push away from the wall, testing my footsteps. I've never felt this weak in my life. I didn't know it was possible to feel like this.

This could kill me too, I realize for the first time. My attempt to save Rune might kill us both.

I stagger another few steps, to where Sorace lies unmoving. Half his body is visibly shattered, but he's still breathing. His eyes open and shut, expression hazy, like he's only half in this world. He makes no move to lift his hands or even to speak. He only blinks at me, each breath ragged.

I can't risk passing out, so I keep my hands tight on Rune. Rather than casting, I plant my foot against Sorace's throat. His mouth parts, but still, he says nothing. Stepping gently, I turn his face and force it beneath the water's surface. His weak thrashing lasts less than a minute. And then, he stops, his eyes frozen in shock beneath the surface.

With an unsteady breath, I stumble backward. I had to kill him—I had to. His magic drifts out of him, swirling into the air like wisps of smoke. I should steal it. I know that. I'm dizzy and weak and it would make my trip back to the Chapter Building so much easier. I should steal it, and yet, I only stare as it floats higher, out of reach.

Murderer, I think. The word infiltrates my mind without permission, until it's my only thought. I've never crossed that line. I was positive I never would.

After allowing myself a moment, I hug Rune tighter to my chest. I'm squeezing so hard I'll probably leave bruises, but I'm too scared to loosen my grip. With a final look at Sorace's corpse, I stagger back to the Chapter Building with her between my arms.

"Holy shit," Joran says as I come through the door. I crash to the ground with Rune still held against me. She rolls out of my arms, unmoving aside from her labored breaths. I'd stopped every block to check for them, for the strained rise and fall of her chest.

I shift onto my side, moaning as I rotate her face-up.

"My prince," Joran says. He steps over Rune to get to me, and something about the movement awakens my magic again. It's a hard pulse, an echo of the transfer's pain.

"Get her into bed," I say, batting at his outstretched hands. My breaths are ragged. "Call for a healer. A female servant too. She needs dry clothes."

"Yes, my prince," Joran says, making no motion to leave.

Instead, he places the back of his hand against my forehead. "What happened?"

"Get her into bed," I repeat. My voice is so weak, as if I might be using my last breaths for this command.

This simple command that Joran *still* doesn't do.

"You're burning up," he says instead. "We need—"

"Get her into my bed. Now." I try to scream the command, but it comes out like a broken sentence. "That's an order, guard."

Joran makes an unpleasant grunt, like he's tempted to disobey. I open my mouth to threaten him, with what I don't know, when he finally lurches to his feet. He scoops Rune into his arms, without half the care I'd managed while fighting a blackout. Within seconds, he's back, calling not for extra blankets but for as many medics as the Chapter Building can offer.

21

RUNE

I wake in a luxurious bed with a feathery blanket and multiple fluffy pillows. I've never felt this comfortable in my life. My body feels powerful. My joints don't hurt. My head doesn't ache. I feel *wonderful*, and that's not a word I ever thought I'd use to describe myself.

I open my eyes, blinking up at a white ceiling. Despite the comfort hugging my body, I jolt into a panic. I am back in the Chapter Building, tucked into the bed of Harrick's master suite, but I have no idea how I got here. I steady my breaths and try to remember, but memories don't rush back to me like I expect. I have to search the corners of my mind, pulling them one agonizing piece at a time.

Alven and I snuck into the City of Mirrors.

A hunter saw us and attacked.

Alven left me.

The hunter—no, Sorace—caught me.

He—

My face is wet, and it takes me a second to realize I'm crying. He degraded, violated, hurt me. He *killed* me. At least, I was sure he did. That pain was unlike anything I'd ever suffered. But if Sorace didn't kill me…

I sit up, surveying the room, only to startle when I notice Harrick at the foot of the bed. He's slouched over in a dining room chair, his eyes closed, breaths even. I have no idea how long he's been there—how long I've been asleep. I almost don't want to wake him, but I have too many questions to let him sleep.

"Harrick," I whisper.

His eyes snap open, and he's instantly on his feet, striding for me. I'm not wearing a mask, but I don't flinch from his gaze as he cups my face. His hands are warm and gentle, but purposeful too. He tilts my chin, leaning closer.

"You're awake," he says. He lets out a shaky breath, as if he thought I might not wake at all. "How do you feel?"

His fingers trail over my skin, drawing an unexpected shudder from my spine. I can't help it. I've never felt so comfortable, so healthy in my life. Despite all the questions rattling through my mind, I'm tempted to kiss him.

"How did I get here?" I ask, resisting the urge. "I don't—you saved my life. You did, didn't you?"

"I carried you here," he says. I notice he doesn't address my other question, but I assume I'm right. "How are you feeling, Rune? Do you feel weak? Have a headache? Anything at all, I need to know."

"I'm wonderful," I say. I can't keep the smile from my face. "I've never felt this good in my life. Truly."

"Good," he whispers. His lips tilt into a gentle smile, and I can almost feel physical relief rolling off his shoulders. "That's so good."

He kisses me then, as if it's taken all his effort to wait this long. With his hands still cupped around my jaw, he leans into me, kissing with more desperation than the last few times. His tongue impatiently presses against my mouth, and as soon as my lips part, he's devouring me. Kissing me until my head is dizzy and I realize I've forgotten to breathe.

I pull back, satisfied by the glossy haze in his eyes. He's looking at me like I'm the most beautiful woman in the world, and for the moment, I let myself believe it.

"I don't understand," I say quietly. "Sorace...I thought he was going to kill me."

Harrick lowers his gaze. His hands are still on my face, his fingers tense along my jaw. When he looks back at me, there's something tortured in his expression.

"He did, Rune," he says, words trembling. "You were cold and limp, and your eyes...they just stared off into nothing—"

Harrick breaks off. He opens his mouth, but rather than words, a horrible choking sound comes out. He closes his eyes, the tears are already falling, trailing silently down his cheeks. My heart pitches at the sight, even as my mind reels from what he's said.

"Harrick," I say. I place my shaking hands on his shoulders, begging him closer. "I don't understand."

Without answering, Harrick crashes against me. He rotates us until I'm straddling his lap and he's clutching me to his chest. His hands roam my body, brushing up and down my spine, over my sides, keeping me as close as physically possible. His lips press against my forehead, my temple, the curve of my ear.

I have no idea what's going on, only that I want to make him feel better. I curl closer to his chest, wrapping my arms around his shoulders. As his breaths slowly even out, I place a tentative kiss to the side of his throat. I've never been so bold, and I've certainly never been the one to initiate affection, but I'm desperate to make things okay.

I press another, this time letting my tongue taste his skin.

It's meant to be comforting, distracting, to take us from whatever haunts him and back to the kissing from before. Instead, Harrick stills beneath me. His hands clench my hips, as if to stop me from moving.

I do.

"Fuck," he groans. I can feel him growing hard beneath me, but he seems unexpectedly displeased with that. "Hold on a second. *Fuck.*"

I pull back from him. Without meaning to, I look down at our bodies, separated only by my coverall and his pants. I can see the thick outline of his erection, and a flutter of excitement courses through me. He's turned on, whether by me specifically or this position. I rub my hips against him without fully deciding to, and he hisses through his teeth.

"Sorry," I say. I try to move from his lap, but his hands tighten their hold.

"Don't be," he says, teeth still gritted. "You're fucking perfect. I just—I need to make sure you're okay first."

"I am," I say. I bite down on my lip, asking the question I know I should, but still don't want to. "How am I okay, Harrick? You said I looked dead, but I feel the best I ever have."

"You didn't look dead," Harrick says, choking the words out. "You *were* dead. He killed you, and I—I didn't know what to do. I gave you magic, Rune. I had to, just enough to get you breathing. I have no idea if I gave you too much or not enough, but the worst had happened. I had to do something. There's a chance it could still go wrong, so I need you to be completely honest with me. If you're experiencing any pain or anything strange at all..."

He trails off, and I study his face. Only now do I notice there's a paleness to his skin that wasn't there before. He looks *unwell*, which is such a foreign concept I didn't know to look for it. The heir, the Architect's strongest descendant and Savoa's greatest hope, looks sickly because he gave magic to a random, indebted servant girl.

I let out a strangled sob. I'd been in the process of betraying him, and he'd risked his life to save mine. Sorace has to know what Harrick did to save me, and once the Committee finds out, I'll be killed. And worse, I've hurt Harrick in the process.

Ruining someone from the crown should be a good thing, but I've never hated myself more. My hands shake as I absorb too much information at once. Harrick is so *good*, and it's being wasted on me.

"What were you thinking?" I whisper. I look over his entire body now. He's dressed in the same suit from days ago, the shirt wrinkled. His hair is messed up, as if he's been laying at the foot of my bed for days. I realize he probably has. "What were you thinking, Harrick? That could have killed you."

I want him to correct me, to say giving mortals magic is easy, something they've been doing for cycles.

"There was a chance," he admits after a long pause. His face twists with a grimace. "I didn't have another choice."

"You should have left me," I snap. There's an unexpected punch of horror and guilt racing through my organs, and the panic is strong enough I don't hold back. "I was already dead! You didn't need to do anything. Of course you had choices, Harrick! You should have left me."

"Never," he whispers. He pulls me closer, until my head is against his chest again. I tense as he touches me, not because I think he's going to hurt me, but because I know it's the last thing he would do. He's too good, and I don't deserve it.

He strokes the back of my hair, fingers gently tangling through it. He touches me as if I'm precious.

"Harrick," I say. My next words feel like blades up my throat, but I can't keep myself from denying the truth any longer. He's genuine and good, risking himself for the life of a lowly, indebted servant. He hasn't asked where I was or what I was doing in the City, when he surely must be wondering. He has only been worried about *me,* whether I am okay, and not whether I deserve his help. I sit back, forcing him to look at me. "You will be the one to save Savoa. I can feel it. The people here, they need you too much for you to risk your life for someone who doesn't matter. I'm not worth—"

I'm interrupted by the crash of his mouth against mine. He kisses me with an urgency I've never experienced. He is a man suffocating, and I'm his final breath. His lips part mine, tasting me, devouring me. His calloused fingers tilt my jaw the way he wants, allowing him to deepen the kiss. He's confident and commanding, growing bolder with each touch of his lips. And yet, it feels like he's losing control of himself, like he's losing himself to *me.*

I shudder against his touch, suddenly impatient for more. I give into my base instincts, moving my hips against his, feeling the hard ridge of his cock with each stroke. I twist my hands into his hair, and when I moan, I'm too frenzied to be embarrassed.

He grabs my hips, urging me faster and harder against him. Then he's breaking away, rotating me beneath him, planting kisses down the column of my throat. I writhe, so desperate for him I'm not thinking of anything but his touch.

"More," I say, and it comes out like a plea.

Harrick pulls back, his eyes dark with lust and desire, but also something tender, gentle.

"More," he echoes. He kisses my neck again, leisurely, before whispering against my skin. "Tell me what you need, Rune."

"I-I don't know," I admit. "I've never...I don't know how to do this."

"You're doing so well," he says. His lips tickle the bottom of my ear. "So fucking well. So perfect for me."

My entire body tingles, whether from his hands or his lips or his whispered praises. Nerves tumble through me, but they're overshadowed by deep, demanding arousal. I don't just want him to make me feel good. I want to make *him* feel good too.

"Tell me if I should slow down," he murmurs. He's kissing my neck, softly sucking the skin above my collarbone. "Tell me if anything doesn't feel good."

"Okay," I say. I bring my hands back to his hair, weaving my fingers through the thick locks. "It feels good, Harrick. Please. I want more."

22

HARRICK

"It feels good, Harrick," she says, curving toward me. "Please. I want more."

I can't process how I went from worrying Rune wouldn't wake up to *this*, and I decide not to try. Instead, I push away any fear or doubt until I'm focusing only on her and the way she lays beneath me. Her legs shift as she chases her relief, and I swear, I've never seen anything so beautiful, so fucking perfect, as her stretched across my bed.

I suck on her neck, grazing her skin with my teeth and chasing the sting with my tongue. With one hand cupped behind her head, I use the other to undo her zipper. Only once I've reached the end, exposing a sliver of her smooth, pale skin, do I pull back to look at her.

She blinks up at me, blue eyes darkened with desire. Though she doesn't say a word, I can almost hear the demand on her lips.

More.

I separate her top with excruciating slowness, and she watches, biting down on her lower lip. She's every bit as beautiful as I pictured and more, slipping out of her sleeves until she's bared to me from the waist up. With my eyes intent on hers, I run my hand over her soft skin and the slopes of her small breasts. I circle her nipple, and her hips jolt upward, as if searching for my cock.

"Gods," I say.

I replace my fingers with my tongue, tracing her breast, sucking her nipple and drawing out her moans. I trail down her body, until my hand disappears beneath her coverall and between her legs. She's bare and wet, and when my thumb brushes her clit, she cries out again.

"So wet for me," I murmur. I memorize every angle of her face, all the colors in her eyes, while my fingers touch everywhere but the spot she needs me most.

"Is that bad?" she asks. Her voice hitches, and she tries to move away.

"No, it's good. Really fucking good," I say, catching her hip. Once she loosens beneath me again, I roll my thumb against her clit in small circles. "Just relax, sweetheart. Not a single bad thing about you, all right? Spread your legs for me."

I've never called a woman sweetheart. I don't think I've ever used an endearment at all. With Rune, it rolls off my tongue, as if the word was invented with her in mind. She parts her legs, and I press a finger into her tight heat. I suck a breath between my lips, my cock so hard it's difficult to think straight.

She's fucking tight, barely accommodating a single finger. I move slowly at first, letting her adjust, but soon she's rocking against me, her sweet moans filling the bedroom. My erection is painful against my stomach, and I realize I'm dangerously close to coming in my pants. I could, I realize. Watching Rune Ealde come apart on my hand could easily be my undoing.

And she's close. Her hands fist the sheets and her eyes fall shut. I want her to look at me when she breaks apart, but I'm too afraid it'll take her from the moment. I suck her nipple into my mouth instead, teasing her with my teeth.

"Come on, sweetheart," I say. I press my thumb back to her clit, curling my finger inside her. "Come for me."

When she finally does, she cries out, louder than I would have expected. It's the prettiest sound I've ever heard, but it seems to startle her. Before she's fully come down, she's pulling away, a vibrant blush on her cheeks.

"Gods, you're so beautiful like that," I say. Because I can tell she's in her head, and I desperately need her to stay here with me. She looks down at herself, top fully exposed, glistening pussy visible at the bottom of her coverall. I've never seen such a stunning view in my life, but she looks nervous.

If she bolts now, I don't know how I'll recover.

"Breathe, Rune," I tell her. I draw imaginary circles over her hip, smiling when she does as I say. After a few moments, she relaxes against the mattress. "Are you all right?"

"Yes, sorry," she says. Her voice is quiet, and she's flushed from her chest to her ears. "And, um, thank you."

I should tell her she doesn't need to thank me. I'll give her an orgasm any time she asks, and I'm already hoping she will...a lot. For now, I just grin at her. I'm sure I look stupidly happy, but I don't care. I *am* stupidly happy, and I want her to know it.

"You'll have to show me what to do," she says. She's staring at my pants, where my cock strains against the fabric. She rolls her lips into a flat line, fear straining her features. "I've never done anything before, Harrick. I don't...I don't want you to be disappointed."

She leans toward me, but I capture her hands before she attempts anything. I guide her onto her back again, using one hand to hold her wrists above her head and the other to keep my weight off her. Then I kiss her jaw before nipping at her bottom lip. Three soft kisses, and then I suck her tongue into my mouth. She gasps in surprise, but she's quick to arc into me.

When I eventually pull back, we're both breathing hard, and my cock feels ready to explode. Rather than letting Rune touch me, I keep her hands away. I'm determined not to fuck this up. I can't rush this—*her*.

"You could never disappoint me," I tell her. "This was already the greatest moment of my life."

Rune smiles, and it's one of the few real, genuine ones she's given me. It lights her whole face, and I'm scrambling, trying to figure out how to make it stay like this forever.

"We don't need to rush, all right?" I tell her. "We can do that another night."

"Oh," she says, her smile fading. "You don't...you don't want me to touch you?"

I can't stop myself from laughing. Rune frowns now, and she looks away from me. I release her hands and lean to follow her gaze.

"Of course I want you to touch me," I say. "I want to do just about every imaginable thing with you."

She swallows, but her eyes light with the promise.

"We just don't need to do everything tonight," I say. "I don't want to push you. You've been through a lot, and it's a long journey back to the Tower. You should rest."

Her face sombers at that, and I hate myself for ruining the mood. I'm tempted to slip my hand back into her coverall to see that glazed look in her eyes again. But I don't. She really *should* rest, and I can take care of my own needs later.

"Sorace..." she starts, trailing off with his name. She swallows, then sits up beside me. Even as she tries to sound unaffected, I can hear the fear lurking beneath her words. It makes me wish I could kill him all over again. "Do you think he'll remember it was *me* he killed? It might cause problems if we return and he realizes I'm still alive."

My magic pulses, and I have to clench my fists to keep it from sparking through my fingers.

"Sorace won't be a problem," I say. I haven't told anyone, not even Joran, what I've done to my cousin. If anyone deserves to hear the truth though, it's Rune. "He's dead."

"What?" she asks. Her expression is unreadable, but her eyes widen. "How?"

"I killed him," I say. The words sound funny in my ears. I never expected to kill anyone in my lifetime. That was always Malek's way, the Architect's and Mother's, never mine. And yet, I haven't felt a morsel of regret murdering my cousin.

"Oh," Rune says. A pause of silence hangs between us. "On purpose?"

"Yes."

Something flashes through those blue eyes. Relief, I realize. She's looking at me with a mixture of relief and satisfaction and appreciation. I'm melting under her gaze, tempted to admit I'd kill anyone she wanted me to.

"Good," she says finally.

I stroke the side of her jaw. For a moment, I consider asking her why she was out in the City at all, and why Alven was with her. I don't though, if only because I can't bring myself to face the answer. Instead, I help her get dressed, and when she offers me a timid smile, I know I'm completely ruined.

A few stolen touches, and I'm ready to burn this kingdom at her feet.

On the long drive back to the Tower, Rune barely says a word. The majority of our group traveled home while she was still unconscious, leaving only Joran and one carriage behind. Now, the three of us return together. Rune doesn't speak unless we're alone, and that doesn't happen often. It is only when Joran stops the carriage, stepping out to go to the bathroom, that she acknowledges me.

"We're getting close," she says, but it comes out as a question. The weather is dismal today, gray skies and heavy rain, making it impossible to see our location. I've made this drive enough times to know it's almost over. Less than an hour, and we'll be stripped of whatever privacy we've found.

Part of me wants to change the destination to take us somewhere no one will ever find us. Unfortunately, I doubt there's such a place in all of Savoa. With enveloping mountains, we couldn't run for long.

"Yes," I say after a tense pause. I glance at her mouth. A few hours ago, her lips were red from my desperate attempts to claim them. Now, she's barely looking at me, her mouth set in a thin line.

"Tell me what you're thinking," I say. It comes out like a plea.

She considers my words for a long moment before scrunching her eyes, scrutinizing me.

"You lost your first battle," she says. The unexpected topic makes my stomach drop. If she notices, she doesn't show it. She only continues. "You shouldn't have. You're the better fighter."

The compliment swirls through my chest, but it's overshadowed by a heavy pressure. Because she's wrong—I'm not the better fighter. No matter how sweet she is for attempting to mollify me, I know the truth.

"I have more magic," I say carefully. "But there's something unnatural about Malek. Something sinister. He's going to best me every time, Rune."

She tilts her head, face tightening like I've caused her physical pain. Before I have a chance to argue more, she inches toward me. She glances out the window, maybe to check for Joran, and leans over the gap between us.

"You knocked him unconscious with a single strike, Harrick." Her words are velvet, soft, inviting. "You can do it again. Every single time."

"It's not that simple," I say, shaking my head.

I shouldn't have told her about my encounter with Malek and Alven, but I wanted her to know her friend had survived, that Malek had tried to kill him but he'd gotten away. She didn't flinch when I explained he'd sold her out to me, and that only made me more curious of what they were doing and who they are to each other. Clearing *that* unpleasant thought from my mind, I continue. "I only beat Malek because I caught him off guard. If he'd expected my attack, he would have deflected it."

Joran's darkened silhouette passes by the window opposite Rune. She shifts back in her seat, shoulders tightening, only to lean forward when his shadow passes the door again.

"You're wrong," she says. Her voice vibrates as she speaks, and there's a too-familiar tinge of fear in her eyes, like she thinks her words will anger me. Despite that, she presses on, "You're not losing because you're weak, Harrick. You're losing because you're not desperate to win."

My mouth slackens. A sliver of ice infiltrates my veins at the accusation, this idea that I'm failing because I'm not *trying*. Rune has no idea what I've done to strengthen my abilities. She hasn't seen the hours of training or the blackened bruises on my skin. She has no idea, and my instinct is to point that out.

But she already looks nauseated. Her face darkens with

blush, her pale eyes flickering around my face. She's embarrassed and scared, waiting for the fallout. I want to ask how she does things, says things, when she's clearly terrified of doing them.

Instead, I only sigh, letting the disappointment curdle through my stomach.

"I do try, Rune. It may not look—"

"I know you try," she interrupts. Her skin flushes again, and she drops her eyes. "It's just...you're unstoppable when you feel you *must* win. When you're not battling for the sake of hurting someone, but for the sake of saving someone else."

Heat washes through me, boiling the ice from my blood. Though she didn't outright say it, I heard between her words: she thinks I am unstoppable when I'm fighting for *her*. Maybe it should annoy me, this idea that I'm stronger for someone else than I am for myself. It doesn't though. I feel a swell of pride, a satisfying twitch that my magic might be stronger when used for good.

"I don't mean to overstep my place..." Rune trails off, twisting her fingers together. She finally returns her eyes to mine. "But it might help you."

I watch her for a long moment, enjoying the openness of her expression. Even with her mask, I can see her vulnerability.

Gods, I want to kiss you.

Before I can, Joran bursts back into the carriage, falling into the nearest seat. He's soaked, dripping rain over the leather. A pool of water collects at his feet as the door again closes and we lurch back on course.

"Really?" Tora shrieks.

My bedroom light whirs to life, casting an eerie glow over the scarlet room. I squint through the jarring colors to glare at my sister. She stands at the foot of my bed, arms crossed as she glowers right back at me.

Rune, Joran, and I arrived at the Tower less than an hour ago. I've just crawled into bed, letting my freshly-bathed limbs mold into the mattress. I had mentally prepared myself for facing her first thing in the morning. I should know my sister better than that by now.

"Can we do this tomorrow?" I ask, unable to keep the irritation from my voice. "You have no idea what I've dealt with these past few—"

"You're right. I *don't* have any idea," she interrupts. She drops onto my mattress, landing roughly on my shins. I grunt, shifting out of her way and she quickly claims the space, leaning toward me. "Because you *left me* here to deal with that fallout. The Architect is pissed. Mother has lost her damned mind. And Malek, well, I'm sure you've already heard what he's done."

I shift at Malek's name. Joran informed me two days ago that he had survived an attack in the City, and that Sorace had been found dead. My brother couldn't remember what happened, but the Committee suspects the two got into a deadly brawl while drunk off stolen magic. The irony is not lost on me. Joran didn't say anything more about it, but I have a creeping suspicion he's pieced together the truth.

"Yes, I heard," I confirm. "It's hard to feel sorry, given what they were doing, don't you think?"

"Regardless," Tora snaps, poking me in the chest. "I can't believe you actually went without me. It was *our* plan to run,

Harrick. Ours. But you left, and all because you lost one stupid battle—"

"It's not stupid," I say. "I'm letting everyone down, Tora. So don't act like that's nothing. And it's not like I was leaving permanently. If I was going to leave for good, obviously we'd go together."

Her face sours, like she doesn't believe me. Surprisingly though, she doesn't push it. She sags at the end of the mattress, ducking her face into her hands. When she doesn't move, I twist into a full sit, winding sideways until we're shoulder to shoulder.

"I'm sorry, Tora. I was mad. I had to get out of here, and I wasn't thinking clearly."

"You thought to invite Viana," she says, lips pursing.

Even though I know it's a chance to confide in her about Rune, I don't. I can trust Tora—I've never doubted that trust for a second in my life, but even saying the words out loud feels like betrayal. The fewer people who know about Rune, the safer she'll be. So instead of being honest, I grin at my sister, nudging her shoulder with mine.

"*Exactly*," I say. "You know she didn't come though. We didn't even make it out of the gates before I told her to leave."

"Yeah, I heard about that," Tora admits, snorting out a laugh.

"Did you also hear I broke off our betrothal?"

"You *what?*" she asks, turning to face me. "What are you talking about, Harrick?"

I shrug in response. There's nothing else to say, really. I was mostly just wondering if news had circulated yet.

"Mother will never let you," she says, eyes wide. "You aren't allowed to break a betrothal."

"I'm not asking for permission," I say. I think back to what

Rune Ealde told me, about having something to fight for. This might be the first time I feel like I do.

23
RUNE

"I'm glad you're all right," Vale tells me as we enter the twenty-seventh level corridor. I've been back in the Tower for a few days now, but this was our first chance to break away unnoticed.

A blackened sky watches us from the elongated windows, and this section of the Tower is blissfully quiet. According to Vale—who heard from Alven—the Committee is meeting tonight regarding Harrick's broken betrothal. He gave me a curious glance as he told me, but he didn't push for information like I expected. I'm sure Alven told him many things about our trip, like the fact I rode in Harrick's carriage and shared his room, and that he saved *both* of us from hunters.

If Vale is suspicious or confused by any of it, he doesn't say.

"Me too," I say, realizing it's been a beat too long. "Yeah, I'm feeling much better now."

"Alven was sure you were going to die," Vale says. "He saw you when Harrick brought you back and swore you might already be dead."

"Did he remember the number?" I ask, trying to change the subject. I don't know what to say about Harrick. I can't tell Vale how gentle he is, or the fact he risked his life to save my own. I'm definitely not ready to admit I've felt strange ever since Harrick brought me back to life. Even now, I stretch and flex my fingers, half-expecting magic to appear.

"He did," Vale says. He glances sideways at me. "Wouldn't have done me much good if you'd died though. I still don't know where we're going."

"We're almost there," I say, rather than admitting I don't really know either. Once we find Berg's hidden elevator, I have no idea what waits for us.

Minutes later, we stop at the end of the final hallway at a locked door. It's identical to several others, but I'm sure we're in the right place. That being said, I have no idea how old Berg's information is. He certainly didn't appear like he'd lived in the Tower recently. Whatever secret he thinks we'll find here might be long gone.

I suck in a lungful of air. Hesitating isn't going to do us any good. If anything, it might get us caught. I type the number before I lose my confidence.

846538.

I open the door, fingers trembling. I don't allow myself to look at Vale or even over my own shoulder. I'm too busy moving, through the door, onto an all-metal lift. It smells like iron and the air is stale, like oxygen doesn't often get circulated here.

There's another keypad, and as soon as Vale's closed the door behind us, I am again typing Berg's code. It feels almost too easy, the way the lift rumbles at the final number and sinks us deeper into the Tower. I glance at Vale, and his expression mirrors my own worry.

"Do you think it's a trap?" I ask. My voice echoes in the tiny space, and I flinch at the sound.

"No. Berg's good," he says. I pretend I don't hear the nervousness in his voice.

We don't speak for the rest of the ride. By the time the lift settles at our destination, my stomach is tangled in knots, ugly and ravenous. The metal doors slide open, and an instantaneous chill blankets around us.

I can barely think straight. Between my nerves and this unheated dungeon, I'm shaking where I stand. I clutch my arms, rubbing heat into them, before leading the way off the lift. Thankfully, Vale is only a step behind. He remains a shadow in my peripheral, head tilting as he takes in the black room around us.

"What is it?" I ask. My voice sounds more awed than I'd like, but I can't help it. I've never seen so many lights in one place. There must be hundreds of tiny lanterns in here, all dyed red to imitate glimmers of magic. They float in symmetrical rows, stacking back as far as I can see. Forget hundreds...this room has *thousands* of red orbs floating through the dark.

"I think..." Vale starts, only to swallow the rest of his sentence. He takes a few more steps, finally bypassing me. Aside from the red lights, it's pitch black in here, leaving us silhouetted in the dark. "I think it's *magic.*"

I blink wordlessly at the nearest shelves, trying to process Vale's words. *Magic.* Not mimicked, but real.

If that's true, if this is bottled magic lining the hundreds of shelves before us...there has to be enough to save Savoa. Enough to fertilize the farmlands, to fatten the livestock, to mine for every jewel and precious metal, to rebuild the destroyed city. There's enough to cure the sick, to feed the starving, to free every servant from their debt.

"No," I say. It comes out as a cracked sob because there's no way. It's impossible. No one would do this—but *Harrick...* Harrick would *never.*

We stand in silence for far too long. I keep waiting for Vale, or maybe even me, to snap. To charge the nearest shelf and shove at the towering metal until one structure collapses into the next, into the next, and so on. Until all the bottled magic has been released into the air. If it had somewhere to go, I might do it. If I could send all of this hoarded magic into Savoa, toward people who need it, I would.

If I do it now, it will sit in this room, impossible for anyone but magic casters to absorb. Still, I step toward one of the shelves anyway. I place my hand, my shaking cold fingers, on the lowest shelf. I don't touch any of the black bottles. I wonder if it would burn me. I wonder if I could hide it in my coverall and smuggle it into the Tower.

"What do you think it's for?" I ask. The awe is still there, clinging to my words like foolish hope. The things we could do with this...

"We need to go," Vale says. His voice is unexpectedly steady, and when I look back at him, he's already walking for the lift.

"What are you talking about?" I demand. I grab his arm, forcing him to turn. "Look at what we've found. We can't *leave*."

"We have to," he snaps. His words bristle against my skin. "What do you propose we do instead? Break the bottles? Steal them? Try to use them?"

I run my tongue over the inside of my teeth, dropping my eyes to the floor. I hate that he's correctly assumed my thoughts, and I hate more that he's right. There's nothing we can do about this now.

"We'll come back," Vale says. He steps farther into the room, head shifting as he takes in the endless rows of greed. "Knowing it's here, knowing they're *choosing* for their people, their land to suffer...We don't know what we're up against. We need to make a plan before we do anything drastic."

Another shiver rolls through me, my thoughts returning to

Harrick. His entire family should pay for this, but I don't want to imagine it. I don't want to think of him suffering.

Maybe he doesn't know.

I don't realize I've spoken the words out loud until Vale leans in front of me.

"Who?" he asks.

"Berg," I say. My cheeks flush at the pathetic lie. It doesn't make any sense, and I'm not sure what I'm going to say if he questions me.

Luckily, he only starts walking toward the lift again. This time, I am quick to follow.

"We're going to die," I say. It's a bizarre realization, one I am having not for the first time in the past few days. The first time, I was right, so I have no reason to think I'm *not* right now.

We've been sitting in this lift for an hour, staring at each other and the ceiling and out at the glowing magic. It's taunting us, as if to say, *you knew it couldn't be this easy.*

Without magic, the lift might go down, but it doesn't go up.

"Just let me think," Vale says, which is approximately the fifteenth time he's said it.

I sigh and get to my feet. I pace the floor in front of the lift, counting the steps it takes to get from one side to the other. This area is even bigger than I originally thought. Fifty paces to the left, eighty to the right. With all this time, I'm tempted to count every single bottle of magic. Just how much have they stolen from Savoa? And what exactly do they plan to do with it?

Hoarding magic to decimate Savoa's population and resources doesn't make sense, even if the crown is evil. There has to be something more, something bigger at play.

"Maybe I need to enter the code backward," Vale says when I pass him next. As he once again crouches in front of the gray numbers, I continue to the right.

It doesn't matter if the crown has a sinister plan. I'm going to be a rotting corpse by the time it happens. I wonder what will kill me first: the thirst, the hunger, or the guards that eventually find us.

"Dammit!" Vale screams as I reach the end of my pace.

I hesitate at the wall, craning my neck toward the ceiling. This room, unlike the low servant levels, has a distant, vaulted ceiling to accommodate all its shelves. There's nothing to indicate a way out. No bits of light or openings that could be an escape.

I walk down one of the elongated rows, letting Vale's muttered curses fade behind me. My eyes have been burning since we first realized the lift was stuck, but only now do the tears start to fall. The acrid taste of salt drips into my mouth and I press my hand over it to keep from sobbing.

Harrick gave me a second chance at life, and *this* is what I've done with it. I wonder what he would think of me now. I roughly swipe at my face, smearing tears over my cheeks. I don't deserve to cry.

"Ah, fuck!" Vale shouts, followed by the distinct sound of glass breaking.

I run up the nearest aisle, skittering to a stop in front of Vale and a pile of shattered black glass. Red mist swirls around broken fragments, magic floating with nowhere to go. It bobs slowly, easy to avoid in such a small quantity. Vale clutches his hand, the edges already welting.

"What were you thinking?" I hiss. I dodge around the magic, careful not to let it touch me.

"I don't know," he groans. He holds his palm to his chest, teeth clenched as he speaks. "We're running out of options here! I thought, *maybe*, the black bottles kept the magic fully contained. I was just going to pour it...And now I've left a nice fucking mess for someone to find."

He drops to his knees, letting his head hang.

"That was my last idea," he says, voice bitter. "I think we're fucked, Rune."

I swallow. Rather than respond, I stare down at the magic. It looks the same as it always has in its raw form: transparent and wispy, more like fog than anything tangible. I've been burned by it enough times to know not to touch it, especially not in its raw element. Vale touching the black bottle was stupid enough.

And yet, my fingers tingle. That impulse to stretch my fingers takes over, and I step forward without meaning to.

"Get in the lift," I say. I don't look at Vale—my eyes are locked on the magic. "I want to try something, but you need to be ready."

"Try what?" he demands. He dips into my view, blocking the loose magic. "Burning your hand like I just did? Breaking another bottle?"

"I'm not going to grab a bottle," I say, finally looking at him. "I'm going to grab the magic."

"Are you crazy?" he asks. I don't realize he's gotten up until he's suddenly at my side. "Don't—

"Just...trust me," I say. "If it doesn't work, then it doesn't work. Like you said, you're out of ideas, and we're going to die if we can't get out of here. I want to try."

Vale purses his lips, studying me. Finally, he shrugs and waves a hand toward the loose magic, as if officially giving his blessing. I resist rolling my eyes. Once he's back in the lift, I move for the swirling magic.

I don't let myself overthink it. I bend and stretch my fingers, channeling whatever magic I hope Harrick has left within me. Surging forward, I sweep my hands toward the mist. They go right through it. I frown and try again. My fingers touch nothing but air.

I've never tried to grab magic in its raw form, but I know that should have hurt. It should have burned my fingers, blistered my skin like Vale's is now. I might not have claimed the magic like I hoped, like it was my own, but it didn't hurt me either.

Stepping away from the fog of magic, I grab a black bottle from the nearest shelf. I'm careful, barely lifting it in case it burns me. The glass is as cold as the air down here, and shock bursts through me.

I was right.

Maybe not completely. I can't claim this magic as my own, but I am suddenly sure that it recognizes Harrick in my bones. It knows I am not a god myself, but it must sense I'm not fully mortal either.

I grasp the bottle and don't allow myself to overthink it. I run for the lift, legs pounding, as if the bottle might suddenly burn me as it should. It doesn't.

"How is that possible?" Vale asks, his jaw dropping.

Without answering, I crash against the back wall. My heart pounds, hard enough I can feel it everywhere and not just against my ribs. I tilt the bottle toward the control panel, not fully sure if this is how it works. Vale slinks against the far wall, and once the gray buttons flash red with magic, I type 846538.

Vale hollers as the lift surges upward, and I grin back at him. For the first time, freedom feels like more than just a lie I tell myself.

24

HARRICK

I sit on the edge of Rune Ealde's bed, a well-worn text opened on the spot beside me. It's an updated version of *Illia's Tome*, Savoa's most in-depth literature on our history, traditions, and laws. It starts with the Architect's origin story—half of which is clearly a lie—and continues with enough propaganda to make my head hurt. Still, there's useful information in here too. Maps, transcriptions, and sector guidelines. Right now, I'm reading and rereading the chapter, "Descendant Law".

In the days since I've returned to the Tower, I've been obsessively studying anything on descendant marriage and kinship. I read it again now, leaned against the off-yellow wall of Rune's quarters. Her room is as hideous as mine, made worse by its tiny size.

Nothing about this place indicates it belongs to Rune. It could be any servant's quarters, reeking of sharp disinfectant and misery. The blankets are stiff, like they're made of paper, and there's nothing on the wall except a single hook.

There's not even a nightstand, dresser, or lamp.

I've no more than thought the word *lamp* when the light

disappears from the ceiling. It's followed by a buzz in the corridor, signaling it's officially midnight. I forgot their lights turn off like this, throwing them into complete blackness. Fumbling with the ancient book, I tuck it beneath the bed so I don't step on it when I get up.

Where is she?

I light a spark of magic on my fingers, casting an eerie glow around me. My stomach twists the longer I sit here. She'd insisted on remaining in her own quarters, at least until my broken betrothal mess quieted down. I'd agreed, but now I feel like a fool. I have no idea where she is, if something has happened to her. She's obviously not with Viana, and I've ensured she hasn't been assigned any new duties in the meantime.

She should be here. There's nowhere else she *could* be at this hour.

I pull the magic back into my bones before rising. Something is *wrong*. I move through the darkness of her room and stride into the corridor. My anxiety spikes as I walk the silent hall. I shouldn't have waited so long to look for her. I should have sensed an hour ago that something was keeping her. Or *someone*. I imagine her standing against a wall again, her face bloodied and maskless.

If Malek comes across her or Viana or—

I round the corner, and Rune collides into me. She's faced away, as if checking behind her, and her head thumps against my chest. She sucks in a breath, making a tiny squeak, and wheels around to look at me. Her face is tight, mouth gaping.

"Shhh," I say, before she makes another sound. "It's me. What are you doing?"

I wait for the terror to slip away like an uncomfortable coat. I want it to disappear, for her to see me and smile and lean into me. But she doesn't—she never does right away. No matter what I do, it feels like I have to work for her trust every single time.

She takes a step back hugging her arms over her chest. I scan her body, checking for any signs of injury. No cuts or scrapes, no visible blood. It looks like she's been crying, but her mask makes it difficult to tell.

"What's wrong?" I ask.

She sucks a heavy breath through her teeth, wide eyes darting around us. She still hasn't spoken. She tilts her head toward her quarters, and without waiting for my response, she hurries away from me. By the time I reach her room, she's already tucked inside, but the door has been left ajar.

I enter her quarters for the second time tonight, and only now do I wonder if it would bother her, me coming here without permission. There's nothing personal in her room, but I suppose I didn't know that before I entered. Maybe she'll hate me for the invasion of privacy.

I swallow. This woman is doing something to my mind, making me question everything, making me worry and over-think. I close the door behind me and lean against it. Once again, I'm trapped in the absolute darkness of her room. Only this time, I can hear her breathing, feel her presence, within arm's reach.

Despite everything else, I feel a pressure release from my chest.

Safe, I think. *She's safe.*

"I don't have a light," she says after a long pause.

I lift my hand and form an orb of magic at my fingertips. Rune is closer than I thought, and she comes closer yet, chin tilted toward the glowing red. Her lips part, and it might be the first time she's looked at me like this. In full wonder, like she's mesmerized.

I imagine that's my expression every time I look at her.

"Take off your mask," I murmur. "Let me see you."

It isn't the first thing I should say. I should ask where she's been. If she really was crying. If someone hurt her or if she was doing something that would hurt *me*. Whether it was sneaking around training with weapons, or worse, kissing lips that aren't mine.

There's a lot I need to say, but I can't think of anything beyond the fact she's hidden from me.

She unties her mask and knots it around the leg of her bed. I wonder if she does this every night, if it's her way of knowing where to find it, even in the dark.

"Did the meeting go all right?" she asks.

I don't ask how she knows about it—word travels fast here.

"They're not happy," I admit. I don't clarify just how *unhappy* they are, Mother in particular. Apparently, I've strained her relationship with Demetrius Llroy. She doesn't realize I take that as a personal win. I cup Rune's face with my opposite hand, tilting her chin until her eyes meet mine. "They'll get over it. I'm—I'm working on something that will fix everything. Trust me. It's all going to be okay."

I don't want to tell her about my research, or my plans, until I'm sure something will come of it.

"Okay," she says quietly. "I trust you."

Her words sweep through me with an unexpected force, easing the strain in my lungs. There are so many unanswered questions between us, and when she says things like that, it makes me wonder why. If she trusts me, why did she go out in the City when I warned her what could happen? Why is she learning how to use weapons when no one is looking? What is she plotting, and am I secretly just a pawn, playing into her game?

Worst of all, why haven't I dared to ask her?

I'm still working through the reasons when she touches my

shoulders. Her fingers tremble against me, and I forget everything else. I don't dare breathe, terrified she'll stop if I do. She's holding *me,* and I can't be the reason she lets go.

"Kiss me, Harrick," she says, voice soft and tender. So fucking sweet, and I realize there's not much I wouldn't do if she asked.

So I don't ask the questions I should. Instead, I withdraw my magic and bury my fingers into her hair. I claim her mouth, rougher than I was the last two times. Rune doesn't seem to mind. She's arcing into me, breathing soft moans as I kiss her deeper, harder. Her hands slide up my shoulders and settle against the nape of my neck. She leans into me, like she's craving this moment as much as I am.

It's all I need to lose whatever bit of common sense I have.

I tug Rune against me, holding both sides of her face now, tasting her lips until they part, until she gives me full access into her mouth. She gasps as I pull her into my arms and turn us for the bed.

I want to lose control, almost as much as I want *her* to lose control. Even if it's only for the night, I want her to forget titles and consequences. *Just be here,* I want to say. *Just let me make you feel good.*

She moans, and the sound shoots straight to my cock. I drop her onto her bed, crawling over her, covering her body with mine. I break away from her mouth, laying kisses across her jaw and down the column of her throat. Her fingers dig into the back of my shoulders, as if silently urging me forward. *More,* her touch says, *give me more.*

My body is corded with tension. I'm imagining my cock buried inside her, the way her eyes would roll back when I made her come. I want to taste every inch of her and listen to her breathy noises when my mouth is elsewhere.

I've kissed a lot of women. *Fucked* a lot of women. But I've never felt this strange mixture of lust and longing and determination that I do now. Even more than I'm chasing my own release, I'm chasing *hers*. I want her to enjoy this. To crave it. To crave *me*.

It's late when I finally leave Rune and arrive at my quarters. Regardless of everything I've read and everything that's been beaten into my head since I was born, nights like tonight remind me why there *has* to be a way for us to be together. Losing my place as heir will only help. Mother and the Committee might not approve of me marrying a low-class commoner, a criminal servant at that. But so long as I'm not making her queen, I think they'll get over it.

I *hope*.

I push into my room, more surprised than I should be to find Tora once again on my bed. She's sorting through a gigantic pile of rings, all varying shades of red, that she must have brought with her. With a quick glance in my direction, she continues sorting, her mouth furrowed into an unpleasant grimace.

"Where have you been?" she asks. It comes out more as a grunt, punctuated by the sound of one ring falling amongst others. She grabs one with a black metal band and an exaggerated red stone, shaped like a bolt of lightning. Scoffing, as if personally affronted by its design, Tora adds it to the pile of discards.

"Why are you here?" I counter. I already know, but the sooner I can get her off the subject of my whereabouts and onto whatever wedding anxiety *she* has, the better.

Rather than answering, she only glances at me, eyes hardening. Then she's back to sorting.

"Do you know what he said when I asked about a ring?" she asks, not elaborating and not needing to. She inspects the next one, a smaller ring with multiple oval-shaped stones. It follows the lightning bolt atrocity before Tora pauses. Her fingers twitch in her lap as she looks at me. "He said I should just pick whichever one I liked best. Said he didn't have a preference."

"You want him to decide for you?" I ask. I try to be gentle with the question, but even I can hear the judgment in my voice. When Tora's glare deepens, I drop any act of subtlety and shrug. "Why would you want him to pick? I thought you didn't like him anyway."

"He's going to be my husband, Harrick," she says, working her jaw. I wonder how long she's been here, if she settled on my bed at about the same time I settled on Rune's.

"So you want him to tell you—"

"No," she snaps. A heated blush spreads over her face, darkening her golden skin. "I don't want Nordan to tell me what to wear or what ring to choose. I just...I want him to *care*. I want him to act like this matters. It's a business transaction—trust me, I understand. But it's also a marriage. It's going to be miserable if...if he doesn't..."

She trails off, watery eyes moving back to the rings. With her lip between her teeth, she squints at the next option. Her breath quickens, like she's about to start sobbing.

Suddenly, my mind feels far less electric and far more exhausted. My sister can have that effect on me.

"It's stupid, but I want Nordan to care about me and I want to care about him. Even if it's forced, it can be good. Right?"

I don't let myself respond, because I can't lie. I can't tell Tora that I believe a marriage can be forced *and* good. Forced is scratchy sleeves and false laughter, pretty lies and hideous truths. Good is terrified bravery and earned smiles, trusting eyes and soft whispers.

"I suppose I could always try to break my betrothal too," she says, sighing. She leans against my overstuffed pillows, finally abandoning the mounds of jewelry. "How's that going, by the way? Have you been stripped of your title yet?"

"Pretty sure they did that *before* I broke my betrothal," I say, earning a tiny smile.

I sit at the foot of the bed and pick through Tora's rings. A few are nice, but most are gaudy and bulky. I grab a delicate ring with an oval-shaped stone. Without permission, I imagine this ring on a certain servant's finger.

"Thinking about Viana?" asks Tora. Her voice is soft, hesitant. "You never told me why you ended things with her. You can talk to me, you know. If you've changed your mind—"

"I despise that woman," I say with a stiff laugh. I rotate the ring between my fingers. "I don't regret breaking my betrothal. I only wish I did it sooner."

"Are you going to ask for a new match?" Tora asks. "Maybe you should approach them with a suggestion in mind. You always did like Gielle Fosfen."

"I've fallen in love," I tell her. I'm not sure why I do, only that the truth spills from my lips like overflowing water. The confession eases the pressure in my chest. My feelings for Rune have built so strong, so quickly, I haven't known what to do with them. I haven't wanted to admit them out loud, not even to myself, terrified what they mean and what happens if this all falls apart.

I know better than to talk about Rune with anyone, even Tora. It's dangerous and stupid, and yet, I can't take it anymore. I want everyone to know. Maybe the sooner it's out in the open, the sooner I can have her on a throne beside me.

"You're...*what*?" Tora asks. Her jaw is slack as she leans toward me. "With whom? Since when? If you're messing with me—"

"I'm not," I say, though surely she already knows that.

"Wow." She twists her hair over her shoulder, looking at me with an unfamiliar expression. "Is she why you ended your betrothal?"

"Yes," I admit. "I despise Viana, but if I hadn't fallen in love, I would have tolerated the marriage."

"Love," Tora repeats. Her mouth twitches into a frown. "What happened to *love is not for us, sister*? What about it being for the best?"

"She happened," I say. My voice softens when I speak about Rune, and I look away, hoping Tora can't hear it.

"Wow," she says. She scrutinizes me for a long time before breathing out a harsh puff of air. Finally she nods. "So you'll ask the Committee to wed this woman. Is she of high enough rank?"

I swallow. I should look Tora in the eye so she doesn't get suspicious, but my brain suddenly doesn't feel like it's working. Everything feels mushy and slow, and I swear I can hear Tora's mind working through all that I've said.

"She's not, is she?" she asks, confirming my suspicion. "You don't think they'll say yes."

I want to laugh. Of course they wouldn't say yes. Rune would be blamed for seducing me, for pulling me away from my duties. Whether or not I'm made king, the Committee won't approve.

"Oh Harrick," Tora says. Her expression has turned pained, pitiful. "You're going to get her killed."

25
RUNE

I don't know why Harrick left this book in my quarters. It must have been why he was here last night, and yet, he didn't mention it while we were together. We'd gotten distracted, but it still doesn't make sense.

What do you know, Harrick?

I absently touch my lips. Even thinking of him makes my skin tingle. I told myself I needed him to kiss me, that it was the only way to keep him from questioning where I'd been last night. I wasn't sure I could keep myself from confessing everything, from demanding to know what the Architect planned with all that excess magic—and whether he was in on it.

It was all too easy to steer him off course—but it was harder than I imagined to keep myself on mine. Far too soon, I was leaning into him, kissing him, devouring him as much as he was devouring me.

And now, flipping through the chapters of this *Illia's Tome*, I feel a pang of guilt. He may have left this as a gift, as a show of trust, and I just used his lust against him. I squint at the crisp pages. Most of this is too advanced for me to understand. Luckily, the maps are easy. It only takes a few minutes to figure out what's being depicted: the Reaping Grounds, the Pit, the City of Mirrors. Each section breaks further into featured buildings, major landscapes, and divided property lines. For the Tower, that means a map of the main sections and noteworthy locations within each.

Without Viana to serve—and until I'm reassigned elsewhere—I have the luxury of wasting time. I've spent all morning memorizing the military section and certain levels within it. There's nothing to indicate the lift Vale and I used, and of course, there's nothing in the book that references the magic at all.

I think back to Caleah. She'd found hints of this last season, and though I doubt even she knew how much magic we'd find, she was still right. I hope she's alive so I can tell her. It's foolish to even hope for it, but I resolve to ask Harrick the next time we're together. If anyone can find out for me, it's him.

For now, I study the maps, memorizing weak points and potential exits. I look through the pages until the lines start to blur and I can't make sense of them anymore. I doubt Harrick will take back the book anytime soon, but it's a risk I can't take. With my breath held tight, I rip out two pages. The first, a broad map of the Tower. The second, a detailed series of military floors.

I force myself not to dwell on the potential consequences. Instead, I consider all the possible rewards.

<hr>

Two nights later, I wait in a pantry closet for Vale. I sit cross-legged on the floor, back propped against a stiff bag of flour, and attempt to clean the permanent layer of dirt under my fingernails. I came down here early, and I've been alone with my thoughts for too long. It's not Vale I'm thinking of though. I haven't seen Harrick since we kissed in my quarters, and despite logical explanations, I'm feeling anxious about it.

Is he planning to frame me with that book?

Is this all an elaborate trap?

Is he mad at me? Disappointed?

Does he notice the dirt under my nails?

The door opens while I'm still obsessing over my insecurities. It's too dark to see anything, but I can tell it's Vale from the way he breathes. He shuffles through the room, bumping into the far shelf as he finds a place to sit.

"What do you have for me?" he asks. He sounds even more stressed than usual.

"A map," I say. I twist my hands together. "Two, actually. From a copy of *Illia's Tome*. The Tower as a whole, then a few floors of the military section."

"Good," he says. Then, "Where did you find it?"

"It was one of Viana's books," I say. A moment too late, I realize it's a bad excuse. I don't work for Viana anymore, and Vale likely knows that. I chew on my tongue, bracing for him to call me out.

"Escape routes?" he asks instead.

"A few options," I say, releasing a tight breath. "It'll depend on the plan though. How many people, whether we're carrying anything, or if we try to save Caleah."

"Caleah is dead," Vale says. His voice is matter-of-fact, but it doesn't stop the sting of his words. I flinch away from him, as if trying to dodge the truth.

I guess I don't need to ask Harrick after all.

"Oh," I say finally. My stomach roils, and I have to resist curling over myself. "I didn't know."

There's a long pause.

"It is what it is," Vale says. His voice wavers slightly, the only indication that he cares. He clears his throat, as if forcing the emotion from it. "We'll want to find an exit near the bunker. We're going to take as much magic with us as we can."

"That won't be much if I'm the only one carrying it."

"We'll figure something out," Vale says. "Who knows, maybe some of the others will be able to carry it too."

I debate telling him to give up on that hope now, but for some reason, I can't. I'm too afraid to admit the truth, even to Vale.

"Even if they can't," he says, as if sensing my concern. "We'll figure something out. I'm having Alven look into it."

"All right," I say. After a short pause, I ask, "Why is Alven helping us anyway?"

It's something I've been meaning to ask. He said he was only offering limited help, but when it was clear I couldn't navigate the City alone, he immediately volunteered. He might not *want* to risk his neck, but he certainly proved he's willing to.

"He's an elite, right? What's he doing working against the Architect?"

"We aren't the only ones who suffer from the crown," Vale says. His voice is heavy, almost resigned. "That family takes from *everyone*, not just the servants, Rune. Savoa will never know peace with descendants destroying everything they touch. And once we can figure out how to use the magic ourselves, we won't *need* them here at all. We can kill them, every last one, and finally build the world we deserve."

I swallow, but I don't say anything. A vicious cold flares through my body as I imagine someone hurting Harrick. After everything he's done for me, I know I could never hurt him. It's more now, though. I can't let anyone else hurt him either.

"The crown we live to serve—they want to destroy us. But we *will* destroy them first," Vale says. He squeezes my fingers. "Together."

If he notices I don't join in on the final word, he doesn't say anything. He asks a few more questions about the maps, and I give him the pages I ripped from the book. The whole time, my heart pounds and my mind whirls at a nauseating speed.

Can Vale feel the hesitation and guilt building within me? I've always wanted to escape this Tower—and I still do—but if it means Harrick eventually has to die, I'm not sure I *can*.

26

HARRICK

My second duel with Malek is tonight, and I've spent the past several working my ass off to prevent another embarrassing loss. I've gone back and forth over whether I even *want* to win against my brother. On the one hand, it will be far easier to be with Rune if I'm not king. On the other, I can't be with Rune if Malek helps the Architect abandon Savoa, leaving us both to rot. The more I think about it, the more it's clear this is a lose-lose situation. Still, I haven't been able to let either option go.

I stand in the center of the shadowed training room. The magic in my bones vibrates, anxious to be released. I grab a weapon off the wall. It's Rune's sword, the one that sent her crashing into my life. It feels right to practice with it, even though I won't be able to use it later.

I twist the neck of the sword in my palm. It had knocked Rune clear off her feet when she used it, but I'd shown her how to keep her balance. I smile at the memory. Despite everything I've noticed about Rune—all the details that hint she's up to something I wouldn't like—I'm surrounded by warmth when I think of her. I'm so pathetically smitten I don't *want* to figure out what she's doing. I like being with her, even if it's all a lie.

I wonder what that says about me.

A tiny click sounds, and my stomach jolts. It's too early for any of the trainers to be awake, let alone here. My heart leaps, hopeful that maybe *she's* here. I spin on my heel, dropping my sword, a wild grin spreading. By the time I realize it's not Rune, it's too late. Tora has already seen me, seen how hopeful and excited I was.

"Sorry, it's only me," she says. She's wearing a red gown, fancy enough for this afternoon's fight, but her clothes and hair are still a mess, like she's just woken. Her eyes narrow at me, quietly assessing.

"I wasn't expecting anyone," I say. It's not technically a lie.

"Right," she says with a scoff. She leans against the door frame, looking almost bored. It's forced, like she wants to act calm but isn't. She's probably waiting for just the right minute to scold me. She clears her throat, "For the record, I waited to make sure she wasn't here."

"I wasn't expecting anyone," I repeat, words harsh. "What are *you* doing here anyway? It's early. I'm trying to train."

"It's Rune, isn't it?" Tora asks. "The woman you love?"

My entire body clenches and red flashes behind my eyes. There's a good chance my fingers are sparking right now, but there's no time to hide them. If there was any doubt in Tora's mind, I've all but confirmed it.

"I see the way you look at her," she whispers. "Honestly, I'm surprised I didn't notice it before."

I don't move a single muscle in my body. I have no idea when Tora would have even seen us together, but I don't say that. I face away from her, desperate to hide my expression.

"It's so obvious now," she continues, voice still low. "Every time I thought you were drooling over Viana Llroy, and all along, it was the sickly little handmaiden."

I see nothing but red, and I'm too afraid to speak. Anything I say will give me away, and if I try to move, I'm afraid of what I'll do. I would never hurt Tora, but the thought of her unraveling everything, of getting Rune killed... I suck in a breath, and it sounds wet. I realize I'm crying.

"This isn't just someone below your rank, Harrick," Tora says. She speaks as if I don't know that, like I haven't realized the potential consequences of loving Rune Ealde. "She's a *criminal*. When the Architect finds out, he's going to kill her. He'll rip her apart and make you watch."

I finally turn. My body is in front of hers before I've fully decided to move. I dig my hand against the doorframe to Tora's left, squeezing the metal so hard I swear it flexes. She gasps, mouth falling slack as I corner her.

"You cannot tell," I say through gritted teeth. "Tora, I swear —I will do anything you ask of me. Relinquish the throne. Demand the Architect give it to you. Kill your enemies until the end of time. But you cannot tell."

I'm breathing so hard I might pass out. Tora doesn't respond, and I can't read her expression. The red of my vision is too hazy and my mind is shattered glass, each thought too broken to put back together.

"Tora. Do you understand? If you tell anyone, they'll kill her —and I can't let that happen. I *won't*."

"Breathe," Tora says, glancing out the doorway. I follow her gaze, just long enough to confirm we're still alone. There's a curious look on her face when she turns back to me. "You know I wouldn't."

"Sorry," I say, forcing myself to relax. "You're right. I'm sorry. It's just—"

"It's okay. You protect the people you love, Harrick," she

says. "That's why I'm here actually. I overheard Malek talking about her. I didn't tell him anything. I *swear* it. I don't even think he knows about you two, though I wouldn't be entirely surprised if—"

"What did he say." It comes out, not as a question, but as a demand. My magic pulses, hot and electric, until I'm sick with it.

"The thing he did to that other servant. The redhead—"

I surge past Tora, running before I've even hit the corridor. She calls my name, but I don't stop. My head pulses and I'm dizzy, imagining every fucking thing he could do to her. Plant evidence, have her thrown in a cell, have her murdered right where she's standing. No time for an explanation, a defense. No time for me to kill everyone within five hundred feet of her.

I don't stop moving until I reach the lift at the end of the hallway. I smash my hand against the panel. One. Two. Three. It's taking too long, the soft whir sounding twenty floors away.

Rune should be in her room, but what if she isn't? What if she crosses paths with him—

Tora reaches me just as I strike the panel for a fourth time. She grabs my arm, not rough but not timid either.

"Harrick. Calm yourself," she says, sounding strangely like our mother. "If Malek knows you care, he'll only want to hurt her more. You can't admit anything."

"You suggest I ignore this?" I ask, smacking my hand against the panel again.

"I didn't say anything like that," she says. Even though I'm not looking at her, I know exactly the cross expression she's wearing. She tightens her hold on my elbow. "If you want to protect Rune—not just now but forever—you know what you need to do."

I look at her expectantly.

"You need to win, Harrick," she says. "If you want Rune to live, you *have* to win."

I don't see her. With the spotlight over the fighting dome, I can't see much of anything. The Architect, Mother, and Tora are off to my left, highlighted on their thrones. Rune isn't here. Now that she's not serving Viana, she doesn't have an excuse to come. I wanted Tora to bring her, but of course that was a stupid idea.

Even without Rune here, she's still the one I'm thinking about as I pace the length of the arena. The announcer is still introducing Malek, and I can see him sneering from beyond the glass enclosure. I don't let it get to me.

It all ends tonight.

This duel might not be intended as a fight to the death, but no one will be surprised if it ends that way.

They'll only be surprised that I'm the one left standing.

I remain motionless on my side of the arena as Malek enters. Like last time, he's working the crowd, a deceptively charming grin on his face. I stare at him, letting every horrible thing about him fill my mind.

Malek at six, breaking Tora's arm after she'd already surrendered.

Malek at nine, killing the injured tree cat I rescued from the Wilds.

Malek at thirteen, coming home from the City of Mirrors with his first scar.

Malek at seventeen, bragging to Sorace about his favorite kills.

"Prince Harrick, Prince Malek. Please prepare for battle."

The automated voice is loud enough to hear over the crowd, to break through my flashing thoughts.

Malek framing the red headed servant. Malek pinning Alven Tjor against the wall, his eyes glazed with pooling magic.

Now, my brother stares at me. His pose is relaxed, but there's a crinkle between his brows, like maybe he can sense the chaos rising within me. Maybe he realizes I've lost my sanity, my rationalization.

He cocks his head to the side, an amused smile lifting his lips. No, he doesn't realize a thing. Malek only ever notices himself.

Beep.

The first buzzer goes, and Malek's smile widens. I let his grin infect my mind, let it soak into every good moment I've had with Rune. I make myself imagine it: him taking every precious future moment away in an instant, just because he can.

Beep.

There are more to come. More buzzers. A clash of cymbals. A shock of darkness and light. Fighters are required to wait. It's the rule, and no honorable contender would strike before the flashing light, the final note. But if our society allows the murder of defenseless commoners, who are we to say what's honorable?

I scream, launching Malek with a force of wind that knocks us both off our feet. Only where I stumble, he slams across the arena and against the protective shield. His head snaps back, making a hideous thud against the glass. The crowd screams in protest, the buzzer continuing its automated countdown.

I'm already back on my feet, screaming again, wrapping vines around his body like they're a hundred vipers. Squeezing harder and harder, so tight on his neck that his skin is purple.

His mouth opens, but there's no sound. For the first time in his life, he's forced silent and helpless.

"You want to play dirty?" I scream. The words aren't mine. They're from a thousand versions of me in time, from a boy who desperately wanted a brother and got a monster instead. Every ounce of anger I've harbored in our twenty cycles, pouring out now, amplifying my voice to the entire arena.

I thrust my hands harder, squeezing the vines until I hear bone cracking. The crowd boos, as if they think their judgment will stop me. Nothing but Malek's lifeless eyes will silence the roaring in my bones, the determination in my blood.

"You want to cheat and lie and thieve? You want to murder and destroy?" My voice has gone hoarse, but I don't care. It doesn't matter if the crowd can hear—only that Malek does. I want my hatred to be the last thing he hears. "I'm done following the rules, just to watch you break them. You made an error, targeting *her*, brother. And it will be the last one you make."

He loses consciousness, body falling slack. His eyes roll to the back of his head, but I'm still squeezing. I don't stop, even as they try to pull me away. I'm not sure who *they* are, but I don't care. I'm staring at my brother's limp body, falling motionless as the reality of what I've done creeps over me. Guards hold my arms at my side, but I could throw them through this whole fucking Tower, if I wanted.

As my breathing slows, I wait for the guilt or horror to flood my senses. Instead, I don't feel anything at all.

27
HARRICK

Once I'm released from medical evaluation, I wait in the arena lounge. Compared to most places in the Tower, the decor is muted and boring, looking almost unfinished. There's a full kitchen on the eastern wall and an array of plush chairs and short tables throughout the remaining space. There's a bookshelf on the western wall that I'm pretty sure is an entrance to one of the Tower's emergency tunnels. While I count the minutes, waiting for the official verdict, I study the bookshelf. And yes, there it is: a faint seam in the wall, almost impossible to see from this distance.

"The ice helps more if you put your hands in it," Tora says, startling me. She strides into the room, wearing the same gown from this morning. Unlike then, she's put together now. Hair in tight coils and vibrant glitter on her eyes. She glances pointedly at the bucket of ice chips to my left.

She circles the table, knocking my feet off it, and sits on the edge. I pick up the bucket of ice, but I still don't use it.

"I should have told you I planned to kill him," I say. I struggle to maintain eye contact, terrified of what she'll find there. "I thought maybe that's what you meant earlier, but I didn't want you to talk me out of it if I misunderstood. I just... wanted to end him."

"I know," she says softly. She places her hand on my knee, a trembling frown twisting her expression. "He's alive, Harrick. Alive and going to recover."

"Fuck!" I don't mean to scream, but I can't help it. Of course my brother has to be a literal cockroach. Of course I didn't do enough to finish him. I shove to my feet, pacing the length of the room.

"On the bright side, the Committee has ruled in favor of your win," she says. She twists to follow my movements. "The Architect seemed pleased too—"

"Malek won't let it happen again," I cut her off. "Next time will be a true fight to the death, and we both know I won't survive it."

"We've found your source of power," Tora says, finally standing. She comes in front of me, blocking my path. I could push past her, but I don't. I'm craving her reassurance, false as it may be. "You fight for Rune. As if her life depends on it— because it *does*, Harrick."

"It won't be enough," I say. I run my hand through my hair, weaving around her. "I used my best weapons—cheating and the element of surprise. My only chance at besting Malek was killing him. And even cheating, I failed."

I pace the room. Once, twice, three times. Tora watches me silently, her red lips in a tight line.

"He's going to kill her, and I won't be able to stop him." My voice cracks, but I'm too worked up to care.

The words worm into my brain like parasites. I'm striding the room faster now, hands jittering as I try to make a plan. Something to get Rune out. Not in a few weeks, but tomorrow or the next day. Before Malek is well enough to ruin her.

"Stop," Tora says. She catches my arms, craning her chin to look at me. "You're going to work yourself into a panic."

I don't tell her that I've been far past panic for days now.

"I lied, okay?" She says, worrying her lip with her teeth. "Malek isn't planning anything against Rune."

I reel backward, ripping out of her grasp. I'm slow to process the words, but it all snaps into place at once. My sister *lied* to me, forced my hand before I was ready. If I hadn't been impulsive, I could have made a better plan. Instead, I'd been reckless —and look what it's cost.

"Why." Not a question, a demand. It'd be a roar if I weren't in a state of shock.

"I was afraid you were going to lose," she whispers. A soft pink colors her cheeks. "And in the training room, you'd gotten so furious when I mentioned her. You crushed the doorframe with your bare hand, Harrick. Did you even notice?"

I didn't.

"That's not possible," I say. Then, shaking my head, I continue, "But it doesn't matter. I acted rashly because of what *you* told me. Your lie won this battle, but it's lost me the war."

"Don't say that. We'll figure something out," she says quietly. She's squirming, a dark blush coloring her cheeks. "I'm sorry, Harrick. I was trying to help."

I close my eyes, squeezing them until my head aches. Tora is being honest—I fully believe that—but it doesn't change the fact that she's completely screwed me over.

"Malek isn't plotting against Rune?" I ask. Despite everything else, I need to hear her say it again.

"He's not. I doubt he even knows who she is," she says. She looks me in the eye, but I can tell she's squirming inside. "I wanted you to hate him enough that you didn't fear him. That you wouldn't hesitate to kill him. I thought it was the only way you'd come out on top."

"Well, it didn't work," I snap.

"You held back!" she yells, shocking us both. Her chest heaves, and her voice shakes, even as she lowers it. "You could have cut through him with those vines, and we both know it. You didn't. You held back, Harrick. And *that's* why he's still alive."

We stare at each other for a long moment. Me, waiting for her to take it back, to admit she's wrong. Her, waiting for me to acknowledge that she's right, that I *could* have cut through him if I tried.

"Leave!" I snarl. "Haven't you done enough?"

"I'm not going anywhere," she says. Her jaw is tight, her shoulders stiff. "I know you don't believe me right now, but we'll find a way to make this right."

I don't respond, don't say another word. Tora sighs and moves to the couch, settling in beside me. She doesn't say anything else either. She only takes my hands and submerges them in the bucket of ice.

"I forgot I left this here," I tell Rune as I sit on her bed. I flip through the pages of *Illia's Tome*, nerves spiking as I look through the chapters. I was a fool to forget this here. If anyone had searched her room, she would've been killed.

When Rune doesn't respond, I glance up to find her anxiously watching me from against the wall. She's said exactly two words since I arrived. *Hello* when I knocked on her door. *Yes* when I asked if I could come in. Now, she stands with perfect posture, hands clasped. Back to being frustratingly nervous and timid. She bites her lip as I study her, shifting under the weight of my gaze.

"Do you want to sit?" I ask. I close the book, scooting to make room for her.

She blushes like I've asked her to get naked, but she still joins me. I'll take any progress I can get. She smells like the cheap soap servants use. I wish I could gift her something better, something that smells sweet yet bold, like her. But the best I can do right now is food and clean clothes. The room still carries a hint of the dinner I sent an hour ago.

"Are you okay?" she asks.

My shoulders loosen at her question, at the softness of her voice. It's been two days since my victory against Malek, and this is the first time I've been alone with her. It's well past midnight, but her lights are on. There are perks to Joran knowing my secret—so long as he doesn't threaten exposing it.

"Somewhat," I say truthfully. "I'm glad I won. I just...wish it ended differently."

Rune stares at me curiously but waits for me to continue.

"I hate that he survived," I admit. "That was my best chance of killing him, and I failed."

I expect her to blanche or give any indication she's offended by my cruelty. Sometimes, I forget that she's lived a far more brutal life than I have. She may be soft-spoken and timid, but she's undoubtedly seen terrible things.

"Enough of my brother," I say, clearing my throat. "We need to talk."

She nods slightly, blue eyes wide and full lips parted. I'm tempted to forgo all my confessions and use my tongue for more enjoyable things. I have to resist though—there's no time to waste on my selfish desires.

"Two people are aware of my relationship with you," I say, slowly, carefully. I give Rune a moment to digest that information, hating the way her skin pales. Knowing that I've put her life at unnecessary risk, whether I meant to or not. "Tora figured it out on her own. She saw the way I look at you. I'm going to be more careful." I pause, waiting for some sort of reaction. When I don't get one, I force myself to continue, "Joran had suspicions after the City of Mirrors, but I've all but confirmed it now that I have him guarding you."

"Harrick," she whispers. Her lip quivers and wetness fills her eyes, like she's trying not to cry. When the tremble of her lip moves through her whole body, I move instinctively. I wrap my arms around her, pulling her onto my lap. She doesn't resist, but she doesn't stop shaking either.

"I'm sorry," I say. "I didn't do it to put you at risk, and if anyone were to know our secret, those two are the most trustworthy. I'd leave my life in both of their hands. But if you ever get nervous or if they say anything, you tell me. I'll take care of it. I won't let *anyone* hurt you—I promise."

Rune doesn't respond. A tear leaks from the corner of her eye, and then another. My heart splinters, and I'm wiping her tears before they dip into her mouth. I've frightened her and I hate myself for it. I hate even more that she has every right to be scared—that I can't protect her the way she deserves.

"Rune, look at me," I say. When she does, I gently cup the sides of her face, thumbs smoothing over her cheeks. "I will protect you with my life."

"Don't," she says sharply. Her voice pitches as she stares at me. "Don't you dare. If you die protecting me, I'll die anyway. You realize that, right? If someone tries to kill me, and you get in their way, they will kill me as soon as you're out of it. So *don't*."

I study the planes of her face. She's the most beautiful woman I've ever known, and yet she's so determined to convince me she's worthless. Like her death would be nothing but an unfortunate casualty.

"I won't be able to stop myself," I say, tracing her jaw.

Rune opens her mouth to argue, but I cut her off with a

kiss, cupping the back of her neck. Her hair is damp, probably from the shower that's left her smelling like that soap. I let my hands drift down her sides, keeping my touch feather light. I settle my hands on her hips, feeling the press of her bones against my palms. She's a little softer than she was when I met her, a little fuller. Still too thin, but healthier every day.

When she pulls back, her face is red from where my stubble scratched her. Swollen lips, a dazed but happy look in her eyes. I wonder if she can feel how turned on I am. She must, and yet, she doesn't acknowledge it. She smiles though, the shy half-smile I've come to crave.

"I am yours," I whisper, pressing my thumb to her puffy lower lip. She stills in my lap, but I don't slow my words. "I don't know how, but I'm going to find a way for us to be together. I promise."

I return my eyes to hers, hoping I look calm and confident and not at all like the bundle of nerves I am. Rune's eyebrows scrunch together and her mouth dips into a frown. My nerves coil, and I'm desperate to shove my declaration back down my throat.

Too soon. Clearly, too fucking soon.

"I love you," she says.

I'm too stunned to respond, and she looks almost as surprised by her confession as I am. Before I have the chance to process it, let alone say it back, Rune kisses me. Her hands, small and thin and cold, cup my jaw. I've barely managed a shock breath when she settles over my lap, growing bolder by the second. I've never seen her like this, so confident and *sure*. The fact she's behaving this assuredly for *me* has my cock straining against my slacks.

She's kissing me so desperately our teeth keep clanking together. It's hurried and wild, and easily the most erotic kiss

I've ever shared. I slide her hips against me, grinding her over my rapidly hardening cock until she's moaning into my mouth.

"Fuck," I say, breaking away to unzip her coverall. Her lips chase me, mouth trailing open kisses down my throat. We've done this enough times now that she doesn't get flustered as I peel off her sleeves. The coverall pools around her waist, baring her breasts to me. I claim one nipple before tasting the other.

"More," she says. She links her ankles behind my back, pulling us together until our hips collide. "Please, Harrick."

Her words have clouded every other thought in my mind. All I can think of is her. Her smell, her taste, her touch.

"How much more?" I ask, because I'm too dizzy with arousal to draw the line myself. "Tell me what you need, sweetheart."

I hope she wants me to taste her. I'll do it all night if she lets me, bury my face between her soft thighs until all other men are ruined. Even thinking of another man touching her has me pulling her closer, trying to imprint myself on her skin.

"Take this off," she says. Her words are barely a whisper as she tugs at my shirt.

I don't hesitate. I flip her onto her back and sit on my heels, undoing my buttons until I'm able to pull my shirt over my head. She stares up at me while I do, shimmying out of her coverall as I toss my shirt to the ground. Her clothes join mine on the floor a second later, and I look back to her in surprise.

She's fully naked, her smooth pale skin on display. She looks terrified, but excited too, and her eagerness sets my heart on fire.

"Is this okay?" she asks. She still has her hands over her breasts.

"You're so beautiful," I say. I move her hands to either side of her face, letting my eyes drift over her naked body. I commit every curve, every soft line to memory. "You are beautiful, Rune. I am so in love with you, I don't know what to do with myself."

"You could have sex with me," she says. Her voice hitches when she says it, but she doesn't shy away from my gaze. "If you want, I mean."

The entire world stops as she looks up at me. Her blue eyes are open and affectionate, and I've never been so determined to deserve someone's love. I trail my hand down her face, over her throat and breast, stopping only when I reach her hip bone. I can imagine it all too easily, slipping into her wet heat and fucking her until we're drunk off each other.

"It's okay if you don't want to," she says. Though she blushes, she still doesn't look away.

"I absolutely want to," I say. As if to prove my point, I lower my hips to hers, rocking my erection against her stomach. Only my pants separate our skin, and I've never hated a piece of clothing more.

I lower until our bare chests touch, my eyes falling shut without permission. Her skin is unbelievably soft and smooth, and every time I thrust, she writhes impatiently beneath me. She keeps gasping, mouth parted in a way that begs me to kiss her. So I do, thrusting my tongue into her mouth, savoring the way she tastes.

"Are you sure you're ready?" I ask her. "Don't feel like we need to rush, okay? We've got time."

"I want to," she says. She runs her hands over the planes of my chest, drawing a shudder from deep within my bones. "But you need to tell me how to make it good for you. I've never—I haven't done this before."

I groan, leaning more of my weight against her. Her nipples brush mine every time she breathes, and her hips keep jerking toward me, seeking me.

"I was made to fuck you," I whisper. I palm between her

thighs, spreading her wetness before pushing a finger inside. She gasps, and I lean back to watch her. When I curl my finger, her hips jerk toward me. "See that? You know what to do, sweetheart. You were made to fuck me, too."

I remove my hand, smiling as she arcs at the emptiness. She's fallen silent, but she watches me, her eyes wide with love and lust. And when I lick her from my finger, her mouth falls open.

"You're perfect," I tell her. Then, "Tell me if it's too much, and we'll stop."

She nods, her attention already drifting from my face to my pelvis. She pulls her lip between her teeth, and with a darting glance toward me, she reaches for the button. My self-control is hanging by a single, frayed thread, and it snaps the moment my cock springs free.

I kick out of my pants and settle between her thighs. They're warm and smooth, and when I pull her ankles over my hips, she instantly latches around me. I lean onto my elbows, rocking my cock against the front of her pussy as I kiss her neck. She slowly relaxes, hips jolting every time I brush against her clit.

I move my hand between her thighs, running my thumb over her slit. Once I've spread her wetness, I slip a finger into her tight cunt and groan against her neck. She continues rocking against me, moaning when I add a second finger.

"*Harrick*," she says. I've never heard someone say my name like she is now, and I'm certain no one could.

I line my cock with her entrance, watching her as she watches where we connect. I press forward, slowly, groaning as she surrounds me. She's warm and wet and so unbearably tight I have to clench to keep from bursting immediately. I've thought of this too many times, dreamt of it when I was sure it would never actually happen.

Rune's mouth parts as I rock into her, inch by agonizing inch. Once I'm halfway, her face tightens and she grabs my hips to slow me.

"That's it," I tell her. I slow my movements, keeping my thrusts shallow and letting her adjust. "Look how well you're taking me, Rune. You're fucking perfect."

She follows my gaze, and I pinch her nipple between my fingers, twisting gently. My attention flickers between her face and the place we're joined.The sight is almost too erotic, and it's only the fact she looks uncomfortable that keeps me from exploding inside her.

"It feels...*big*," she moans. She's saying it like it's a nuisance, but my male ego swells with pride anyway. So does my cock.

"Breathe for me," I tell her. "You're doing so good, sweetheart."

She does as I say and I continue moving, until finally—fucking finally—my cock is fully buried inside her.

Mine, my body demands. *She is mine.*

"Fuck," I say. The word shakes, and so does my entire body. "I'm not going to last. You're too tight. Too fucking beautiful."

She cries out at my praise, mouth gaping in pleasure. She's louder than she's been before, and her legs clamp around me, like she's determined to keep me close. I lean against her, until we're fitted together too perfectly. We were always made to find each other, I realize. We were destined to collide again and again, until inevitably we'd find ourselves like this.

I thrust, deep and slow, circling her clit with my thumb as I kiss her neck and shoulder. When her ankles slip away and her back arcs, I realize she's close. Only then do I pump faster and harder, filling the room with the sound of our bodies connecting. Rune's head falls back, and her mouth opens in a silent gasp. Just as her eyes start to roll back, I slow my movements.

"Eyes on me, sweetheart," I say. Because there's no way I'm

missing the first time she comes around my cock. "Look at me when you come. Let me see your eyes."

She obeys immediately, giving me those blue irises. Her brown hair flows around her face, draping over her pale skin and across her breasts. I press my thumb more firmly against her clit until finally, she's coming. Breaking apart beneath me with a breathy moan, until I'm sure I'll never feel whole without her.

I'm less than a second behind her, coming so hard my vision goes black at the edges. I slow my thrusts until her cunt is so full of my cum, it's leaking out of her. I keep most of my weight on my elbows, but our chests rest together, and our heartbeats align.

"Rune," I whisper. I kiss her collarbone. Her neck. Her jaw. The side of her mouth.

I ease out of her, slowly to avoid hurting her. She groans once I'm gone, bringing her legs back together and placing her hand against her entrance. She blinks at me, giving me a sated smile, before letting her eyes drift shut.

"I love you," she whispers.

"I love you more," I say. I need to get something to clean us up, but I'm in no rush to move. I roll to her side and tuck her against me, my cock already stirring with her ass pressed against it. I resist the temptation. As fucking incredible as that was, Rune is—or was, I guess—a virgin. She'll need a break before we go again.

With her lithe body tucked against mine, Rune eventually falls asleep. I try to do the same, but instead, I stare at the ceiling for what feels like hours. I think about what she's been through, and what we've been through together. I think of the people in power, and the way Savoa suffers beneath them. And finally, I whisper the truth of it all into her sleeping ear.

"You're better than all of them," I tell her. "Every single one. You're a queen, Rune Ealde, and someday, they'll bow to *you*."

28

RUNE

I wake up several hours later. Harrick is still here, shirtless but wearing pants. He's wrapped my blanket around me, and his arm is trapped beneath my head as a makeshift pillow. I roll over, blinking up at him, half-expecting him to disappear. There's a part of me that's still sure this is all a dream, and that at any moment, I'll wake up and realize it never happened.

"Hey," he says, voice gravelly. He's reading *Illia's Tome*, and by the dark bags under his eyes, it's gotten incredibly late. It doesn't look like he's slept.

I glance at his lips, blushing. Only hours ago, he was *inside me*, and I'm inexplicably aroused by the ache he's left behind. I shift my legs, feeling the soreness and hoping it never goes away.

As if he can sense my wandering mind, Harrick's mouth slants into an easy smile. He brushes the hair from my face, looking at me with the utmost care and affection. This man loves me. Even if he wouldn't have told me, I'd know. I can feel it in the way he's gazing at me now, as if I'm precious and important and *his*.

If there's a single person in this world to trust, it's him.

I study him. It feels like my lungs are shriveling and curling up my throat, like I could puke half my organs on the bed if I tried. Harrick quirks his head, concern sketching his features. I should say something light, something casual. But there's a blaring sensation in my chest, begging me not to let this—*him*—go.

"I've been planning my escape for over a cycle," I tell him. It comes out in a rush, making it sound like an impossibly long word, rather than a sentence. When Harrick blinks at me, his face stunned, I clarify in a low whisper, "My escape from the Tower."

"I knew what you meant," he says, voice quiet. His eyes sweep over me, as if he's seeing me in a way he never expected. I can't tell if he hates it.

I bite my lip hard enough that it starts to bleed. Harrick hasn't gotten angry or shown any sign he's about to imprison me. He only stares, but it's enough to make my entire body shiver. I recoil slightly, tugging the blanket higher on my chest.

"Hey," he says, gentle as ever. He touches my face, pressing his thumb to the bleeding spot on my lip. Even when I flinch at his touch, his face remains steady, patient. "Careful, sweetheart."

"Are you mad?" I ask. His endearment settles the nerves in my gut, but cycles of abuse keep me on edge.

"Of course not," he says. His throat bobs as he swallows. "Is that—is that what you were doing that day in the City?"

"Kind of," I say, not sure how much I want to admit. Harrick takes a deep breath. He's still holding my face, a gentle sadness crossing it.

"I don't blame you for trying to leave," he says. He strokes my cheek. "But do you have any idea what I would have done if you disappeared? Not attacked, not hurt…just *gone*. Rune, I would have torn this world to shreds looking for you."

"We weren't leaving," I say. I lean against Harrick's hand, but I move my eyes away from him. I'm tempted to ask about the hoarded magic, but then I'm sharing more than just my secret. It's one thing to risk my life, another to risk the entire faction's. "I don't want to say more."

"Thank you, for telling me," he says.

His fingers slide to the back of my hair, squeezing gently. He tilts his head, reclaiming my line of sight. He pulls me tighter against his side, and though I'm embarrassed at my nakedness, I don't pull away. Once I'm settled, he kisses the crown of my head, sweeping my hair to the side.

"Gods, I can't wait to hold you like this all the time," he whispers against my hair.

I let his words wash the insecurity from my skin. I lay my head against his chest and lose myself in the steady rhythm of his breaths and his heartbeat. His thumb strokes over my hip, again and again, like a silent lullaby, until I find myself drifting to sleep once more.

Harrick is gone when I wake the following morning. There's a breakfast tray in my room, and it's by far the best thing I've eaten in my life. It's better than the ones Mom made before she got sick, and it's so far superior to servant meals there's no comparing them. I sit cross-legged on the bed, cutting into the final egg on my plate. I'm already stuffed, but I'd be a fool not to eat every crumb.

The six o'clock buzzer sounds. I've been waiting for reassignment ever since being taken off Viana's service, but so far, a notice hasn't come. I imagine Harrick is behind it. One way or another, I've had ample free time. Today, I'm going to take a long shower and see if I can snag anything useful for Vale. While I'm not sure what I'm going to do now that I've told Harrick the truth, I can't bring myself to abandon the mission entirely.

I take my last bite and check that I haven't spilled yolk on my coverall. Relieved I haven't—since Harrick sent this new one only yesterday—I slip into my shoes and open the door to the hallway.

I'm startled backward when Harrick himself pushes into my quarters. He looks handsome as ever, but he's exhausted too. Dark bags color beneath his eyes, and he's blinking like he's ready to fall asleep.

"What are you doing here?" I ask, stumbling back a few steps. "Why are you up this early?"

"I never went to sleep," he says. He closes the door behind him and leans against it, and I realize he's still wearing the same clothes from last night. I flush at the reminder of what we did, only to shake my head.

"What are you doing here?" I repeat. "Someone might see you and think—"

"What *will* they think, Rune?" He asks, giving me an almost goofy grin. He's *giddy*, I realize, like this is somehow a joke.

"I don't know, but I'm the one they'll punish," I say. My arms start shaking without my permission, only for Harrick to press his hands to my shoulders, steadying them.

"No one is going to touch you," he says. Despite the severity of his tone, the easy smile remains. "Because by this time tomorrow, you will be their queen."

I stumble a step backwards, surprised at the high laugh that bursts from my lips. I can't remember the last time I've laughed at all, but this sneaks up on me. No one has ever said such ridiculous words.

"Is that right?" I ask. Despite everything, I smile at him and his inexplicable excitement. He's proven time and time again that he'll keep me from danger, so if he's not worried for my safety, I'll trust he knows what he's doing.

Harrick freezes, staring at me with wide eyes and a parted mouth.

"What?" I ask. I shift on my feet, feeling the weight of his gaze scouring over me. I suddenly worry I didn't check for egg yolk well enough.

Harrick grabs my waist, pulling me against his. His mouth crashes against mine, and he tangles his hand through my hair, tugging gently. He pulls back all too soon, breathing hard and eyes bright with electric energy.

"You are so beautiful when you smile," he says. "Most beautiful woman I've ever seen."

I blush, feeling the heat everywhere. I want to say something back, but it all feels inadequate. Before I can think of anything, Harrick breaks away, pulling a few folded documents out of his coat pocket.

"I found what we need," he says. He speaks with hesitant excitement, as if he's not sure I'll feel as happy about this as he does. "Well, technically *Tora* found what we need."

I know she's his sister, but hearing him refer to the princess so casually is strange.

"After I left here last night," he continues. "She and Joran helped me do research. It took us hours, but..."

He trails off as he unfolds the documents. After handing the stack to me, he waits with lifted eyebrows. My stomach pulses uneasily as I look at the different texts. I squint at the top section, because that's a trick Vale taught me. Focus on the first paragraph and hope it gives an insight to the entire page.

Event. Illegal. Crown. Honor.

Shame heats my face.

"I can't read," I finally admit. My voice cracks, but I tell myself not to cry. It's not my fault I was taught too late, and that my teacher barely knows how to read himself.

Harrick doesn't laugh or tease me. He gently takes the papers from me, laying them on the bed beside us. He takes my hands and leans in, our lips almost touching.

"It's how we can be together," he says. His warm breath fans over my skin, tickling softly. "All those papers say a variation of the same thing: if we're married before I'm made king, you'll be queen. So long as we keep it a secret before I'm crowned, there'll be nothing they can do."

Harrick dips to meet my eyes, and my breath catches. When he said Tora saw the way he looked at me—and that's why she suspected us—I'd shrugged off the comment. Now though, I think maybe it's true. I think he might look at me differently than he looks at anyone else.

"Married?" I repeat. The word ricochets between my ears, refusing to settle in one place. A strange and lovely numbness burns through my chest. Still, there's no way he's being serious. He hasn't *actually* thought about marrying me. It's absurd and unrealistic and pathetic...and yet, my shredded hope begs that's *exactly* what he means.

"That's not how I planned to do it," he says, blushing. His words shake, but his gaze is as steady as ever. "Marry me, Rune Ealde. Nothing makes me feel half as brave and worthy and *good* as you do. Let me spend the rest of my life making you happy. Safe. *Powerful*."

I don't realize I'm crying until he's wiping at my face again. But for the first time, these are hopeful tears. Stunned tears. Completely and utterly happy tears.

"Are you sure?" I ask. I move my hands to his neck, unable to stop their trembling. "Don't do this because you feel guilty or because you feel like you should. You don't have to—"

"I'm in love with you, Rune," he says, cutting me off. "I *want* to marry you."

I rise on my toes and pull him down by the collar until he's close enough to kiss.

"Yes," I say. It comes out as a quiet breath, but by the way he surges to kiss me, I know he's heard. I lean into him, chasing his tongue with mine, tasting him and losing myself in the way he holds me. My usual insecurities are shadowed by pulsing adrenaline and the unbearable need to get closer.

I break away from his lips and trail kisses down the column of his throat. He groans, lifting me against him until my feet don't touch the floor. I wrap my legs around his waist, pressing our chests together and relishing the soreness between my thighs. I'm desperate to feel him inside me again, but before I get carried away, I lean back to look at him.

"When?" I ask, chest still heaving.

"Whenever you want," he says. "We won't be able to have a ceremony until after I'm king—obviously—but we can still make it nice. If I have a few days, I can arrange for flowers and have your favorite meal made. We can go pick out—"

I smile at him like the complete, lovestruck fool I am.

"I love you," I tell him. His face softens at those three words, as if they're the most beautiful thing he's ever heard. "Today. I want to marry you today."

29
RUNE

I stand in Harrick's bedroom, surrounded by scarlet...*everything*. I don't know how he bears to sleep here, how the red doesn't give him a constant headache. If his sister wasn't here, shooting me skeptical glances, I might ask him. Instead, I haven't spoken a word since we arrived.

Princess Tora sits on Harrick's bed, cross-legged, scrawling furiously over a fresh sheet of parchment. Brow furrowed, she only pauses to reference one of the wrinkled documents from earlier or to ask her brother a question. The few times I've seen her, she's either worn training gear or a frilly dress. Right now, she's got loose-fitting bottoms and a matching top.

It's inexplicably endearing, watching Harrick interact with her. They clearly love each other, even as he makes fun of her handwriting and she accuses him of smelling like sweat. He most certainly doesn't.

"Do you have a surname, Rune?" she asks. Up close, she looks perfectly golden and beautiful. I haven't dared to meet her eyes, but I can tell she's looking at me.

"Obviously," Harrick says. His tone instantly shifts to agitation. "She's a person, Tor. Not an animal."

"I didn't say she was an animal," Tora snaps. "Some servants don't have—"

"Ealde," I say, interrupting them. My voice is so quiet I'm not sure she's heard me. "My number is 247, if that's more useful."

"You won't be needing *that* much longer," she says with something between a laugh and a scoff.

I shift on my feet, unsure whether she's mocking, pitying, or judging me.

"All right, that's everything," Tora says. She shoves off the bed and stands between me and her brother. Looking at him, she asks, "Ready?"

In response, he looks to me and I give a sharp nod.

Much like sex, marriage is something I didn't consider before Harrick. Servants don't marry and having a child was the last thing I wanted. Maybe I would have married if I ever escaped the Tower, but my plans didn't go that far into the future. Now that it's actually happening, I wish my parents were here—my dad especially. He'd be tearing up, telling me he loves me and that he's proud. He wouldn't care that Harrick is heir to Savoa, he'd only want to know whether he's good to me.

He is, I tell Dad, wherever his magic may be in this world.

"Join hands," Tora says. Even though I don't meet her eyes, skepticism is heavy in her expression. Aside from Joran, who stands guard on the other side of the door, she's the only one who knows about me and Harrick. I hope, someday, she comes to like me.

"Can I take off your mask?" he asks, stealing my attention. I look at him, and unlike with Tora, I don't hesitate to meet his gaze. The warm darkness of his eyes fills me with a sense of comfort. It reminds me of home, a feeling I haven't had in cycles.

Rather than answer, I untie my mask and pass him the thin

fabric. He loops the band around his wrist before taking my hands in his. He's smiling now, that same giddy grin from earlier.

"Gods, you're so pretty," he whispers. He captures my mouth in his, not seeming to care that we're in front of his sister. I'm pretty sure I'm blushing from head to toe by the time he pulls away.

"You're supposed to wait until after you sign," Tora says pointedly, but her expression changes from skepticism to curiosity. Harrick pulls away from me, still grinning, and roughs her hair. Then leaning into me again, he whispers, "Are you ready? Say the word, and we don't do this."

"I'm ready. I want to," I say, breath shaky. "I'm just...scared."

"You're safe with me." Harrick tucks my hair behind my ear. "Give yourself time, sweetheart. One day, *soon*, you won't be scared of anything."

That seems impossible, but I believe him anyway. I breathe through my nose and close my eyes. When I open them again, I push onto my toes, pressing a quick kiss against his stubbled cheek. Harrick smiles, and I do my best to block out the rising nerves.

Whatever happens after this, I could never regret *him*.

"Rune Ealde," Tora says. "With your word and your name, do you vow to protect my brother's heart and love him for the remainder of your days?"

"Yes," I say, surprised when my voice cracks. A rogue tear slides down my face, and Harrick's hand is immediately there, wiping it away.

"And Harrick Ademas," Tora says, shifting to look at him "With your word and your name, do you vow to protect Rune's heart and love her for the remainder of your days?"

"Yes," he says. He keeps one hand on my face, and the other grasped between both of mine. He smiles at me with so much love it sends a physical ache through my chest. "I will love you forever, Rune."

"I love you," I whisper back, fighting another wave of tears.

"Sign here," Tora says. She lays the parchment on the foot of Harrick's bed, and he signs his name in beautiful calligraphy. Once he's done, she turns the paper to me. My hand trembles and there's a good chance I've misspelled my name, but it's there.

When I return the pen to Tora, she glances over both signatures before adding her own.

"There," she says. She blows out a heavy breath, pausing to dab at her eyes. "It's done. Welcome to the family, *Princess Rune.*"

Hours after marrying Harrick, I walk the third level of the Tower alone. He'd wanted us to spend the rest of the day in his quarters, and it took more willpower than I knew I had to say no. Even now, my body is itching in frustration. I could be lying in a luxurious bed with the world's most wonderful man —my *husband*—and instead I'm here, counting dingy doors on a low level servant floor.

The one I need is marked by peeling paint and a cracked doorway, and within it, Vale sits in the far corner. The brief splinter of light casts over his face, showing his drawn expression. He looks like absolute shit, and I feel an immediate pang of guilt.

I may have had the best day of my life today, but he clearly hasn't.

"This better be important," is his greeting.

I leave a crack of light for the room and crouch at his side. I unzip the front of my coverall, just far enough to pull out a single folded map. It's strange knowing I won't escape with my faction as I originally planned, but I know deep in my soul, this is for the best. Not only for me, but for all the rebels. For all of Savoa, hopefully.

Once Harrick is king and I am queen, we will work to get that magic redistributed. I haven't spoken to him about it — he doesn't even know I'm aware the bunker exists. Still, I know who Harrick is in his heart, and I trust he will do what's right. It won't matter if we have to face the Architect himself —we will fight to save this kingdom, and we will do it together. Maybe someday, Vale will come back to help, but for now, I want to give him the thing he desires most: his freedom.

Using the light from the hallway, I show Vale the map.

"Is that—"

"An escape route," I confirm. It was crafted by Harrick himself, the surest way to get out without getting caught. "If you can make it through here, you'll get out before anyone realizes you're missing."

There's a long stretch of silence as Vale studies the map. He scoffs, tapping the exit point.

"This goes into a wall," he says, lifting an unimpressed eyebrow.

"It's a secret door, hidden by a bookshelf. You'll see it once you're in there. It will lead to some stairs, and at the bottom, a tunnel."

"A tunnel?" Vale repeats. He narrows his eyes at me. "The Tower doesn't have tunnels."

"Just like it doesn't have a bunker full of magic," I snap, then soften my voice. "Trust me, Vale. This is your route."

"I'm supposed to believe you just happen to know about a secret passageway? And that you didn't know about it until now?" he demands. He takes the map from me, turning it as if expecting to find a hidden agenda. "What aren't you telling me, Rune? And why are you talking like you aren't coming?"

"Because I'm not," I say. I let out a tight breath. "I'm working on something, something that I think will help Savoa. I need time though, and I need…I need to be here to do it."

Vale's lips form a tight line, and his eyes scrutinize my face. I can't tell what he's thinking, only that he's not convinced.

"Trust me, Vale," I say. "I realize I'm not giving you much to go off, but I need you to believe me. The map is good, I promise."

"Fine," he says.

He's no more than said the word when he lunges forward. At first, I think he's attacking. He clamps a hand over my mouth, pressing hard enough my jaw will bruise. It's only when I hear a distant yell that I realize he's acting on instinct. Someone is screaming—and they're coming this way.

I hold my breath, praying it has nothing to do with us. Somehow, deep in my gut, I know it does.

An old man with weathered skin bursts into the closet, throwing the door shut behind him. I only saw a flicker of his face, but it was enough to recognize him. Arnelian. One of the rebels who'd joined in the days before I became Viana's handmaiden. He collapses against the door, panting hard.

"He. Knows." Arnelian is breathing so hard he's difficult to understand. "He knows. And they're coming. *Now*."

"Wha—" I start, but Vale cuts me off.

"What did you do?" he demands, shoving me against the shelf. I struggle against him, staggering to my feet. His reaction shouldn't sting, but it does.

"I didn't do anything," I snap.

"It was Larken," Arnelian says, still gasping. "I don't know if anyone else was involved, but it doesn't matter. We need to go, *now*, before they get here."

"Who?" Vale asks

"The Architect's guards." With that final declaration, Arnelian slumps against the door. There's barely a pulse of silence.

"Use the map," I say. "It's your best shot, Vale. Your only shot."

"Right into your trap, Rune?" he sneers.

"You're dead if you don't use it," I say. "I'm going to buy you time. Do whatever you can to get out. Don't look back until you're in the tunnels."

I shove Arnelian out of the way and crack open the door, only to stop when Vale grabs my wrist. I look back at him, at the line of light that falls across his face.

"You promise?" he asks. I've never seen him look so young, so *scared*.

"I promise," I repeat. "Give me thirty seconds before you follow. I'll lead them away."

"You'll never outrun them, Rune. They'll catch you," he says. His expression is caught somewhere between shock and horror.

"I know. That's the plan."

"That's a *terrible* plan." He tightens his hold.

"Thirty seconds," I repeat. Pulling out of his grasp, I add, "Don't you dare try to save me, Vale. You get out and you don't look back."

With that, I push into the hallway. There are too many things that can go wrong with what I'm planning, but this is the only way I can see Vale and the others getting out. We'll all die if I don't buy them time. Even if this doesn't work, at least I can say I tried. At the end of it all, I would rather die good than live cruelly.

"Find me, Harrick," I whisper.

And then, I run.

30

HARRICK

After Rune leaves to deliver the map, I walk the 182nd floor with Joran. I'd much rather be with my *wife*, whispering that word in her ear while I fuck her senseless. I've been consumed with thoughts of it, of having her under me, now that she's officially mine. It's more than that though, obviously. Soon, all of Savoa will see Rune for what she truly is—a queen—and all who hurt her will be forced to beg her for forgiveness.

I stop in front of one of the small storefronts. This floor has a variety of shops, selling everything from bouquets of flowers to basic weaponry. There are something like eleven jewelry stores, but Tora insisted only this one has rings fit for a queen. I'd smiled at that, and as soon as Rune left with my map, I headed here.

I scan the rows of glittering jewelry. Gems in all shapes and colors, bands of all widths. I select a simple ring for myself, handing it to the blushing cashier.

After asking for Joran's opinion on a few for Rune, and getting lackluster responses, I browse the rings alone. Most options have green stones for the elite class or purple for the royals. There are several red rings, and a few of random colors. Dark bands with orange stones. Red bands with translucent stones that catch the light.

I stop at a thin-banded ring, black like mine. Rather than a red gem, as typically worn by members of the crown, this one has a delicate blue stone. It's shaped in an oval, and it's vibrant, shocking, alluring. The color reminds me of Rune's eyes.

"This one," I say to the cashier. Despite being several cycles my senior, she smiles coyly at me.

"Lady Viana is a *very* lucky woman," she says. She's clearly fishing for information, trying to see if my betrothal is back in place.

I don't respond. I have nothing to say to this woman—or anyone else—about Viana. An undercurrent of relief pulses through my body that soon, everyone will know the truth. Rune Ealde is my queen, not Viana Llroy, and Rune will be the one to raise Savoa from its ashes. I only have to beat Malek in one more battle. Though I don't know how yet, I can feel it in the pulse of my magic. I am going to defeat my brother, no matter the cost.

Once I've settled both rings, Joran and I leave the shop and head for my quarters. I steal a final peek at the blue gemstone before tucking our rings into my coat pocket. I want to wear mine now, though not half as much as I want to see this ring on Rune's finger.

I enter the lift, fingers tapping against my thighs. In my head, I'm planning the next several hours. Once Rune returns, I'm going to enjoy her, uninterrupted, for the rest of the day. I don't let myself stress over the fact she's with another man right now. He might not know she's mine, but she does. She doesn't want someone else—she wants *me,* and I'll be eternally grateful for that.

"I want lion steak," I tell Joran. I'm studying my reflection in the mirrored ceiling. "Have two sent to my room this evening.

And nightwater. Wyhel. I doubt she's ever tasted hard drink. Just a single bottle then. And a dress. Even if only for the night, I want her to feel—"

Joran's hand clamps over my shoulder, hard and sudden, like he's done a hundred times during earthquakes or storms. I tense, bracing my hands against the glass walls. But it's perfectly still, everything moving slowly and gently as ever. It's Flood Season, after all, and we're rarely affected by it here.

"What is it?" I demand. He doesn't respond, and I finally notice the faint mark on the side of his mask. He's getting a message, and by the red hue, I know it's from the Architect. He rarely sends a system-wide message.

The lift settles at my quarters, and the glass door slides to reveal the scarlet corridor around my room. I make no move to get off, glancing from Joran to the patterned wallpaper. There's a beat of silence before he closes the door and enters a new address for the lift. I track the numbers across the keypad as he types.

I close my eyes, hard enough that spots break through the darkness. He's directed us toward the low courtyard. It's too early in the season for a planned execution, which means someone has done something terrible. Something requiring an *instant,* public death.

Without opening my eyes, my next words are a harsh whisper.

"Tell me it's not her." It's not a question. It's a pathetic hope against what I already feel deep in my bones. It's like my magic can sense her—a tangle of fear and panic—even as my brain tries to convince me otherwise. It's a creeping, nauseating pulse that thickens when Joran doesn't respond.

I curse, slamming my hand against the wall of the lift. My hand glows red against the glass, and I thrust us toward the ground in a freefall. Magicked wind, stolen from the Wilds, sends us hurtling downward. I count the seconds in my head, catching us occasionally to ensure we don't crash.

Joran clings to the corner, muttering rushed prayers to the heavens as we fall. Catch. Fall.

Finally, we reach the ground. The lift shudders into place and Joran slouches, hands to his knees like he might vomit. When the lift doesn't instantly open, I send another gust of wind, this one shattering the glass doors into the corridor. I break into a run, Joran's footsteps only a breath behind mine.

"They've caught rebels, several of them," Joran says. Holding my pace, he adds, "They're going to execute. My prince—"

"If I fail, they'll kill me," I interrupt, looking over my shoulder. I take a sharp left, away from the Tower's main entrance and toward the low courtyard. I'm not sure Joran is still behind me. I don't look back to check. I only pick up the pace and say the rest in bursts. "And anyone. They see. With me."

"I'm with you," he says. There's no hesitation in his voice. Even if there was, I wouldn't have time to reason with him. He speaks louder now. "There are others. Once they've apprehended them all—"

"Save my wife," I say. "That's our goal. Everything else is secondary. Even me."

"Understood."

Another turn, and we're there. I force myself to stop and take three full breaths.

"Don't reveal anything." It's barely a whisper, but I know Joran heard it. I don't wait for him to respond before I push into the courtyard.

Forcing a relaxed posture, I tally the opposition. Six high guards, five with descendent crests, one without. Three line the bottom of the stage, two stand with the prisoners near the fence-line, and one stands beside a pair of thrones. The Architect's chair of bones is empty, but Malek occupies the black one. He looks bored, his crown lopsided over messy hair and his dress shirt wrinkled. His mouth is twisted into its trademark grimace, and a fresh scar decorates his throat. He grins when he sees me though, leaping to his feet with arms spread in a welcoming gesture.

"Brother!" he calls. His guard shadows him, leaving little space between them. My brother may not hold our close match against me, but his guard certainly does. Magic dances beneath his palms, close enough to the skin I can see it. Malek strides closer, hands loose at his sides. "Shall I call for another chair?"

"I hadn't been informed of an execution," I say. I keep my voice carefully level, but I have to put my hands into my coat pockets. They're vibrating with tension, the magic burning for release. I don't allow myself to look for her in the huddle of servants. "What's the occasion?"

"Another rebel cause," he says, voice mocking. He turns, giving me his back, and I'm tempted to strike him down right then. It's too dangerous when I don't know where the Architect is. Malek settles into his throne, sighing. "There's always something, isn't there?"

"It seems that way," I say.

I finally look at the servants. Three of them, all knelt in a shallow pool of water. Their heads are bowed: two men, one woman. Rune is in the front, mask removed, eyes focused on the ground before her. I want her to look at me, if only so I can see if she's injured.

It's better she doesn't. I force myself to return my attention to Malek.

"Call a throne for me," I say after a lengthy pause.

"Delightful." He nods to the guard beside him, and the man hurries from the stage. Once he's crossed into the Tower, I join my brother, standing between him and our father's chair.

"There are supposedly several more," Malek says. He tilts his chin toward Rune and the other servants. "The Architect has instructed us to wait for him, but..."

He glances at me, that horrible, mischievous glint in his eyes. With a lazy flick of his wrist, he waves for the servants to be brought before us. The guards shuffle them to their feet, and for the first time, Rune's eyes find mine. Stark blue and utterly terrified.

It's all right, I try to convey. But it isn't all right, not at all. Unless I can play this exactly right, she's going to die, and I'm going to die trying to save her.

"I won't tell if you don't," Malek says. He settles into his chair, smirking at me. "Servants die of natural causes all the time. Who's to say it didn't happen on our watch?"

I stiffen, not at Malek's cruel words, but the fact he's saying them to me. He's baiting me, I realize. Goading me into action, and that can only mean one thing.

I don't respond. I tighten my jaw and look at Joran, who remains near the Tower entrance. His stance is steady and casual, but I can tell he's cataloging every detail in this court-yard. His hands are balled into fists, and flickers of red dance between his clenched knuckles.

"I am not playing your game, Malek," I say. When I turn back to him, he's still grinning. "If these servants are guilty, the Architect will punish them. Not you."

"If?" he asks, eyebrows lifting. "I didn't take you for a servant sympathizer, Harrick. Then again, you've given one our fucking name, so what do I know?"

I can't keep myself from reacting. I lunge forward, grabbing Malek by the throat and ripping him from his throne. He makes a horrible wheezing sound, and I squeeze, feeling his life pulse against my palm. There's something ridiculously satisfying about the thought of killing him, not with magic, but with my bare hands.

His hand lifts, and at first, I think he's going to lash against me. But then, I realize he's waving off the guards. Three of them are on the stage now, one to each servant. Rune and the two other rebels stand against the far corner. A quick glance finds her at the center of them, hands braced as if she's holding them behind her.

As if she could possibly protect them from the malice that's about to be unleashed.

"How." The word drops from my lips before I can stop it. I know it doesn't matter *how* he knows, only that he does. Only that my options just became excruciatingly limited.

Don't be rash, I remind myself. *Learn what he knows.*

"You thought you could hide it?" he asks. "From *me*? I've been watching you, Harrick. Fucking a servant was one thing, but having a marriage agreement drawn...I had to intervene."

I tighten my fist, relishing the way his breath strains. Malek, of course, only grins at me. His words are rough, choked from my hand, but his eyes light with manic glee.

"The Architect was furious. Didn't help when he realized the rat-whore had a whole scheme built up with her friends." Malek grabs my wrist, sending a flicker of magic from his palm. I flinch at the raw sting of heat, but I don't loosen my grip. "The only question now is...did you know, brother? Were you in on whatever pathetic scheme they've spent cycles building?"

I don't respond. There's nothing to say, nothing that will get me out of this horrible reality. One where Rune dies if I say the wrong thing, one where I'm imprisoned and she's slaughtered and—

"The Architect will be here soon," Malek continues. Both hands are on my wrist now, his eyes wide. He can still breathe, and I hate that I'm letting him. I can almost hear Tora in the back of my mind, whispering *you held back*. Malek lets out a wheezing laugh when I look away from him, my eyes settling on Rune. He sparks my wrist again. "If you're smart, Harrick, you'll back down. Admit defeat. Beg for his mercy. He'll kill you if you don't."

I look at Malek now, not because he's stung me but because his words awaken something in my chest. I can't remember the last time he's spoken like this, like we're just talking, not verbally sparring. He's not taunting me, I realize. My brother, the cruelest of jokers, is being serious.

I think, in his own twisted way, he's trying to save my life.

"You made an error," I say. It comes out as a snarl, ripping from my throat. "You made a fatal error, Malek, in targeting *her*. I will fucking *die* before anyone harms her. I will *kill* anyone who tries, and that includes you."

Malek's eyes narrow and his upper lip curls. He sends a wave of magic against my wrist, shocking me hard enough I lose my hold and stumble backward. We're both casting before we've fully regained our balance. Red mist swirls from Malek's palms, transforming into a bear-wolf hybrid. Standing on massive haunches, the creature looks down at me, baring long, curved teeth. Its eyes are translucent, and yet, I can feel the hunger in them, the rabid determination.

I take another step back, casting thorn-covered vines from each hand. Distantly, I'm aware of the guards, their palms lit with magic, and the servants, still huddled in the corner. I whip my vines around us, smacking them against the wooden stage and forcing everyone else back.

"He's mine!" Malek shouts. The guards don't release their magic, but they maintain their distance. "Nobody fucking interfere."

"I wanted us to be brothers!" I scream. I don't look at

anyone else, just Malek. He stares back at me, the rain pounding harder over the courtyard.

"I wanted that too," he says, surprising me. There's something unreadable in his expression. Pity, perhaps. Or maybe it's guilt. "It wasn't supposed to end like this, Harrick, but you make it too hard to let you live."

Panic flares in my chest. I've lost to Malek too many times, and if I don't win now... I shut the thought out. There's no time to be scared or hesitant. If I'm going to do this, I can't be afraid.

I look at Rune in the corner. Her blue eyes are already on me, and her lips are moving. I can't hear what she's saying, but she's crying. Her shoulders tremble, and she steps toward me, against the guard's hold, like she wants to help. Like she might *try*.

I look away. Raising my arms, I feel every ounce of magic pulse within my bones. It collects like a rising storm, like the brutalest of seasons in this godsforsaken land. It builds to the point I'm vibrating, until my vision tints red.

Malek's eyes light, not with fear, but excitement. For a moment, we are children again. We're standing in the Royal Training Arena for the first time, and the Architect is pitting us against each other. We're gaping at each other, shocked at what we're expected to do.

Like then, Malek is the first to strike now.

His beast surges across the stage, reaching me in only three lumbering steps. It is almost twice my height, with the body of a bear and the gaping jaw of a wolf. It swipes me with its massive paw, launching me across the stage. I don't even attempt to block the blow. I crash against Malek's throne, using my vines to keep me from falling over the edge.

I lurch back to my feet, forcing my movements to slow, as if I'm injured. He needs to think I'm hurt, that he's already won.

The bear-wolf hybrid charges me, knocking me back down.

Its clawed paw slams into my ribcage, and I feel every bone crunch in my chest. I cough, straining my lungs, waiting. Because even though I don't understand Malek, I know him well enough. I know that no matter the circumstance, he can't help but treat everything like a game. Even this.

He has to taunt me, to tease me. Maybe because he's a monster, but maybe just because he's my brother.

"Is that all, Harrick?" he calls with a pitying laugh. Right on cue. "And here I thought—"

He's so busy watching my face, he doesn't see my vine until it's too late. It's wrapped around his throat, cutting his sentence in half. With my teeth gritted and the edges of my vision going black, I force all my attention on my brother. Twenty cycles of him expecting me to lose, of me being too afraid to win.

"I wanted us to be brothers," I say again. I'm not sure why.

As Malek struggles to breath, his beast shudders and fizzles, dissolving into mist above me. I suck a full breath of air into my aching lungs and rotate onto my elbow. Malek is staring at me, face purple and eyes bulging.

"I'm sorry, Malek," I say. I hate that I am. I hate that for so many cycles, I hoped we could end any other way. "I'm *sorry*."

"Harrick—"

He barely manages to speak the word, but even if he says more, I don't hear it. I scream, unleashing every drop of magic and energy and hatred I have in my body. For the first time, maybe in my entire life, I don't hold back. I clench my fists, tightening my vines against his skin. I don't watch his dark blood seep over my magic. I stare only at his eyes, at the way they look when the light finally goes out.

A rough sob breaks from my throat.

Malek is dead.

A strangled scream follows, bringing my magic back into my palms.

I killed him.

I lurch onto my knees.

I killed my brother.

I crawl across the stage, not letting myself think. I act on instinct alone, on the pure need to find her, to save her, to protect her. I stretch for Malek's magic as it swirls above us. With my hand extended, I capture it all, pulling it deep into my bones, taking more than I probably should. I'm nauseated, even as the magic soothes my wounds and sharpens my spent magic. I lurch to my feet, drunk with power, overcome with immense magic.

I don't let myself look at Malek again.

Instead, I survey the mess around me. In a matter of minutes, everything has changed.

I am alone on the stage with my brother's corpse. The servants have disappeared, and the courtyard is overrun by guards. Thirty of them, at least, some in their usual attire, but many without their masks. I waver on my feet as I watch them, sure that I'd be unconscious without this rush of adrenaline— and stolen magic.

I blink at the chaos. It takes me a moment to process what I'm seeing through the excess of crumbled rock and root, hazy shadow and sharp magic. Those with masks are fighting against those without, and it is only when I see a familiar face that I put everything together.

Joran shouts orders from the center of the battlefield. His head is exposed, revealing the bright red hair I haven't seen since before he entered the military. The maskless guards are fighting, not against me, but *for* me.

I launch off the stage, throwing myself into the madness. Through the blur of violent magic and wielded blades, I search only for her. With every guard I kill, I scan the surrounding area.

I find two bodies of male servants, their corpses sprawled near the stage. She isn't with them.

Get out, I plead silently to her. *Don't let anyone find you.*

A hand clasps my shoulder, and I spin, palms raised and ready. I lower them when I realize it's Tora. Dae stands at her back, blocking her from the onslaught of approaching guards.

"Tora," I say. Her name is a breath of relief and terror at once. She's okay, but she's here.

"Joran had me take her inside," she says. "She should be safe."

"Where?" I ask. I glance over her shoulder, checking for threats, for Rune, for anything. When she doesn't answer, I demand louder, "Where?"

Before she responds, a chilling voice breaks through all else.

"Stand down," the Architect calls. His words are no more than a whisper, and yet, it becomes the only thing I hear. Tora stumbles against me, and Dae blindly steps closer until she's shielded behind him. The Architect's voice raises, "Anyone who is not on their knees in the next five seconds will be slaughtered."

Tora stares up at me. She's crying, lips trembling as she tightens her hold on my shoulder.

"Five," the Architect calls.

"What do we do?" she asks, the words almost impossible to make out.

"Four."

"Kneel," I tell her. Before she can protest, I roughly shove her to the ground. Dae's exposed eyes meet mine. He's somehow more terrifying without his mask, his features so much sharper than I remembered. His jaw is clenched as his gaze flickers between me and my sister, and it is only then that I realize I'm not the only one here he's protecting.

"Three," the Architect says.

Behind Dae, almost the entire courtyard—masked and not —kneel before my father. He is so much weaker than they realize. His magic could infiltrate half our minds at once, but the rest of us could kill him if we struck at the same time.

"Two."

We're too divided. It's too late. We've already lost.

"Kneel," I snap at Dae. Then, louder, to the remaining soldiers, "Everyone, kneel! That's an order!"

The remaining guards do as I say, kneeling with their heads bowed. Once Dae is on his knees, he adjusts, placing his head against the top of Tora's.

"One," the Architect says.

With everyone knelt between us, I have a clear shot at my father. His suit is not red in color alone. Splatters of blood cover his clothing, but it's clear he's only just arrived to the fight. He moves his head slowly, as if surveying the dozens of guards between us. His magic collects at his palms, and I already know he's going to kill them. All my unmasked men, whether they're bowed or not, have made an unforgivable statement.

"Don't," I say. My voice is a sharp crack through the slanted rain. "They've kneeled."

"They have," he agrees. He steps between the guards, leisurely working his way toward me. "And yet, you have not."

I'm the only one strong enough to open the Architect's portal—especially with Malek dead—but I'm not sure he cares in this moment. His magic pulses, until there's a swirling mass at either hand. I can feel his attention on mine too. It's brighter than his, but less contained. I have too much of Malek's magic mixed with mine, and it's making everything sloppy. Still, I don't dare release it. If I'm going to kill my father, I'll need every drop I have.

"I will not kneel," I say. "But I *will* offer a trade."

"Is that right?" the Architect asks. He chuckles, head tilting not in confusion but amusement. "You think you've something to offer?"

"Yes," I say. My voice rasps as I lift it, making sure all can hear. "You cannot escape Savoa without me. If you leave everyone alive, I will do it. I will open that portal, even if it fucking kills me."

The Architect halts. He stands halfway between me and the Tower, and I wish now, more than ever, I could see his face. He is utterly motionless, but whether he's debating my offer or readying for the kill, I have no idea.

"You cannot do it without me," I repeat. "I've killed Malek. Tora and Mother aren't strong enough. *No one* is strong enough. But let them live, and I will do it."

The Architect begins walking again. His steps are as slow, as unconcerned as before, and yet I notice the way his magic pulses. The guards around us might not know what I'm talking about, but I'm giving them enough to wonder, to question whether this man truly has their best interests in mind.

"You think you're irreplaceable?" he asks. A few more strides, and he's here, standing on the other side of Dae. He presses against my guard, as if he's nothing more than an inanimate barrier between us. "You think I can't fuck another woman? Make myself another set of heirs? It will be easy to replace you, and I've got nothing but time."

I step away from Tora and Dae, carefully leading my father a few steps to the left. He pays them no attention, shadowing my movements until we're close enough I could lunge for his throat. I don't. The Architect is not Malek. He'll kill me before I leave a bruise.

"You're dying," I say. I spit the words like they're poison, like they might kill him faster, and I make sure everyone can hear me. "You need my help *now*, and if you want it—"

"I don't *want* it," he interrupts. "I *have* it. I own you, child. You are mine, and you are here to serve me."

I don't respond. My chest heaves, my magic burning hotter with each passing second. I need to strike, but I already know I'll lose. He'll see any attack coming. He'll block it before it lands.

"I won't," I say. I lower my voice. "So if you ever want to leave this wretched place, you'll take the deal."

The laugh that leaves him now is different from the first. It's ragged and spiteful, and it's clear he's tired of this conversation.

"All right, Harrick. You've made your point," he says. He steps away from me, and for a moment, I think he's going to agree. "How about I offer a deal of my own? You stop acting like a petulant child, and I promise to let your whore live. You get on your fucking knees, right now, and I won't murder her, like you did your brother."

Everything inside me goes cold. My mouth opens but nothing, not even breath, comes out. A flicker of movement catches my attention, and then I see her. Framed by two bulky guards, she struggles to keep up as they drag her across the yard. She's lost her shoes and her hair is a tangled mess around her face. The sleeve of her coverall is torn, and even from here, I can tell she's crying.

"Fine," I say, the response immediate. My voice is hoarse, the word barely a whisper. It is opposite the chaotic rage of magic and fury, swirling within me. I don't let the Architect see my terror, my wrath. I keep my face perfectly neutral, revealing nothing at all. With my eyes still on my father, I lower to my knees. "Fine. You win."

My mind races as we sit in momentary silence. There's nothing but the sound of heavy rain and dozens of ragged breaths. I can barely see Rune from where I kneel. They've taken her to the stage, and she stands in front of my brother's remains.

"Disappointing," the Architect says, pulling my attention back to him. He touches his mask with a flick of magic, and it dissolves into his suit. I study his cruel, ordinary features, and the cold, empty glare of his eyes. He looks at the stage, then back to me. "Forsaking your own blood for a *criminal*."

"Like father, like son," I spit. "Isn't that why we're all here? Banished because you betrayed your own. If anyone has forsaken—"

The Architect's lip twitches. He lifts his hand in a slow, all-too-familiar gesture. Without a word, he's commanded his men to attack. There's no time to react, to defend myself.

His guards are on me, one on each arm, another behind me. Magic burns against the back of my neck, and I scream until my throat turns raw. The pain is blinding, scalding, unbearable. I thrash against my captors. Cast magic in futile bursts, hoping that something, anything breaks their hold. It doesn't. Their magic spreads around me, burning my skin, twisting my limbs, breaking my bones.

I don't know how long I'm tortured, only that eventually, I lose consciousness.

31
RUNE

The slaughter has ended, but this nightmare is far from over. I kneel in the center of the lifted platform, staring out at the wet courtyard. The Architect sent everyone away, and it was almost surreal, watching chaos dissolve into strained compliance. Masked guards led bare faced men into the Tower, the latter with their hands bound behind their backs. Tora was taken away screaming, calling for Harrick, even after he could no longer hear her.

The Architect remained on the stage with me and two guards, and together, we watched the masses work. Servants were brought out to scrape the dead from the cobblestone, and I clenched my teeth to keep from crying. They left the rebels in their haphazard pile to the right of the stage. I can see the bodies still, and I imagine it's a warning for me to behave.

"Rouse him," the Architect says.

I tense at the command, looking down at Harrick. After they'd beaten him into someone unrecognizable, they laid him out in front of me. He's been sprawled across the cobblestones ever since, unmoving with his left arm twisted in the wrong direction.

One of the guards descends the stage and delivers a sharp kick at Harrick's side. I flinch, unable to stop myself. Harrick groans. It's long and drawn out, pained but alive. Despite everything, a streak of relief courses through me. Alive. He is alive—which means we still have a chance.

The guard wrenches Harrick up by his shoulders. His head lolls to the side, then drops to settle on his chest. His dark hair hangs over his face, hiding most of the bruises, but I know they're there. I watched each strike land against his face, his body, his limbs.

I suck in a watery breath, unable to stop the tears. This is my fault. All of it—and I *knew* it would happen. I thought, hoped, it would end differently, and now I hate myself for being wrong. For being a fool. A selfish, impulsive fool.

I look at the murdered servants, abandoned in the rain. There are four of them, and I know them all. Arnelian's corpse stares at me with an empty gaze. He's the reason the guards found me. Tora had left me with a good hiding place, and I'm sure the guards never would have seen me. It was only Arnelian's odd angle, as they dragged him through the entryway, that allowed him to notice me. And whether on impulse or out of anger, Arnelian called my name, stretching a hand toward me. Again and again, until the guards realized I was there.

"He's waking," the second guard says, the one still on the stage.

Harrick's movements are loose and unsteady, but the guard is right: he's waking. Those dark violet eyes blink, slowly at first, then faster. His attention snaps around the courtyard, at the darkness that has fallen over us. When his eyes finally find mine, a terrible sob breaks from his lips.

"I killed your men," the Architect says, sounding bored. I

don't know if he's telling the truth. "Pitiful deaths. Your sister barely fought. I expected more from her."

Harrick doesn't respond. He takes haggard breaths through his teeth, and I let out another involuntary sob.

"This is what happens when you lose focus," the Architect continues. He makes a tsking sound in the back of his throat. "I told you your duty was to me, not these vile mortals. You defied me, and now, you will suffer the consequences."

Harrick's eyes rake over me, and I can only imagine what he sees. I am filthy and soaked, bruised and bloodied. He must know the truth, that every second of this misery is my fault.

"I'm sorry," I say. I'm crying so hard I'm not sure he can understand me. "I'm so sorry, Harrick. I didn't—"

Something strikes the back of my head—a fist, maybe. I fall forward, catching myself just before my face hits the wood. The Architect grabs me by my hair, twisting me up to my knees and then my feet. He roughly drags me, and I fumble to stay upright, closing my eyes as we stop at the stage's edge. His rancid breath is hot against my cheek, a stark reminder he's still not wearing his mask.

"You promised!" Harrick shouts. "You promised to let her live!"

He lets out an animalistic scream, unlike anything I've heard. By the time I open my eyes, he's fought his way to his feet. He's unsteady, but still straining against the guard, trying to reach me. He raises his hands, only for the barest of sparks to light his fingers.

The Architect heaves a disappointed sigh. He maintains his cruel grip on my hair as he pulls me back to his chest.

"I've drained your magic, Harrick," he says. "Go on, feel for it. It's gone, almost to the last drop. It will come back, don't worry. But not tonight."

He lets his words hang in the air, and I watch as Harrick

realizes the truth of them. He flexes his hands, the color draining from his face. For the first time in his life, he is as weak, as powerless as I am. And without his magic, we don't stand a chance.

"Don't," Harrick says. His entire body trembles as he speaks, and each word sounds physically painful. "I'll do anything. *Anything.*"

"Ahh, I'm sure you would," the Architect muses. He releases my hair, curling his hand around the back of my neck instead. I clench every muscle in my body, as if being perfectly still will allow me to disappear. "Unfortunately, the time for begging is past. Now, you must face the consequences of your actions."

Harrick attempts another step forward, only to crash to his knees. The guard behind him lets out something dangerously close to a laugh, and it's echoed by the other guard. The Architect doesn't join. He only sighs again, as if impatient for all of this to be over.

"Hold his arms," he says. "And keep his eyes open. Make sure he watches."

Harrick's head lifts before the guard reaches him. He fights, even though he must know it's a battle he will lose. Magic sparks uselessly at his hands as the guard restrains his arms behind his back.

"I'm here," Harrick says. His voice is strangled still, and tears trail through the blood on his face. "I'm here, Rune. You are not alone."

"I'm scared," I say. I don't know why I admit it, but I do. "I don't want to die."

"I will be with you soon," he says. "As soon as I can, sweetheart."

I shake my head. There are so many things I need to tell him, but I can't find my voice for a single one.

I'm sorry.

I love you.

Live for both of us.

Don't let him win.

A flare of magic lights beside my face. For one foolish moment, I think Tora has returned to save us, that the Architect lied and she is still alive. But when I turn my head, it is the Architect's magic I see. It flares in a misshapen orb, creeping toward me like a starved animal. I lean away from it, even though I know there's nowhere to go.

The Architect's hand clasps tighter over my throat as his magic presses against the side of my face. It is warm, but not scalding like I expect. It caresses my cheek, sliding across my skin and slipping into my ear. I feel it inside my skull, dancing past the bone and into my mind. I try to look back for Harrick, but my vision is clouded until I can't tell what's real and what's not.

I am on this stage, the rough, bloodied wood beneath my bare feet. But I am also at my mother's deathbed. I am begging her not to leave me, even as she's struggling to breathe. I am selfishly demanding she stay, telling her I will never forgive her if she dies.

I am in that cramped servants' bedroom, asking too much of a father who has already given more than he has. I am telling him my cruelest thoughts, pushing him to be reckless, foolish, selfless. I am racing down poorly lit corridors, tripping over my own feet, shoving into this same bleak courtyard. But he's already dead. I'm too late and it's my fault and he's already dead.

I am convincing Harrick to marry me. I am abandoning the rebel faction. I am ruining every life that comes into contact with mine.

All the horrible, terrible things in this world come back to me, and there is only one way to keep them from continuing. To stop the hurt I've forced on everyone around me.

"Creature," the Architect whispers. For the first time, I realize his voice is not cruel at all. It is honest, bare, true.

When I open my eyes, it is his I find. They are darker than Harrick's, without even a hint of violet. They are black, endless, all-knowing.

"This is for you," he tells me.

I look to his outstretched palm. He holds a dagger between his fingers, delicately, as if it's precious. And it is, I realize. It is the only solution to the damage I've caused, to the hurt I've inflicted. I study the Architect's wide, omniscient eyes. I'm not scared anymore. I am at peace. For once, I know exactly what I'm meant to do.

I take the dagger from his palm, careful not to touch him with the blade. I look at my reflection within it, at the dark circles beneath my eyes.

You are so tired, the Architect tells me.

And I am. I feel the exhaustion of this life on every bone in my body.

It is time to let go, he says.

And I know he's right.

I hold the handle, rotating the dagger, just like Harrick taught me.

If you were to stab someone, he'd said. *You'd do it like this.*

I point the blade to my pulse.

I will be your friend. He said that the very same night.

The dagger shakes in my hand, and I'm caught off guard by this second memory. It is not from the Architect, I realize, but from myself. I'm suddenly desperate to hear more. I want to stay, if only so I can hear his voice for another moment.

Gods, you're beautiful. He'd said that the first night he kissed me for real.

Somewhere, I feel the Architect's hand tighten on my neck. I feel him shake me, as if rattling me into submission. But I still don't move the dagger. I want more, just one more.

Marry me, Rune. That was only yesterday, and I can still feel the warmth low in my stomach. *Nothing makes me feel half as brave and worthy and good as you do.*

I blink against the warm haze of the Architect's magic. Bits of reality come back to me, as if I am waking from a deep slumber. I can feel it then, the presence of not just the Architect's magic within me, but Harrick's too.

I will protect you with my life, he said once. And he has, over and over again.

And I will do the same, I whisper into the void.

I cling to Harrick's magic. It is softer yet so much more vibrant than his father's, and I let it lead me away from the Architect's distorted reality. I claw through muddled visions and memories, until I blink and find the rain-streaked court-yard before me. I still hold the Architect's dagger against my throat, but it no longer feels like an answered prayer.

It feels only like a cold piece of metal, meant not to heal, but to destroy.

Harrick fights his captor, screaming my name again and again. Straining to get to me, to keep his promise. This time, the voice I hear is not his or the Architect's or even my own. It is Alven Tjor's, the dark-haired servant who didn't want to risk his neck but did anyway.

That's our strength, you know, he'd told me in the Wilds. *They always underestimate us.*

I look at the Architect without turning my head. Even as he pinches my neck, urging me to kill myself faster, he doesn't look at me. I am so little a threat, he's not paying me any attention. His eyes are solely on his most powerful descendant. Because this moment is not about me dying, not really.

It is about Harrick *watching* me die and being unable to stop it.

I tighten the blade in my hand and take a thick breath through my nose.

And then, I lunge.

The Architect turns, his eyes widening in surprise. He's too late. My blade slices through his exposed skin, hitting somewhere between his throat and his pulse. I jerk my hand back, drawing out the blade with it. I stab him again. And once more.

He falls like many of his victims. First to his knees, with his fingers grasping at his throat. Then forward, onto his hands. Blood sprays in thick pulses, soaking his leather gloves. I stand over him with the dagger still clutched in my hand.

His blood is everywhere. On my clothes, my hands, my face. I can taste the sharp iron of it on my tongue.

His guard crashes against my side. At first, I think it's to kill me, but he only shoves me out of the way. He's knelt before his leader, pressing both hands against the man's throat.

"Get a healer!" he screams at the second guard.

The man doesn't wait to be told again. He abandons Harrick's side and sprints for the Tower's entrance. I stare after him in disbelief before looking back to the Architect. He's ruled this land since its creation, and he's terrorized my kind every day of it. It's fitting, I think, that he should die by a mortal hand. Despite this guard's effort, I can tell by the empty glaze over his eyes.

The Architect is already dead.

"Rune," Harrick says. His voice is a desperate plea. "We need to go."

I stumble off the stage, half-collapsing at Harrick's side. I gently hold his bruised face between my hands, and even though there's no time for it, I place a frantic kiss to the top of his forehead.

"We need to go," he says again. His eyes dart between me and the stage. "Help me up."

It's a struggle but I manage to get him on his feet. He's covered in blood and bruises and swollen flesh, and I'm terrified he might lose consciousness at any moment. The guard on the stage has his back mostly to us as he tries, uselessly, to stop the Architect's bleeding.

"If I collapse, leave me," Harrick says as we cross the court-yard "If I collapse, go until you find—"

"We're going together," I interrupt. "So stay with me. Okay? Stay with me, and we'll go together."

We don't speak again as I drag him into the Tower. The entryway is thankfully vacant, but we're quick to escape it, just in case that changes. We head down a series of hallways until we reach a concealed military lift. Only once we're inside, moving upward, does he kiss the top of my head. Again and again, until he lets out a shaky sob.

"I love you," he says, breathing the words against my hair. "So much, Rune."

"I love you too," I say. I'm trembling again, not from Harrick's weight but from the reality of all that's happened. "What are we going to do now?"

"I need to get my magic back," he says. His voice is strained, tight. "We'll rest tonight, and in the morning, I'll be ready. We'll call a gathering—and then, we'll take what's ours."

"Harrick, you need a healer," I say. A quick glance at the side of his face confirms my worst fears: he's fading, and fast. I tighten my hold on him. "Forget the kingdom. You're going to die if you don't get help. Once we get to your quarters, I'll go find someone—"

"No," he says, but even his words are growing weaker. "It's too dangerous, Rune. Tomorrow. I'll see one tomorrow, I prom-ise. Just, please..."

I don't answer him. The lift reaches his floor, and I lead him to his quarters. Once we're in his room, he stumbles into bed. He's still soaked and covered in blood, but he's rapidly losing his fight to stay awake. I tuck him beneath the covers, not strong enough to change his clothes by myself. Once he's settled, I hurry to the wardrobe for more blankets.

I've no more than turned when a flare of red magic erupts through the room. I startle, spinning to face Harrick again. He's sitting upright in bed, arm shaking but lifted. Thin, reedy vines twine around the door, as if to lock us in—and everyone else out.

Harrick manages two strands before his eyes roll back. He collapses against the mattress, finally succumbing to unconsciousness.

32
RUNE

After checking on Harrick, who is unconscious but still breathing, I stand in front of his door. The vines are too small to keep me from leaving, but that also means they're too small to keep others from coming. I lean against the door, listening to bursts of chaos. People are screaming, sobbing, running. I suck in a breath, forcing myself to breathe. Too much has happened in too little time, and I need to stop and think. I look around the room, evaluating, calculating.

Harrick is unconscious and dying.

The Tower is in complete turmoil.

All of our allies are dead.

I wait for a plan to formulate, but when nothing does, I return the wardrobe. I rummage for extra blankets, pausing when I spot a stack of dry coveralls, tucked beneath his clothes. I wonder how long he's had these here, ready for whenever he needed to send me a new pair.

I grab the top set, pressing my face against the rough fabric to muffle my sobs. I'm crying before I can stop it, leaned against the side of the wardrobe, legs shaking as today rushes through me. I risked Harrick's life. I watched old friends die. But most of all...

I killed the Architect.

With the coverall clenched in my fist, I run to the bathroom. I fall to my knees before the toilet, puking until there's nothing left. My chest burns with each breath, and I squeeze my eyes shut, sure this is all a dream. I'll wake at any moment, back in my servant quarters. No husband, no freedom, and none of this blood covering my clothes.

Murderer.

I retch again, even though there's nothing left. I'm shaking and crying, and feeling a strange whisper, telling me I'd do it all over again.

It is with that thought that I force myself back to my feet. I dress in dry coveralls and return to Harrick's bedside. His breaths are heavy and labored, as if each one hurts his ribs. I gently brush my fingers through his hair, combing them from his bloodied face.

"I'll be back soon," I whisper against his temple.

I swallow hard, refusing to let myself cry again. I've already wasted too much time. I leave him with a final kiss on his forehead.

It takes more effort than I expect to open the bedroom door. Three hard shoves, and Harrick's thin vines finally snap. I stumble into the hallway. It's loud, but the sounds are distant, echoing from other corridors, other floors. I move quickly, my head down, as I head for the medical wing.

By the time I reach it, it's nearly impossible to move through the crowd of waiting people. There are several elites and royals packed into the corridor, all clamoring to get into the infirmary. They're families of the guards, I realize. Mothers and fathers and siblings, desperate to know their relative survived.

Many will not get the answer they want.

People look down at me as I squeeze through any open spaces I find. There's no point in asking them to move—I'm dressed in servant's garb, and the less attention I draw, the better. With my elbows tucked to my side, I press forward, until I'm faced with a guard. He stands, centered in front of the open doorway to the infirmary. The black walls swallow the commotion behind them, but it does nothing to quiet the moans of agony. The man crosses his arms, giving me an unimpressed expression.

Behind me, someone yanks on my shoulder. I'm ripped back a step, but I fight them off, ignoring their shocked outcry. I focus only on the bare-faced guard before me. Without a mask, I don't know his rank.

"I need a healer," I say. My words are too quiet, my voice stolen by the crowd. I try again, louder. "I need a healer. Immediately."

"Get out of here!" a man yells behind me. He grabs the back of my head, fisting my hair between his fingers. My scalp is still tender from where the Architect grabbed me, and I cry out. The man snarls against my ear. "They don't serve fucking vermin here!"

The guard lifts his hand in a lazy, dismissive gesture. The royal releases me, and I surge forward again.

"A healer—"

"He's right, creature," the guard says. He's bald with a sloping nose and a deep crease between his eyebrows. He tightens and releases his fist, tiny flickers of magic sparking with each movement. "Elites and royals only."

"It's not for me," I say. "The prince! The prince needs a healer."

"The princes are dead," he says. He flinches as he speaks, but he otherwise remains still.

"No," I say. "He's alive. I will take you to him. I just—"

Someone, maybe that same royal man, grabs my shoulder again. They wrench me backward, and I stumble, falling onto my ass and then struggling back to my knees. I can feel my heartbeat through my entire body.

They're not going to help him. They're going to let him die.

"Go on," the guard says. "These people are anxious. They're looking for something to distract themselves, and if you stick around, that's going to be you. I'm too fucking tired to keep them from beating you. So *go*."

I swallow, but I can't back down. I can't leave. Harrick will die, and if he dies, I will too.

I scramble to my feet and lunge forward, clasping both hands around the guard's wrist. He blinks at me in shock, the magic sparking brighter from his fingertips.

"You will get me a healer," I say. I raise my voice, until I'm yelling, until I'm louder than I've ever dared to be. "I am your queen—and you will get me a healer! Right. Now."

"Wyhel, it's fucking deranged," the royal man says, lurching away from me.

"Three seconds," the guard says. He stares at me, and despite my veil between us, I'm terrified he might actually kill me. "Three seconds to release me, or I'll end your pathetic, worthless—"

"Unhand her."

My head jerks toward the familiar voice. The Architect said everyone was dead, but she sounds like...

"Princess Tora," the guard says. He turns toward her, probably to point out I'm the one holding him, not the other way around.

I'm too busy staring at Harrick's sister to know if he says anything at all. Tora wears a frilly red dress that's been torn and muddied. Her usually plaited hair is messy and tangled around her face, but there isn't a spot of damage on her.

If she was hurt, they've already healed her.

I'm still staring, eyes wide, when she pushes between me and the bald guard. Her hands wrap around my shoulders, crushing me into a tight hug. I freeze, too surprised to return the gesture.

"You're alive," I say. My mouth bobs a few times as I try to decide what to say before finally managing, "He said you were dead. That you were all—"

"Where's my brother?" she interrupts. She pulls back to look at me, her pale violet eyes cataloging me from my wet hair to my bare feet. "Is he alive?"

"He's alive," I say, choking through the words. "He's alive, but he needs a healer. Please, believe me."

"I believe you," she says. She tucks my hair behind my ear with a touch far too gentle for someone like me. I can only imagine how the royals are staring, whispering at the two of us. I don't have the energy to look. "Let me get Joran."

Before I can reply, Tora sweeps back into the infirmary, glaring down the bald guard as she passes. It's only seconds, and she's back. She's joined by a heavyset healer, dressed in simple black clothes, and a maskless Joran. His hair is red, like Caleah's, but brighter. It sticks up in every direction like a wild flame.

"They'll go with you," she tells me. "I need to stay. Dae isn't doing as well as the rest of us, and I...I want to be here when he wakes."

"Okay," I say, but I'm rooted in place. My mouth dries as I peer into the infirmary. I can't imagine the frenzy that's bleeding through every level of Savoa right now, only that most of it is my fault.

I killed the Architect. Harrick killed Malek.

I'm overcome with the realization that might be unforgivable, even if Harrick is strong enough to claim his throne.

"Tora," I say, shaking as I step toward her. She doesn't lean away in revulsion like I fear, instead placing a hand on my shoulder as she comes closer. I whisper, turning my head so only she can hear. "It was me."

"I know," she says. "I figured that out when you were being held with the other rebels. But it's okay. None of that matters now—"

"No," I say, cutting her off. I can't fight the tremble in my hands as I force myself to say it. "I killed the Architect. That... that was me."

"Oh," she says. She keeps her hand on my shoulder, but she's tense now. "I...see."

"He was going to kill me," I say, as though she didn't already know that. "I didn't—"

"Don't explain yourself," she says. She squeezes my arm. "I'm glad you did. Just... Just go be with my brother. I'm glad that he has you."

They're words I never imagined I'd hear from, well, *anyone.*

"Thank you," I whisper. "And I'm, um, glad you're okay."

"Go," she says again. Then, she gives Joran a sharp look. "Don't leave her side. Understand?"

"Understood," he echoes. Then, "Keep me updated on Dae."

Tora gives me a final, quick hug, before darting back inside the infirmary. I don't look at the bald guard as Joran leads me away from the blackened room, but I feel a twitch of satisfaction when the crowd parts for us. Joran places his hand between my shoulderblades, guiding me through the masses. I keep my chin raised as I pass the gawking royals, not allowing myself to shrink like my instincts beg.

As soon as we clear the 195th floor, Joran's touch vanishes. We don't speak until we've reached Harrick's quarters, and even then, he waits for the healer to enter the bedroom before he catches my shoulder.

"Is it true?" he asks. "You killed the Architect?"

I swallow, giving myself a moment.

"Yes," I say finally.

"Thank you," he says. I startle, meeting his dark gaze. He dips his head, and it takes me a moment to realize he's bowing. To *me*. "You did for the prince what I failed to do myself. I shall be indebted to you for the rest of my life, princess."

"No," I say, the word sharp and quick. Joran looks up at me in surprise. "You are not indebted. I don't—I don't..."

Joran's face wrinkles in confusion at first, only to soften.

"I understand, princess," he says. He straightens, offering me a gentle smile. "Then at least accept my thanks."

I nod, trying but failing to clear the emotion from my throat. Joran has never been cruel to me, but he's also never been outwardly kind.

"After you," he says. He gestures for me to enter Harrick's bedroom, and I do, still struggling to process his gratitude. I know others won't be so quick to acceptance, but I can't keep the hope from blooming in my chest.

For so long, I dreamed of ruling Savoa, of overthrowing the crown to claim it for myself and the rebels. I wanted this kingdom to grovel before me, to suffer for the way they made me suffer. Only now do I realize what a waste that would be. Savoa needs *hope* to heal, not vengeance.

I sit at Harrick's bedside for the next several hours, turning these thoughts around my mind. I envision myself, finally in a place of power, and try to envision what that could look like. With my husband's hand in mine, I watch the healer work to repair his body.

Tora enters Harrick's quarters after another hour passes, and it is only then I notice how quiet the Tower has grown.

"Well?" Joran asks.

"It's in progress," Tora says. She sits primly on the foot of

Harrick's bed, watching him breathe for several seconds before continuing. "I've got every available guard restoring order through the Tower. We'll send a few troops out in the morning to make sure the outer sectors are all right."

Joran nods, and Tora sighs.

"I've spread news to the elite's biggest gossips," she says. "It won't be long before everyone knows. Many already know Harrick is the only surviving heir, and that the Architect and Malek are dead. My mother is in a state of shock, and from what I've heard, she's refusing to leave her quarters."

I twist the edge of Harrick's blanket in my fist. My chest feels weak, like my heart might beat right through my ribs. I can't bring myself to look at anyone, instead keeping my attention on the red duvet.

"Rune," Tora says, her voice growing softer. I can feel her studying me, but I still don't look her way. She sighs softly. "I considered lying about what you did, but...I couldn't."

I swallow, but the knot in my throat is almost too much to manage. I force myself to meet her gaze, even as I shake with the implication. She's told the truth, and that means *everyone* knows I killed their ancient leader.

"You were a hero today, Rune," she says. Her words are harsh, fierce. "You deserve to be remembered as one."

I don't say anything now—I can't hardly form a thought.

"I told everyone the truth. When they asked what happened, I told them a servant killed the Architect to save the prince's life," she says. "You defied magic itself to save someone you love—and what's more powerful than that?"

"They won't see it that way," I say. I don't realize I'm crying until I feel the tears on my cheeks. "They will kill me for this."

"Who?" she asks, and her words are as hard as a blade. "They will have to get through Joran and Dae, through me, through Harrick...through *you*, Rune. No one can touch you."

"We will kill them if they so much as try," Joran vows.

I can't find the words to respond, probably because there aren't any strong enough to describe the relief and gratitude I feel in my chest. Finally, I settle with the bare minimum.

"Thank you," I say. I wipe the tears from my face. "Truly."

"We'll let you rest," she says. She squeezes my shoulder as she rises, and I somehow keep from flinching. "It looks like the healer is finishing up."

I follow her gaze, to where the healer pulls his coat back into place. He looks exhausted, sickly almost, as he steps from Harrick's side.

"He may need more work," the man says. "Fetch me if he does. For now, I think his best healing will happen through sleep."

"He should heal your face," Joran says. I realize he's speaking to me. "You're bruised."

"It's all right," I say. Maybe I imagine it, but I think the healer sighs with relief.

"Princess—"

"I don't want to be healed. I just want to sleep." I do my best to sound confident and assured, like there's no room to argue. I've never spoken like this in my life, but if I ever want to help Savoa, I can't fear my own voice.

I expect Joran to argue, but as if realizing my nerves, he nods. Within minutes, he leads Tora and the healer from Harrick's quarters.

"I will be right outside, if you need me," he says, lingering at the doorway.

"You should rest—" I start, but Joran is already closing the door.

I curl against Harrick's side. Joran and the healer changed his bedding and clothes, so there is only soft warmth surrounding us. He is safe and alive, his wounds closed and the bruising faded. The healer placed magic to help him sleep, and his breath comes gently, smoothly.

"I love you," I whisper against his neck, and then I drift to sleep too.

———

I wake to Harrick screaming my name. I jolt upright, heart leaping into my throat. I've got my hands raised—to do what, I'm not sure—when I realize Harrick is still asleep. He lies rigid on the bed beside me, eyes closed but body tense. His arm swings blindly, and I tumble off the bed to avoid his fist. As I return to my feet, the door crashes open.

Joran's attention jumps between us, and he instantly slouches against the door in relief. He looks half-dead, his eyes so shadowed with exhaustion I'm surprised he's still awake. Or maybe he'd fallen asleep in the hallway, and that's why it took him an entire two seconds to get in here.

"My prince," he says. He glances over me before crossing the room and pressing his hand to Harrick's chest. Magic sparks from Joran's fingertips, faint, but enough to shock Harrick awake. He flings upright, narrowly avoiding a collision with his guard's forehead.

"Where is she?" Harrick demands, stumbling out of bed. He's got his hand on Joran's collar, only relaxing slightly when he realizes who stands before him. His chest heaves as he frantically looks at his surroundings, and it's clear he doesn't know how he got here.

"It's okay," I say. I'm trembling as I reach for him. "I'm right—"

Harrick crushes me to his chest, pulling me into an embrace. His lips land on my temple, my cheek, my neck. Joran says something, but I don't hear a word of it.

"You're alive," Harrick says. He's still breathing hard, lips tickling the side of my neck. "Gods, you're—are you okay? Look at me. Are you okay?"

He pulls back, then in a single move sweeps me up and places me back onto the bed. He balances his weight on one hand and traces my cheek with the other. His touch is so gentle it tickles, and I smile up at him. Hours ago, I was sure we'd both be dead. The fact we're here, tangled in the sheets of his luxury bed...

"I love you," I say.

He kisses me then, hard and fast, pulling back entirely too soon.

"I love you. Why haven't they healed you?" he asks. His hands skim over my sides, gently, as if afraid to hurt me. "They've clearly healed me. They should have...Joran!"

He leans farther from me, looking surprised to find us alone. I, on the other hand, am immensely relieved.

"He tried," I say. I touch Harrick's jaw, tilting his face back to look at me. "The healers needed to rest. They've had a long night."

As if my words jolt something in his memory, Harrick shifts off me. He's crossing the room with wide strides, flinging open the door. Having his backrest ripped away, Joran falls into the room.

"Wyhel," he mutters, but he's already scrambling to his feet. "Apologies, my prince. I was only—"

Harrick doesn't let him finish. He pulls Joran into a hug, one nearly as tight as how he'd just held me.

"You're alive," he says without pulling back.

"Yes," Joran says. "Most of us are. Princess Tora, Dae, Meyra—"

"Tora," Harrick repeats. He drops his head against Joran's

shoulder. "Good. That's... Thank you. What's happening out there? Has the Committee—"

"Everything is under control," Joran says. "The Tower is secure and news of your victory is circulating. I'm keeping tabs on the radio for any sign of trouble. For now, everything is quiet. People are sleeping. You should too."

"Very well," he says. He finally releases Joran, stepping to put space between them. "You should rest too. Send for guards to replace you. Once they're here, you're dismissed."

Joran straightens his shoulders, as if to argue.

"That's an order, guard."

Joran nods, and though I can tell he's reluctant to leave, he looks far too exhausted to stay. Once he's gone, Harrick closes the door and slides back into bed. Rather than lying beside me, he drapes over me again, keeping the bulk of his weight off me. He remains close enough that our clothes brush with every breath.

"You're feeling better?" I ask. I loop my arms over Harrick's neck, tugging his face closer. He certainly looks better. A healthy flush colors his skin and there's nothing to indicate he'd been on the brink of death only hours ago.

"I feel amazing," he says. He presses a soft kiss against my eyebrow, still frowning. "You should have had them heal you."

"They needed rest," I repeat. "I'm not hurting anyway. I just —I'm really happy to be here."

"Me too, sweetheart," he says. His lips trail down my neck, and his teeth nip at a spot above my collarbone. His violet eyes meet mine. "Sorry I woke you."

"I'm not," I whisper. I tangle my fingers through his hair and pull his mouth back to mine. My thighs part, and Harrick settles between them, his erection already pressing against my stomach.

"Does anything hurt?" he asks. His lips brush against mine as he speaks.

"No," I say. It's not exactly the truth, but I don't want Harrick to be delicate with me. After surviving something I was sure we wouldn't, I want to make him lose control.

Even more, *I* want to lose control. I have no idea what the next several days will bring. We'll be inundated with questions and demands, and undoubtedly people will want me to stay in the servant class where I belong. Tora and Joran seem confident that I can do this, but unease still settles in my gut.

I don't want to think of any of that now.

"I want to try something," I say. Heat flushes over my cheeks as I force the words against a wave of insecurity. "I'm not sure it's something people do."

"Tell me," he says. He brushes the hair off my face, looking equal parts curious and patient.

"When we had sex," I start, and I hate that I can't stop myself from blushing. "You were above me. I was just wondering if..."

I want Harrick to finish the sentence for me, but he only stares, waiting. The heat rises sharper beneath my skin.

"Do women ever...go on top?"

Harrick's pupils widen, making his eyes look impossibly black. His lips part as he looks over me, hands digging against my waist. Just when I'm about to take back the question, he flips us in one swift motion, settling himself beneath me. His attention roams over my body like a physical touch.

"Are you asking to ride me, Rune Ealde?" he asks, voice low and gravelly. He stares up at me like I'm brighter than the sun and stars combined.

"Ademas," I say. I grind myself against his erection, drawing a growl from his throat. "That's my name now, right? Rune *Ademas*?"

"Fuck," he swears. He grabs my hips, urging them faster against him. "Say it again, and I'll give you whatever you want."

"Rune Ademas."

"That's right, sweetheart," he says, unzipping my coverall until it pools at my waist. Harrick's lips trail across my jaw and throat and chest. He sucks a hardened nipple between his teeth, only switching to the opposite breast once I'm arching against him, lavishing that one too. He pulls away to snap the waistband of my coverall. "Take these off. I want to see you."

I slide off him to get undressed, but I keep my eyes on him. He is a flawless masterpiece, from his toned chest to his muscular arms and the sharp V that points to the waistband of his pants. Then those are gone too, and I'm settling over him once more. Without anything between us, I can feel the heat from his skin, the way his erection twitches every time I so much as breathe.

I press my thumb to the tip of his cock. Harrick's hips snap up in response, and when I look at him, I find him watching. I've never felt more beautiful than I do when he's looking at me. Even knowing my face is bloodied and bruised, I don't feel ashamed or like I should hide.

I killed the Architect, the man who made people far more powerful than me suffer for countless cycles. I killed him and saved the man I love—and no matter how long it takes, I will save this entire kingdom too.

"You look like a goddess," he murmurs. He cups my breast, pinching the nipple between his fingers. When I let out a gasp, he moves to my opposite breast, stroking it with his thumb. "I'm convinced you may very well *be* a goddess."

I arc against him, sliding out of his grasp and pushing until my chest is level with his face. Those dark eyes dart up to mine, a silent question in them.

"Suck," I say. My voice trembles, but I don't shrink beneath the command. I will not be afraid of my own desires anymore—and right now, I want to feel his mouth on me.

Harrick's gaze drifts from my face to my chest, his hand curling around the back of my neck. With a firm tug, he closes the distance, wrapping his warm lips around my nipple. His tongue traces circles, teeth grazing the sensitive skin. He hums in approval, and the vibration sends tingles across my skin.

I'm grinding against his cock so hard I'm losing focus. My head falls back and I stare up at the red ceiling, only half in this world.

"Gods, you taste so good. Like fucking magic," Harrick says. His hands trail down my back, landing on my waist. "Look at me, Rune."

I do, and when he touches the spot between my thighs, I moan so loud I'm sure anyone on this floor can hear me. Rather than feel embarrassed, the sound emboldens me. For the first time in my life, I don't have to be quiet.

I press my hands to Harrick's chest and raise onto my knees. I nod at him, and he wordlessly lines his erection at my center. Though I'm tempted to ask him for guidance, I don't. I want this to be *my* moment, as much as it is his too.

I sink onto him, groaning as he fills me. He feels even bigger at this angle, and I'm suddenly wondering if it was a mistake. There's no way I'll be able to take him like this. Just as I'm starting to pull back, his hands squeeze my hips.

"You can do it," he says. His attention lowers from mine to where we're joined. He rubs his thumb across my clit, using his other hand to balance me. "Breathe, sweetheart. You're doing so well."

I let out a sharp moan. I've never felt so full, so stimulated, as if he's touching me *everywhere*, all at once.

"That's it," he says. I take him in and in and in, until he's fully inside me and I'm seated against his hips. "Look at you, Rune. Oh gods—"

His hands snap to my thighs, stilling me. It sends a tortuous ache through me, and my body demands to move. I writhe against him, feeling overwhelmingly full yet somehow needing *more*.

"Fuck, hold on," he says through his teeth. "I don't want to come yet."

"Then don't," I say, still straining against his hands. "But let me move."

"You have no idea how pretty you are," he says through a groan. "How *good* you feel. It's a miracle I haven't come already. Just—hold on. Sit still for me."

I do as he says, clenching my thighs against his hips. He steadies his breathing, and by the time he finally nods, I'm a crumbling, whimpering mess. I've passed the point of being cautious, instead lifting off him and slamming back down, taking him in one thrust. I scream out, not meaning to but not caring that I have.

I let the ache between my thighs fuel me, pumping him in and out. His hands dig into my hips so hard I'm sure they'll bruise, and I hope they do. I hope he marks himself on me forever, so that I always carry a piece of this moment with me.

Harrick circles my clit, increasing the pressure as I lose myself to him. And when I come, I let myself scream his name, so that everyone knows he is mine and I am his.

33

HARRICK

"**I** thought you might be here," Tora says. She crosses the upper courtyard, her floor length gown dragging against the black stone. Sparkles in the shape of raindrops cover the skirt, and her heels are frighteningly tall. She's done her hair and makeup as if preparing for her own wedding, rather than a sector meeting.

My sector meeting. It's the first one I've ever called, but it won't be the last.

"Well?" I ask. I lean against the metal railing and cross my arms. I've been up here, watching the skyline and counting the seconds as they pass. I think I'm more nervous about *this* than I am about the meeting. "How's it going?"

"Rune is *fine*," Tora says. She rolls her eyes, stopping a few paces from me. Her eyes drift to the mountains, to the water surging between its peaks. The rain is heavy today, cloaking Savoa in a hazy gray. It thunders against the glass ceiling, rolling over the edge in thick sheets of water.

"I know," I say, even though I'm not sure I do.

So much has happened over the last season that it seems impossible *any* of us are fine. We've all been physically healed, but I doubt I'll ever fully recover from that day. There will always be a part of me remembering the hot, leaden panic of realizing my wife was going to die—and not being able to stop it.

"Joran is back," Tora says, stealing my attention. "He found Vale and that other escaped rebel. They were alive and fine, though they were *not* interested in coming back. I don't think Rune was surprised. She seemed relieved, honestly, just knowing he was okay."

"Good," I say. I never met Vale, but Rune risked her life to save him, and that must mean he's a decent man. "Maybe he will one day, once he realizes it's safe, once he knows things are actually different."

Tora doesn't reply. She's still scared to hope for a future like that, I think, but I no longer am.

"How about Mother?" I ask, deciding not to push her. "Any update there?"

"Not really," Tora says. She shakes her head. "She's furious, obviously, but I don't think she'll be a problem for us, Harrick. Truly."

"Has she changed her mind about today?"

"No. She's not coming," Tora says. "But she's not fighting us either. She's agreeing to a peaceful transfer. I think it's the most we can hope for at this point."

I nod. The wind sends a smatter of rain against us, and I tuck my hands into my pockets. It's getting colder, a stark reminder that Blizzard Season will be here in a matter of days. This time, Savoa will be ready. That's what we're doing at today's meeting: deciding how to distribute the excess magic and on what timeline. We have proxies from all sectors attending, with me and Rune at the lead.

"She looks beautiful, by the way," Tora says, and I know she's no longer talking about Mother.

"Of course she does," I say. "She's the most beautiful woman in the world."

"Other than me, right?" my sister says. She lets out a laugh at the face I make. "Look at you, Harrick. Don't you know *I'm* supposed to be the romantic?"

"Speaking of," I say, letting the unasked question hang between us.

"I ended the betrothal. Nordan wasn't too upset."

"I was asking about Dae, actually," I say. I smirk at the way Tora blushes, as if she thought I hadn't noticed. As far as I'm concerned, *everyone* has. "You could have told me, you know. That you cared for him."

"I knew it didn't matter," she says. And then, pointedly, "It *doesn't* matter."

It does, I want to argue. I don't though—it's something she'll have to decide for herself.

Tora blows out a heavy breath. "Wyhel. Maybe I'll leave like those rebels. Change my name, start a new life—"

"You could, you know. No one will stop you," I say, pausing. "But I think you should stay. We wouldn't be positioned as we are now without you. I'd likely be dead, Rune imprisoned or worse, the Tower in complete chaos…The kingdom needs you, Tora."

"Just say you'd miss me too much," she says. She's trying to tease me, even as her eyes fill with tears.

"I would miss you too much," I say. "So if you're asking my opinion—"

"I'm not."

"I think we should reactivate the emissary position," I continue, ignoring her. I smile when her eyebrows shoot up, something lighting in her eyes. "And I think you should take it. You'd be perfect for it. You could go see the world, learn what

Savoa needs and how the sectors are doing. You can think about it, take your time—"

"I'll do it," she interrupts. She's already grinning, and it's one of her rare smiles. She looks like a kid again, launching herself into my arms. "Thank you, Harrick."

"I prefer *your majesty*," I say, barely dodging her elbow.

"You ruined it," she says, half-whining, half-laughing.

I smile down at her, feeling so much happier than I knew I could. Of all the ways I thought my life would go, I never dared to dream of this. To be king in a land *without* the Architect or Malek, to be able to offer freedom and happiness to my sister, to be husband to the most wonderful woman I've ever met...

The Tower bell chimes, signaling the meeting is about to begin.

"Let's go," I say. I call to Tora as I walk, only pausing once I've reached the courtyard door. "You're sure she's all right? If she seems nervous, we should just go in together. There's really no—"

"Relax," Tora says. She sweeps past me into the stairwell. "In case you've forgotten, she killed the Architect with an old rusted blade. She can handle herself."

I am a man exactly where he belongs.

I stand in the front of the meeting room, facing two dozen men and women. The four sector representatives—Demetrius Llroy, Oris Fhell, Ksana Renat, and Maeve DinSon—are joined for the first time by several proxies, descendants, and guards. Everyone wears the same black mask over their eyes. They are narrow like a servant's veil, but thick like an elite's.

It was one of Rune's ideas. We'd had a seamstress make them over the past couple of days, and people's reactions alone made it worth it. Demetrius Llroy hasn't stopped scowling. I smile at him and Oris Fhell from across the room. Though they don't know it yet, their time on the Committee is running out.

Rune and I have been planning this meeting since the day after the Architect's death. We had a funeral for both him and Malek, one neither deserved. It was what the people wanted, what they needed, maybe, to accept new times were coming. More importantly, it allowed us to announce Rune as a new, unprecedented type of leader. Someone born without magic, who now seemed to defy it.

The Architect is dead, and without his looming presence, a flourishing kingdom feels possible.

Today, Rune and I will finally pitch our ideas and hear from others in the room. Only a few factors have already been decided, and one of my favorites is that representatives will be elected, not chosen by me or any other member of the crown. While I imagine Ksana Renat and Maeve DinSon will maintain their places, I will be surprised if Demetrius and Oris keep theirs.

"Thank you for joining us today," I say. My voice feels so much louder in this room than it did the last time I was here. Maybe it's because the window shields are down, and the glass echoes. Or maybe it's because I know my words matter now, that they aren't only for show.

This time, change is actually possible.

Tora smiles at me from her place on the left side of the table. Only Rune and I have chairs on this end, and hers is currently— symbolically—empty. My sister insisted it would be more powerful this way, but I hate that Rune's not beside me.

"We are in the midst of an unprecedented transition," I say. All eyes are on me, just visible behind ebony masks. "I realize many people are uncertain of Savoa's future, but be assured, I am not. For the first time in our kingdom's history, we have the opportunity to change, to be whatever our people decide—and not what was best for one man. From this moment onward, we are the architects of our world.

"Our kingdom's hardest times are behind us, but there are still many decisions to make. I am proud to be your king, to help lead us through the next several cycles." I pause, letting light and warmth fill my chest. It's the same sensation I experienced the first time Rune stepped toward me. "And I am equally proud to introduce my wife, your queen, and Savoa's greatest hope, Rune Ademas. The woman who saved me, and this entire kingdom."

Tora cheers, and most of the room offers their polite applause. I don't look to see who is—or isn't—welcoming toward my wife. One day, they will all see her exactly as I do. For now, I'm staring at the door, determined not to miss a single moment.

Joran steps through first. He may not have immediately taken to Rune as I did, but it's clear now: the man admires my wife, and nothing has ever given me more peace. He smiles back through the open doorway, giving her an encouraging nod. She must be hesitating. For the past several days, she has worn Tora's borrowed clothing. It's been red and flowy, and even that has made Rune tense any time we were around others. She's expecting someone to threaten her, to challenge her new role here.

They haven't dared, of course. While these people might not accept a servant as their queen, the rest of the kingdom sees her as a symbol of hope, of possibility.

Just as I'm tempted to go to her, Rune enters the room. Her presence steals all other thoughts from me, and a bit of my breath too. The topics for today's discussion vanish as I look at her. Hopefully she doesn't mind taking the lead, because I might be a lovesick fool for the rest of this meeting.

My wife is wearing a dress, and she is simply stunning. Though the bodice is bright red, almost everything else is yellow. Bright gems cover the top; tangled vines circle her waist like a belt; sparkles in the shape of rain decorate her tulle skirt; and her jewelry is made entirely of mirrors. She represents all of Savoa, both as a servant and as a queen. The ring I gave her glimmers on her finger, on the same hand as her indebted brand. When I offered to remove the mark, Rune said she wanted to keep it.

It's part of me, she'd said.

I hadn't understood fully, when she'd said it, but I do now. Standing before us, Rune is more than a queen—she is *everything.*

Pale, sickly handmaiden.

Daring, secretive trespasser.

Beautiful, fucking temptation.

Powerful, unstoppable liberator.

"Rune," I say. I don't mean to speak her name out loud, but when she smiles at me like this, I don't regret it. I finally turn back to the table. Two dozen men and women face my wife, watching her with assessing curiosity. With a sharp grunt, I snap, "Kneel for your queen."

Chairs screech as everyone moves at once. Rune remains in the doorway, cheeks flushed, those blue eyes sparkling beneath her mask. Rather than the black one everyone else wears, hers is a ratted servant's veil.

"Do not kneel," she says, surprising everyone—me most of all. Her voice is loud and unwavering as she approaches my side. With her beside me, I can sense the cracks in her confidence. Her fingers tap her thighs, and her voice tremors, just enough for me to hear. "Return to your seats."

I stand tall at my wife's side, keeping my focus on the table instead of her. Still, my fingers crave her skin. She's too close not to touch, and so I graze my knuckles against the back of hers. With how strong she's standing, I brace myself for her to add distance. Instead, her hand finds mine and she interlocks our fingers.

She's scared. I can feel it, every unsteady breath and twitch of nerves. She's terrified, but she's never let that stop her before—and she won't now, either.

She tilts her chin, and I realize she's not wearing a crown. I'd been too distracted by the way she looks in a dress: soft and delicate and beautiful. I didn't look at her hair. It's been twisted, not around a crown, but itself, forming a loose braid. She'd considered several crowns this morning, and while I enjoyed them all, this is undoubtedly better.

"This crown we live to serve," she says, her voice steadying. "It has failed us. It has left us divided, weakened, and lost... But this is a new era, and we must come together, not as crown and commoner, but as equals. We must rebuild these broken lands. Together."

Chills dance down my arms, and by the quiet of the room, the others feel it too. This sharp tugging, right at the center of the chest, that demands long-forgotten hope.

"Together," I say, echoing Rune's final word. I remove my crown, placing it on the table before us. She turns to me, brows lifted and mouth parted. I squeeze her hand, smiling when those blue eyes soften for me. I say it again, as if we're the only two people in this room. "Together."

THE END

ACKNOWLEDGMENTS

To my readers: Thank you for reading *Between Smoke & Shadow* —I hope you loved Rune and Harrick's story. If you did, please take a moment to review this book on Amazon and/or Goodreads. It makes a monumental impact for indie authors like me! If you want to stay up-to-date with my upcoming releases and behind-the-scenes sneak peeks, make sure to subscribe to my newsletter.

To HJ Nelson: Thank you for keeping me sane in this wild publishing world. We've been through a bit of everything since we first met as Wattpad authors, but I *think* I see our moment coming. I can't wait to buy that Scottish castle together. For now, thank you for talking through random book ideas, for bringing me to your cool author events, and for convincing me to change the original ending I wrote for Malek (it was truly, *truly* a dumpster fire). This book is what it is because of you.

To my parents: I don't know many people who would encourage their starry-eye child the way you've always encouraged me. You believed in me long before I did, and I will always be grateful for your endless support. Thank you for reading all my terrible first drafts and for talking me through my (many) imposter-syndrome meltdowns.

To my husband: Thank you for telling me to publish the book, even when it was rejected by just about every literary agent on the planet. Thank you for convincing me I was worthy, even when the industry suggested I wasn't. I took this leap because you insisted I could.

To my ARC readers: Thank you for taking a chance on a completely unknown author. When I posted a call for early readers, I never anticipated three-hundred people would volunteer. Your willingness to read my book sparked something I haven't felt in years...and your love for Rune and Harrick makes me excited to share more stories in the future.

To my siblings, Brittany, Beau, & Dyston: Thank you for talking through plot holes and strengthening world building and creating badass character art. I probably don't say thank you enough, so now it's in writing. You're welcome.

To: Katrina, Jonni, Cooper, Tiegan, and anyone else I missed. Thank you for supporting me!

To Okay Creations: Thank you for the beautiful book cover. If any authors are looking for a cover designer, you can check out her work here.

And finally, to my younger self: Thank you for reading books beneath your desk in math class. Thank you for staying up too late to plot that new story idea. Thank you for trying and failing and struggling. It all led to this moment, and I am so proud.

ABOUT THE AUTHOR

 Bree Wilde writes romance and romantasy books for adults. *Between Smoke and Shadow* is her debut novel. She lives in Idaho with her family and spends most of her time reading, writing, and yapping about books. Follow her on Threads and Instagram: @authorbreewilde.

www.ingramcontent.com/pod-product-compliance
Lightning Source LLC
Chambersburg PA
CBHW021240190726
48289CB00005B/1413